# THE GOLDEN RHINOCEROS

Ranulfo

ISBN: 978-0-6456023-1-9

Book Cover by Rayhan Ikhwan

**SHIELD WOLF BOOKS**

*"I asked him to admit that there was not a rhinoceros in the room, but he wouldn't."*

—*Bertrand Russell on Ludwig Wittgenstein*

# FOREWORD
## Death of the Author


*I was clearing out my late Dad's garage to make room for my new Mitsubishi Outlander when I came across this dusty old manuscript. I was ready to toss it into the skip bin when the title on the top page caught my eye. The Golden Rhinoceros. Flicking through the tied bundle, I realised that it was a novel written by my Dad. I asked my wife what I should I do with it. My wife said to read it. If it's any good, send it off to the publishers. If its rubbish, publish it on kindle or whatever, and maybe we can get twenty bucks out of it.*

*Well, I've read it and I just can't imagine any mainstream publisher would publish this book.*

*The novel is crazy and hilarious. Wild flights of fantasy. Talking houses, a singing and dancing bottom, talking turds, cockroaches in love, pastiches of films from the Marx brothers to Ingmar Bergman, parodies of literature from Shakespeare to James Joyce. A comic surreal satirical philosophical ride. Insane.*

*My father didn't know a thing about writing a novel. Broke every rule. Like the author shouldn't be in the novel. You don't see J K Rowling popping up in her books, getting involved with the characters or shagging with one of them but my dad did. He fell in love with a cockroach!*

*The novel stated that it was written in 1986. Dad would have been in his twenties. The era of Michael Jackson, Madonna, Reagan, Thatcher, big hair, bright clothes but he didn't mention any all of that. The novel was entirely in his head. He even interrupted a sentence to say he had to go to the toilet. Does Stephen King do that? That's why Dad was not a professional author. He worked as a clerk all his life.*

*One further thing, my father was found dead in a street, completely crushed: flattened like a pancake or a man-shaped pancake. I suspect that one of the characters in the novel killed him—Harry the Farmhouse. He had a vendetta against my Dad for killing him off. However, fiction characters can't get arrested so it's pointless me telling the police.*

*So...enjoy the novel! His only novel...I think. Well, I or my wife or my kids threw a lot of stuff, along with his paintings and drawings, a large collection of books (lots of boring stuff like Thomas Pynchon, no Stephen King!) into the skip bin to make way for my Mitsubishi. That's what a garage is for, right? My man cave now. And I think my Mitsubishi Outlander is a classic! The ultimate in Japanese engineering!*

*So, thank you, buyers, maybe I might use the extra cash to treat my family to a pizza dinner.*

# BOOK ONE
# WAR

# CHAPTER 1

## Tempest

K is crazy, and I'm crazy about her. I guess that's love. Come to think of it, dear readers, I'm crazy too. So beware, this novel, which I shall rip out of my soul, might hold a mirror to my sickness inside. Riddled with conflict am I, and I must out this conflict on these poor virgin pages. But don't you fret, I am a clown/philosopher, and I'll try my best to make you laugh, cry, think, ponder, scare, depress, and transcend. I hope this novel will make a million bucks so that I can marry K because I don't want a job, which is a definite drawback of married life. K, K, K, care you not for an impoverished author and the riches of his mind? No, O well, bumeroo. Now let the novel begin!

Once upon a time...a good beginning that...saves me from doing a lot of historical research...there lived a king and a queen, who ruled over a tinyish kingdom located somewhere between the North Pole and the South Pole. It was a peaceful kingdom, most likely because no one, including myself, the author, knew where it was, and thus no one invaded it. Until one day, two village idiots, Fart and Suck, decided in their discombobulated minds to overthrow the King and Queen...now what were their royal names...let me cogitate upon it...King Prawn and Queen Clytoris! The two first names that popped up in my head. I value the unconscious as I inhabit its realm most of the time, usually supine. In other words, food and sex are always on my mind.

That day was bright and sunny, with very little wind frolicking, but historically, it was a tempestuous day, one of those forked days that tore lives apart like brother from sister, husband from wife, friend from friend, and humanity from God.

"Down with the King!" shouted the two village idiots, with explosive saliva, outside the castle of King Prawn and Queen Clytoris. The castle was one of those typical medieval castles you would find in a B grade Hollywood movie, complete with a moat, a drawbridge, portcullis, keep, baileys, and stuff...good word that. Outside the fortified castle, stretched to the horizon were forests and lakes and stuff and more stuff, especially green stuff. Clouds on the horizon, rising and looming, harbingers of war and doom and possible rain.

Hearing the ruckus and having nothing better else to do, King Prawn stepped out onto the battlements overlooking the village idiots. Two pairs of crazy eyes amid unruly hair glared back at him.

"What is your complaint, my subjects?" he bellowed to them below.

"I'm the rightful arse to sit on your throne, wrong-arse!" Fart shouted back at the robed King aloft in the battlements.

King Prawn scrutinised the insurgents. With their drool and amusing and ill-fitting attire, they were clearly village idiots, so he dismissed the potential danger of the situation.

"Your arse belongs to the dunny. Get thee there, idiot," King Prawn replied.

Stabbing a finger at King Prawn. "Don't you mock me. I may be a village idiot, but I'm a human being as well and deserve just as much respect."

His partner in treason nodded bouncily in agreement. "Yeyes. Respect. R.E.S.P.E.K."

"I'm sorry, village idiots," said King Prawn, with slightly insincere sincerity.

"We village idiots have had enough of all this mockery and humiliation. I am a village idiot and I'm proud of it."

"I said I'm sorry. So why don't you go back to your village where you idiotise in and go suck your thumb or whatever village idiots do."

"We don't suck thumbs!" shouted Fart, indignant at this vile slur on village idiots.

"Yeyes," said Suck, and corrected King Prawn, "We suck dogs tails!"

"And whose dog's tail are you sucking?" Fart inquired of Suck, before snarling, "Not with my dog, I hope."

"What's your doggie's name?"

"Kitty Kat."

"Nono, the name of the dog whose tail I suck is called Leroy."

"Excuse me, befuddled gentlemen," the King interrupted them. "Could you try concentrating on the task at hand?"

"Leroy the Great Dane who lives down the lane?" Fart asked.

"I wouldn't say he was gweat. He's okayey."

"Yes, I agree. Not great, just average. How he got his reputation for being great I have no idea."

"In my oponinion George the bulldoggie is the best."

"He's rather ugly, don't you think?" Fart asked.

King Prawn waved his hands. "Hello, remember me? Hello…focus, please. Eyes on me." He pointed two fingers at his own face.

"I like the ruggedy look."

"For me," replied Fart haughtily. "I have a weakness for the sophisticated type. I like a well-groomed perfumed French Poodle."

Sock laughed derisively. "What a sissisy you are!"

"Don't call me sissy!" shouted Fart angrily, and socked Suck on the jaw.

Naturally, Suck socked back.

Fart was about to launch a fist straight at Suck's chin, but he stopped himself. In disgust he shook his head. "The idiotic things we village idiots must do in order to be village idiots." And he screamed, anguished, pathetic, "No more!"

"Yes," sighed Suck, feeling ashamed of himself. "It's extremely hard work to be village idiots. So demeaning."

Lamented Fart: "The pressure gets to me sometimes. There are days when I feel like chucking it all in. Get a job in an office, get married and have kids, read newspapers for information, eat white bread, suffer heartburn every night, indulge in intolerant remarks towards the minorities and less well off, watch dumb television, have meaningless monosyllabic conversations with my wife and kids, go to church, vote for the mainstream parties, and think that life can't get any better than this. God, I envy normal people. They don't have to work at being idiots, they just are. I work so hard at it, and with an IQ of 300, it's not easy."

King Prawn placed his elbow on the castle thingy (crenel?—according to my pictorial dictionary) and propped his jaw on his palm, yawned, and gazed at the horizon…yearning, big dollops of yearning…wondering what lay beyond the horizon?

"Yes," said Suck. "I've got an IQ of 300 too. But what can a man of intelligence do in this crazy civilisation? Be a scientist, invent new weapons of mass destruction, or new deodorants. Learn all this outer knowledge to compensate for our lack of inner knowledge. Or be a philosopher or a writer and wallow in words so that nothing is real anymore. No, I'd rather be a village idiot. At least I'm not pretending to be intelligent.

Fart nodded his head in assent. "It's the most honest way of living, expressing the true nature of existence, which is that it is absurd. Furthermore, it's the only way for humans to render themselves harmless."

Fart and Suck gazed into each other's eyes and understood at once what they needed to do.

"Whowho said village idiots are harmless?" shouted Suck vehemently and bowed down to ram his head into Fart's stomach.

Thus, angry Fart chased after stupid Suck and Bonk! Pow! Bam! their way back to the horizon, disappearing like dust into a vacuum cleaner.

"Bloody village idiots," muttered King Prawn as he walked down the stone steps, across the cobbled courtyard, and trudged wearily into the tall tower. He was disappointed rather than angry. He had hoped for some action to take his mind off his boredom. His eyes lacked lustre, his mouth sagged, unable to form a smile or a snarl, his skin was grey and bloodless, his flesh sagged in folds of indolence, yes, his body screamed it: King Prawn was bored with his life.

The castle, however beautiful it was, suffocated his soul; he yearned for the world, for horizons of conquest. To wield a sword and spill blood and cut muscle in heroic battle. But something was holding him back. Some Ball and Chain. He fixed his dull, clouded eyes on his queen, who was sitting on the throne.

The court was empty; the only courtiers and knights were dust and cobwebs. Dust and cobwebs invading and clogging his entire body, fogging his brain, choking his soul, crushing him.

"Have they gone away?" asked Queen Clytoris, knitting a garment as if knitting a wall between her and her husband.

"Yes, when you show leadership, people respect you. I am King because I am stronger and wiser than they are."

"Have you told the servants to clean the windows? They are so dusty and grimy."

Dethroned. "No. I was too busy putting down a rebellion."

"But you're not busy now."

He felt defiant, standing his ground like General Custer at Little Big Horn. "But I am. After all, I am the King. I have to deal with so many important issues...like war, famine, high interest rates."

"It will only take a second to tell the servants to clean the windows," she said, persisting like a knitting needle.

King Prawn was losing his patience and pride. "Why do you want clean windows? There's nothing to look at outside. Just stupid, boring natural scenery: mountains, lakes, trees, birds, cute animals. Instead of clean windows, let's have large canvasses of epic battles, with buckets of alizarin crimson for blood, or if you prefer to be modern, paintings of the Irish master, Francis Bacon, with his screaming popes and posing corpses. Now that's beauty—the distillation of horror!"

"Men and your definition of art. Beauty is something you want to rape and destroy," said the Queen.

"Men need to be men, daring, adventurous, dangerous. And women such as you want men to be sissies. You want men to be caring, loving, sensitive, understanding, sharing, as well as be doting parents to spoiled obnoxious brats. Even sex has been sissified. My idea of good masculine sex is no foreplay, premature ejaculation, and a good night's sleep. Instead, you want us to perform to the best of our abilities before the female critic. Men must combine the feats of a ballet dancer, a gymnast, and a marathon runner. Sex takes so much energy that I have little left of it to do the more important things, things that matter, things historical and glorious."

"Why have sex with me then?" she asked, looking up from her knitting and observing his demeanour, sensing something new, ominous.

"Because I need that one second of orgasmic ecstasy."

"Do stop whining. If you were the man you fantasise yourself to be, you would have done something by now."

Now. That word hit him hard like a divine revelation, the hammer of God bopping him on his noggin. For Now existed before a thought was formed. Now!

He spoke, and he was surprised by how passionate he felt. "You think manhood is a childish, immature thing. Men were born to be warriors, to feel power and strength, to kill with their hands. Let there be war!"

He picked up the royal sceptre that slept on his empty silk throne and raised it high like a sword. Be a man now. The time for love and conscience and peace and talk was over. When he felt himself wince at her bright reasoning eyes, he knew that he must snuff the light out of those orbs and bring in the rule of darkness. He swung it down hard on the queen's head, and she slumped and slipped off her throne. The ball of yarn tumbled away and scurried for help. But she didn't die from his blow. Instead, it woke her up from her inner slumber, deep within her psyche, the sleeping beauty snoring her life away. She understood at once that she had to be free from his chains. Blood trickled down her forehead, the pain intensifying and throbbing, but she felt stronger than ever.

She would rise as someone new and powerful.

Oh what a violent beginning to my novel. Blame it on K, she makes me suffer so. Before I get to the next chapter, let me tell you, dear readers, this is an abstract expressionist novel. I can't write about reality. Since birth I have been alienated from reality—family, country, nature, God—so I am not in any position to write about reality. Who is to blame for this separation? Who drove me to this gaping hole in my soul? I don't know. Maybe this novel might enlighten me a bit. Or perhaps drop me into darkness? Anyway, I've always lived in my head, and this is where my novel is set and where the characters live and die. Enjoy! Or maybe not...

# CHAPTER 2

## Trojan Duck

Fart and Suck, the two village idiots, returned to the castle, towing a giant wooden duck painted yellow with blue polka dots and set on wheels. (Did you know my earliest memory was that of a painted polka dotted wooden duck? Thought I might weave this detail into the novel. A novelist must borrow from his life, even though mine is small and pitiful.)

A sentry guard stopped them at the castle gates. Raising his spear, he enquired of the ludicrous duo the reason for their journey.

"We have a gift for the King," Fart explained.

The guard scratched his head in great bafflement. "You want to present the King a big wooden duck? Pray tell me why His Royal Majesty would want this hideous monstrosity?"

Fart rolled his eyes and replied snootily. "Can't you recognise a modern art masterpiece when you see one?"

The guard, an amateur dabbler in cubist art and a part time performance artist, blurted out, "I recognise a big stupid duck when I see one!"

He walked around the giant duck, inspecting it, and noticed a door in the back. "That's a door!" he spluttered.

"It's an anus," Fart corrected him with smug pedantry.

"An anus! Looks like a goddamn door to me!" the sceptic argued vehemently.

"That's what a duck's anus looks like. Haven't you ever seen one before?"

"That doesn't look like a duck's anus."

"It definitely is.

"Bullshit!"

"Duckshit you mean."

"You liar! That's a door!"

"It's an anus! Here is Doctor Suck. He is a professional analogist."

Suck magically extracted a stethoscope from his coat and inserted it into his ears.

"You don't look like a doctor," the guard accused him.

"Carey to checky your anus, sir."

He pointed his spear at Suck. "Don't go near me, you weirdo."

Laughter exploded inside the duck, followed by a cascade of suppressed giggles.

"Hey! What's going on? What's in there?" he spluttered, his knees trembling with fear.

"Innards. I think it has indigestion."

"Open that door at once!" ordered the guard, pointing a spear threateningly at Fart's chest.

"It's not poopoo time."

"Open that door now!" shouted the enraged guard, his whole body shaking.

"You asked for it," and Fart opened the door.

A diarrhoea of soldiers plopped down on the guard. One bloodthirsty soldier thrust a sword into the unfortunate guard's abdomen, sheskebbabbing him.

"I'm slain! I'm slain! But...if I'm dead, why am I still talking?" the inquisitive dead guard asked.

"Because you ain't dead yet, fool," and the self-same soldier whipped out a pistol and shot the guard in the forehead.

"Right through my brains you blasted me. Dead at 20, O woe is me!" the dead guard whimpered.

"Oh shut up and die!" screamed one Xerxes Xenophobia, who was a closet transvestite, dressing himself up in Nadia Comanechi's costume to perform gymnastics inside his closet.

Underarm and underhanded, Xerxes hurled a live grenade at the guard, who then exploded, limbs flying everywhere like a Rumanian gymnast. The judges adjudged him a score of 9.95.

"Pray tell me what have you against me?" asked the guard's severed but articulate mouth on the ground.

"Oh, please don't take this personally," said Xerxes apologetically. "You must understand that I am a soldier, and it is my duty to kill you. Barbaric as it may seem, but a job is a job, and since I am a conscientious person, I want to do my job as best as I can. I will not shirk my duties. I'm sorry that you should lose your life, but that's how our civilisation is. Offer wages for murder and you will get murderers. If you don't like it, then you should find a civilisation that does not allow this. So, if you don't mind, may I continue my job of killing you?"

"Now that you have explained that you are not an evil fellow but an honest, decent citizen that must work to earn money so you can buy expensive toys for your children, a microwave for your wife, and a set of golf clubs for yourself, then I shall gladly lay down my life for you. Please proceed."

"Kill!!!!!" screamed Xerxes, then multi-jumped on the mouth, which, not wanting to make work easier for Xerxes, retaliated by leaping up and biting his balls.

"Enough!" commanded Captain Peeble, a midget who wore polo neck jumpers to make him aseeming six feet tall. "Leave that mutilated mouth alone! We have more esteemed things to transact!"

"Such as killing the King!" surmised all the soldiers.

"No, sillies, tap dance!" and Captain Peeble burst into a spasm of Astaire hoofing. He was quite skilled, having learnt to tap at plumbing school.

Screamed out Xerxes, "Let's kill!"

Upon which the whole army pounced on poor Xerxes and tore him apart like roast chicken gobbled up by the Brady Bunch.

Well…hang on, dear readers, while I go visit the toilet to seek some inspiration. Meanwhile, why don't youse all go to the fridge and devour a snackeroo or two, okay? Hopefully, we'll both return to this novel.

"Let's kill the King!" shouted Tommy Benson, a born again and again and again Hindu. The army scrambled helter skelter into the castle's courtyard, screaming and brandishing their glinting swords. Inside the cobbled yard they stopped to ruminate on their next move.

"What are we to do now?" asked Peter Petano, a worrywart. Once he believed that the world was going to end, and so to spare his wife and children from the horror and the pain, he chivalrously dispatched them to heaven. However, the world lived on, but he was much relieved that he now had less to budget for. "Shall we risk our lives to besiege this castle for the sake of our bloodthirsty delectation? After all, isn't it rather mean, malignant, and most unneighbourly to kill the King, who, after all, is a human being just like us? Aren't we all mature, fair-minded mortals? We don't need war. Let's make love, not war!" he declared.

The soldiers promptly hugged each other while singing John Lennon's famous peace anthem 'Give Peace a Chance'.

King Prawn stepped out onto the balcony above the soldiers and berated them. "What are you? Men or girls? If you are a man, you would storm this castle, pillage it, raze it, and kill all the occupants. But if you are girls, go home and do your household chores!"

He was flabbergasted when the soldiers couldn't reach a decision.

Suddenly, the Queen appeared on the balcony, rivulets of blood running down her face.

Queen Clytoris addressed the soldiers in a calm but firm tone. "Are we human beings or are we monsters? Do we choose creativity, or do we choose violence?"

"I am not a monster; I am a human being!" shouted one soldier with three eyes and two noses and a mouth at the back of his head.

Some soldiers gasped, some fainted, at the sight of him.

"Go home to your wives and children. Love them, take care of them, enjoy life," Queen Clytoris implored them.

King Prawn screamed a tirade at the mouth-agape soldiers. "Women think with their hearts and men with their dicks. Attack this castle right now if you are men. But we all know who the real enemy is. Not us men! It's women! They have turned men into wonderful, loving, caring, sensitive, and understanding wimps. Women have castrated men. Women are the woe of men. But no longer shall they rule our lives. From this time forth men shall be masters of their fates and of women. We shall turn women back into quiet, obedient, giggling, male-respecting, sex objects instead of the independent, opinionated, ambitious, sceptical, University graduates that they are today. The first step in achieving domination is by abolishing foreplay. There shall be no more female orgasms. Women are not meant to enjoy love and sex. They were meant to be miserable housewives. Let's not make love, but rather let's destroy love! Let's destroy the rule of women! Let's be men once again! Tell me, are we men?"

"Is this a trick question?" asked James Picknose. He was an Elvis Presley corpse impersonation. The audience thought his act stank.

A horse bearing Queen Clytoris and her two-year-old son Prince Jotel cleaved through the bewildered soldiers and out of the gates and away, away...

"There's the enemy!" bellowed the King. "She's gone back to the womenfolk to make trouble. She'll make the women get us to see marriage counsellors to discuss our problems. Discussion is for women, action for men. I demand action! As your King, I will give you wars, conquests, and glory!"

"What about interest rates?" asked one Tele Banos, a computer programmer, who programmed his computer to give him a blowjob.

To which the King replied, "I shall give you bank robberies!"

"Hooray!" cheered the soldiers, raising their swords and cans of coke, which they had bought from a nearby vending machine.

"Let's be real men!" hollered King Prawn, with his sword gloriously erect, pointing to the horizon.

The men gnashing their teeth and shaping dangerous faces.

"Let's attack!"

"Roar!" yelled the soldiers as they stormed out of the courtyard, attacking whatever was there to be attacked. One soldier attacked a defenceless tree that was minding its own business. Another stepped on an innocent snail while on his way to visit his girlfriend to propose to her. King Prawn joined them on his steed, and galloped off towards the horizon, leading the men.

"Towards the horizons of conquests!" he hollered, his face delirious with gory prospects.

Meanwhile, our Queen began travelling from house to house, farm to farm, warning women of the impending male invasion and imploring them to join her in forming a committee that would meet every Tuesday night to discuss issues. The women, on the other hand, preferred to have the Queen made General of their newly formed troops to beat the shit out of those wimps.

"I refuse to resort to violence," declared Queen Clytoris, "for those are the very tactics that a man will use. I believe in love and wisdom to solve all our problems."

"How are we going to protect ourselves?" asked Anne Loopie, a farmer's wife.

"With our wits," said Queen Clytoris, pointing to her head.

The women liked and admired Queen Clytoris, impressed with her intelligence and kindness, and decided to join her to form a community where women could run their lives without the interference of men.

"My little boy," said Queen Clytoris to her two-year-old son, Prince Jotel, when you grow up, be wise and compassionate. Don't be a brute like your father. Don't be a man, be a person."

Right this moment Prince Jotel had this disturbing urge to rape his mother and kill his father. But it wasn't too disturbing; in fact, it was a relief because he had been desperate in his desire to rape his father and murder his mother a month before. According to Freud, he now had normal perverse desires and was well on his way to maturing into a normal psychopath who could cause serious damage to the world.

"What a sweet looking baby you have!" gushed Jane Fonda over the a-bed Prince Jotel. She was of no relation to the famous Hollywood star. Just the same moniker. Her dad was called Henry, but that was also coincidence. And that of her brother Peter. Not to mention her niece Brigitte…

"Yes, babies are wonderfully innocent," said Queen Clytoris, beaming with pride at her baby.

"A perfect little angel!" gushed Jane Fonda.

"What an ugly witch you are!" thought the little baby as he beheld the large woman.

"It is bad upbringing that destroys a child's innocence," Queen Clytoris lectured. "Children are brainwashed and miseducated to believe in destructive beliefs that destroy love and wisdom."

"Yes, I absolutely agree," Jane Fonda said, nodding unctuously, her eyes as blank as JD Salinger's typing paper.

"You look like a baboon's arsehole," thought Prince Jotel of the large looming face.

The Queen went on. "Intelligence can only grow on the fertile ground of Liberty. Our minds must be free to think, enquire and comprehend. Our education fills our minds with thoughts but never with thinking."

"How true, how true," Jane Fonda agreed, sheepishly nodding, and staring at Prince Jotel, wondering if the baby was looking at her with disgust or if the baby simply had a disgusting face.

"You make me spew," the baby said in gibberish, and the woman smiled innocently.

Later...

"Come and join me, not as a follower, but as an equal," the Queen told a group of women. "We will have a community in which everyone grows to enlightenment together, a community that helps and cares for its members so that there is no injustice, poverty, or alienation."

Cilla Billa, who had joined Queen Clytoris, addressed the crowd. "The men are coming to rape you, burn your houses, steal your belongings, and then expect you to serve them refreshments." She paused for emphasis. "We must leave this Kingdom immediately and establish our own Kingdom elsewhere. We will face death and slavery if we stay here."

"We should stay and fight!" shouted a woman, Carol Prag, from the crowd.

"Let's castrate them all!" shouted some women.

"No," said Queen Clytoris adamantly. "There will be no violence. Come with me and I'll take you to a new world where we shall be one big happy family."

"Show us the way, Queen Clytoris. We will follow you," the women spoke in unison.

"To our beautiful new world then!" exclaimed Queen Clytoris, pointing joyously at the horizon.

Jubilant, Jane Fonda picked up Prince Jotel and kissed him.

"Get this horror face out of my sight!" cried the baby in babbling screams.

"Ah, poor innocent child," said Queen Clytoris, tenderly gathering him from Jane Fonda. "Such a fragile creature in a cold, hard world. Don't fret, my love, I'll make you strong and wise."

"Oh, Mommy, can you chop off the lady's head?" asked the baby. "And feed it to the dogs."

"It's trying to communicate to you," gushed Jane Fonda. "I bet it wants to tell you how wonderful life is."

"Life is shit, Mommy," cried the baby, "I'm so helpless. I want to be tall and strong so I can cudgel this ugly twit into pulp! I want to speak so I can tell her to fuck off. Oh Mommy, I'm so miserable, can I suck your tits?"

Hey, dear readers, didn't I previously write that Prince Jotel was a two-year-old infant? That's a bit old for a prattling suckling! Oh, what the fuck, on with the novel, and all its inconsistencies. I love human imperfection, of which I am a perfect example. Fuck Literature! Fuck its prissy authors, its prissy books, its prissy prose, and its prissy critics! I am a gangster writer, a peasant prophet, a minority messiah!

"I adore babies, and babies adore me," Jane boasted, her nose flaring. "Queen Clytoris, may I be his nanny if you need any assistance?"

"I don't want servants. But you can be his friend."

"Aaaaaaaaaaahhhh!" screamed Prince Jotel, his mouth swallowing his face.

"Thank you, Your Royal Majesty!" and made a curtsy

Queen Clytoris shook her head. "Please don't call me Royal Majesty, in our community we are all equal. Just call me Clytoris."

"What's a clitoris?" queried a village idiotess, sucking her hair and dancing like Isodara Duncan on crutches.

A few women started giggling. Jane threw an admonishing glare at the village idiotess.

The Queen smiled good-heartedly. "Yes, I must admit that it is a funny name, but as far as I'm concerned, it's a beautiful name for a beautiful part of the body."

"It's a woman's best friend," added Sister Katrina. She belonged to the Sisters of Sin convent, which had a long waiting list.

"I'd rather have a dog," said the village idiotess, dancing, "and suck his tail."

Dear readers, don't you think women are too moral?

Q: Why did the woman cross the road?

A: To assist the chicken in crossing.

I think it's about time I introduce myself. My name is Ranulfo. I was born in Bohol, Philippines. I moved to Sydney, Australia when I was ten. I can't speak my native language, Tagalog, nor do I have an Australian accent. I don't know who the fuck I am. If anything, I am a lost soul, whose nation is Nothingness. To Nothingness I owe my allegiance. To Nothingness I salute. It all means nothing—God, Truth, Art, Money, Success. Maybe deep down I'm still a brown savage who worships trees and sharks, and my dark soul remains indifferent to western civilization. But my dark soul remains a stranger to me, and perhaps this novel, which will dig deep into my psyche, will make my dark soul a friend to me, and, who knows, an enemy to the world.

Let me introduce K. She is my Russian Jewish girlfriend. She was born in the village of Vitebsk, Russia, the magical setting for many a Chagall painting. My problem is she loves freedom like it's all brand new. She wants to be free! After all she escaped from Soviet Russia. And she hates the chains of love I give her. We met at the University of NSW during an anti-racism rally. East met West. We had travelled thousands of miles to meet. Yet sometimes when we are together, I feel that there is a thousand miles between us in terms of understanding. Can we work it out? Can East learn to live with the West? Jew with Christian? Male with female? White with brown?

# CHAPTER 3

## Prince Jotel in Love

Queen Clyot...damn I HATE TYPING!...holding back my urge to hurl this crummy typewriter at the wall. Liquid paper, come to my rescue once more. Queen Clytoris, beloved leader of the Women's Support Group, had gathered all the women in the nasty kingdom of King Prawn and sallied forth to seek a land where they could settle and build a Queendom of joyful wisdom.

Three thousand women followed Queen Clytoris in her quest for this virgin land that no man could desecrate, trekking across mountains, forests, plains, and deserts. A most arduous journey but one made easier by the strong emotional support within the community. A community of friends. The desert stretched on forever, the horizon encircled them like a prison, and the sun felt like an electric heater on a hot summer day. A hell without flames, doomed to turn angels into demons. The cloudless sky shed no tears of pity.

The women were getting antsy.

They were becoming increasingly impatient and irascible by the minute. In this sea of sun, Queen Clytoris feared mutiny on her ship of love. What the women feared was not falling over the edge of the earth but that there might be no edge. Women feared the Eternity Queen Clytoris offered them. Deep down in each of us was the need to crucify Eternity.

Finally, Queen Clytoris and co had triumphed over the desert and reached verdant lands. It was a land where the weather was kind, the ground fertile, and a river flowed with the purest of waters. It was a valley hidden like a vagina in the comely folds of the labia majora, surrounded by a forest of silken hairs. It was perfect.

A large pool of water quenched their parched, exhausted bodies, making them happy and hopeful once more. They took a vote and decided that this place was home. The desert was a trying experience. Queen Clytoris learnt that the tribulations of life could trigger people to become selfish and hostile. To knit her women together, she had to encourage them to be concerned and attentive to one another. By doing so, she had created a genuine community.

Surely, since Queen Clytoris can be regarded as a saviour of sorts, there must be a Judas figure. Of course, there is one, and if there isn't one, I'd make one, for a novel needs a villain to create tension and excitement. Hero/Villain...the yin and yang. Our Judas was a woman called Carol Prag, a university graduate in Economics. People were in awe of her as if she was a strong beast like a boa constrictor. She was a powerful woman; she knew how to manipulate people, not by bullying them, but playing on their fears and their conceit. As a pragmatist she was precise and formidable in the map of political and economic reality (or unreality). You felt emotionally neutral with her, neither invoking love nor hatred as she confronted you with facts and statistics. Yet she was a good woman. She just lacked the ability to understand the human soul or even care for it. Carol would never admit to being frightened of anything, though it was true that her fears had become abstract and intellectualised. Carol was afraid and she made everybody afraid. She was too limited, seeing only the earth, never heaven or hell, only the little reality, never the greater. In her small world, she made everyone feel small. Carol's world was populated by grubby, grasping rats.

A most beautiful world Queen Clytoris could see through her loving eyes. The sky was shining blue, so blue as if one were swimming in a sea of cerulean oil paint You could feel the blue, inhale it like it was a blue rose. And the water of the pool was so sweet to her flesh as she waded into it, her flesh intoxicated. The surface of the water sparkled like diamond rings in the rays of the sun. Surrounding her was a bevy of naked women. So many varieties of bodies, all beautiful to her.

Prince Jotel sat back and ogled at them, judging the naked women rating them on a scale of ten: 2...6...2...10! —Prince Jotel's eyes popped out when he saw the most beautiful girl in the world standing in the water.

Twenty years later, Prince Jotel rhapsodised to his drinking chum, Jimmy Mouse, a fellow alcoholic, brother (he claimed) of a famous acting mouse:

"She was an angel with luscious legs for wings. I still remember her then vividly, her back towards me, she stood in the pool, the water up to her knees. I gazed at her face, and I was caught in the whirlpool of her perfection, and I loved her. She gazed back at me as if she was desire itself. I can't describe that passion in her eyes, it wasn't human, it was some unnatural force, a drug, an idol, a devouring inspiration. She laughed at me when she saw my stunned look as if I was going to die. She turned around, and the sunlight made her white flesh glow with desire and tenderness. I knew I had to love her."

"For twenty years I chased her. I couldn't catch her because she wasn't real, she was a dream. She was a performance of womanhood, an actress playing the seductress, and I wanted to lose myself in her unreality inasmuch as she had lost herself. She was a priestess of lust, who knew everything there was to know about men while knowing nothing about herself. It was this flowing, giving, generous self that ensnared me. Yet it also ensnared herself, for her gift to attract men would eventually bleed and kill her. Having failed to capture her, I feel as if I'd missed out, not on the reality, but on the Art of Love, the Mozartian symphony, the plastic unreality of Beauty. Love, which was purely Art, calculated, rehearsed, perfected, pure abstraction distilled from reality."

"Her name was Virginia. She was perfect. The Perfect ones destroy themselves, the fate of the Marilyn Monroes of the world."

# CHAPTER 4

## Harry the Wanker

God, I hate newsagents! I've just been to a newsagency at the University of NSW to read the papers. The woman tending the shop told me that I couldn't read them unless I bought them. I wanted to say to her "Why do you make the world so small? Why do you make an issue about nothing? Why should you care if I read the papers? Who cares? Why care about the trivial things when you should care about the important stuff! Following that trite incident, I came across a lovely black and grey striped cat. I followed that cat, who walked nonchalantly around the university, so proud, composed, and sharp like a true aristocrat. Every time it sat down, it was ensconced in a golden throne, and every time it ventured into the bushes, it was a lion in the jungle. How serene and majestic it was. How superior was that cat over that newsagent lady.

King Prawn despised the world. He had to wage war on it because he had no love for it to leave it in peace. He cursed its pettiness and mediocrity, which he wanted to crush, this bureaucracy of stupidity, and transform it into a jungle of adventure where people were strong, proud, and dignified. Human beings had become jokes; small wonder comedians weren't running out of material. Humans had become trite matters, earning little respect, as if misery and destruction were their just wages. King Prawn believed that he could save the world...through war. War, according to King Prawn, was a struggle to live, to live to the utmost. The purpose of war was to free the lions from their cages. The cage of the mind. Never in the history of humanity had humans thought and felt so much. Perhaps there was a time when the mind was a beautiful island, but now that island was a Manhattan Island of concrete wilderness, a traffic gridlock of pollution, technology, overpopulation, skyscrapers, ghettos, consumerism, racism, politics, crime, corruption, impotence, and insanity. The mind had become Leviathan. Billions of thoughts and feelings running amok through its narrow streets and boulevards. And the mind kept expanding, becoming an obese monstrosity, piling up, and devouring more space, more fuel, sucking everything up like a black hole, while spewing out pollution, cemeteries, PR, and Art. That city must be levelled to the ground, and the ground must be made fertile again, a place for indigenous Indians to hunt their buffaloes: this was King Prawn's sacred duty.

Everything would revert to its natural state. The end of artifice, the end of Art. He would destroy Art and her theatres of tortured self-consciousness, these kitsch daydreams, sanctuaries from our fear of nothingness, this retreat from reality and escape into the nightmares of Art, the Finnegans Wake of Art, Art, Art, stimuli of abstraction, the mirrors of mental glorification, the diarrhoea of self. Away, away, always a further retreat from reality. How sick he was of the cowardice of Art.

Damn this cowardly world! So many cowards, afraid of eating red meat, losing one's job, running out of money, being lonely, dying from cancer, missing an episode of Melrose Place, not having an erection. These little fears making Lilliputians of us all. And King Prawn sought to destroy these fears that were paralysing the world, not by giving them a super safe world where no one got sick or died, but by giving them a dangerous world where courage, not greed, was the driving force. The soul, fearing Death, chose not to face God, who was Death. The soul had degenerated from the godly to the ungodly, the spiritual to the frivolous, from Yahweh to Ronald McDonald. The ungodliness of our civilisation like Sodom and Gomorrah, people so afraid of Death they lived in desperation, losing themselves in an orgy of pleasure. Pigs of pleasure, pigs of sex, pigs of love, pigs of Art, pigs of money, pigs of food, pigs of happiness. These contemptible, sordid little pigs weren't alive; they were merely stimulated into life, electrocuted into feeling. What copious amounts of hatred the King had inside his mind; all these years buried by the sham of Love. He felt like a Death's scythe slicing through life.

King Prawn had travelled for miles through the forest when he arrived at the top of a large hill. He could see a clearing below where a forlorn farmhouse stood. At long last, he was able to launch an attack. At long last, he could be a man.

"What a pretty place to have a picnic!" commented one Fredric Hudson, whose brother was the famous Hudson River. Everybody despised him because he was a newsagent. In five years', he would be murdered by one of his disgruntled customers. His skull pummelled by a rolled-up newspaper.

"Okay, men!" hollered King Prawn. "You are true soldiers now! Fight, be courageous, and do not fear death!" On his black steed, he loped down the hill and towards the farmhouse. Men swarmed behind him, screaming with their swords and spears raised high. Soon the green paddock would be a grey mass of running soldiers like a run amok charging porcupine. Despite the din of men, King Prawn could still hear the immense silence of the farm; he was sure it was abandoned, and his heart sank. Reaching the farmhouse, a soldier knocked politely on the door.

"I don't think anyone's home, Your Royal Majesty," said General Motors, who was neither a general nor a multinational company, just a mere private who acted like a real general because people thought he was a real general.

"Bust the door down!"

General Motors kicked the door, then again, and again, but to no avail.

"Burn it down!" ordered King Prawn.

"Does anybody have a light?" General Motors asked the soldiers.

"We don't smoke. Smoking is bad for you," the soldiers answered. "Smoking reduces life expectancy by 6.8 years."

"Surely this lone house is no match for us strong men," said King Prawn, getting annoyed with his soldiers, and he screamed, "Attack!"

The men drew their swords and charged at the brick farmhouse, striking the walls with their swords and spears, but their brick enemy blunted their assault.

Eventually, the men relinquished the fight and took up sedentary positions.

"I'm sorry, my Majesty," said General Motors, "but I think we have lost the battle. The men did put up a courageous fight, but the house proved much too formidable."

King Prawn alighted from his horse and surveyed his vanquished army. Amid the heavy respirations of exhaustion were the reverberations of snoring.

"I think we have a battle casualty," said General Motors, pointing to a man clutching his stomach.

"Don't worry about me, sir, it's just indigestion. Too much chilli con carne for lunch," explained Tobey Olson. He was a bank clerk who had been embezzling millions of dollars from his bank to pay off his mother. She was blackmailing him, having caught him in the act of masturbating to a photograph of Andrew Peacock, dashing Australian politician.

"I don't accept defeat," said King Prawn irately. "Every enemy has his weakness, and this house is no exception."

"What a sore loser you are," said the house to the King. The house's eyes were two upper windows, and his mouth...egad! was the red front door.

"I haven't lost yet, foe," replied the intrepid King Prawn, drawing out his sword and brandishing it provocatively at the smirking house. King Prawn screeched a war cry, which sounded like a constipated bull, and assailed the house, repeatedly striking it with his sword.

"It's no use," laughed the house. "I'm impervious to pain."

"Yes, impervious to physical pain," said King Prawn with a malignant smile, "but are you impervious to emotional pain?"

"What a smart cookie you are," said his adversary admiringly.

"Then take this: your mother was an outhouse!"

The house laughed, a low booming concatenation. "You call that an insult! I despise my mother! She was a barn, a simple woman really, but because she got married to a hotshot New York skyscraper 60 storeys high, she got ideas put into her simple head that she was a superior woman. And she wanted me to become superior too, be like my father, and work in New York as a skyscraper. Boy, she really nagged and bullied me. She sent me to New York, and what a joke, me a simple farmhouse trying to find work as a skyscraper. I was laughed out of New York. So I returned to the country to be a simple farmhouse. My mother never forgave me for that. God, she likes to make me feel inferior."

"But you are inferior," King Prawn insulted him.

"I am not inferior," the farmhouse reacted hotly

"Yes, you are, Shorty!" King Prawn baited him.

"Don't call me Shorty!" shouted the house, flushing red in his face.

"Shorty! Shorty! Shorty!" King Prawn teased him, while doing an irritating jig.

"Why you!" The ground began to rumble, and the farmhouse suddenly broke free from its foundations and heaved toward King Prawn. Opening his mouth, the house roared.

The soldiers speedily stood up in fright and fled in panic as the house chased them. Fortunately, the house was a slow runner, so King Prawn and his cowardly men were able to escape into the woods.

"Shorty! Shorty! Shorty!" King Prawn kept shouting back as he retreated.

In the safety of the woods, he plotted to defeat that farmhouse. He needed to win this battle because it was his first, and it would serve as a springboard for his future conquests. He went to a vantage point to study his adversary. There in the sun, sat the farmhouse, smoking, reading a magazine, and sipping a refreshing glass of enamel. The house looked so pathetic all alone out there. Its loneliness bothered King Prawn, who did feel an affinity towards lonely creatures. He understood loneliness. He hated it, knowing loneliness was a sign of weakness, a telltale of cowardice. Loneliness was exile from reality. King Prawn was now determined to seize control of reality.

"All right, my lonely farmhouse, you'll have female company tomorrow, and your dreams of love and lust will turn into a nightmare that will destroy you."

Returning to camp, King Prawn ordered his army to construct a female bungalow, a real hotsy-totsy to inflame the farmhouse's lust.

Meanwhile, Harry the Farmhouse was poring through the pages of House and Garden, admiring the beautiful exteriors and interiors of beautiful rich belles that would never love him. He was getting quite horny looking at the intimate bathrooms, the photographs soft and glossy, why, just like Penthouse magazine. What a huge bathtub she had! round, pink, and equipped with five gold jet faucets, sunk in the middle of a mirror-walled bathroom. But they were mere photographs. He had never seen the real thing before. If photographs were beautiful, how much more beautiful the real thing would be? He was depressed. It was his loneliness that pained him, the unreality of his life that tore him inside. Isolation was so unreal. Like a movie being screened to an empty movie house. His life needed to be seen and appreciated by someone he loved and cared for. To love and be loved. That was what living was all about. And without love, there could only be the negation of life.

Hate, despair, fear...he thought back to the incident with King Prawn and his army. It was all so ridiculous and petty, yet he was dragged down to their madness. There was no love there, just hatred and destruction. He knew that the king was lonely, for there was something desperate about his actions. A desperation to overcome and annihilate his innate, introverted philosophical nature. The house was desperate as well, wanting something wonderful to happen to him, yearning that his dreams would come true, so he needed dreams no longer. But reality was beyond his dreams, which remained inside of him unwilled to being. He wasn't free to do anything. There was something in him that kept him a prisoner. For a time, he called this his Ball and Chain. But when he met other houses, he discovered that they, too, had balls and chains; and these houses weren't shy like him. Then it dawned on him: life was a ball and chain. We were all caught in a pattern of behaviour that we couldn't break. Living was habitual, with the same thoughts, emotions, actions, repeating endlessly. We lived the same day over and over again. The Past was the Present was the Future. The Ball and Chain. For Harry the farmhouse, tomorrow would be the same day. No, not really, for tomorrow would be his death, the day his Ball and Chain were smashed to smithereens to give him freedom. Death is freedom, my friend, so cheer up. Life is a just prison.

So, what did Harry the Farmhouse do on his last day? Nothing at all, except daydream, think, and reminisce. For shy people or cowards, the purpose of memory is to regret it. And Harry regretted all his yesterdays, especially those moments we all had in our lives when we encountered an opportunity that had to be seized, an opportunity that would break the ball and chain. It was in New York that Freedom came and visited him for the taking. He met a lovely, young American female bungalow in Central Park. She initiated the meeting when she struck up a conversation with him while he was feeding the pigeons.

"You come from the country?" she asked him, her smile so lovely. "Here for a visit?"

"I'm here looking for a job," was his shy reply.

"Job as what?" she inquired, puzzled as to how a farmhouse in New York could possibly be employed.

The farmhouse answered with embarrassment. "My mum wants me to be a skyscraper."

She smiled and laughed. "My mum sent me here to marry a Wall Street skyscraper."

He smiled tentatively, hurt.

"But I don't like cities much," she promptly added, noting the sadness in his face. "Too much concrete and steel. I prefer to live in the country."

He smiled shyly.

"My mother would be shocked…" she paused, and said coyly, "should I marry…a farmhouse."

Harry blushed.

Harry and Winnette got along fabulously, like a house on fire. They spent a lot of time together; they went to the movies, watched Broadway shows, ate at restaurants, and danced in nightclubs. They were in love with each other. The only problem was Harry's shyness. He could relate to her abstractly but remained at a physical and emotional distance. He felt safe just talking. He could not tell her that he loved her and wanted her. Those emotions provoked so much distress in him. He had never had the opportunity to express those feelings to anyone. His relationship with his parents was empty of love and affection. Those feelings were never nurtured to become strong and confident. They hid inside him like scared mice. So nothing eventuated between him and Winnette. Harry went home alone, and so did Winnette.

He wrote her some abstract letters, but she lost interest, convinced that he didn't love her. Harry suffered tremendously but chose to suffer alone rather than to declare his love. He could never accept the possibility that he could be loved. Always, always, was the feeling of great unworthiness. Perhaps he was too aware of the sky above him, a great, big, fat eternity sitting on his face, God the bully. Never again did Harry have the opportunity to have a woman to love. We need love. We need to be loved in this world, which makes us so small and insignificant.

Harry was bought by the Retnik family, a big family, a couple with two boisterous boys, two mischievous girls, and a poopy pet dog. He found humans exasperating. They were obstreperous, shouting at each other whenever they spoke, or incessantly playing the idiot box, or the radio, or the record player, as if silence was a terrifying ordeal. Having to watch their daily lives appalled him, like watching a boring soap opera played by melodramatic actors. He rejoiced when they left. Being alone in the country was quite a splendid life, for nature was like a beautiful and wise wife. But he felt something was lacking. He wanted a real wife.

Harry always waited for something to happen. Every day, he hoped that this would be the day when everything would fall into place. Today he woke up with the same positive feeling of anticipation. Today was the day. And he never suspected that today was the day of his death. Poor Harry, dying unfulfilled, unloved, unfucked. Oh Harry, you died the day you left New York without Winnette. You killed yourself, Harry. Freedom is Life. Freedom is Choice. You couldn't choose because you were shackled to your Ball and Chain. Oh poor Harry, poor virgin, now you are going to die, and Death is going to fuck you real bad.

Harry was astounded when he saw a beautiful bungalow crossing the fields towards him. She was looking at him with a seductive allure. What a sexy hotsy-totsy she was! Could she be Winnette? Of course not, Harry, Winnette is dead. She died a year ago, demolished to make way for a parking lot. That's why I'm going to kill you, Harry, so you can join your Winnette up in that big land development in the sky. I, the author, created you, and I shall make you happy. I take care of my creation unlike you know who...

"Hello," she greeted him with oozing sensuality.

"Hello." Blush, blush, blush.

"What a handsome hunk you are," she blarneyed.

Harry, eyes meeting the ground, too afraid to look up. "Geez...thanks." Blush, blush, blush.

"Guess what?"

"What?"

"I've been checking you out for the past few days, hiding behind those trees, and you know what?"

"What?"

"I fancy you," she whispered seductively.

Harry, reddening into neon red.

"You know what?"

"What?" Jesus Christ, Harry, can't you be a bit more articulate?

"I want you."

He could not believe his ears...or um windows. She was so beautiful!

"Hey, big boy!" she said, winking at him with her window shades. "Why don't you open your door and show me what you've got. Show me yours and I'll show you mine."

How much Harry yearned to open his door to a female house and show off his wonderful and beautiful interior. It was like opening the cage to free the bird. But Harry grew shy and shook his head in fear.

"You stupid twit!" said King Prawn inside the female bungalow. King Prawn was pat at female voice impersonation. He was brilliant doing Judy Garland and Liza Minelli singing a duet. For the voice of the female bungalow, he did Marilyn Monroe. He knew every man was in love with Marilyn Monroe because she was beautiful, sexy, and fragile. And every man fantasised he was the special man to make her happy forever. Fools!

"Don't be shy," she said to Harry.

Harry blushed like the setting sun, and like the setting sun, he wanted to hide behind the horizon.

She opened his door, and Harry, instead of freezing, felt wonderful, the bird of his soul liberated from his cage. The opened door revealed his living room, which was a horrendous mess, as the last family who lived there were slobs. There were dirty plates and glasses and old newspapers and rotting food in plastic Chinese take away containers and broken umbrellas and battered old shoes and beer bottles and paper wrappings and God knows what else, maybe radioactive waste. The living room was a garbage dump, and it would turn off any female house in the world.

"Oh yuk!" said King Prawn, feeling nauseous. Then he turned to his men in the house. "This is it, soldiers! When I open the door, go run inside and tear him apart!"

"How handsome you are inside," she lied to him. "Now I shall show you mine."

The reality of love at long last. No more photographs, no more daydreams, no more Art. From now on, reality was his. He would be connected to the world at last, not a separate, isolated object, lost and unwanted. He would belong! The strength of the world would give him strength. No more the weakness of his isolated self, impotent and afraid. The force of the world behind him.

Slowly she opened her door and...everything became so unreal...it was a dream...no, a nightmare...as soldiers ejaculated out of her house and into his. He was being rent asunder inside, the guts of his self being ripped out.

Harry could not react; he was shattered. The death of dreams was a great wound. He was staring at the female house in front of him. Looking through her door, he saw that there was absolutely nothing inside. Just nothing. No living room, no kitchen, no bathroom. He had waited all his life for this...nothing...just your Ball and Chain, Harry, the Past was the Present was the Future. He felt hot inside, was it rage he was experiencing? He saw soldiers leaping out of his mouth, scampering to the woods. Smoke plumed the air, and flames kicked about his eyes. He was burning. Instinctively, he ran. He screamed in pain and desperation. He could see nothing in front of him; all was smoke. He crashed into a tree, then into another. He was reaching the extremes of pains. Dying was too painful for him to have any last thoughts. Perhaps he wanted to think of Winnette before he died. But he couldn't.

Just pain, the utterness of it. And like sleep, he didn't know when he finally died.

Later, when King Prawn viewed the charred remains of Harry, he felt that something had died inside himself. Was it his soul? A soul is not separate, it is linked to other souls, and today he severed that link with the utmost brutality. He was glad, it was like a ball and chain.

# CHAPTER 5

## Adventures of Prince Jotel the Cat

You came to my apartment for the first time, and we lay on the floor browsing through art books. You wore brown corduroy jeans, which fitted snugly to your body. My hand wandered to touch and caress your legs. You said nothing as you flicked through the pages. I can't remember the artist's name. His genius had slipped into my memory's black hole. Then when it was time for you to leave, I kissed you for the first time. How soft your lips were, I felt I was falling into air.

I need a plot! My plot is a blur, a hazy suburb in a mist. My intention so far is to establish both King Prawn and Queen Clytoris and their jolly little kingdoms. These kingdoms will represent the flaws and flights of humanity, an allegory of a soul in search of a home, a God, or Truth. These two kingdoms will clash, not only on the battlefield but also inside me, ultimately for control of my soul, because King Prawn and Queen Clytoris form two parts of my Gemini self, the Yin and Yang, the male and female, the good and evil. I hope, in the end, peace will come to me, my conflicts resolved. Perhaps I can understand K and myself, and we can be happy together.

Prince Jotel despised his nanny, Jane Fonda. He disliked her superficial niceness. It was too contrived, too overdone. Jane Fonda had no talent for being nice, and he wished she would stop forcing herself on others and just keep to herself. He was sure that homo sapiens were the lowest form of life on earth, all the animals and insects having learnt a long time ago the wisdom of silence.

"Prince Joty!" called out Jane Fonda in a shrieking voice. "Prince Joty! Come out, come out wherever you are! "

Prince Jotel, disguised as a ginger cat, sat in the corner of the room, watching Jane Fonda and contemplating his hatred for her.

"I know you are hiding from me, you naughty little boy." She crawled on the ground, her round, hideous head probing under here and there. When she saw the ginger cat from under the bed glaring at her, she hissed. "You get out of here! No cats are allowed here! Shoo! "She grabbed the cat by the tail, stomped to the front door and kicked it outside.

Prince Jotel the cat landed on his bottom and immediately a rabid Alsatian barking ferociously charged at him. The dog was suddenly stopped in its tracks with one solid whack on the nose by the cat. The cat, fuming, stomped his way back to the house, kicked the door open, and like two gunfighters in a showdown, Jane Fonda and the cat glared at each other.

"Didn't I tell you to scram!" yelled Jane Fonda.

The cat growled, then lunged at her, grabbing her throat and shoving her to the ground (BLANG!). Jane slipped out of his grip and hurled him against the wall (SPLATT!). She rushed towards him, ramming her head into his stomach (BOOOG!). She headlocked him and punched him in the ribs repeatedly (BINGBANGBOO!!!). He bit her tits (CRUNCH!!!!) and kicked her fat bottom (BOING!!). In reply, she headbutted him (GRONK!!!). Finally, he gripped her throat, threw her to the floor, and smacked her head on the ground (BANGBANGBANG!).

Jane lay exhausted on the ground, bruised and beaten. Prince Jotel the cat went out to take a stroll around the community.

It was autumn, and strong winds cooled the air. His cat costume kept him warm. People were baffled by seeing this ginger cat walking on his hind legs with his front paws in his hip pockets. The village was bustling; some were gardening, some building things, some cooking, some resting and chatting with friends.

"We should build a castle," Carol argued with a group of women standing around her. "We need a castle to protect ourselves from any invaders. What if King Prawn discovers where we are? He'll burn our village down and make us all his slaves. To further protect ourselves, we need an army. We should be trained to fight. We need to make weapons. If this community is to survive, it has to be strong, and it won't survive merely on the strength of Queen Clytoris's wisdom. What good is a strong mind if we have a weak body? Our bodies have been our downfall throughout history. We have been oppressed because women are physically weaker than men. This wouldn't have happened if men and women were physically equal. And if we don't build this castle, then you're virtually asking to be oppressed by men again. We don't want that to happen again, do we? You don't expect King Prawn or any other invader to leave us alone. Let us not wait on this issue. We could be attacked any minute now. Now is the time to be strong!"

When Prince Jotel saw Jane Fonda emerge from his hut looking enraged, he decided to make himself scarce. He had no desire to fight her again; she was as tough as nails. He decided to travel by rooftop, casually jumping from roof to roof like a cat with nine lives to kill. By chance he caught a glimpse of his paramour, Virginia, gazing out of her window. His heart pounded as he gazed upon her beautiful face.

"Oh pussycat!" she called to him when she spotted the cat crouching on the rooftop across from her.

"Here pussywoosy!"

Prince Jotel leapt to the ground and dashed madly to her arms.

"Oh beautiful kittykat, beautiful kittykat."

How wonderful it was to be held by her! To feel her warm body and to smell her sweet fragrance, it was like being enveloped by a rose.

"Oh kitten, are you owned by somebody? Do you want to live with me? You'll be my prince, my own handsome prince. You and I are going to be great friends...I adore you so much. And you adore me too...I could see...your eyes are so full of love...you hug me as if you didn't want to let me go...God answered my prayers. I asked God for a friend...and he sent you to me...You are an angel cat sent from cat heaven. Tell me, have you seen the Virgin Mary? Is she beautiful? She must be very nice. Is Jesus Christ very handsome? I bet he has very beautiful eyes. I also bet heaven is made of fluffy white clouds."

"This is heaven, "said Prince Jotel to himself. "This is heaven." And he nestled his cheek on her unbloomed breasts.

Prince Jotel became her pet, albeit part time, for he had to be Queen Clytoris's son as well. They had a wonderful relationship; it was purrfect. It was love only love that bound them together, no fights, no betrayals. She loved the cat like her best friend and confided in him with everything. He watched her body grow from girlhood to womanhood. He listened to her joys, her sorrows, her dreams, her opinions wise and foolish, her playful humour, her peeves, her seriousness, her nightmares, her confusion, her. It was like watching a stem, seeing a node struggling out to be a bud, then unfold its flower then slowly rot till it fell to the ground. He witnessed her living, and he witnessed her dying. When she died, and she was still young, the only friend she had was a cat who wasn't a cat. She despised all men and, ironically, it was a man disguised as a cat that she loved most. But, dear readers, I'm getting way ahead of myself.

"Do you want me to tell you a bedtime story?" Virginia whispered to Prince Jotel as they cuddled in bed. "Once upon a time, there lived a beautiful princess who was sad and lonely. Her parents, the King and Queen, wanting to make her happy, threw a ball and invited all the princes in the world. And whoever could make her happy would marry her and have half of their kingdom. All the handsome princes of the world came to the ball to try and make her happy. All the princes were so handsome, so courageous, so rich, so charming, but alas, none could make the princess happy. Then she saw happiness. There it was—a cat curled up on a cushion. She approached the cat and held him up, and instantly became the happiest girl in the world. Observing all this, the King said. 'That cat made my princess happy. He should marry my daughter and have half my kingdom.' Do you know what happened? She kissed the cat. Like this," and she gave Prince Jotel a kiss on his whiskered cheeks (Prince Jotel had to resist himself from grabbing her and giving her a French kiss).

"Tell me, do you think he turned into a handsome prince?" The cat nodded. "No, silly, she turned into a beautiful cat. They ran away, lived in the woods, they would have got married but cats don't marry, they had heaps of kittens and they lived happily ever after."

"And we lived happily ever after," thought Prince Jotel to himself and the wishing stars outside in the night before nodding off into a beautiful, dreamy sleep beside Virginia.

# CHAPTER 6

## Friday the 13th

I hate love, love is so unloving. You see, dear readers, the author is not a man, he's an artist. I'm sorry, K. I cannot love you as forcefully as a lover should. I was born to dream in this real world. This is the 5th chapter, and I haven't got a clue what to write about. Today is Friday the 13th, so maybe I'll write something scary with ghosts, goblins, monsters, and the Osmond teeth. Maybe I'll kill off a character. Say, how about rubbing out Queen Clytoris? She's a bit of a bore. Hey, were you sad to hear about Harry the Farmhouse biting the dust? Why do you feel sad? It's only the death of words. Mere words. Like Hamlet. Or Martin Chuzzlewit. Perhaps God. Just words, which pose as reality. Pure fiction, nothing else.

"I am real!" protests Harry the Wanker, now materialising before me.

"Hey, you're supposed to be dead!" I shake and tremble, soiling my pants with my own piss.

"I'm a ghost," he explains to me.

"A ghost!" I let out a petrified scream. My hair stands on end, my brown face blanches into white chalk. I want to flee, but my legs feel like frozen drumsticks. I hold up two pens, cross them like a crucifix, and point them at Harry.

"I'm not Dracula, silly," laughs Harry. "I'm Harry the Friendly Ghost."

I sneer at him. "I hate friendly people."

"Who do you think you are?" snaps Harry. "What makes you think you're better than everyone else?"

"My self-awareness," I reply. "I know I'm a fuckwit idiot. This is profound self-knowledge. Self-awareness is a step towards enlightenment."

"Yes, I agree, you are a fuckwit idiot."

"Thank you."

"But tell me, Mr. Author, why did you kill me off?"

"Out of mercy. Wankers should be put down."

"I resent that I had no choice. You created me, my plot, my actions, my words. You were responsible for everything that I did. Yet you chose to give me a lonely life and a horrific death. I am your abused creation."

"You should at least be grateful that I created you."

Suddenly, his face darkens. "I hate you!" he hollers.

"I can destroy you." I point my pen at him like it was a knife.

"Don't you dare point that at me, you bastard!" His massive body moves aggressively towards me.

"You don't scare me," laughing at his face. Of course, I am terrified. But I try to bluff him out.

"I don't scare you, do I?" Harry, grinning maliciously. "Then take this! BOOOOOOOOOOOO!!!!!!!!!!!!!!!!!!!!!!"

I jump so high that I orbit the earth twenty-three times before splashing down in the middle of the Pacific Ocean, where I am immediately swallowed by a whale. The belly of the whale is a dark, quiet, stinking place, from where I shall do my writing from now on. Most people would find it too dark to write in. But I don't care, for I have chosen darkness to be my inspiration. Yes, the belly of the whale is a wonderful place, the smell can be overpowering, but one grows to love it for it is the smell of passion, the stinking heart of the ocean. It's not boring inside here. There are beautiful views of the deep aquatic life through the blowhole, mouth, and arsehole. The ocean is really weird, and all these strange creatures appear and disappear in the mist of the deep. Crazy wall-eyed creatures like drowned tourists stare back at me. It's the underworld here. Here in the underworld, everything is deepened, your senses, thoughts, emotions, reaching the bottom of reality, losing its humanness. You get the suspicion that God is not human, but something beyond. The ultimate weirdo.

Reading what I have just written, what a super wanker I am!

Queen Clytoris was hopeful about her new community. She envisioned peace, love, and understanding flourishing here. She had abandoned the mammon of economic growth. Only the soul, the mind, and the heart mattered in her new kingdom. Politics was supposed to be about the rule of wisdom. But politicians were only concerned with power and profit. The egotistic, self-serving politics of today where each person must look out for number one, damn the poor, damn the elderly, damn the sick, damn the failures, damn the minorities, for all that matters is to be a success, a millionaire, a celebrity. Politicians must lead, and they must lead people to Wisdom. Queen Clytoris wanted to create a caring community where each person mattered. No one in her community would be neglected. This was family. Compassionate politics.

No blinkered idealist, Queen Clytoris was well aware of the enormous challenges. People were obstinate. They were reluctant to change. People were impervious to wisdom. She recounted how she could never convince a Christian that Jesus was not God but a wise man. Nor could she ever convince a rich man to share his money with the poor. What could she do with our belief-ridden species? Set up a dictatorship like Stalin did and terrify and massacre the masses into submission. This would only unleash the monsters. But she had come to despise the madness of human affairs to the point where she couldn't sit idly by any longer; she had to try to change the world, or the world would destroy itself.

One of the reasons Queen Clytoris was quietly optimistic about the future was St Claire, an orphan girl of indeterminate age (undetermined by the author). She was very intelligent, and she found a mother figure in Queen Clytoris. St Claire visited her often and enjoyed asking her philosophical questions. She listened hungrily to her answers. Ideas were like Tim Tam biscuits to her. Sometimes she understood, and sometimes she did not, but that did not seem to matter because she felt good inside. She desired wisdom. Queen Clytoris never spoke down to her; she spoke intelligently.

"I believe in reason. There must be no compromise on reason: because once you do, there is no limit to what irrationality can let loose. History has shown that we have paid a bloody price for our irrationality. We must not even sacrifice reason for God. The first step to madness is faith. If there were a God, he or she or it would want us to think, rather than simply believe. Faith is blindness."

"But," said St Claire, "aren't some people born more intelligent than others?"

"We all grow. We are not born wise. We go through life, making mistakes, learning things, understanding, and changing. We grow through understanding. People who don't grow have given up on trying to understand life. They have made up their minds about everything. Their minds have become ossified."

"Is it bad to have emotions?"

"No, one should leave reason for thinking and emotions for feeling. Don't mix the two. The emotions can't think properly, so leave it to reason to do its job. In the same way our bodies should do the sensing, we must see and hear and touch without being distorted by our thoughts and feelings. Our emotions are a battle between darkness and light. The victor possesses the heart. We must help the light win the battle so that the heart can love. If darkness wins, the heart will hate and wreak destruction."

"Will the world ever be a better place?"

"Not if people expect Messiahs to save them. It's a silly, romantic, rescue fantasy. Everyone must work out his or her salvation on their own. The world will change when people change. But people do not want to change. It is a job for politicians to encourage them to change rather than indulge them in their weaknesses and superficialities. The wisdom motive is more important than the profit motive."

Queen Clytoris watched St Claire hanging on to every word she said. She didn't like that; she wanted her to be independent, not a mere follower.

"Of course, you don't have to accept blindly what I say. I might be wrong. The evillest people in the world have been the ones who believed absolutely in their being right. Always leave room for doubt, for there is no end to understanding."

"Shouldn't one fight evil?" asked St Claire. "There are monsters out there that have to be destroyed."

"Yes, one should try to prevent people hurting other people. But never fail to see the humanity in other people, or else you will lose your humanity. Don't divide the world into them and us. We are all imperfect humans."

"Do you believe in God?"

"I don't know if God exists or not. Only Death will tell me the answer. Nonetheless, God exists as a concept and does affect our lives considerably. God is a mirror of our souls. If we are narrow-minded, we believe in a narrow-minded God. If we are modern, we believe in a modern God. If we are vindictive, we believe in a God who will be the instrument of our vengeance. If we are cynical, we create the God of nothingness. We shape our God to fit our personalities. In fact, people should use the genitive 'my' whenever they talk about God. However, God becomes the justification of our negativity, our limitations. Then God presents an obstacle to our personal growth. We must remember God is infinite, so we must not limit God and therefore not limit ourselves. To believe in God is to believe in the infinity of our souls."

St Claire wondered to herself what kind of God she believed in. Her God would be female, and she'd be wise, loving, and protective. She'd be a big fat Mama, who'd always have cookies, cakes, and apple pies ready to eat, and she'd always give you a big loving hug, and lovely fairy tales to tell at bedtime. That was her God. She thought about the gods of the people she knew. Prince Jotel's God would be his personal pimp, butler, Santa Clause, and hit man. Virginia's God would be tall, dark, handsome, with a cute butt, small brain, and a mushy romantic. Yuk! thought St Claire.

Carol's God would be a tight-arse, strait-laced asexual who would always be too busy administering the universe to look after the personal side of her creation. St Claire laughed as the images of God rolled through her mind. She had no idea religion was so amusing. Just as a dog resembled his or her master, God resembled his or her worshipper. Like owning a pet God. Yet she couldn't simply laugh at life. There was something scary about life. Death, disease, loneliness, old age, and sorrow await us all. And what did all this suffering mean? If only for the reward of eternal happiness at the end of a hard life. If that was the case, there had to be a God to make sure this happened. If there was no God, Death ruled the universe. Death, the Eternal Nothingness.

St Claire wasn't always philosophical. In fact, she was quite in love with Prince Jotel. She didn't know why. It was all so irrational.

St Claire walked up to Prince Jotel, who was playing Rambo with his teddy bear.

"I'm going to marry you."

Prince Jotel made a rude gesture. "Look here, little girl, you don't know what love is. Take it from me, I'm an expert."

"Teach me," she said, and then kissed him on the lips.

"Yuk!" cried Prince Jotel, grimacing, and spitting out her kiss.

She kissed him again and held him tight; then she said to him, "Now look here, Prince Jotel, you can't tell me what to do. I'm going to marry you one day because you're mean, rotten, awful, and I'm going to make you nice. I don't deserve you, but you deserve me."

"I won't marry you. You stink! I'm going to marry Virginia."

She sneered at him. "She's silly. I admit that she's very beautiful, but she's not smart like me. You have to marry me because I'm smart, and I'll make you smart. If you marry her, you'll be silly for the rest of your life, just like her."

"I love her, that's all that matters."

"She's too silly, I tell you. I played with her once, and all she wanted was to play make-believe. I wanted to play chess, but she insisted we play pretend husband and wife. I was the husband and all I had to do was sit and do nothing while she cooked, cleaned, and entertained. I sat there rotting to death. You marry her, and you'll rot."

"Sounds perfect."

"You deserve better."

"She's the best."

"Shut up and kiss me!" She pushed him to the ground and smacked one long, super-duper, super wet kiss on his scrunched-up mouth.

When she released him, he screamed, "Yuk!!!!!!"

# CHAPTER 7

## Kissing Mammon's Arse

The year is 1986. I am 26, unemployed, and I spend my days writing, reading, and studying at the University of NSW library, and my nights painting, daubing thick oily paint on large canvasses, bringing to shiny life my dark nightmares. I live in a large upper-story house with four young men, all of them students at the university, just down the road lined by fig trees, across the racetrack. My darling K was also a student there, studying commerce. That was where we met—at an anti-racism rally. Now she's studying to become an actress, and I'm writing a play for her. My rent is only $25 a week. I eat nothing during the day, and for dinner I have a luncheon meat sandwich, or, on occasion, I treat myself to half a roast chicken and a bowl of cheap instant noodle soup. I sleep on a single mattress, I have a bookshelf of my favourite authors like D H Lawrence and James Joyce and the great Shakespeare, and my paintings and drawings decorate the walls. I am young, free, impoverished, and in love. Golden days indeed. Yet I dread thinking about the future, both the world's and mine. I see a bad moon rising: Aids, Margaret Thatcher, Reaganomics, Ayatollah Khomeini, welfare crackdown, and the Challenger Shuttle Disaster live on TV.

Onwards, from one horizon to the next, King Prawn and his army invaded and conquered Italy, Germany, USSR, Fiji, University of NSW, McDonald's, and were now about to invade Hollywood.

"Hurray for Hollywood," sang one of King Prawn's soldiers, Jiminy Crimson. He used to be one of Henry VIII's wives; he was beheaded, which would explain why he sang out of tune.

"We have just caught a spy," announced Mitty Balinos, a former middleweight boxing champion of the world, who, after retirement, became President of the United States, who, after retirement, became Premier of the Soviet Union and who, after dying from old age, became a prima ballerina for the Eskimo Ballet Company and who, after losing his tutu, became Pablo Picasso, the greatest painter in history.

"What's your name, spy?" asked King Prawn to the whaa…hey, this here is a cartoon mouse!

"It was Jimmy Mouse, who claimed to be Mickey Mouse's unsuccessful and alcoholic older brother.

"You have a voice of a sissy," King Prawn said, contemptuously.

"I'm a cartoon. I don't have testosterone."

"I can turn you from a mouse to a rat." I'll call you Ricky Rat. How would you like that?"

"I don't want to alienate the public," explained Jimmy. "They hate rats."

"God damn Mammon," King Prawn exclaimed. "Everyone desires to kiss Mammon's arse. There are no individuals any longer, only public personalities who'll do anything to be famous. A bunch of degenerates they are. I'd like to kick Mammon's arse."

"What shall we do with our prisoner?" asked George Balkan. Occupation: Accountant. Favourite TV show: Sliders. Favourite dish: Spaghetti Marinara. Favourite Music: Beatles. Favourite Actor: Clint Eastwood. Turn ons: Wet socks. Turn offs: A woman's vulva.

"Shoot him," King Prawn decreed.

Jimmy Mouse laughed. "You ding-a-ling, you can't shoot me. I'm a cartoon.''

"Then shoot the projectionist!" retorted King Prawn, the smart-arse.

"No!" screamed Jimmy Mouse, as they dragged him away to the editing room.

Suddenly, this huge fleshy mountainous thingamajig landed right on King Prawn, smothering every part of his body except his crowned head, which was just poking out.

"It's a bird!" shouted Tommy Coyle, who was really Thomas Pynchon, American novelist, who was really Roger Moore, who was really Sean Connery, who was really JD Salinger, who was really Bill Cosby, who was really Barbara Eden, who was really Vivien Leigh, who was really dead.

"No, it's a plane!" shouted Geoffrey Cabe. He held the record of swallowing one hundred piranhas.

"No, it's me! Mammon's Arse!" The large arse spoke through his anus. "I heard that you want to kick me. Nobody kicks me, thank you very much." Mammon's Arse let out one supersonic supersmelly fart. PPPYYRRRTTTTT!!!!!!!!

Poor King Prawn was choking and suffocating in fart exhumes.

"Kill this shithead!" commanded King Prawn to his stunned soldiers.

His soldiers surrounded the creature and charged at him with their swords. The creature stood up and splattered them all with...oh yuk...wet shit! SSSPLECHHHH!!!!

"Yukkypoo!" screamed Yerros Golt, Managing Director of Lullaby Laxatives

Corp.

"Help! I can't see!" screeched Leonard Best, running in circles, lost in shit. He worked part time as a cadaver for the UNSW School of Medicine. One student, as a prank, tied his oesophagus into a bow.

"Does anyone have any toilet paper?" queried Gil Armour. Now this was a really sad story. At 5, he died of Cystic Fibrosis. At 7, he died of leukaemia. At 10, he died of typhoid. At 15 he died of overmasturbation. At 18, he died of acne. And now at the age of 21, he would drown in shit.

In the meantime, Mammon's Arse bounced up and down on King Prawn, singing:

*I'm Mammon's Arse*
*which youse all love to kiss*
*And if you don't love me*
*I'll sit and shit on your face*
*I'm Mammon's Arse*
*I may be big, ugly, and smelly*
*but if you love me*
*I'll make you succeed*

*I'm Mammon's Arse*
*Kiss me and I'll give you fame and fortune*
*Kick me and I'll give you a bucket of shit!!!*

"Get off me!" shouted King Prawn.

"I will get off you," said Mammon's Arse to King Prawn, "if you choose to kiss me."

"Never!" yelled King Prawn.

Mammon's Arse blasted out a huge turd, cannonballing all the way to the King's cavalry and annihilating it, no survivors except one Jojo Coot, who at the time was at the latrine.

"I'll destroy your whole army unless you kiss me," warned Mammon's Arse, oozing wet shit on King Prawn.

"Kick him!" spluttered out King Prawn.

The army charged at Mammon's Arse but were repelled by a huge explosive blast of faeces on their faces. Spitting and coughing, King Prawn managed to get free before delivering a great nasty stinging kick at the creature. The creature yelped in pain. King Prawn struggled to run across the slick ground, feeling a certainty he would be recaptured. Luckily, Mammon's Arse slipped on his own shit and crashed heavily on the ground. Taking advantage of this opportunity, King Prawn commanded his troops to charge once more; but the creature quickly defended himself with a blast of diarrhoea sweeping over the troops like heavy surf. They were washed back to the King Prawn helplessly like sea wrack. There was no choice but to beat a retreat. King Prawn needed time to think, to outsmart this wily opponent.

King Prawn realised his army was unreliable and inept and would be hard put to deal with a vicious 10-year-old girl. So it was all down to his wits and cunning to save the day. He probed for the weaknesses of his adversaries. Usually, it was their dependence on their great strengths and their complacency about their weaknesses. And one weakness was their narrow sense of expectation. They were restricted by a narrow field of behaviour that limited their actions. His opponents were so bound up in routine that when the unexpected arose, panic and confusion overtook them and defeated them. They lacked the versatility, flexibility, and depth needed to deal with the new situation effectively. They had been conditioned to cling to the old and resist the new. The past was the present was the future. The Ball and Chain. Apeman, Urbanman, Spaceman—all the same. There was no evolution. People were slaves in soul, and King Prawn's main weapon in his arsenal was throwing freedom at them. Freedom was the greatest enemy of humanity. Like sunlight to Dracula. King Prawn knew his fellow men were vampires who thrived on the blood of bondage. A world of slaves.

Mammon's Arse was a slave to his vanity, sitting in front of a mirror admiring himself. He was without doubt an ugly creature, but to his eyes, he was the most beautiful creature in the world. After all, he was the most kissed creature in the world. Millions of people loved him, and this love gave him the strength of armies. This love justified everything he did, justified his evil, his conceit, his insanity...Thanks to Mammon's Arse, ambitious people achieved success, but only after first paying a price. The price was kissing Mammon's Arse. It was a kiss of success, and millions of people kissed him. Mammon's Arse thought the world needed him. The world thought so too except King Prawn. He didn't need him because he believed in the heroic individual. King Prawn shunned success: he wanted victory. Success was climbing the ladder; victory was smashing the Ball and Chain.

We see Mammon's Arse seated comfortably on a throne in his opulent palace. A long queue of politicians, businessmen, movie producers, etc, waited nervously for their turn to kiss him so he would grant them their greedy wishes.

## AT THE COURT OF MAMMON'S ARSE

"Yes, what is your name?" Mammon's Arse asked this rather handsome fellow.

"Ranulfo is my name," I answer him, getting down on my knees. I make the most sycophantic bow I can muster.

"What is it you want, my woebegone fellow?" he asks, acting bored with the proceedings, but he relished the obsequious behaviour proffered to him.

"I want to be a successful novelist and make millions of dollars, sir," I tell him, as if I were a small child on the lap of a department store Santa.

"What kind of novels do you write?"

"Unfinished novels so far."

"I will grant your wish if you promise to write novels that are entertaining, suspenseful, sympathetic to the public, and uphold the values of Christianity, Capitalism, and Consumerism."

"Yes, I promise," I answer him, crossing my fingers behind me.

"Good, now you may kiss me."

I reach forward to kiss him, but I am interrupted by one of his advisers, whispering into Mammon's Arse's ear, assuming he has one.

Mammon's Arse glares at me. "I have just been informed that you are the author who created that fiendish character King Prawn. Is that true?"

"Um…um…ah…eh…eh…ah….um…yes," I answer him.

"That King Prawn kicked me!" Mammon's Arse growls at me. Angry utterances of disapprobation behind me.

"Don't blame me, I'm just a writer," I explain lamely, my heart boomarabooming. "I'm an instrument of Fate. My Fate is to be an author, my ambition is to be a lowly clerk. What is written doesn't come from me, it comes from…Fate."

"Who is this Fate fellow?"

"Well, you see, I'm an atheist, and an atheist needs authority figures too. Fate is my God, I guess. Fate dictates what happens to me."

"Are you an atheist because you believe there is no being higher than the homo sapiens?"

"No, I'm an atheist because I believe that we're too inferior to have been created by a superior being."

"Don't you believe in Life after Death?"

"I'm still yet to believe that there is Life before Death?"

"I like comedians," he says, "because nobody takes them seriously. They're harmless anarchists. They're of no danger to the public whatsoever. Well, my dear Ranulfo, I shall grant you success, but on one condition…"

"What is it, my Excellency?"

"You must kill off your character King Prawn."

Should I sacrifice my artistic integrity to gain public success?

"Gladly, my most Perfect One," I answer him, bowing and kowtowing.

"Good, you can kiss me now."

Gladly do I kiss Mammon's Arse, first his right cheek, next his left, although his flesh is scabrous, pus-ridden, and smells horrendously. I do it because I'm sick of being poor, sick of going to the library of UNSW every day, sick of working my guts out for nothing, sick of not being able to take women out to restaurants, opera, ballet, islands, sick of living in my apartment with four crazy strangers, sick of not having a car, sick of being able to travel, sick of writing unfinished novels, sick of the dole, sick of failure, sick of daydreaming, sick of going to the end of my tether, sick of this great big hole in my head…so I kiss Mammon's Arse, hoping that he will cure me of my sickness. And lo and behold, I am now a wealthy and well-known novelist. I am immediately surrounded by the media. I thank Mammon's Arse who grins, and he throws me a Time Magazine with my smiling face on the cover with the caption "The Richest Novelist in the World".

"Is it true you're having an affair with Madonna?" a top American television network interviewer asks me, shoving a microphone in my face.

"Um…I don't know…but I hope so," I answer her.

"Can I have your autograph?" asks a little boy.

My first autograph! What a strange phenomenon a person requesting your signature. People wanting your name. Ranulfo. Without knowing them, I have affected them. Like all those names who have inspired me: Shakespeare, DH Lawrence, Sylvia Plath, Emily Bronte, Krishnamurti, Jackson Pollock, Michael Jackson, Stanley Kubrick, Fred Astaire, Neil Young, Muhammad Ali, E M Cioran, Kafka. Names which made a lonely boy enjoy his loneliness so he too could dream and create a world of his own. All these names are superheroes saving the world from darkness and dullness. Now I too want to be a superhero so I can fight the darkness that has inundated the world. Super Ranulfo will bring the light of the sky down to the earth and into people's eyes. Up, up and away, skyward, Ranulfo, your home…

"Let's fuck?" asks a beautiful red-haired woman, emerging from the crowd of reporters and fans.

"What, now?" I answer nervously.

"Yes, let's do it here."

"Here? In front of everybody, the photographers, the TV cameras, the public?"

"Of course, you're now a celebrity. From now on, you will do everything in public."

…meanwhile, in the privacy of a living room, a family watches television.

"We have for you live via satellite," speaks the TV anchorman, "film of famous novelist Ranulfo making love to that beautiful TV actress Ketisha Antro. Here we are in the court of Mammon's Arse where Ranulfo is besieged by his fans and the media. You see Ranulfo and Ketisha undressing in front of everyone. There you see Ranulfo nibbling on her large scrumptious nipples. He brings her to the ground where she spread eagles herself for him to perform oral sex. Here's a close up of Ketisha's wet vulva. You've seen it first on Channel 53 the first live shot of Ketisha's quivering vulva. Here we have a shot of Ranulfo's erect penis…can we get a measurement here, John…as it enters the vagina of Ketisha. Here's a replay of the penetration. Here's an inside view, a vagina cam located inside showing Ranulfo's penis burrowing into her hole. Now we speed up the film as they go through various positions: missionary, doggie, upside down, 69, triple somersault, and, finally, the climax, which we shall show in slow motion. Close up of Ranulfo's face, which looks like a baboon pleading for mercy. And a shot of Ketisha, who is smiling at the camera, waving her hands, and saying hello to her mum. Now our roving reporter, Josie Buffner, approaches the couple to interview them.

JOSIE BUFFNER: Ranulfo, how was it?

RANULFO: Great.

JOSHIE: How was it for you, Ketisha?

KETISHA: He's rich and famous and that's why I love him.

JOSIE: Now we'll cross back to our newsroom. This is Josie Buffner, Channel 53.

"Thank you, Josie. That was one of the best fucks I have ever seen on television.

43

These famous people are so talented. And talking about famous people, next up we have live via satellite, Robert De Niro's appendix operation."

"Daddy, what is sex?" asks a little girl to her father as they watch television.

"Sex, Patti," he answers her, "is when two people love each other's bodies."

"And what is love?" she further asks.

"Love, Patti, is when two people enjoy each other's minds."

"And what is hate?"

"When two people have tried to love each other's minds."

"NEWSFLASH! The pope admitted today that he is an atheist, although he still believes in the Easter Rabbit. He has handed in his resignation, and tomorrow he will take up the job offer as coach of the Brazilian soccer team."

The serenity and solemnity of the court of Mammon's Arse returned soon after I left, along with the backwash of my admirers. The noise and density of the crowd had obscured me from seeing my character, King Prawn, who was standing in the queue, observing everything in utter disgust. He was a most unrecognisable person because he owned no face. I, the author, have purposely obscured detail in my characters and their surroundings because I refuse to suffer them a particularity which bound them to a nation or race. Nor do I want myself to suffer that fate of being regarded as an ambassador to any nation, as I detest all patriotism. Patriotism is a politician's trick to send people to fight their dirty wars. The world I belong to is the one I create. My battles are fought on the battlefield of my soul.

Mammon's Arse was taken aback to see that the person before him was King Prawn. As King Prawn approached and knelt humbly, Mammon's Arse glared at him, still resenting the kick the King had bestowed on him.

"The nerve of you coming here after the indignities you inflicted on me," Mammon's Arse reprimanded him.

"I apologise, my beautiful one," King Prawn replied, "but I come here as a soldier, not to fight, but to acknowledge your superiority in strength. I am a true soldier, and every true soldier respects a better soldier."

The speech did much to appease Mammon's Arse, but he still sulked.

"My ever great one," King Prawn continued, "if you can find it in your heart to forgive me, I will do anything you ask of me."

Mammon's Arse was a sucker for compliments, both true and false. He didn't want to know the difference between truth and lies. If the truth was that he was ugly and unloved, then damn the truth. Leave truth to the beautiful, happy, and fortunate.

Mammon's Arse learned early in life that life was one son of a bitch, and that people in general were mean, selfish, and shallow. There was no point in being a profound person in a trivial world.

"I will even kiss you," King Prawn proposed. "Every day and every night for the rest of my life."

"And in return, what do you want?" asked Mammon's Arse.

"All I ask, my most perfect one, is your forgiveness."

"You have humiliated and insulted me, King Prawn," sobbed Mammon's Arse with a sorrowful face of a victim. "And I am a very sensitive creature who gets easily hurt. It's not very nice to hurt people. It's not very nice at all. Wouldn't the world be a better place if everyone was really nice to each other? I think that everyone here in court should hold hands and sing."

And lo and behold, everyone in the court, including King Prawn, was linked together with their hands, swaying, and singing. They formed a circle around Mammon's Arse, who sang and danced.

*Hey, everybody, let's be happy*
*The world is a fantastic place*
*Be good, work hard, enjoy life,*
*And never be unhappy.*

Mammon's Arse loved entertaining his arsekissers; it gave him a high to watch people laughing and smiling. He felt so talented, knowing he could never disappoint the audience. Of course, he refused to believe that his audience were merely pretending. Our creature was not a realist, one who investigated reality, but a fantasist, one who believed only in his fantasies. Our King Prawn was not amused at all. In his eyes, Mammon's Arse was one big idiot. It was idiocy to want everybody to love you. Mass produced love, plastic love. Love, instead of being focused and deep, becomes silly and meaningless, spread out like ugly roads in the metropolis of greed.

King Prawn regarded the whole court as ridiculous. He wanted to destroy this civilisation which made idiots of everyone in it. He wanted to destroy the false gods and false truths. He wanted to destroy Religion, Capitalism, Communism, Money, Drugs, Alcohol, Hollywood, Television, Romance, Fashion, Fast food, Shopping Centres, Diet books, Therapy, Cars, Pop Music, and Politics.

Mammon's Arse was in a cheerful mood and was charitable enough to accept King Prawn's apologies. He bade the king come hither to kiss him on his left and right cheeks. The King stepped forward, knelt solemnly in close approximation to the creature, and kissed him on the left cheek, then on the right. Mammon's Arse went blind all of a sudden, and he felt as if some clothing had covered him and trapped him. King Prawn had put underwear on him, quite ugly underwear, those horrid, unflattering gigantic cotton Y-fronts. Mammon's Arse was unable to extricate himself from the underwear, and he screamed for help. All the arse-kissers were cowards and fled when King Prawn brandished his sword at them. Mammon's Arse was defenceless as his powers of bowel movement were incapacitated; he growled in fury inside the white jockeys, and hurled himself forward towards the King, hoping by chance to crush him with his massive weight. He landed heavily, but he missed King Prawn, who was now a taunting voice in the darkness.

Desperately, he gave one blast of shit to break through the underwear, but thanks to scientific progress, the underwear was hole proof. He was choking on his own shit. Once again, he catapulted towards the cruel voice of King Prawn. Again, he missed. Mammon's Arse felt hopeless. It was like fighting against the night. The enemy was not one particular object, but rather the entire darkness of his soul, which had grown enormously large. Again he hurled himself at the voice of darkness, as if he would crash straight through a wall which would bring him into the light. But it was still darkness besieging him, darkness which seemed to have no depth, as if he was still standing still as he threw himself forward. How flat the darkness was? It was a wall made of emptiness. "I'm over here, shitface," the voice of the darkness called out to him. He jumped forward. The sensation of going nowhere unnerved him, demoralised him. He was ready to give in. He knew he was weak in character: diffident, insecure, and terrified of life. At this moment, he felt he was a little boy in his bedroom, scared of the dark, wanting a teddy bear, or a mother, or even a lamp, to reassure him and console him. So much love he craved for, love to light up the immense darkness of his existence. The hostile darkness, where lurked monsters that did not love him or care for him, darkness that was impervious to mercy.

"Get up!" taunted King Prawn, giving him a painful kick. "Get up!"

Mammon's Arse began to cry copiously.

"Stop crying, you big fat baby!"

"Why are you so cruel to me? Why can't you leave me alone?"

"Because you won't leave anyone alone."

"But I've made so many people happy."

"Bullshit! If you want to make people happy, make them strong, proud, and independent. But you make them into idiots of success."

"I hate you!" screamed Mammon's Arse, who then mustered all his strength to hurl himself at the voice. He expected to land right on his head, but instead he landed with a splash in the middle of a large pool of water. Face down, he was swallowing water that was slowly choking him. He knew he was drowning, and this was Death. The darkness was infiltrating his inner body. Darkness was flowing through his veins, his heart, his brain, his soul. In the throes of death, he clutched at the final straw. It was Jesus Christ, who was going to rescue him. Jesus said to him, "Ye have been a good Christian, Mammon's Arse, and now ye shall be rewarded for ye shall enter the Kingdom of Heaven."

"Hold me and kiss me, I'm so scared."

Jesus kissed him. "I'll take care of you for ever and ever…"

Then Mammon's Arse heard a loud flushing sound, and angry waters whirled around him before he vanished into the final hole…

Mammon's Arse would not have liked his demise. He'd be humiliated to read the front page of the papers:

MAMMON'S ARSE FLUSHED TO DEATH IN GIANT TOILET

But why should he care? He belonged to the world no longer.

*Do you love me, Ranulfo, K writes on my manuscript.*

Yes

# CHAPTER 8

## St Claire

Most sagacious readers, isn't there anything more real than money? Don't you think that Love, Happiness, Art, Truth, and God are all illusions for which we suffer meaninglessly?

Speak for yourself, Ranulfo, you, the reader, say to me.

"Okay," I answer you.

"Just get on with the fucking novel, will you?" you tell me.

"Yes, my Master, whatever you command. Please pull down your knickers and let me kiss your blessed arse, my ever-wise reader…"

When St Claire closed her eyes, the world vanished. Most terrifying, this isolation. She was the world, and the world was her, and it would always be that way till she existed no longer. The world could never be the world, it would always be seen through her eyes, distorted by her. Knowing this made her cry. To be herself seemed terribly lonely. Never could she be anyone else, nor could anyone else be her. Her body was a prison, and her windows were those two tiny cracks on the wall called eyes. She longed to be outside the window, enter inside people's heads, see through their eyes, feel their emotions. She wanted to transfuse herself with the cosmos, to flow with the rivers and oceans, to burn with the stars. She was tired of herself, tired of her thinking, thinking, thinking, tired of her insignificant perception of the world. As she walked through the woods, she felt so vulnerable, her small body carrying her precious soul. Her fragile body was so easily wounded, so easily dead. If only her body were made of sterner stuff, not this flimsy wallet. How she feared that this world was such a dangerous stranger.

St Claire had been thinking for so long that she had forgotten the time and had wandered far. She looked up at the sky and noticed that the light was fading. She grew anxious. She felt the night could gobble her up. The trees around her were so tall that she couldn't tell where she was. She was lost. She continued on. Then darkness descended. She ran and ran, but she could not outrun the night, which pursued her like a wolf. She prayed, "Please, God, please help me, please…"

She came to a halt, her legs too weary to go on. She sat on the cool grass and cried. She wanted to sleep because sleep was a kind creature. She wondered whether

Death was kind. But the thought made her tremble.

"Can I help you, St Claire?"

She is startled. She looks at me but shows no fear of me. She is relieved. She can speak to a human, if not to the deaf stars.

"Who are you?" she asks.

"I'm Ranulfo. I created you."

"Are you God?" she asks innocently.

"No. I'm an author," I say self-importantly.

"I'm lost. Can you help me?" Her eyes are so full of trust that it unsettles me. I'm more accustomed to wary adults.

"I can take you anywhere you like."

"I'm hungry."

"I'll get you something to eat."

I take St Claire back to my apartment. She sits down on the lounge chair, while I cook her some pasta. I live in this five-bedroom apartment with these four other blokes, university students, one Vietnamese, two Malaysians, one South Korean, and me, a Filipino. Yes, mates, we're all Aussies, Fair Dinkum. Lost in Oz. I read in the papers that 70 % of Australians want a reduction in Asian migration. That doesn't bother me. I hate myself!

"You're not very rich," she says to me when I come back with a tray of food.

I scan my hovel. "Money is not important to an author."

"Why did you become an author?"

"Novelists are philosophers who prefer feeling to thinking."

"I want to be a philosopher," she tells me.

"That's good."

"There's so much to philosophise about."

"It's wonderful you like to philosophise."

She looks at my bookshelves, scans the titles. "Have you read all these books?"

"I'm afraid not. I don't seem to have the time."

"What do you do most of the time?"

"Suffer."

"How silly."

"Yes."

"Do you have a girlfriend?"

"Yes, I do. I think. We didn't fight this week, so I guess she's still my girlfriend.

K is her name."

"Is she pretty?"

"Too pretty. And do you have a boyfriend?"

"No, but I'm in love with someone."

"Yeah, with whom?"

"Prince Jotel."

"Since I'm your author, I can make him your boyfriend if this is what you want."

"You can!"

"Sure. But isn't he in love with Virginia?"

Her face sours. "Yes, but she's not right for him. She's so silly."

"But Prince Jotel isn't exactly bright."

She staunchly defends him. "But he is. He's just not interested in intelligence right now because he's only a kid."

I laugh. "But you're a kid too."

"I gave up on being a kid a long time ago. It's a silly phase of life."

I study her wonderful face. "You look just like her."

"Who?"

"This woman I based your character on."

"Were you in love with her?"

"Yes, but that was a long time ago."

"When I'm older, you could marry me if you like. I think you'd make a better husband than Prince Jotel."

"Anyway, I can't marry you. You're a fiction character."

"Why?" she asks, puzzled, and hurt.

"Um..." realising my tactlessness, "I don't know. I had a love affair with Catherine Earnshaw from Wuthering Heights, and it didn't work out. Heathcliff beat me up."

"You're a sad man," she tells me.

"I'm not sad. I love self-pity, that's all."

"You're a sad clown."

"That sounds like a cue for a song."

"Anyway, what's the ending of the novel I'm in?"

"I don't know yet. I'm not sure if I can even finish the damn thing. I've written five unfinished novels. I can't seem to finish what I start."

She studies the place I live in. "Your room is a mess. Is it a mess because your life is a mess as well?"

"Yes, definitely. That's why I'm a writer and why I can't finish my novels."

"We should marry. You need a woman who'll put some order into your life. A woman who'll make you write and have lots of fun.''

"A happy writer," I say ironically.

"Your girlfriend K is not doing her job properly. She should make you happy."

"I'm not making her happy either."

"Why do you stick together?"

"I can't finish what I started, I guess."

"Well, we must get married, and you'll write lots and lots of novels. Finished novels."

"And you'll write lots of philosophy books, of course."

Seeing her plate of food untouched, "Hey, eat your pasta before it gets cold."

"All right."

What a wonderful gal St Claire is? And she's only a kid. So much potential in her. She'll grow and grow and grow to be the tallest woman in the world.

Later in the night I ask St Claire, "Do you want to go home now?"

"Let's go somewhere and have some fun!"

"Where to?"

"Into the world of your imagination!"

There is a nervous pause. "I'm not sure I can live up to the challenge."

"All right. Let's go ride on a Bopper."

Excitedly, "What's a Bopper?"

"I'll show you," and a Bopper appears in a puff of smoke before our eyes. Planted on four sturdy feet is a purple hippopotamus patterned with yellow dots, and across his back are gigantic eagle wings. As we board, the Bopper starts flapping his wings. Wind howls inside, my room, the pages of my novel fly up helter skelter. Buzzing like a million bees, the Bopper elevates into the ceiling—CRASH!—and we burst into the night sky. We fly straight up over the sleeping suburb of Randwick, where I can see the racecourse, and next to it, the University of NSW, and eastward, the luminous, glittering city of Sydney is beckoning us, but above us, a greater luminosity, a greater beckoning.

"Let's go to another planet, Ranulfo," St Claire shouting from behind me. The wind, turbulent, noisy wolves.

"Okay, but hold tight!" She embraces my torso tighter, and zoom, zoom, we blast through the ozone layer, flying at the phenomenal speed of Art. Flying past the acned moon, past vain Venus, and doing some fancy wing work, the Bopper evades the over familiar asteroids, then past the regal Saturn, bullyboy Jupiter, and neurotic Neptune, then away from cold harlot Pluto, out of our solar system, and towards the stars, the wishing stars.

"This is so wonderful, Ranulfo."

The mischievous Bopper makes a loop and poor St Claire nearly drops off.

"Are you okay?"

"Yes, you won't let me die, will you, Ranulfo? You created me."

"No, of course not."

"And you will live forever too."

"I don't know. That's up to my creator."

"Why shouldn't your creator take care of you?"

"Well, it depends on his plans for his creation."

"You won't ever hurt me."

"No."

"You won't hurt Queen Clytoris, Prince Jotel, and the rest of our community?"

"Um...I can't do that. I'm writing a novel, and I have to think of plot, conflict, tragedy, and all those things that novelists have to write about."

"I don't believe that you could ever be that mean to hurt any of us."

I keep quiet, not wanting to pursue the subject anymore as I know I have some nasty things in store for my characters. I'm not sure of the details but I'm hatching...bwahahaha!

"Ranulfo, you won't hurt us, will you?"

Silent, guilty creator.

We at last reached a star, and the funny thing about this star is that it is shaped like one of those cartoon five-point stars. We snoop around its solar system, searching for a nice, cosy planet to land on. We come across this pink planet made entirely of soft silk cushions. The Bopper tips us over, and we fall headlong onto the planet, and when we land, we bounce a few times. St Claire does a triple somersault in the air.

"This is fun, Ranulfo."

"Yes."

She turns over on to her stomach and looks at me with her typical studious gaze.

"But you look so sad," she says to me.

"It's just me. I can't really let go. I'm anchored to some heavy object inside."

"You should marry me when I'm older. In fact, why don't you make me older? You're my creator."

"Don't you want to grow up and enjoy the stages of adolescence and teenagerhood?"

"No, I don't want to wait that long and risk losing you to some tramp."

I touch her face, and she changes into a 25 year-old woman. Rather beautiful, I might add. She walks about like she was trying on a new outfit. She laughs at her new strange self. "I can't believe how tall I am. Look at my hips, my boobs, good heavens!"

She comes to me. "Kiss me! She grabs my face and kisses me on the mouth. When she releases me, she studies my expression. "You're still sad…"

I don't answer her.

"I'll learn to kiss you properly," and before she can kiss me again the planet begins to wobble like jelly. The ground grabs the two of us as it liquidifies. We sink helplessly into the guts of the planet, falling headlong, and tumbling out to the other side and into an abyss.

"Help me, Ranulfo," she cries out.

I try to grab her hand, but she falls further and further away.

"Don't let me die."

"No, I won't, St Claire," but I seem to have lost control of my imagination, which is crumbling apart, and we are falling deeper into the abyss. I try to regain control, but I can't overcome this sadness, which is killing the artist in me, the dreamer inside, this sadness, this craving for reality…

"Ranulfo, help me," cries her distant voice, the gap yawning. Suddenly, we crashed into my apartment. St Claire lands safely on my bed, while unlucky me lands headfirst on my TV set. Ouch! Extricating myself from the wrecked television, I rushed to St Claire's side. She is in a daze, and seeing me, she accuses me, "You said you'd never hurt me."

"I'm sorry, St Claire." I hold her delicate hand. She is a child again.

"Why did you hurt me?"

"I don't know."

"Take me home," she cries. "You kissed me, and you found out that I'm nothing. Just a dream…a silly dream. A fiction character."

And when St Claire woke up, she thought that all that had happened was just a silly dream and she had been in her room all night. Yet she could not shake off the sadness that was so real.

# CHAPTER 9

## Virginia

K would ring me in the middle of the night, and we'd talk for hours. Sometimes we said nothing. Yet it felt we were physically together. I liked it when she was calm and peaceful before the storm clouds gathered, broke, and blew me away.

Carol's daughter was Virginia. Carol's father was an accountant who divorced Carol to marry a young, beautiful nymphomaniac. Carol was humiliated by her divorce. It came as a complete surprise. She had not seen a storm on the horizon during her marriage, which she saw as a sunny, though windless, climate. The marriage was so static that she thought it couldn't get any better or worse. In her pragmatic way, she loved her husband. She believed that she had done everything she could to make the marriage work. She even did things for him that she disliked, such as fellatio and anal sex. She had worked hard at her marriage, hoping for a secure future; then he fired her, for no reason other than he had found someone younger and prettier. Her efforts had been for nothing.

After the divorce she became more cautious and wary of men and set high standards for herself. She approached each date like a job interview, with her acting as the interviewer and the date as the interviewee. The date had to convince her that he was worth taking aboard. She queried them intensively about their lives, philosophy, past relationships, and future hopes, but stopped short of asking for references, although she believed a woman should have the right to interview previous girlfriends and wives to get a more rounded and accurate picture of the man. She had a few guidelines on what would constitute a desirable man. Divorced men were out; they would only do to her what they had caused their ex-wife to divorce them. She even had issues with single men; they were either philanderers or just plain losers. Perhaps what she was looking for was a widower. Of course, this depended on how her wife died, for if she died of a disease, it was likely psychosomatic, triggered by her husband's toxic deficiencies. If she had to accept a death, it would be that of a wife dying of old age. But somehow, she couldn't fire herself up to date octogenarians.

There was no man right for the job. This confirmed her dim view of the male species. The folly of all those women who think they can find happiness with a man.

The male—a sorry bunch of bananas. So she gave up on men, just like one would give up on cigarettes. It was a bad, useless habit to be weaned off. She saw it as a purely rational decision, arrived at not on the rocky road of bitterness but on the wings of reason. She was mighty proud of herself. She had liberated herself. Loving men was like worshipping a false god. Man is dead, she would say if she were Mrs. Nietzsche.

She had hoped to impart this scientific fact to her daughter, Virginia. She shuddered at the horrifying thought of her daughter suffering needlessly at the false shrine of men. She wanted her to be strong, independent, and intelligent. But a major obstacle to reaching this state of grace was men, who could ensnare Virginia in an endless cycle of stupidity. The merry-go-round of stupid love. The thought pained Carol immensely. But children are born if only to disappoint their parents. Virginia was a hopeless romantic who believed love was the be-all and end-all of life. It would be futile for Carol to teach Virginia, a dreamer, about reality.

"Is that your cat, Virginia?" Carol asked, seeing Prince Jotel seated at the dinner table disguised as a cat.

Virginia eyed Prince Jotel mischievously. "No," she answered, "he belongs to someone else. I'm his mistress. He visits me when he can. Isn't that romantic?"

"Being a mistress? No," Carol reprimanded her. "There is nothing more abhorrent than a man who wants to have his cake and eat it as well. Such men are greedy, selfish pigs. If a man truly loves you, he must choose you and only you. If a man wants more, then it's a woman's duty to kick his balls and tell him to get lost. A woman must never fall so low as to allow herself to be a concubine in a man's harem. You will find out in the due course of sordid experiences that men treat women like doormats. Men are bad. Hammer that into your head."

"I want to be a slave to a man," said Virginia wantonly. "Do everything for him and expect nothing back."

"And nothing you shall become," Carol said sharply. "You're still a child. You don't know what love is about."

"The greatest love affairs are tragic. Like Romeo and Juliet."

"They're just fiction characters. Like everything you say is fiction because everything comes from your imagination, not your intellect in conjunction with reality."

"I can make all my dreams come true," Virginia boasted.

"Can you?" Carol said, unbelieving.

"Yes. If I concentrate hard enough, my dreams become real. Like my cat here, I brought him out of my dreams."

"Don't be silly," Carol frowned.

"I'm a magician."

"There are no such things as magic, there are only magic tricks. And now you've tricked yourself into believing that you can make magic. Now you want to trick me? Well, prove it. Virginia, make your dreams come true right before my eyes."

"Okay," answered Virginia confidently. How could a child refuse a dare? "In fact, I can make my unicorn, Ulla, appear before you."

She closed her eyes and summoned a unicorn with her imagination. She coaxed it to come out of her head and prove her sceptic mother wrong. "Come on out, Ulla, come on out and play with me. We can have a lot of fun."

Ulla nodded and neighed.

"Oh, thank you, Ulla, thank you."

The unicorn poised himself to make a great leap to burst through the walls of imagination and into the world of reality. Off he went, galloping faster and faster, until he sprang his heavy, white body into the wall.

Virginia opened her eyes, excitedly searching the room for Ulla. She could only see her mother, who was looking concerned. There was no Ulla. She shut her eyes to see if Ulla had gone out of her head. There was darkness as she peered into her imagination, then she saw the gleaming mass of Ulla sprawled on the ground. Dead, her neck snapped from crashing into the formidable wall.

"Ulla, Ulla, are you all right?" she called to him. "Please, Ulla, say something."

She looked into his eyes. There was no arrogant glint in his eyes; they were dead eyes, unreaching, unreachable. Virginia burst into tears.

"Ulla is dead! Ulla is dead!" she screamed, heartrendingly. "I've killed him."

"You killed no one, Virginia."

"He died when...he...tried...to...get...out...the wall...I killed him!"

"It's only your imagination."

"My imagination is real...but the walls were too hard...Ulla could not get out...no one can get out any more...no one...it's a prison...someone built a wall and all my friends are trapped inside."

Carol embraced Virginia, stroking her soft hair, which ran as long as her imagination. "Don't cry, Virginia, don't cry."

"My friends are trapped," she cried in terror.

Carol tried to soothe her. "They want to stay inside you forever. They don't want to get out. It's a cruel world out there. It's safer and nicer inside yourself."

"Ulla is dead!"

"She isn't dead. Nobody dies in your imagination unless you want her to."

"Ulla is alive, if you want her to be alive."

Virginia closed her eyes and searched her imagination. Her mother was right! Ulla wasn't dead! There he was standing, as lordly as ever, though suffering from a few bruises and cuts. His eyes glinted as before, and his muscly white flesh glowed in the darkness of her imagination. "I'm sorry, Ulla," she said remorsefully to him. "Would you ever forgive me?"

The unicorn did not answer her, still chagrined, and humiliated by her own failure.

"Please, Ulla, forgive me."

The unicorn glared at Virginia; she withered at the hard, angry, penetrating fire of his eyes. Gradually, the angry eyes softened. Ulla neighed magnificently, swivelled around, and galloped into the darkness...

"He's alive, Mother," she said, her face bright with joy. "He's forgiven me too."

"That's good. Now, let's go wash up, shall we?" Carol said, happy with relief.

But she felt defeated. Tricked into sentiment.

"Okay," Virginia said cheerfully, skipping to the kitchen.

Carol smiled, but she was sad. She knew that dreamers like Virginia would suffer a lot in life. They all became martyrs to their dreams. If only she could protect herself, make the world a servant to her dreams. If only she could create a wall to ward off the bad world...little did she know that she would only succeed in building a wall between her and her daughter. Once you build walls, the first prisoner you take is yourself.

## THE TALE OF MING AND TANG

"Shall I tell you a bedtime story, my little prince," said Virginia to Prince Jotel, nestled in her arms in her bed. The cat nodded and miaowed. "Let me see what my friends are going to perform for me tonight...let me see...I see a Chinese man...he's standing on a dirt road in a little village somewhere in China...the houses are small and simple, made of thatch, bamboo, and mud...I see no cars...no electric poles...he's wearing a peasant's costume, grey, loose, comfortable, a bit worn and dirty…he's looking at me…he is weary from having worked in the fields all day long and now he is paying a visit to his brother…so go on, now, what's your name, sir?"

'Tang!'

"Hello, Tang. He opens a low gate, enters a small, neglected garden, and knocks at the wooden door. A fat Chinese person answers the door."

"Tang greets his brother Chang, who has a very sad face; he has no smile creases at all. They sit in the hard, dark furniture, and talk…they talk as if they need to talk…as if they had spent the whole day alone in silence…like being inside a box and talking to someone gets you outside.?"

Virginia stood up, cradling Prince Jotel the cat in her arms, and strolled to the moonlit window. She gazed at the half moon sitting like a cup. "Let me drink that cup of moon," she whispered. Then she gazed deeply at the stars. "How far away they are? They are made of diamonds, those stars. When I die, I shall fly to one of those stars and live there. It's so far away…It's eternity…only eternal people live on those stars…only eternal people…if I drink that cup of moon, I shall be eternal."

"Where was I in my story? They were talking…Tang and Chang…there was a framed photograph propped up on the centre table…it's a faded black and white photograph of a beautiful Chinese girl."

'It's been ten years to the day that I last saw her,' Chang said to Tang, referring to the photograph.

'You must forget her and begin living,' his brother Tang advised, but rather indifferently, as he had given that same advice countless times before.

"Chang's face weighed heavy with sorrow. 'I can't forget her…I can't. I have no present, no future to forget the past…I have never loved any girl but her. I am an ugly man…The thought of her fills me with beauty. What a treasure she was…so beautiful…so beautiful…I still remember her vividly…I was twenty-two, a young, lonely man who had only dreams to make himself happy…Now I have no dreams but only memories. A travelling acting troupe came to perform in our village, to sing, to dance, and to tell stories…'

"Oh yes, did I tell you Chang had a cat called Mita…beautiful feline, who was very shy and loved Chang very much, and whenever his brother Tang or anyone else visited him, she would scurry away as if she was being chased by a monster. She only trusted Chang and believed that the rest of humanity was evil and terrible, like dogs. So, while Tang and Chang were conversing, she hid under Chang's bed, feeling safe. Oops! I'm digressing, aren't I? I'm sorry."

"Chang continued his tale…"

'She was the leading lady. Her name was Ming Ling. I have never seen a more beautiful woman' his voice suffused with bittersweet nostalgia. I kept my eyes fixed on her throughout her performance. She was doing a melodrama…she was married to a cruel villain…she fell in love with a handsome prince who wanted to take her away to his castle in a beautiful land…and on the day they were going to depart…the prince reveals his true identity…he was none other than her villainous husband…he laughed at her and gave her a savage beating…she then commits suicide by drinking poison. Her last words were, "I am dying because I cannot love…"

Virginia, with light magical steps, returned to her bed, which was seductively cool. She lay on her stomach, her flesh immersed in the luscious tingly-ness of the cool sheets. "This is heaven…moonlight and cool breeze having a midnight tryst on my bed. Love—that's what I was created for…Love."

"Shall I go on with the story?" she asked Prince Jotel in her soft, whispery voice.

Prince Jotel gazed into her eyes. Her pupils were dilated; she was lost in her dreams and secret wishes.

"Please continue your story, Chang."

'After the show, I couldn't stop thinking about her. I could not sleep. I had to get out of the house. I went out into the night, which was blustering…a tempestuous night that suited my mood…I pushed against the bumping wind. I walked towards the travelling troupe's camp, hoping to see a lit window, which would be nearly as good as seeing her in person, as if her soul beamed her rays at me like a star. But I got more than a lit window. I got her. At first, I thought I saw a ghost who had come to scare me. Then it hit me: it was her. She didn't see me, her face raised, whipped by the wind, her eyes closed, choked by some grief. I dared not intrude upon her sorrows, so I turned away sadly…Besides, I was terrified of meeting her, terrified of meeting a dream…Then suddenly, as if Fate had conked me on the head for being so shy, a tree branch dropped bang on my head and knocked me down. She saw this and came to my rescue. Blood streamed out from some unseen wounds on my head. "Come quickly to my room and I'll bandage your wound."

'She appeared like a guardian angel to take me to heaven. Back in her room, we started talking. I asked so many questions…I had nothing to talk about, you see. She told me about her childhood…she was a dreamer, endlessly dreaming. She said she had a house inside her head where lived all her imaginary friends, mainly animals and magical creatures. She was very happy being in that house. When she turned 15, she joined this travelling theatre and became an actress. She travelled from village to village, town to town. In one town, she met Tasho, a very handsome man. He was also an actor. She fell in love with him.

'They got on very well and soon became lovers. They had one wonderful month together. One day, she asked Tasho to go inside her head and meet her imaginary friends. She closed her eyes and saw him, radiant and beautiful, like a prince.

'Then he opened the door and told her it was a beautiful world out there and to come with him.

'She told him she was scared. But Tasho assured her not to worry and promised to love her and make her happy. He took her hand in his and walked her out of her dream world. She looked back to say good-bye to her friends, but the door was shut on her. She was sad but was also very happy. She was going to live happily ever after, just like a princess.

'Next day he was gone. He left her a note, which read:

*Dear Ming,*

*I'm sorry, but I must go. You should understand you are an actress travelling from place to place, performing for my selected audience. Actors like you and me do not love the audience but love their applause. We cannot be loved by one but by many. Please understand. Love is just a show, it is not real. Goodbye.*

*Love,*

*Tasho*

'She cried and cried. She returned to her house inside her head, and it was empty. She burst into tears and cried for a very long time.

'I mustered the courage to touch her shoulder and say consoling words. She then looked at me with sad and pleading eyes.

"Come inside my secret room."

"How?" I asked, bewildered, yet flattered.

"Close your eyes."

''Yes."

"Can you see my room?"

"Yes," I lied to her, for my eyes were open, fixed on her beautiful face. "Can you see me?"

"I can't see you, I see…no, it's Tasho! He's back!!"

"Yes, I'm Tasho," I ventured to say. "I've come back to you."

"Oh my love, I miss you so much."

"I miss you, too.' I kissed her. It was heaven. Her body was soft and exquisite.

'When she lay asleep, I stole out of the room, afraid of her discovering it was me, not Tasho. The next day, I returned, feeling guilty that I should not have left her. But the troupe had packed up and left, as had she. I set out to track her down. Two years later, I caught up with her troupe and asked after her. "She's gone nuts. She lost touch with the real world and stayed in the twilight of her dream world. We committed her to a mental asylum." I went to the asylum she was sent to. The nurse informed me that she had starved herself to death, never having come out of the shell of her dream. Now it's been ten years, and I still think of her.'

Virginia paused. She was in a reverie, lost in her story.

"Tang, his brother, who had grown tired of hearing this story countless times, excused himself to leave. He was sad for Chang. 'How humiliating it is to love somebody who does not love you. Ming was an idiot for falling in love with that scoundrel Tasho, and Chang was even a bigger idiot for falling in love with that crazy woman. And what an idiot I am staying in this village where the only females are cows and hens. I have to get out of this small town!'

"Later that night Tang packed his belongings and left for the city of Peking, where there were lots of women and all the cows and hens were chopped sueyed. Meanwhile, back at Chang's house, he heard a voice inside his head. It was Ming. He looked inside his imagination, and there she was. She was smiling at him and beckoning him. 'Come inside, Chang. I miss you very much.' 'I miss you too,' and he went inside and kissed her. 'Stay with me forever,' she asked him. 'I'll never leave you,' he promised her. And they lived happily ever after. The end."

"Wasn't that a romantic story?" she asked, but Prince Jotel was fast asleep.

She yawned. "Good night, sweet Prince," and she kissed him on the nose.

"Oh yes...what happened to Chang's cat Mita?" she wondered, her eyes fidgeting in her search for a denouement. "I guess she either starved to death or found herself a new master. I'll leave the choice up to ..."

She curled up in her bed like a foetus and drifted into the arms of the sandman.

# CHAPTER 10

## The Golden Rhinoceros

Queen Clytoris, weary of the politics, the arguments, and the discussions that Carol liked to stir among the women, took off one morning to walk around the surrounding countryside. It occurred to her that she could just keep on walking, away from it all. She realised that she was no politician like Carol, who thrived in the turmoil. Carol was a fighter and would fight her to the bitter end. Queen Clytoris did not want to fight her, but she feared Carol would take control and destroy everything she believed in.

This morning, the sky was effulgently clear, the blueness and sunlight colliding into a brilliant glare. The valley was mingling with bright light and melancholic shadows. The trees were soft and tender and softly glowed. Among the leaves, sparrows twittered and gossiped. A dark male sparrow sat like a fat ball of yarn, chirping away, calling for a mate. The sparrow glanced quickly at her, espying her from moment to moment as he took everything in his vigilant glance at the environment. His head movements were sharp and quick. Then it darted away, shooting through the greenery. She followed a trail, stepping lightly on the fallen leaves. Her eyes watched, noticing so many things. There was always something to discover in the infinite details of nature. On the ground, she could see ants busy at work; up in the sky, various birds flew. Flowers of different colours, leaves of many shapes and hues of green, trees looking like a cast of characters in a movie.

There was something this morning she had never expected to encounter: a golden rhinoceros. She saw it from afar, the creature browsing some berry bushes. Slowly, she sneaked forward to get a closer look. The creature was massive, its golden armour bright and shining, its horns sharp and solid. When Queen Clytoris approached it, she looked into its eyes. The creature's eyes were an impenetrable forest of darkness. She backed away, overwhelmed with awe. The rhinoceros perplexed her. She searched for sentences to clarify her confusion, sought symbols to pacify her, like a signpost to pinpoint her place in the cosmos. Her disturbance was unpleasant. Her mind failed her; its limitations weighed heavily on her. She wandered around the valley, trying to regain her serenity and composure. Words poured into her mind, words trying to create meaning and order, but ultimately failing. She sank to the ground, lay on her back on the grassy floor, and looked up at the sky, which belittled her. She was humbled. The universe was infinitely superior to the human species; there was knowledge beyond the knowledge of humanity. It was impossible to know. The secret was concealed in the eyes of the Golden Rhinoceros. The only true response was silence. So Queen Clytoris silenced her mind and listened. Initially, she could hear the wind and the leaves and the birds. Then she heard the words in her head, trying to shatter the silence. But she let the words disperse and disappear. Words dissolving into silence. Then she listened deeply to the silence inside her. Terrified, she steeled herself to confront the silence. Was it merely emptiness at the heart of the universe? Did the Kingdom of Nothingness rule the universe? Then the fear subsided. The silence soothed her. The silence sang a beautiful song. The silence filled her with bliss. But it was like the voice of a siren which could drive the listener raving mad.

# CHAPTER 11

## The Stone

We rented a boat at Berowra Waters. We hitchhiked our way there. It was your idea to hitchhike. Men were willing to give you a lift. It was perhaps a dangerous thing to do. But I don't regret being in the boat with you. You sat and enjoyed the scenery, while I rowed across the serene waters. The day was hot, and your bright green dress glimmered. The dark green bush stood still and silent. I didn't want the day to ever end.

The hard, rough surface of the stone impressed itself on the soft, pink palms of Carol. She was squatting before the stone, ready to pitch her strength against it, lift it, and triumphantly haul it away to the village. One stone for her stone castle. Instead of rising with the stone, she found herself being pulled down, the ponderous stone resisting her and clinging to the breast of soft grass. Carol relinquished her grip. Unlike the hard, solid stone, Carol was soft, her body a sleeping beauty, unaccustomed to actions requiring bodily strength. Get up! she commanded her body, which must now match her mind in strength. No more ideas, action was the imperative. The stone must be raised. She tried again. The stone stayed; she despaired.

"What a beautiful stone!" gushed Virginia, in a dulcet mood.

"Yes, it will prove strong and reliable when we build the castle." said Carol.

"How romantic to have a castle! It would be just like the fairy tales!"

"This castle is not for romance," said Carol, miffed by Virginia's silliness. "Its purpose is to protect us women from the violence of men."

Virginia sang, "I want my husband to be as solid as a stone."

Carol rebuked her, "Surface features. Look deeper. Inside, men are incorrigibly stupid and vain. Be wary of them!"

A yellow dab of butterfly was sprinkled on her gaze. Virginia flapped her arms and pursued the butterfly, which fluttered like heartbeats in the sun.

Carol blamed it on her husband's genes conspiring inside Virginia's mind. If only women could be born solely of women, without the extra insidious ingredient of men.

A pure woman, uncreated by fathers.

Carol turned to the women that accompanied her. "This is our first stone for our castle! Let's get this thing moving."

"It looks rather heavy," said Sharon Fing, grimacing at the formidable stone.

"Together we can carry it."

Like soldiers encircling an enemy, the four women gathered around the stone.

Maylene, a tall, spindly woman with knobbly joints, made the first move, slipping her fingers under the stone. A startled spider underneath skedaddled away, eight furry legs scurrying. Eight human legs scurrying. Carol stopped, regaining her composure.

"Don't be frightened. It's only a harmless spider."

"I hate spiders," squeaked Maylene.

"Men are worse than spiders. Come on, we have to build this castle."

"Maybe Queen Clytoris is right. Maybe a castle is injurious to our soul."

"Screw the soul!" shouted Carol. "We're talking about security and protection here. We can't allow King Prawn to destroy our community."

"Queen Clytoris won't allow him. She's his wife."

"That's the trouble with us women—we have placed our trust and faith in our husbands, our boyfriends, and we have made ourselves defenceless and vulnerable to them. I'd like to believe that there's one safe sanctuary in this men-infested world where women can come to and feel safe."

With one explosive effort Carol and the women heaved up the stone and dislodged it from the earth. Beneath the stone: wet, slimy, light-fleeing insects. The women trudged forward; the stone heavy like a pregnant woman carrying a stone baby. They made some progress, then the stone returned to the earth, thud!

"Let's up and go!" Carol barked.

"We need a break," pleaded Maylene.

"This is one meagre stone. We still have to haul in a thousand more."

"Thousands," groaned the chorus of women.

"It's nothing. We'll get stronger and stronger and stronger."

"My fingernails are broken," whimpered Maylene.

"Let's get this straight. The past is over. No longer are we dolled up and painted for men to gawk and drool over for cheap entertainment. Those ornamental days are over. Now starts our new era of strength, when we have to dig deep to find the strength and will to overcome the obstacles that keep us weak and limited. The future is ours. Who will follow me into the future?"

Carol had no doubt that the women would follow her. She was their leader, not Queen Clytoris. People asked for clarity, success, gain, and hope. Queen Clytoris offered mere Truth, a road pocked with doubt, failure, and isolation. Carol offered them a castle, which was real and provided them with security and a feeling of achievement. Carol's castle stood on the ground while Queen Clytoris's fantastic castle of truth floated in the air. The women would choose Carol, even if it meant sacrificing Truth. Carol grasped the black heart of politics.

Virginia was still playing with the butterfly when Carol resumed work on the stone. The vignette of her daughter larking in the sun distressed and infuriated her. How long must she wait for Virginia to get sensible about life? She was tired of waiting. They started once again on the stone.

Virginia picked up a small stone the size fitting her small palm. "Here, Mum. Isn't this a cute baby stone? Look, baby stone wants to be with Mummy stone. Baby stone wants to kiss Mummy stone. Kiss kiss kiss." Virginia pressed the little stone to the large stone.

"Stop that!" Carol snapped at her. She accidentally lost her grip on the stone, dropping and grazing Virginia's knee. Virginia let out a cry and sat on the grass and nursed her scratched sore knee. She expected sympathy from Carol. Instead, she yelled at her. "That's what happens when you act stupid. You get hurt. It's all your fault."

The women wanted to pamper Virginia, but Carol ordered them to continue on with the work. "Let this be a lesson, Virginia, life is not all about fun. If you are not careful, life can hurt you really bad."

They bore away the stone and left Virginia in tears. "Oh Baby stone, I'm sorry. You've lost your Mummy stone." And Virginia and Baby stone cried together in the middle of the forest.

# CHAPTER 12

## The Invasion of Hollywood

### SHOT 1

*The army of King Prawn descends en masse on Hollywood. Defending Hollywood is a battalion of famous Hollywood stars, including legends such as Clark Gable, Gary Cooper, Marilyn Monroe, and an assortment of extras, stuntmen, film directors, cartoon characters, B-Grade stars, and celebrity wannabes. They have barricaded themselves with props of trees, moons, building facades, rubber boulders, and a giant cutout of Arnold Schwarzenegger in Conan the Barbarian costume.*

### SHOT 2

*General Barbara Stanwyck in full military attire, inspects her troops, and orders them to take their positions and hold fire until ordered. She sees Marilyn Monroe posing seductively for the cameras.*

BARBARA STANWYK: Private Monroe! Where's your helmet, your rifle, don't you know there's a war's going on?

MARILYN: I'm sorry, General, but I was boosting the soldier's morale.

BARBARA: I can see that you've quite boosted their morale. Now how can the soldiers fight when they can hardly walk? Monroe, stop your boosting and get back to the barricades.

MARILYN: Yes, sir! *(Marilyn salutes her then walks sexily back to the barricades. Soldiers gawked at her with popping eyes, lolling tongues, and boosted morale.)*

BARBARA: How does she do that? She must have a double-jointed crotch.

### SHOT 3

*King Prawn and his soldiers charge through the barricades. The Hollywood stars shoot at them to no effect. They are shooting blanks. Spencer Tracy falls melodramatically. Paulette Goddard swoons. The Hollywood army panics and scatters helter skelter in retreat.*

BARBARA: Get back to your positions and fight, soldiers! I'll have you all court marshalled!

MARILYN: We're all going to the Surrender Party. Wanna come?

BARBARA: A party! Why didn't you say so sooner? Let's party!

MARILYN: Hurray to Hollywood!

ELEANOR POWELL: Everybody dance!

NELSON EDDY: Everybody sing!

JERRY LEWIS: Everybody laugh!

ERROL FLYNN: Everybody fuck!

BOMB: Everybody die!

KABOOOM!!!!!!!!!!!!!!!!!!

## SHOT4

*Gary Cooper and Rita Hayworth in embrace. Bombs explode around them.*

GARY: I guess this is goodbye, darling.

RITA: Yes, my love.

GARY: I love you, darling. We shall meet again in eternity.

RITA: I think I'm going to puke!

GARY: You can't say that!

RITA: Why not?

GARY: Because we're on camera.

RITA: Fuck! Why didn't you tell me! Um…yes…I love you, I love you, my darling!

*(They kiss passionately. A gunshot. They look into each other's eyes for the last time. They both fall dead, with melodramatic music playing loudly.)*

## SHOT 5

*Robert Duvall is running and then stops when he sees the cameras.*

ROBERT: This is not fair! They're using real bullets!

GEORGE LUCAS: Cut! Robert, can you say it again with more feeling?

ROBERT: I thought I did it rather well.

GEORGE: Camera! Action!

ROBERT *(He runs then looks at the camera.)*: This is not fair, they're using…aak!

*(Robert is shot dead by a sniper's bullet.)*

GEORGE: Wonderful, Robert, but let's have one more take. Um…Robert…Robert…

ASSISTANT: Mr Lucas, I'm afraid that Robert Duvall's dead.

GEORGE: He can't die. It's not in the script!

ASSISTANT: It's not a film, Mr Lucas. It's real. There's a real war going on.

GEORGE: Real? You don't mean…reality?

ASSISTANT: Yes, reality.

GEORGE: Didn't I say that this is to be a closed set?

ASSISTANT: But war respects no rules.

GEORGE: Who's responsible for this war?

ASSISTANT: A King Prawn.

GEORGE: I'll make sure he never works in Hollywood again!

ORSON WELLES: Cut! That was great, George! Now I need I shot of your death scene.

JOHN FORD: Cut! That was great, Orson. Now I need a shot of your death scene.

STUNTMAN (OF ORSON WELLES): I'm ready, Mr Ford.

(Explosions behind the stuntman, who throws himself into the air, and crashes into a stack of cardboard boxes.)

### SHOT 6

King Prawn enters the studio and shoots down John Ford and Orson Welles.

### SHOT 7

Close up of the dying Orson Welles.

### SHOT 8

Flashback of Orson Welles as a child riding a snow sled on the snow. The sled does not move. Orson is too heavy.

### SHOT 9

Harpo Marx is running, collapses from a gunshot. Enter the Marx Brothers.

CHICO MARX: Harpo! Speak to me! Are you dead? One honk if you are dead, and two honks if you are still alive.

(Harpo honks his horn three times.)

CHICO: Three honks? Whatya mean wid a three honks?

GROUCHO: Maybe it's time for breakfast.

CHICO: Itsa too late for breakfast

GROUCHO: Lunchtime?

CHICO: Itsa too early.

GROUCHO: Why am I hungry then? My stomach is always punctual. It visits me three times a day-breakfast, lunch, dinner. Except yesterday it visited me only lunch and dinner.

CHICO: Where was it at breakfast?

GROUCHO: I don't know. I wasn't home.

CHICO: I know why you're hungry. You gotta hole in your stomach.

GROUCHO: Why, you're right. I have a hole in my stomach. In fact, it's a bullet hole. I might also add that I'm bleeding to death, which is the only way to bleed when you're in New York.

CHICO: We're not in New York. We're in Hollywood.

GROUCHO: You better book me a flight. Nobody bleeds real blood in Hollywood.

CHICO: Why don't you stick a finger in the hole, maybe that'll stop you from bleeding?

GROUCHO: Are you a doctor?

CHICO: I cured a man once.

GROUCHO: Yeah? How did you cure him?

CHICO: I left the room.

GROUCHO: How did that cure him?

CHICO: He was sick of me.

GROUCHO (*putting the back of his hand on his forehead dramatically*): It's too late, Chico, I'm dying, I'm dying. Goodbye world, it was nice while it lasted.

CHICO: Stop complaining. My uncle never complained when he died. In fact, he's been dead for ten years and he hasn't complained at all. Except for the neighbours about his smell. But we don't tell our uncle on account we don't wanna hurt his feelings.

GROUCHO: When I die, I'm not going to take it lying down. This is a grave situation. I must take drastic measures. Chico, go to the drugstore and get me a bottle of drastic measures

CHICO (*peering into Groucho's stomach*): Hey, look what I found in your stomach. A can of baked beans.

GROUCHO: That's canned food for you. Tastes better in the can.

CHICO: There's plenty of stuff in your stomach. Let's see. Here's a leg of ham, a pepperoni pizza, and an orange duck.

GROUCHO: Duck L'Orange.

CHICO: Hey, what's this? (*A live horse jumps out of Groucho's stomach.*)

GROUCHO: I was very hungry.

CHICO: Don't be ashamed, I coulda eat a horse too and sometimes an elephant even.

## SHOT 10

*Chico crawls inside Groucho's stomach. Inside he finds a delicatessen store.*

CHICO: Pretty big place in here. *(He sees James Cagney, smoking a cigar.)*

CAGNEY: Hello.

CHICO: What are you doing here?

CAGNEY: I came here on recommendation. They say they serve the best pastrami sandwiches in all of U.S. of A. in here. Say, you want a cigar?

CHICO: I don't mind if I do. Thanks, pal. *(He takes a cigar.)* I hope Groucho doesn't have gas or we both get blown up.

CAGNEY *(lights Chico's cigar)*: I like this place. It's swell.

CHICO: Needs a better interior decorator.

CAGNEY: It's good to be away from the lights. I'm sick of facing those studio lights. It feels like I'm being interrogated for a crime I've never committed.

CHICO: The lights—they never turn off in Hollywood.

CAGNEY *(despondently)*: I'm always playing a gangster in my movies. When all my life I've always wanted to play beautiful blonde sex bombshells like Jean Harlow.

CHICO: You've got nothing to gripe about. I'm always playing Chico the dumb wop. I ain't even Italian. Don't you think it doesn't bother me that I can't play Rhett Butler in *Gone with the Wind*?

CAGNEY: What a coincidence. I wanted to play Scarlet O'Hara.

*(A man enters the delicatessen. He is John Smith, an unemployed actor. He had a face no one, even his mother could remember.)*

JOHN SMITH: I wanted to play Rhett Butler. In fact, I want any role. I've been a struggling actor since they made the first movie. So stop griping. If there's anyone who has the right to gripe, it's me, not you rich and famous Hollywood stars. I've got nothing. All I have are my dreams.

CAGNEY: Don't feel bad, Jack. All success does is give you a swell head.

BILLY WILDER: Cut! That was not bad…*(looks at appointment sheet)*…Joe Smith. If we're interested, we'll give you a call. Next screen test!

KING PRAWN: Hello.

BILLY WILDER: You can't be a movie star. You have no face!

## SHOT 11

*You see though the camera and see King Prawn drawing his sword and slaying Billy Wilder. He then runs toward the camera. You die.*

## SHOT 12

GROUCHO: I knew I should have opened up a hotel in my stomach. Hey, you in there! Quiet it down! Can't a dead man rest in peace? Next time I have a hole in my stomach, I'll charge admission.

## SHOT 13:

BING CROSBY: The trouble with the cinema of today is that it's so ugly. Everything and everyone were beautiful in the golden days of Hollywood.

*(A soldier enters and throws a grenade at Bing Crosby. His death is shown in slow motion. Blood gushing everywhere, his torn limbs flying apart.)*

HEAD OF BING CROSBY: Nowadays, it's all about special effects!

## SHOT 14

MARGARET DUMONT *(kneeling over Groucho)*: I came as quickly as I could. Is it true, my love, that you are indeed dying?

GROUCHO: Yes, my love, it is true. I'm going to the great big pie in the sky. Do you have a napkin? I guess it's over. No more moonlight swims, no secret trysts in the forests, no passionate kisses and embraces, no gazing at each other's eyes. Well, I'm glad that's all over between us. I don't think I could have survived another of your embraces. I could barely breathe!

MARGARET: I will miss you terribly.

GROUCHO: I'll miss you too. I've never loved a woman as rich as you. I also never loved a woman as big as you. Come to think of it? I've never loved such a woman. But I'm jesting...I love you, I love you, I love you. I love all three of you.

MARGARET: You will always be in my heart.

GROUCHO: In your heart? Wouldn't it be spacier for me to be in your stomach, considering you're ...but let's not talk about elephants for this is not the time and the place. I'm dying, and I just want to spend the last minutes of my life gazing into your eyes, which remind me of...but let's not talk about elephants. By the way, I shot an elephant in your pyjamas the other day. Your pyjamas fitted him perfectly.

MARGARET: I will never forget you. I'll be in mourning for the rest of my life.

GROUCHO *(dramatically)*: Don't mourn, my darling. Live...for my sake. Get married, be happy, and forget about me. Let me take one last look at you, my darling. *(He gazes long into her loving eyes.)* Say, you didn't by any chance get shot in your pyjamas the other day?

MARGARET: Oh Groucho, you're so brave. Joking to the end.

GROUCHO: Who's joking? I'm speaking the truth. Go look in the mirror, a very wide mirror. I thought I saw you last night. But it was only a truck passing by. Ah! I guess this is it! I'm about to kick the bucket. Where's that bucket? Give me some dust that I can bite? But before I die, let me have one last kiss with a beautiful woman.

MARGARET: Of course, Groucho, I'll grant you your last wish. *(Margaret kisses Groucho.)*

GROUCHO: I said I want to kiss a beautiful woman!

*(Margaret kisses Groucho again.)*

GROUCHO: And I thought a bullet in my stomach was the worst thing that could happen to me. *(He dies.)*

MARGARET: *(cradling Groucho)* Oh Groucho, Groucho, my love.

*(Enters Susan Hayward.)*

SUSAN HAYWARD: You should be glad that cad is dead.

MARGARET: I'm only an actress. I just read what the script says.

SUSAN *(handing a script to Margaret):* Here's a script for you to read. This time you be the funny man and he the straight. You humiliate him for a change. *(She kicks Groucho.)* Groucho, get up, stop playing dead, you're called on the set.

GROUCHO *(sitting up and skimming through the script)*: I can't read this. I'm not funny.

SUSAN: Take One!

MARGARET: I came as quickly as I could. Is it true, are you dying?

GROUCHO. Yes, my darling.

MARGARET: Then you'd better pay the two hundred bucks you owe me.

GROUCHO: Money! Is that all you can think of while I'm dying. Don't you love me?

MARGARET: You're so funny, Groucho. *(She laughs loudly.)*

GROUCHO: Aren't you even going to miss me, darling?

MARGARET: I didn't miss you. The bullet hit you right where I wanted it.

GROUCHO: You shot me! But why?

MARGARET: I killed you for the money.

GROUCHO: But I don't have any money.

MARGARET: Someone paid me a buck to kill you.

GROUCHO: I'm dying. Will you kiss me before I die?

MARGARET: One person dying is enough.

GROUCHO: But you will never see me again. Won't you even be sad?

MARGARET: I have to go now. I'm late for a lunch date. As for the two hundred dollars you owe me, I'll take all your possessions. That should add up to a grand total of one buck. For the remainder of your debt, I'll sell your body to science, most likely archaeology.

GROUCHO: The pain of unrequited love. (*He dies.*)

SUSAN: Cut! Now that's better, don't you think so, Margaret?

MARGARET: I love it.

GROUCHO (*getting up*): You must be kidding. That was atrocious.

(*Enters John Wayne acting as King Prawn*)

JOHN WAYNE: Surrender or die!

SUSAN Excuse me?

JOHN: I'm playing King Prawn.

SUSAN: Who says so?

JOHN: Paramount. They're making a 90-million-dollar epic on King Prawn. I'm the star.

SUSAN: Who's playing Queen Clytoris?

JOHN: Haven't you heard? Katherine Hepburn.

SUSAN: That bitch!

### SHOT 15

*The Globe Theatre. John Wayne in Shakespearean garb. He wears tight tights, and where his crotch is, is a concealed Colt.45 calibre pistol. He struts about the stage.*

JOHN: King Prawn am I, and I am the King of men.

This world methinks too safe and nice,

it is a cobbler of cowardly souls.

A world of men it's not! A pitiful ant colony

crawling with the slaves of a castrating Queen.

In a word she is woman.

Woman is the rust that eats your iron,

Woman is the cage for your proud cock,

Woman is the woe of man.

The time is now that we be men

and act like men

and free ourselves from their dangerous embrace.

The hour is now when these witches

must sweep the floor with their brooms.

*Enter Mickey Rooney dressed as Shakespearean page.*

MICKEY ROONEY: Your Royal Majesty,

I have the news your appetite

ravenously waits for.

The castle which houses the lair

of the man-eating lioness,

Queen Clytoris, has been sighted,

and at the risk of losing

your appetite altogether,

we have sounded out a bold escapee

from her ungentle claws,

and he has many a horrendous tale to tell.

How he survived know not I

but certainly, many bits of his mind

have not journeyed back with him.

JOHN: Bring this poor brave wretch here.

I know what he will relate.

I am not a prophet, but I know that witch well.

It shames me to recall my love for her,

our marriage, my subsequent hell.

Her visage, the brightest and sweetest flower

adorning this beautiful earth,

and when I plucked this lovely flower

I thought as foolish youths do

that I had possessed the amulet

to shake off misery forever.

But she and misfortune hand in hand,

and the noble soldier that I was,

the craven fool I became.

Each day of our marriage

laid heavily on my mind's shoulders,

A burden that only jackasses bear.

MICKEY: Your Royal Majesty,

Here before you is the brave Coldbutt,

who is not mad angry, but mad mad,

from his sad encounter with the bad Queen.

JOHN: Tell us your torrid tale,

my courageous Coldbutt.

TOM HANKS (*as Coldbutt*): Once upon a time there lived a rabbit named Randy, a randy rabbit was he. Oh! I'm scared, poor Coldbutt, his mind is now a half-loaf, not Randy the rabbit whose wife must be fun, and Queen Clytoris, spider's bottom, baboon's nostril, she took hotbutt Coldbutt away from his happy, happy farm, and to the castle, the dungeon where she, oh beautiful but ugly Queen, she took Coldbutt's handsome pecker into her beak for supper. Oh poor Coldbutt Nopecker, forever cold, for nothing oh nothing to keep him warm in the frozen nights. Oh, where are you, my handsome tool, come back to me I am so alone, alone, alone, will you forgive me, my sprucey spunk. I thought a favour I do you if inside the Queen keep you hot and warm, but it was not inside her tummy I intended. A pecker! A pecker! A condom for a pecker! (*He holds up a unused condom.*)

JOHN: Disgusting was her deed!

Foul! Horror! Shame! Rank!

Now emboldens my blood to blot out this blight.

No remorse shall I feel when I crush this vile insect.

My dear Coldbutt I cannot bring your pecker back,

but her head on a silver platter I shall for you.

Let's on! This world needs a saviour!

## SHOT 16

*The dark, expressionistic interior of Queen Clytoris's castle. Queen Clytoris and her two witches are standing around a large cauldron chanting incantations, with Queen Clytoris stirring the obscene, hot brew with her broom.*

KATHERINE HEPBURN (*playing Queen Clytoris*): Sisters, how many cocks have you collected for our emasculating casserole?!

BETTE DAVIS (*as Witch 1*): Five from five brothers,

of five different sizes,

from thick to thin,

from tiny to biggie.

JOAN CRAWFORD (*as Witch 2*): I have just one

but a giant was my catch.

He was a ten-foot ogre

who terrorise the village women

with his whipping whopper.

"A two-foot friend have I," he said to me.

"And dearly would he like to meet

your little furry friend that hides inside your dress."

Replied I, "Show me this lengthy friend of yours,

for around my mouth I'll caress him."

Out with his serpent with no fangs,

and into my mouth did he slither.

One bite was enough

and here I have his two-foot creature.

KATHERINE: Well done, sisters two.

A cocky casserole we shall have,

and now into the pot I pollute:

One ugly toad, two chopped ears,

cat's guts and used tampons.

If anyone of you care

to relieve yourself, please do,

it will add zing to the flavour.

And now a sprinkle of dried horse dung

will make a wonderful stink.

ALL: We are witches three,

and we are wicked we all agree,

though fat and ugly are we,

beautiful and slim to men we seemed to be.

No hearts and souls have we

and those men who think with their dicks

cannot expect the next morn to be

the whole man they used to be.

We are wicked witches three,

and we are wicked all men agree.

*(Enters John Wayne with raised sword.)*

KATHERINE: That fool looks familiar.

I remember him at our Wedding Night,

I shouldn't have come then,

for he didn't make me come.

JOAN CRAWFORD: A man knows not how to please a woman.

BETTE DAVIS: And a displeased woman becomes a witch.

JOHN: Foul is the air I breathe,

and with a swipe of this sword

I shall clear the air.

Prepare for death, wicked witches three.

KATHERINE HEPBURN: How presumptuous of you

to assume we women are weak

and easy to defeat.

Now, my sexist, sex-incompetent,

prepare for death, and I'll prepare your cock

for a sumptuous supper.

*(She and the witches draw their brooms, which transform into swords.)*

JOHN: Three against one.

How wise of you to be cowardly.

KATHERINE: You, a man, cannot understand this,

but we are sisters three who do things mutually,

unlike you men whose joys are singular.

Up your sword. Perhaps it'll stay up longer

than your selfish toy.

JOHN: Die, most horrendous witch!

And may the life after be a hot stove

for your soul to fry.

*(They fight. Witch 1 is killed. Followed by Witch 2.)*

Now it's just you and me,

and it's not our honeymoon.

KATHERINE: Prepare to meet Death, your bride.

JOHN: Love I did you.

Hate I you now.

Die you must.

*(They fight. Queen Clytoris is fatally wounded.)*

KATHERINE: I am cruelly cut,

Death be kind to me.

Death be a woman not a man.

*(She dies.)*

JOHN: The witch is dead.

Now the vapour of her wicked reign

is lifted up from this suffering earth,

so that the neglected sun

may illume Beauty and Truth.

The night is dead. Long live the day!

*(The real King Prawn enters the stage.)*

JOHN: Who are you?

KING PRAWN: I'm the one and only King Prawn.

JOHN: I'm King Prawn. I signed the contract.

KING PRAWN: You're an actor, that's who you are. Stupid circus animals performing for the masses.

## SHOT 17

*An old western town, a dirt road, two gunfighters facing each other.*

JOHN *(now wearing a cowboy outfit, guns and all.)*: You take that back, mister, or you're dead where you're standing.

KING PRAWN: Or else you won't sing and dance for me, huh?

JOHN: Or else I'll have to ask you to draw.

KING PRAWN: You don't scare me. I'm the fastest draw in the west.

JOHN: That's nothing. I'm the biggest drawcard in the world.

KING PRAWN: I guess one of us will have to mosey down to the local cemetery and lay there for eternity.

JOHN: You ain't fit to be buried in the local graveyard, mister. You're meat for the buzzards.

KING PRAWN: I'm going to get rid of dirty scum like you. This Hollywood is the Sodom and Gomorrah and I'm going to burn it down with my fire and brimstone. Last night I went searching for ten Hollywood Superstars with integrity so I can spare this tinsel town. I didn't find one.

JOHN: You talk too much, villain. Let your gun do the talking from now on. Get ready to meet your Maker.

KING PRAWN: I wasn't made; unlike you, I was born.

JOHN: The good guy always wins in the end. I'm ready when you are.

*(They exchange glares, their fingers twitching before their guns in their holsters. In the middle of a twitch, they draw as quick as a flash, and the air cracks with a loud blast. For a moment, they stand motionless, until John Wayne crumples to the ground.)*

JOHN *(clutching his bloodied stomach)*: Where's my stuntman when I need him? This ain't fair, I shot you first. You're supposed to play dead.

KING PRAWN: This is not a movie, this is for real. My bullets are real, not blank like yours.

JOHN: But my contract specifically states that I can't die in my roles.

KING PRAWN (*picking up a handful of dust*): Here, kiss the dust. (*He throws the dust at John Wayne, who drops down dead, rather undramatically.*)

## SHOT 18

*World War 1 trenches.*

MONTGOMERY CLIFT: War is Hell.

WOODY ALLEN: Oh yeah? Love is hell. War is a bed of roses compared to...women...th-th-they're the enemy

MONTGOMERY: Let's get drunk. (*He takes a swig from his whisky bottle.*)

WOODY: I don't drink. Alcohol calms me down. I need...anxiety. Wh-which is why I need women.

YOUNG SOLDIER: I'm 18 years old and I'm still a virgin.

WOODY: You think you've got problems. I'm 45 a-and I'm still a virgin.

YOUNG SOLDIER: Why don't you get married?

WOODY: Wh-what are you talking about? I've been married twice.

MONTGOMERY: You mean to tell me that you didn't make love to your first two wives.

WOODY: My first wife, I was young and desperate, so I married Godzilla. As for my second wife...we just never got around to it. I suppose I was too shy to broach the subject. Hey, I'm Jewish, life is not a straight arrow, we are a wandering people. I'm not German, I don't blitzkrieg women, march over them, call myself fuehrer. I just wander and hope something, besides plagues, happens. I guess nothing happened between my wife and me.

MONTGOMERY: What did you do in your wedding night?

WOODY: Um...my my wife and I went to watch an Ingmar Bergman movie. *Face to Face* I think it was. Wonderful movie. I can't count the number of times I got depressed and wanted to commit suicide. There's n-nothing more intimate than feeling suicidal with a w-woman one loves.

MONTGOMERY: Your wife enjoyed the movie.

WOODY: She snored throughout. But...it wasn't his best movie. Should have taken her to *The Seventh Seal*, it has death, murder, plagues. Rivetting. A must for dating couples.

MONTGOMERY: Whadja do when you got home?

WOODY: Um…-m-my wife got really romantic. We talked about love and sex…she referred to Freud, Plato, Fromm, and *Cleo*…W-while I quoted some letters from *Penthouse*. Well, things led to other things and before you know it we were talking about Sartre's *Nausea* and I threw up in bed…well, it was hard to get romantic after that. A bed of vomit is no bed of roses.

YOUNG SOLDIER (*standing up and screaming*): Oh God, we're all gonna die!

WOODY: Hey, speak for yourself. I have no intention of ever dying. It's not my scene. But look on the bright side. Who knows, maybe D-D-D-Death might not be too bad. Maybe when you die, you'll be surrounded by beautiful angels, and all of them are into free love and Dostoevsky. You'll be happy forever. You needn't worry about money, and what's more, you'll look like G-G-Gary C-C-Cooper. Everyone will look like Gary Cooper. I mean the guys, and all the women look like Marilyn Monroe. B-But I'm talking about Heaven. Hell is another thing. All the guys look like Adolf Hitler, and all the women, Mussolini. But that's assuming there's life after death. There might be nothing. Nothingness…wh-which, probably, looks just like my bedroom.

YOUNG SOLDIER: Why do people want war? It's not just politicians to blame. We all want war. We all want conflict.

WOODY: I joined the army to keep away from women. Um…despite bombs exploding around me and any minute now I could look like Boris Karloff…I-I feel absolute peace.

MONTGOMERY: (*sings in a drunken stupor*)

Let's have a jolly good time

Life is too short

So put on your party hat

we'll have a jolly good time

(*"Let's have a jolly good time!" shouts ten gorgeous women decked in glittering red, white, and blue sequined costumes. Fred Astaire comes out in his debonair top hat and tails and sings and dances in a battlefield of corpses.*)

FRED: Let's have a jolly good time

Let's sing and dance

Let's not get too serious

For this mean old earth

full of suffering

for the poor and the rich

for the dumb and the wise

There's a mean old God

who wants to make you cry

But let's forget the bad times

let's forget the pain

let's forget our troubles

Let's just sing and dance

and have a jolly good time

(*Fred Astaire breaks off into a razzle-dazzle tap solo. The finale is Fred Astaire being blown to pieces by a bomb landing on his top hat.*)

YOUNG SOLDIER (*getting hysterical*): Enough is enough. No more suffering. No more violence. Let's have peace. Let's not fight any more.

WOODY: That's the exact thing I said to my last wife. Just before she punched me on the nose.

YOUNG SOLDIER: Let's hold hands and learn to understand each other

MONTGOMERY: This is getting a bit much for me. (*He aims his rifle at the young soldier who is dancing in the field and shoots him dead*)

(*Enters Cary Grant in his tuxedo*)

CARY GRANT: Hello.

WOODY: Hi.

CARY: How are you?

WOODY: Fine. And you?

CARY: Not bad. The weather's fine.

WOODY: Yes, a nice day to be killed.

CARY: Yes. Good day for horse riding.

WOODY: I can only ride carousel. I don't like horses that breathe.

CARY: Um...how's Diane Keaton.

WOODY: Well, ladeda, I guess.

CARY: What did you have for lunch?

WOODY: Why are you so boring?

CARY: My scriptwriter was killed by King Prawn. I've been improvising since.

WOODY: Now I understand.

CARY: It's been a struggle. You have a scriptwriter?

WOODY: I write my own scripts. Masturbation taught me to be self-reliant.

CARY: Um...yes...um...

## SHOT 19

*A clock on a white wall. It's 3 O'clock in the afternoon.*

## SHOT 20

*A cow is hacked to death live on stage. The audience are cheering.*

## SHOT 21

*A carousel. The Grim Reaper is riding with his four-year-old son, a skeleton wearing a Lord Fauntleroy outfit and Mickey Mouse cap. He is biting into a pink fuzzy cotton candy, smearing his mouth and chin.*

## SHOT 22

*Liv Ullman rises from her bed, and looks at the camera, and reaches out to touch it. "Don't touch the bloody lens, you stupid twit!" shouts the director, Ingmar Bergman, from behind the camera.*

## SHOT 23

*Liv Ullman and Bibi Andersen are facing each other. One of them farts. Nobody laughs.*

LIV: My father died yesterday. I laughed and laughed.

BIBI: My father died yesterday. I made love to my ten-year-old son.

LIV: My husband raped me on our wedding night. He wore a trout outfit, put a knife at my throat, and raped me. Next night, he cut off his penis and sodomised himself.

BIBI: When I was a young girl my father showed me his penis. Then my uncle showed me his penis. So did our milk man. One day Aunt Margaret showed me her husband's penis, which she kept in her handbag.

*(Enter Gladys Smith, an ordinary Australian woman. She sits with them in the lounge. Liv and Bibi do not look at her.)*

GLADYS: Hello, Livi and Bibi.

LIV: My husband died.

BIBI: I'm sorry to hear that, luv.

LIV: He ate his brain.

GLADYS: Men eat the funniest things. They're goats really. My husband Stan would eat anything served on his plate. But look, sweetie, I went to Grace Bros today and did I snap a bargain, pantyhose at half price.

BIBI: I caught my husband masturbating before the mirror. He was calling out God's name.

GLADYS: Oh, men are a weird mob. The stories I can tell you about Stan. Once he had two different socks on. One red, one blue. He didn't notice until I pointed it out to him. All he said to me, "A sock is just a sock." I suppose there's some wisdom in that.

LIV: My husband defecated on the floor and asked me to eat it.

GLADYS: Men are such pigs. When Stan cooks for me, you should see the kitchen! All the drawers and cabinets were opened, and practically every can and ingredient were left outside. He was only cooking me steak. And the steak he gives me! I think he gave me the whole cow.

BIBI: My husband hates the smell of me when we make love.

GLADYS: I hate the smell of the toilet after my husband uses it. I think I smelled better corpses.

LIV: "Don't touch me," my husband said to me after I touched him. "My body is pure. It must not be defiled by woman. I am the son of God.''

GLADYS: Stan lords it over his car. You have never seen a cleaner automobile in the world. I think he loves his car more than me.

### SHOT 24

*Full frontal shot of a woman's vulva. A rat enters it.*

### SHOT 25

*City traffic in fast motion.*

### SHOT 26

*Enter Cary Grant, who sits in the lounge with Liv, Bibi, and Gladys.*

CARY: Hello

LIV: I see this man before me. I want to seduce him. But I mustn't. I haven't taken a bath today.

CARY: Um...so how's things?

GLADYS: Good. How about you, Cary?

CARY: Swell. Um...the weather's been fine the past week.

LIV: He listens to me, but he does not hear. He only wants to fuck.

CARY: I had steak for lunch. What did you have?

(Harpo enters. He sees Liv Ullman. His face: bulging eyes, his tongue wagging like a thirsty dog. He jumps into her lap and puts his arm around her. He beeps his horn. She is annoyed and tries to push him away. But he is persistent, and as quickly as he falls off her lap, he jumps back on again. He cuddles her, pressing his face against hers. He looks mischievously at the camera, wide-eyed and wide-mouthed.)

(Banging at the door. "Open up! This is the Gestapo!" Cary answers the door.)

GESTAPO OFFICER: We are looking for Shirley Temple.

CARY: Hi, how are you? What did you have for lunch?

(Harpo beeps his horn and gives his leg to the Gestapo officer's hand. The Gestapo officer blows him away with machine gun burst. Innards come out of Harpo's bloodied trench coat. Ten Gestapo officers enter the room and search for Shirley Temple, overturning furniture, rifling through the cabinets.)

(Enter Groucho and Chico.)

GROUCHO: I'm looking for Shirley Temple. We have a date.

CHICO: (taking out a desk calendar) I've got a date. January 1. I got lots of dates. January 2…January…

CARY: I had steak for lunch.

GROUCHO: What a coincidence. I had lunch for steak.

KNOCK KNOCK KNOCK

(Enter Fred Astaire.)

FRED: I'm the great Fred Astaire. I'm looking for Shirley Temple. She's my new dance partner.

(Harpo jumps up and gives his right leg to Fred Astaire. Fred pushes him away. Then Harpo grabs Fred and dances with him.)

KNOCK KNOCK KNOCK

(Enter Bob Hope and Bing Crosby.)

BOB HOPE: I'm Bob Hope, I'm a comedian.

BING CROSBY: That's what he thinks.

GESTAPO OFFICER: Do you know where Shirley Temple is?

BOB: You're a soldier. Care for some entertainment?

GESTAPO OFFICER: No. (He blasts Bob Hope with his machine gun.)

BING: Now that's funny.

*KNOCK KNOCK KNOCK*

*(The Mickey Mouse Club enters.)*

MICKEY MOUSE CLUB: We're friends of Shirley Temple. We've come to play.

GROUCHO: Come right in. The cat was just looking for you mice. Try walking on the ceiling you might get somewhere.

MICKEY MOUSE CLUB *(singing)*: *M.I.C.K.E.Y.M.O.U.S.E.*

LIV: My husband's only friend was a mouse. He kept it in his anus.

*KNOCK KNOCK KNOCK*

MERYL STREEP: I'm Meryl Streep. I'm the greatest actor in the world. I want to play Shirley Temple. I can play anybody. Now I am a Gestapo Officer. *(She goosekicks.)* Now I am Groucho Marx. *(She bends, struts, tugs her eyebrows, and smokes a cigar.)* Now I am a bird. *(She flaps her arms and flies around the room, dropping an egg on Cary Grant.)*

*KNOCK KNOCK KNOCK*

TEN DANCING GIRLS: We're looking for Fred Astaire. Is he here?

GROUCHO: He must be here. Everyone else is.

CARY: The room's getting a bit crowded, isn't it?

MERYL: *(landing)* Now I am an elephant. *(She transforms into a large elephant.)*

GROUCHO: I had a feeling she'd do that,

*KNOCK KNOCK KNOCK*

ROBERT DE NIRO: I'm Robert De Niro the greatest actor in the world. I want to be Shirley Temple.

GROUCHO: Come right in. We have a table for you in the next restaurant. Say, you can't do an impersonation of an elephant impersonating Fred Astaire?

ROBERT: You bet! *(He turns into a fat elephant, stands on his hind legs, and tapdances.)*

MERYL: If you can be Fred Astaire the elephant, I can be Ginger Rogers the elephant. *(She gets on her hind legs and dances with Fred Astaire doing the Piccolino and they whirl around the room.)*

GROUCHO: We should thank our lucky stars that Margaret Dumont isn't here.

*KNOCK KNOCK KNOCK*

MARGARET DUMONT: Hello.

GROUCHO *(shouts to the crowd)*: Tsunami!

GESTAPO OFFICER *(to Margaret)*: Are you Shirley Temple?

ROBERT AND MERYL: I'm Shirley Temple!

LIV: No, I'm Shirley Temple.

GLADYS: No, I am.

BOB HOPE: I'm Shirley Temple. *(aside)* Anything to get a laugh.

GROUCHO: I can't pretend any longer. I'm Shirley Temple and has anyone seen my tap shoes?

GESTAPO OFFICER: No, I'm a transvestite at night and go by the name of Shirley Temple.

FRED ASTAIRE: I'm Shirley Temple. I had a sex change and called myself Fred Astaire and became the greatest tap dancer in the world.

*KNOCK KNOCK KNOCK*

SHIRLEY TEMPLE: I'm Shirley Temple. Has anybody seen the good ship Lollipop?

EVERYBODY: She's Shirley Temple!

SHIRLEY: Yes.

EVERYBODY: Who cares!

## SHOT 27

*The Academy Awards Ceremony night. A gala evening. On stage is the beautiful Elizabeth Taylor presenting the Oscar for the best Male Actor. Before her the glittering array of actors and actresses and directors and producers of Hollywood.*

ELIZABETH: The nominations for Best Actor in a motion picture are: Sylvester Stallone in RAMBO THE MUSICAL.

## SHOT 28

*Rambo walks through the streets of Moscow billowing in flames. He is armed and military dressed cap-a-pie, and the cowering Muscovites in droves are surrendering to him. He bursts forth into a song which has the same melody as Don't cry for me, Argentina*

SYLVESTER: Don't fight for me, America

The truth is I don't need you

I can fight on my own

Wallop the Russkies and the Arabs

Have I boasted too much?

There's nothing more I can say

But all you have to do

is to glance at my pecs

to know that all is true

## SHOT 29

*The audience applauds. Close-up of Sylvester Stallone in tux, looking nervous, smiling at the camera.*

ELIZABETH: Clint Eastwood in BATTERED HUSBAND

## SHOT 30

*The living room of an ordinary couple. Clint Eastwood wearing a flower print apron greets his wife, Bette Midler, wearing a businesswoman's suit.*

CLINT *(kissing Bette on the cheek)*: Hello, honey. How was your day?

BETTE: Don't honey me, you dirty lowlife scum! (*She belts him one with her black leather briefcase.*)

CLINT *(terrified)*: What have I done wrong, darling?

BETTE: You BEEP put butter not margarine on my sandwich you demented BEEP BEEP twit! You know how much cholesterol there is in butter? You wanna BEEP kill me, *you BEEP BEEP! I'll BEEP* kill you! (*She kicks him, punches him.*)

CLINT *(cowering and bawling on the floor)*: Please, honey bunny, you're hurting me. I'm so sorry. I ran out of margarine. I won't do it again. (*His tears do not stem the violent fury of Bette Midler.*)

## SHOT 31

*Enthusiastic cheers and applause among the audience attending the Oscars. Nominee Clint Eastwood mutters under his breath, 'Go ahead, make my day.'*

ELIZABETH: Mo in THREE STOOGES RULE THE WORLD.

## SHOT 32

*The Oval Office at the White House.*

MO *(as President of USA)*: President Larry, I believe that America and Russia should develop stronger ties.

LARRY *(as President of Russia)*: In Russia we build the strongest ties. Look here (*holding up his tie to Mo*) this tie is made of stainless steel.

MO: You nincompoop! (*He pokes two fingers into Larry's eyes*) I don't mean that stupid tie, I meant relations between our countries.

LARRY *(offended)*: Don't you nincompoop me! (*He tweaks Mo's nose.*) Anyway, what's my Uncle Vladimir and my other relations, got to do with international politics?

MO: You stupid nitwit! (*vibrating Larry's nose with his hands*) I don't mean that stupid relations.

LARRY: My uncle isn't stupid. He just looks stupid. Hey, look, there's a spot on your shirt. (*Mo looks down at his shirt and gets his nose finger flicked by Larry.*) You're the one who's stupid if you fell for that trick.

CURLY (*as Prime Minister of Britain*): Gentlemen, let's behave in a more civilised manner.

MO and LARRY: Shut up, fathead! (*They punch him in the stomach.*)

## SHOT 33

*Loud cheers. Mo in a neck brace acknowledging the audience and the camera. Larry beside him, slaps him on the back. Mo falls over and hits his head and bleeds to death.*)

ELIZABETH: Meryl Streep in KING KONG MEETS GONE WITH THE WIND.

## SHOT 34

*The interior of a Southern mansion. Rhett Butler and Scarlett O'Hara are having breakfast*

RHETT: (*played by Meryl Streep*) Why don't that damn ape go back to Yankee New York? There ain't any skyscraper in the South for him to climb.

SCARLETT (*played by Meryl as well*): I believe that handsome gentleman has fallen for some beautiful Southern belle. He comes to court her.

RHETT: No respectable Southern family aint gonna let a giant gorilla marry into their family.

SCARLETT: I believe that he wants to take his wife to Africa.

RHETT: Africa! What fool woman would marry that oversized chimpanzee and live in savage Africa.

KNOCK KNOCK KNOCK

RHETT (*answering the door*): Yes. (*He sees a hairy big toe and looks up.*) Good God!

KING KONG (*you guess it, played by Meryl*): Me want Scarlett!

SCARLETT: I thought you'd never come, my tall, dark, and handsome man.

KING KONG: Me marry you. We live in Africa. Live in big tree. Biggest tree in Africa.

SCARLETT: How can a woman refuse you, shy big boy you?

RHETT (*astounded*): Why, Scarlet, you aint serious about wedding this here ape and gallivanting off to Africa, are you?

SCARLETT: Why, I sure am serious, Rhett, honey. This Mister Kong is the man I love.

RHETT: What about me? You aint leaving me behind all lonesome?

SCARLETT: Frankly, my dear, I don't give a fuck.

## SHOT 35

*Wild applause billowing through the sequined glittering audience. Meryl Streep sits nonchalantly reading her acceptance speech.*

ELIZABETH: And, lastly, King Prawn in THE INVASION OF HOLLYWOOD

## SHOT 36

*A crowded room*

*KNOCK KNOCK KNOCK*

*Groucho opens the door. A ten-year-old Shirley Temple, wearing a knee length dress with a big bow tie.*

SHIRLEY TEMPLE: I'm Shirley Temple. Has anybody seen the good ship Lollipop?

EVERYBODY: She's Shirley Temple!

SHIRLEY: Yes.

EVERYBODY: Who cares!

SHIRLEY: I do, because I'm not Shirley Temple. I'm really (*she takes off her mask*)...King Prawn! (*He pulls out a machine gun from under his skirt and mows all the people down. Everybody dies in slow motion, blood dancing like a Jackson Pollock painting.*)

## SHOT 37

*Stupendous ovation. King Prawn sweats profusely in his black tux wishing the unbearable suspense would end.*

ELIZABETH: And the winner is (*tearing open the envelope, reading silently, smiling*) ...King Prawn!

(*A rising souffle of beauty as the audience stand up to applause King Prawn, who trots up the side aisle, pounces on the stage, hugs Elizabeth Taylor, and receives his Oscar.*)

KING PRAWN (*in tears and disbelief*): I just don't believe it...it can't be true. Thank you, thank you (*kisses the Oscar*). I didn't think I'd win so I didn't prepare any speech...I was up against such magnificent stars. I still can't believe it...this is a dream come true. There are so many people to thank...my producer, my agent, my Mum and Dad, but most of all I like to thank...(*Suddenly his face turns serious and sardonic.*) That's how you wanted me to react, wasn't it? (*He slams the Oscar down on the table and throws the broken figurine at the hushed audience.*) This Oscar means nothing to me. This fake religious icon. You all mean nothing to me. I don't care that you're rich and famous. I don't care about your movies at all. They're just opium for the masses. You have deluded yourselves that you are artists. Art is about Truth and

Beauty—your Art is all Lies and Ugliness. You have created false gods and false heavens. You have murdered reality! You are all murderers! You are all found guilty! The sentence is Death! (*King Prawn extracts a TNT detonator from his coat. Grinning like a B grade villain, he pushes down the plunger.*)

KAABBOOOOOMMMMMMMMMM!!!!!!!!!!!!!!

## SHOT 38

*A mushroom cloud over Hollywood.*

## THE END

*No credit roll as the film burns.*

# CHAPTER 13

## Heaven and Hell

Dear Readers, I am alone, and only through Art can I truly communicate. K and I, we do not speak, we fight. A colliding of private spaces. Without Art, I shall be mute, my inner world trapped inside this black hole called my soul. I wish I could talk to K and she would listen and understand I am not the enemy. I am merely human, crazy, but full of good intentions.

The last time we heard from King Prawn, he blew himself up along with Hollywood, thus making him as good as dead. So, dear readers, since I can do whatever I like with my characters, should I have my hero die or not? Should I? Speak up! I can't hear you. Yes, I agree with you that this novel desperately needs King Prawn and that if I let him die, the novel will croak along with him, for I can't expect Queen Clytoris, Carol, or Prince Jotel, to carry this novel on their puny shoulders, considering they're such a pack of bores. Thus, King Prawn lives, for the sake of this novel. King Prawn, I raise you from the dead!

King Prawn died and went to heaven. When he regained consciousness, he found himself standing in a pizza take-away joint, greeted by a tall, bulbous, hirsute angel behind the counter.

"Yes, large, medium, or small?"

"What are you talking about?" asked the perplexed King, still reeling from the explosion that had blown Hollywood to kingdom come.

"You've ordered a Pepperoni and Anchovy Pizza," answered the uncherubic and ungenial angel.

"Where am I?" King Prawn asked.

"You're at Luigi's Pizza Restaurant."

"Why am I here?"

"Because you bloody came here!"

"Why?"

"To buy a bloody pizza!"

"I can't remember what brought me here."

"Jesus, you're not one of those new arrivals?" the fat angel said with disdain.

"Huh?"

"You're one of the newly dead."

"I don't understand."

"You're in Heaven," he said, with some sarcasm.

"Heaven?"

"Yep, you've died and gone to heaven. Hallelujah and praise the Lord."

"Heaven?" he repeated, looking around.

"What do you expect? Clouds and naked baby angels?"

"No, I was expecting to go to Hell."

"Hell...that was abolished centuries ago."

"Why?"

"You know, reforms, reforms, reforms. There's always someone calling for reforms: better living conditions, and all that human rights stuff. And Darryl, he's such a wimp, he lets everyone have their way."

"Who's Darryl?"

"You know. In Pizza lingo, the big cheese. The big enchilada. Or if you prefer, God. As you see, everyone on earth got it wrong—the Jews, the Christians, the Zoroastrians. Weren't they disappointed to meet Darryl."

"Where can I meet this Darryl?"

"13 Nietzsche Street, Voltaire Hills. That is, if he's there. He's probably making tours of heaven, you know, meeting and greeting the crowds, opening a new museum, doing public relations stuff. So that will be fifteen dollars for the pizza."

"I don't have any money."

"Well, I guess you can't eat, can you?" the angel barked at him.

"I'm quite hungry. Where does one get some money?"

"Well, get a job or go on welfare!"

"You have any vacancies?"

"Are you kidding me? These are hard times. Thanks to all you new arrivals. There are too many people already, too many!"

At that untimely moment, Cary Grant, newly dead, came in.

"Excuse me, but where am I?"

"Get out of here!" screamed the angel, who then hurled a pizza base straight at Cary Grant's face.

King Prawn viewed the street around him. It was too drearily familiar. A typical urban district, filled with shops, buses, traffic, and people. The people consisted of angels and devils wearing jeans, skirts, frocks, and ordinary stuff, very dreary stuff.

King Prawn wandered around, checking the shops he passed by. Finally, he came to a newsagency where he searched for a street directory to locate himself in this dreary wilderness.

From the display shelf he plucked a daily newspaper called THE HEAVEN DAILY. The headline was WOMAN BASHED AT BUS STOP. He flicked through the pages, the same old earth news of crime, politics, show business, sport. Nothing's changed at all.

"This is not a library," chided the woman newsagent.

"I'm only browsing for a second," explained King Prawn.

"If you want to read the paper, buy it," she admonished him.

King Prawn, flabbergasted at the prevalent rudeness of Heaven's Angels, screamed at her, "Who cares? Isn't there more meaningful things in life to preoccupy your pettifogging brain?"

"Look, what if everyone didn't buy the paper, and just read it here. I'll go broke."

"Good!" King Prawn shouted, and he flung the newspaper up in the air, the pages raining all over the shop.

He stormed out of the newsagency. "This is not heaven, this is hell!!!"

SMILE the billboard poster exhorted him. JOHNSON'S ELECTRIC BLANKETS WILL KEEP YOU WARM IN HEAVEN'S COLD AND LONELY NIGHTS

King Prawn successfully applied for a job in the Public Service as a Clerk Grade 1. He was assigned to the Department of Industrial Affairs in the Accounts Section. His job was to fill in blanks. That is, he had to write in the names and addresses of the companies and other details in the form letters he sent out by the hundreds every day. Heaven had no computers because there was no rush to do anything as time no longer mattered. His work was menial. He hated it and was bored to tears by it. But he needed the money to pay his rent.

At lunchtime, he made sure he got drunk enough to make the afternoon pass quickly and painlessly. In desperation, he even resorted to Zen Buddhism, which teaches how to blank out one's consciousness.

As a result, he was able to work without feeling bored or depressed.

For weeks on end, he achieved Nirvana with his non-consciousness. In the midst of filling in a blank, he was overcome with pure, inexplicable ecstasy. However, he gave up on Zen, sick of being happy for no reason at all. He wanted to be human, suffering, mad and all! Therefore, he returned to his drunken stupor. It was the best method of non-existence. When he returned to work in the afternoon, he was too drunk to write, so he scribbled hundreds of illegible letters to addresses no postman could decipher. He eventually gave up trying to write and instead drew and doodled. Occasionally, he sent out love letters or suicide notes to businesses.

*Dear Washo Toothpaste Inc.,*

*I am madly in love with you. I need desperately to see you. Please meet me tonight at midnight outside your premises.*

*Love,*

*FK Stade*

*Commissioner of*

*Industrial Affairs*

*Per: K.P.*

## LUNCH

King Prawn, "One Big Mac meal, please."

"Eat here or take away?" asked the pleasant, smiling angel.

"Eat here," decreed His Royal Majesty King Prawn.

## DEATH OF KING PRAWN AGAIN

He dreamt he was a bird. When he woke up, he could not bear the thought of not being a bird. He glanced around at his small, pathetic, Losersville room. "This is what my kingdom has been reduced to." He got up stiffly and shuffled out in his dirty pyjamas into the hallway. Julius Caesar, who lived next door, greeted him in his old bathroom robe. He asked King Prawn if he wanted to play checkers. King Prawn shook his head. Julius Caesar looked extremely disappointed. King Prawn understood his loneliness and boredom, but he couldn't help him. He had once joined a Tyrant Support Group. There he met a German guy called Hitler. He tried to converse with him, but the conversation was a one-way street: Hitler yelling at him and ranting about the Jews. He grew tired of the people there, all reminiscing about the good old days of pillage and plunder. But it was all yak and no action. Which is the antithesis of being a tyrant. So he stopped going.

Up he plodded the flights of stairs to the roof. His goal: to be a bird. He teetered on the roof's edge and gazed up at the endless blue sky. "That is my kingdom." He leapt to the sky, his arms spread like wings. Momentarily, he flew. Gravity pulled him down and crashed him onto the concrete pavement below. It was a hard landing. He hoped for quick oblivion, sweet emptiness, thoughts running out of his head like blood. But he was still alive, unhurt, undamaged. He could not shed his own blood, so he cried a river of tears. Heaven was a lifeless and deathless place.

# CHAPTER 14

## Darryl—the true story

*Dear K,*

*Your new nest may as well be the moon, and I am an astronaut! How far you are away from me. Good heavens, our bridges are burning! But I assure you that the bridge from my heart to yours shall never turn to ash. Is our relationship a lost cause? I feel like an artist with a masterpiece in his head but have no paint or canvas to bring it to fruition. Our relationship could be a masterpiece, given the time and effort. An artist cannot expect to produce a masterpiece unless he is willing to devote his life to his art. And love is an art, it is devoted to Truth and Beauty. Oh K, don't give up on the artist in you and the artist in me. Stop being a Philistine treating love as a hit and miss thing like dart throwing at the pub. Love is a religion, and scepticism has no place in it. Love is also a science for it has a solution to every problem. K, don't give up on love. Don't give up on me.*

*Love Always.*

*Ranulfo*

My novel bothers me quite a bit. In particular, the neurosis of it all. There seems to be quite a streak of misogynism in it. But that's the point I'm trying to make in my novel. Every work of art is coloured by the psyche of the artist. It cannot be objective. By extension, perhaps we humans are a reflection of our creator. We are crazy, so God must be crazy.

Let us talk about Daryl, our creator's real name. Darryl was short and slim and brown-skinned; actually, he was Filipino, and had a bad habit of sniffling. He had always been since…since always, as he had always existed, neither born nor created; he was just there always…always. Perhaps it was the isolation and the lack of social contact for eons and eons that shaped his inadequacy in dealing with people. He had created the universe coldly and detachedly as a scientist, lacking the moral sensibility to provide the universe a sense of justice and truth. The universe, like humans, was merely intended to be a machine. Just toys for Darryl, the childlike scientist, to play with. Darryl, to his horror, discovered that human beings were not machines but conscious beings that could think and feel. These humans needed love, happiness, and truth, and he could not give it to them. He had just had no grasp of the strange world of emotions. He was just a scientist...and human beings were supposed to be adjustable like Lego.

When he created Jason and Kylie, the first human beings, he had expected that there would be no problems. He expected them to be nice, polite, and eternally grateful to him. But grateful they were not. They resented him. They defied him. They even went so far as to deny his existence, just a Nothing that ultimately did Nothing. But Jason and Kylie weren't always like this. They were affectionate, respectful, and obedient. However, they were looking to Darryl for understanding. They wanted meaning and purpose. Darryl being a "Why not" person rather than a 'Why' person failed to give them conviction and direction. When Jason asked him once what the meaning of life was, he couldn't answer him, so he joked '42'.

Jason didn't get the joke. The show "Hitchhikers Guide to the Universe" had not been created yet, though Darryl watched it, being omniscient. The questions kept on coming. Why me? Why death? Why love? Why the pain? Why should I care? Darryl couldn't answer them, so they stopped caring. Jason and Kylie became selfish and cruel, incapable of real sympathy. Darryl couldn't provide a reason for them to be good. He grew to hate them; they would insult him and throw stones at him. This drove him to retaliate. Never before had he experienced such rage. He was no longer a cool scientist; he felt his hot blood throbbing. He found himself deliberately plotting to get back at this vile couple. And nothing could overcome this feeling. Darryl schemed to remove Jason and Kylie from the Garden of Eden and force these ungrateful bludgers to fend for themselves. The plot he devised was simple. We are all familiar with the story of the serpent and the forbidden fruit. But what we don't know is that the serpent was Darryl himself in disguise.

After that, for centuries, Darryl was one mean and confused dude. You see, Darryl was going through the phases of emotionally growing up. He had never had emotions before, but with the arrival of humanity, they flooded out of him uncontrollably. His flaw was love. Love took away his loneliness and replaced it with a bleak loneliness that degraded him. Darryl demanded that his creation love him. When he didn't get it, he went into a rage. A rage that reached a point where he created a Hell to punish those who didn't love him. His behaviour was inexcusable, except one must remember he was basically a child growing up, learning, misunderstanding. Darryl, in a way, was born on the day he created Jason and Kylie. His rising emotions eventually burst into a great flood which drowned the world. However, the flood filled him with remorse. It compelled him to question his actions and make changes to his personality. He had to...well, grow up.

As centuries rolled on, Darryl naturally mellowed, and he was no longer the vindictive jerk he once was. But he was bored. Heaven was such a boring place, teeming with overbearing religious zealots, all so funless. Darryl decided it was time to take a break, a relaxing vacation, and where better to go than Hawaii or Disneyland? Not wishing to be recognised, people bugging him to save them and so on, he decided to be born as a human being to this married couple: Mick, a carpenter, and his wife Sharon, a housewife, both from Gosford. Mick and Sharon weren't too happy; after all, they weren't part of a divine mission where Darryl would come and save the world. No, they were just used as a hotel to accommodate a tourist who wasn't even paying. They had no choice because the angel that Darryl had sent them told them that if they refused, they would be booked into the Fire and Brimstone Hotel after they died.

To be born, Darryl had to spend nine boring months cramped inside Sharon's womb, and the service in there was atrocious—no movies, no music, and the food was execrable. No way was Darryl gonna come back a second time. Once was enough!

On the 25th of December, year zero, Darryl was born. His birth was not the secret event he had wished for. Obviously, some sticky beaks leaked the news far and wide. For instance, the Three Wise Men, a famous Jewish vaudeville act, a prototype of the Three Stooges. They went on stage and advised the audience about health, love, respect for parents, the consequences of masturbation and chicken soup. They never failed to break up the audience with their advice on masturbation: "Don't masturbate or it'll stunt your growth." Darryl was not amused and cursed the three men with permanent constipation. When King Vince learned of Darryl's birth, he immediately set out to assassinate this so-called God. Gosford was not big enough for two rulers.

Mick regarded this as of good news—he loathed this ungrateful bludger, Daryl—and decided then and there to take the family on a trip to King Vince's Palace. They got lost and ended up in Egypt. Daryl, the tourist, thought the pyramids were over-rated, but nonetheless chipped off some limestone—that was when the pyramids were entirely covered in white limestone. He sent a postcard to his best friend, the Archangel Gabriel.

*Dear Gabe,*

*Here I am in Egypt and am not impressed at all. I saw the pyramids, and all I could think was what is the whole point? Don't these Egyptians have better things to do than drag these humongous blocks of stone across the hot burning desert and stack them together in a neat pile? Get a life, will they? We're going to check out the Sphinx. I'll chip off a bit of the nose and send it to you. What Egypt needs, more than the pyramids anyway, is air-conditioning and carpeting.*

*Check you out later,*

*Darryl*

From Babylon he wrote:

*Dear Gabe,*

*I saw the Babylonian Gardens today. Big deal! It's for the birds and bees. Since I'm just a baby, I can't have too much fun. Rather boring being a baby. There is only one advantage is that Sharon cuddles me a lot. She turns me on. As for Mick, what does Sharon see in him anyway? Gabe, do me a favour, when Mick kicks the bucket, be sure to send him straight to the hottest part of hell. Yesterday, Sharon was breastfeeding me (Hubbahubbahubba!), Mick complained, "Don't do that! He's a pervert I tell you." Sharon laughed at him. "He's only a baby, for goodness sake. Besides, milk is so expensive." Mick replied, "Yeah, well I don't like the look on his face." He glared at me while I winked back with my mouth around his wife's tit."*

*Catch you Later,*

*Darryl*

Mick and his family settled down in Galilee, a small coastal town inhabited by fishermen, carpenters, tax collectors, lepers, whores, and religious loonies of all stripes. At the age of seven, Darryl was sent to school, where he encountered a few problems with the teachers and students. With the teachers, he acted like a know-it-all who looked down on them as if they were stupid. He had all these outlandish theories, such as the Special Theory of Relativity. The craziest claim he made was that the world was not flat but round like a ball. "You say that the world is round, Darryl," said the teacher. "Now tell me, smarty-pants, have you walked around the world and found yourself with the ground above you and the sky below you?"

"The law of gravity," Darryl explained," keeps our feet to the ground."

"Darryl, you're impossible. The world is flat, and to teach you that simple fact, you'll have to learn the hard way. I want you to stand on your head for the rest of the school day, and this punishment will make you realise that we live on a flat earth because walking upside down makes us dizzy."

Darryl was unpopular with his classmates. They considered him a know-it-all. One afternoon, they ambushed him on his way home from school, punching him and kicking him. Darryl broke off and fled. Hard on his heels, they were sure to catch him if he hadn't jumped into the lake of Galilee and ran on the water to safety. He stood in the middle of the deep lake and waited for the boys to go away. The boys went into the lake, got wet and ran home. Darryl returned to the shore, aching all over, his nose bloodied, and sporting a black eye.

For the first time in his life, he experienced pain. Not only physical pain, but also emotional pain. He was angry, humiliated, and afraid. He wanted to exact revenge, but alas, he knew too well his inadequate physical strength. He didn't want to go to school anymore. What was the point if he was omniscient?

*Dear Gabe,*
*Beam me up, Gabe. Gotta get out of this stinking world! They're a pack of savages.*
*Desperately,*
*Darryl*

In reply:

*Dear Darryl,*
*Sorry, mate. Only way to get out of the planet earth is to die.*
*Good luck,*
*Gabe*

Then die Darryl resolved to do. He obtained a knife and proceeded to cut his throat. As soon as he pricked his skin, he screamed: "Jesus H. Fucking Christ!"

Must death be so painful? Instantly, Darryl changed his mind about committing suicide. Then, to his horror, he realised he was living in a prison he was afraid to escape from.

Next morning, Sharon knocked at his bedroom door. "Wake up, honey. Time to go to school."

She saw that Darryl was in bed, groaning with pain. "Darryl, darling, what's the matter?"

And in the most pitiful voice he could muster, he answered, "I think I'm sick."

"What symptoms do you have?"

"I'm sick all over."

"You better stay home today."

"No, I don't wanna...miss...school."

"You better stay home today."

As if heartbroken, "Okay, Mum."

Sharon became suspicious when Darryl was ill every morning for two weeks; yet in the evening he was in peachy health, wolfing down his food as usual. "Come on, now. You're not sick," she said to him one morning when he was acting sick and on the verge of death.

"Yes, I am," Darryl groaned, clutching his stomach like he was preventing his intestines from spilling out of his mouth.

"Why don't you go to school, Darryl?" Sharon asked, rubbing his hair tenderly.

"I want to go to school, Mama, I really do."

"Then you go to school today."

"But I'm sick, Mama."

"You're not sick, and you're going to school."

"I don't wanna."

"Why?"

"Because they hate me at school!" he blurted out, bursting into tears.

"Oh my poor baby," Sharon sat beside him, holding him as his tears drenched her shoulders.

Crying was a sensational new experience for Darryl. He quite liked it. Self-pity—what a wonderful human emotion!

At dinner, Sharon told Mick about the bullies.

"He's asking to be bullied. He's a snotty, up-himself brat. If he doesn't want to be bullied, he'd better work at being likeable. Stop acting so high and mighty—people like to knock people off their high horses. "

"You don't understand me," shot back Darryl, and burst into tears. Sharon rushed to comfort Darryl and glared at Mick, rebuking him, "Darryl is not like you. He's very sensitive. He's an artist—he created the universe. "

"Well, I built this house with my own hands, and in this house I am Lord and Master!"

Darryl was in his self-piteous phase when he wrote to Gabe:

*Dear Gabe,*

*Special people like myself suffer a lot because there is nobody to understand us. We are alone on the mountaintop, and we enjoy and suffer from our isolation. I tell you, Gabby, this coarse and vulgar world will crucify me one day. Mediocrity rules this world. This coarse world crucifies everything that is beautiful and sublime. By the way, I have decided on what career I shall embark on during my earthly stay. My hatred for Mick and his ill-mannered ilk has ruled out carpentry as a career option forever. Although the money and security are tempting, I must set aside such trivial matters. I have decided to become a poet so I can write about my agonies and ecstasies. For in my heart lies beauty and truth. I have enclosed a poem. Read it and be swept into the realms of agonising beauty.*

*Yours Ecstatically,*
*Darryl—Poet*

ALONE
*Alone, alone, alone*
*On the mountaintop*
*I sit and cry for the world*
*O when O when will my teardrops stop?*

*Alone, alone, alone*
*On the mountaintop*
*I am a poet I shout out loud*
*O when O when will my sorrow stop?*

*Alone, alone, alone*
*On the mountaintop*
*I see the dirty rotten world below*
*And long to clean it with a mop*

Poetry was Darryl's favourite preoccupation until he discovered the joy of masturbation. What a strange, wonderful, and extraordinarily simple form of pleasure-giving physical trick! Readily available at your fingertips! Soon, masturbation became a daily ritual, and he even wrote a poem about it.

ODE TO MASTURBATION
*Whose hands do you long for, my bride of joy?*
*Whom do you dream of in your quiet sleep?*
*Is it my fingers you rise to in your majestic poise?*
*Come, my bride, and drink my caresses deep.*

Of course, life was not so simple that Darryl masturbated and lived happily ever after. Thanks to the human mind, things get awfully complicated. At first, it was masturbation for masturbation's sake that drove his addiction. A pure act, self-contained. Not till the intrusion of women and sex crept into his consciousness that the purity of masturbation was poisoned. The serenity and enjoyment that followed the act of Onan were replaced by frustration and self-castigation. Darryl was no longer content with masturbation. His hands were no substitute for the mystery and grandeur of a woman. He wanted to plunge his thingy into the hairy hole of pleasure, swim in its sea of juices, and drown in ecstasy. Although Darryl strove to make masturbation as close to sex as possible. Even with a hole in it, humping a pillow was unsatisfactory. The room snowed with chook and duck feathers as he banged crazily into the ersatz cunt. There was no decent substitute for a vagina. A vagina was a vagina was a vagina. No two ways about it.

Having failed to fabricate or simulate a live vagina for his lascivious purpose, he made plans to obtain a real one. Galilee was a fishing town, and the smell of fish acted as a sort of aphrodisiac for the men. Hence, there were brothels galore. All Darryl had to do to acquire a whore with an authentic love hole was to get some cash. However, since his picayune school allowance could not cover the cost of a whore's time, Darryl turned to petty crime. The victims of his evil deeds were none other than Sharon and Mick. He was a cautious thief. Inconspicuous amounts he pilfered from them, so that neither parent noticed the diminishment of their assets.

Furthermore, he took an after-school job cleaning fish at the fish market. Slowly but surely, he garnered enough money to purchase himself a...Vagina!

Darryl entered the brothel as if it were a supermarket. "One whore, please," he asked the Madame, who greeted him.

She asked, "How old are you, young man?" with a good-natured chuckle.

"18," he answered in his deepest octave.

She laughed loudly. "Sure you are, and I'm sweet 16. Come inside, and I'll show you the ladies."

He was brought into a garish room, resplendent with bright and gaudy interior décor, and on the silk couches lounged four exotic women, sexily dishevelled. "We have a gentleman customer," and Madame introduced him to each temptress. Darryl scrutinised each of them, as if he was picking a toy for Christmas. Finally, "I'll take this one please," selecting a sad-eyed girl called Jena, a lass of 14.

Dear Darrylians, do I offend you with this blasphemous story? Darryl, you see, is just a word to me, like any other, and it must be dissected, analysed, and perhaps philosophised to death. I do not want to be a Darrylian or a Christian or a Muslim or whatever. I just want to be a human being, who is sometimes right, sometimes wrong, makes mistakes, and learns for better or worse. Can you accept me as what I am? Do you need to punish me? Can you see the humanity we both share? We are both on a journey, and it is a journey of the heart, soul, and mind, on this strange, scary, but exciting road...

Darryl grew up and had many women. He was handsome, charming, and women found him irresistible. He was, however, a heartbreaker. Women were so beautiful and delicious that he wanted to try each of them as if he were in a cake shop. Besides, there was not one woman that he really loved. Love was impossible because love came from the mind, and the mind was to him a Pandora Box of evil. The mind was ultimately bereft of love or joy. It was an abyss.

Jena, the prostitute with whom he lost his virginity, was madly in love with Darryl, but she was also very jealous and possessive. She wanted him for herself alone, despising all the other women in his life. She pleaded with him to be faithful to her.

"Unfaithfulness destroys love," she said. "When you destroy love, you destroy everything."

"Leave me alone!" Darryl shouted at her. "I've told you so many times that I like screwing around. Can't you accept that?"

"You're a bastard, you know that," she replied despairingly.

"I'm a man."

"You're so cruel."

"Do you think I'd be less cruel if I married you, made you bear five children, turned you into a dull, fat housewife, and forced you to put up with my obnoxiousness for the rest of your life?"

"If you love me, I'd be happy."

"That's right. Love is sadomasochism. The man inflicts suffering, and the women endure. The perfect couple."

"I want only you."

"I want all the women in the world."

"You'll get your just desserts one day.''

"Do yourself a favour and hate me. It'll be easier for both of us."

"I love you."

"Then love me right now." He lifted his white gown, showing his erect penis. She hated that thing that controlled him. That thing that degraded her. That thing commanding her like a master to a slave. It was like a big rod that beat her.

Tearfully, she took off her clothes and spread herself for that thing to impale her.

Tears, tears, fell all night, while Darryl slept in callous indifference. Something broke in Jena's mind. Broken was her sanity. Her life was utter misery, and all to blame was that thing obtruding between Darryl's legs. It wasn't Darryl's fault. He was at the mercy of the wicked demon that respected no woman. She collected a knife from the kitchen and faced the demon, who stood arrogant and fearless.

"Forgive me, Darryl, for what I am about to do. Evil must be cast out."

She held his erect penis and off it went. Slash! Now he was hers forever.

*Dear Gabe,*

*Help me! Some demented bitch has cut my dick off! Can you do something to restore it? Please! I'm absolutely frantic! I don't think I can survive the planet without a willy to keep me company. Please help me!*

*Desperately Dickless Darryl*

*Dear Darryl,*

*Sorry, Darryl, but you are a mortal being, and, unfortunately, mortal men cannot grow their dicks back.*

*Sorry,*

*Gabe*

*Dear Gabe,*

*Fuck you!*

*Darryl*


Darryl was in a state of shock. He believed that his life was as good as over, and that despair would never depart. He had lived for sex and nothing else. His life was now nothing. No longer would he experience the tumult of an orgasm. Farewell, ecstasy! He supposed he could make love the lesbian way, but it wasn't the same as banging his rod into a woman like a frenzied knife attack. Anyhow, what woman would touch him now? He was a mutilated freak, and no woman would look at him as a man, to be feared. He was a peacock that had lost his tail, shedding his pride, dignity, and vanity. A peacock without a cock. Just a pitiful pea. He was an outcast, like the lepers, the cripples, the whores, and the tax collectors. He was no longer the rich, handsome prince whom the world loved, but the leper whom the world shunned and despised. He was no longer the chosen, but the unchosen....

Darryl wanted to run away and hide, just keep running and running. He left Galilee and set out eastward, into the vast Arabian deserts. As for Jena, Darryl gave her a good thrashing, and bade her never to see him again. Poor Jena, she had planned to keep Darryl for keeps, and now all she had was his dick, permanent tenant of a pickle jar.

Travel consoled Darryl. The constant motion of his body and the ever-changing surroundings distracted his mind enough to keep him from falling into unbearable despair. And the mind was a torturous thing. So he kept moving forward, away from his mind, even appreciating the difficulties and discomfort that assailed him. The desert was a place of pain. After a few weeks, emotional survival was the last thing on his mind; the utmost priority was physical survival. He was ill prepared for the desert. He was hungry, thirsty, and burning from the heat. He was dying.

He was in deep doo-doo. Desert all around him, and not a person in sight. The sun was his only companion. He saw a figure up ahead. Standing, holding a glass, waiting for him. A peculiar sight, dressed in a tux, he looked cool and refreshed. Darryl grabbed the gelid glass of ice water, and gurgled it down, heavenly liquid sliding down his parched mouth and throat. The water in the glass was endless, flowing like a river.

"Who are you, my dearest friend?" Darryl asked.

"Shane."

"Don't you feel the heat?"

"The place I come from is much hotter than this."

"Remind me not to visit your country. What's it called?"

"Don't you remember? You created it. It's called Hell."

"Hell? Oh yes, that's where I throw all the baddies in."

"Baddies?" Shane reacted with loud fury. "Balderdash! It's a concentration camp where you put people who don't believe in you. People who don't kiss your arse. You are a fascist tyrant that refuses to have any opposition. It's either your way or no way. You refer to us as baddies, but you are the true villain. You are devoid of love, sympathy, and wisdom. Your time is running out. We are going to depose you and install a just and benevolent government that will look after everybody. There shall be no more Hell, and there shall be no more dictators like you."

"What are you talking about? I'm a just, loving, wise Darryl. I know everything. Ask me all you want to know about the universe."

"You know everything but understand nothing. You have a dumb heart."

"I'm Darryl! I'm perfect!"

"Perhaps that's why you don't understand us human beings, who are imperfect. Hopefully, your stint as a human being on earth will teach you what being human is all about. You might even gain a feeling of sympathy."

"If you hate me so much, why did you give me a glass of water?"

"If you die now, you'll still be an unchanged soul when you come back to your heavenly throne. I want you to live so you can learn what life is all about. You will learn the elusiveness of happiness. You will learn to be sad, to be afraid, to be weak, to be strong, to love and be loved, and to suffer and die. From that you will learn humility, and from humility you will learn compassion."

"Well, show me some compassion and give me a lift on your wings to the nearest village.

"If you think you are suffering, what about all those people you sent to Hell. Are they enjoying their undying dying?"

"They broke the Law of Darryl and must be punished."

"The Law that forbids anyone to doubt and to think."

"It's my universe and I can do whatever I like with it."

"You can't do that. You're not free anymore. You have responsibilities and obligations. Human beings are your children: You must take care of them all. You are not alone, you are our Father. I'm going to watch you from now on. If you don't come back to Heaven any the wiser, I'll come to get rid of you."

"You haven't got a chance. My angels are the toughest military outfit in the universe."

"Your angels are sadistic thugs."

"I can't have sissies for an army."

"In the end, I shall win. You and your fascist angels will be defeated. There will be freedom for us prisoners of your narrow-mindedness."

"Yeah, right," Darryl smiled smugly.

"The desert will give you a soul, my friend," said Satan before he vanished.

"The desert will give me an unwanted suntan," muttered Darryl as he trudged through the sweltering heat.

He was pissed off. How could Shane talk so rudely to him, the creator of the Universe, the Absolute, the Lord Almighty, and dare question his rightness? Such galling insolence from inferiors. He should act humbly, subserviently, knowing his place. But quickly, Darryl realised as he peered at the glaring sun where his place was, and he forgot his anger and became concerned for his survival.

Night graciously came and bathed him in her cool arms. But gradually, cool became cold, and cold became freezing, and Darryl yearned for the hot sun. Utter exhaustion granted him sleep. He woke up suddenly when he was startled by a tiny voice, which must surely come from a tiny creature. He surveyed the scene, but there was no one around.

"Are you blind? Or have you already forgotten your dear old penis?" said the creature, hovering before his face.

Darryl jumped back in fright. "What the hell are you?"

"I'm the ghost of your dear departed penis."

"What do you want from me?"

"I want you to know the Truth," his penis replied.

"Okay, speak," Darryl beseeched the poor miserable creature, whom he was still quite fond of.

The penis began, "You are the cause of all my sufferings. Because of you, I will live in eternal pain. When I died in my prime, I was dispatched to Hell, the furnace where one breathes, drinks, and eats fire. I went to Hell for your sins. But in a sense, it was good that I was sent to Hell, for there I discovered the truth about you. You are the bane of the world. You have abandoned your creation, humankind, to fend for themselves, bestowing them with a mind not equipped to know the truth of life. Because humanity cannot know the truth, they can only know the lie. And for the lie we lived. They were doomed from the beginning. They were ill-made to bear the greatness of life. But justice has come for you. You have just died in your sleep, and I've come to escort you to Hell."

"I'm Darryl. They can't send me to Hell."

"You are now mortal. But, you see, there has been a bureaucratic slip-up, and Heaven has no record of your visit to earth."

''My friend Gabe will vouch for me."

"Is he really your friend? Tell me who arranged that bureaucratic bungle? No, Gabe is an ambitious angel. He wants your throne."

"You're wrong about Gabe. You'll see."

"Soon we'll see."

Suddenly, a flashing light blinded Darryl, and he found himself in a courtroom facing a beetle-browed, stern-eyed judge.

"What's your name?" the judge asked him imperiously.

"'I'm Darryl! The creator of this universe!"

"Blasphemy! I ought to send you to Hell immediately! You are a mere mortal"

Darryl wanted to vaporise the judge, but he realised he only had his mortal powers and not those of a god.

The judge shook his head as he closely examined a tome. "You have an untold number of sins. I'm afraid there is no way we can let you into heaven. You have committed fornication, masturbation, theft, and shown disrespect to your parents, and worst of all, you have never attended church on Sunday. Is there anything you wish to say in your defence?"

"Yes!" screamed Darryl. "I want to call a witness. The archangel Gabe. He'll explain everything."

They called forth the angel Gabe.

"Do you know this man?" the judge asked Gabe.

Gabe looked at Darryl.

"I've never seen him in my life."

"You bastard!" screamed Darryl. "I created you! I created the Universe! I am Darryl!"

"Take him to Hell at once!" the judge shouted, banging the gavel like the doom of thunder.

At that moment, two hefty angels grabbed hold of the berserk Darryl and dragged him screaming and fighting. They led him to the edge of a large hole where below raged the flames of Hell. "I'm Darryl! You can't do this to me!" and they flung him into the mountainous sea of fire.

The pain was unbearable, and he wanted it to go away, but it would not. There were people around him, screaming, their voices hoarse from years and perhaps centuries of crying out for mercy, and yet there was something fresh, as if the pain could never get old or familiar. He ran and ran, but the pain was relentless, and everywhere there were people writhing in utter agony. He couldn't talk to them because all he could do was scream. This was Hell and this was forever.

Darryl screamed as he woke up.

The sun was out now, and he could feel the terrible heat. He was relieved that it had all been a dream, albeit a nightmare. However, he had been profoundly affected. It had hit him at the centre of his being, undermining his previous beliefs and values. For the first time in his life, he had experienced compassion for humanity. He had felt their pain, their confusion, their limitations, their mortality. For the first time in his life, he doubted himself, that he could be wrong, that he could be bad. But how wonderful that he was wrong. It was so enlightening. Wisdom is the continual discovery of how wrong one was. We might not be able to discover the truth, but we could keep getting less wrong as we grow older. And we had a choice about which path we would take. Either we choose to live in the prison of the lie or in the freedom of the truth. Darryl wanted to be free, and he wanted to set people free.

When he set himself free from the desert, he set off to find the answers to his questions. He set off east, to India, the Land of Wisdom. But he was wary of religions that taught that the world was an illusion. The world was much too real for him. He headed back west, where he joined some esoteric sects. These sects preached salvation for the few. But he wanted salvation for all, for everyone was his child, each and every one he loved and cared for. He was their creator, responsible for their well-being. He could not deny or cast out a single being. He travelled further to seek the all-encompassing truth. In the end, he could not find the inclusive truth; all he could find was compassion and forgiveness for all his children.

"A Mr. King Prawn to see you," said the receptionist to Darryl, sitting behind his desk, cluttered with files and paperwork.

"Send him in," Darryl replied, his voice cheerful and gentle.

A very depressed looking man shuffled into the room. Darryl stood up and shook his hand, which was rather limp. "I'm Darryl. And you're Mr Bing Brawn?"

"King Prawn," corrected Bing Brawn I mean King Prawn. "But you can call me Royal Majesty."

"Please take a seat." Darryl waved his hand to the visitor's chair in front of his desk.

"Thank you."

"How can I be of assistance to you, King Ron?"

"I want to die."

"But you are already dead."

"I want to vanish, disappear, not exist. No thoughts or feelings. Just nothing, nothing, nothing!"

"Why?"

"Because I can't stand it anymore!" shouted King Prawn, on the verge of hysterical tears.

"What can't you stand? The food, the accommodation. I'm sure I can fix something up."

"Heaven is…hell!"

"I'm sure it's not all that bad."

"I want to die!" he screamed, at his piercing loudest.

"I can't do that."

"Why?" His face begging to be shot point-blank.

"Because your soul is immortal. No one can destroy it."

"I can't bear it anymore!" King Prawn sat in his chair looking as if he would explode into little red bits.

"Have you considered taking hobbies like stamp collecting or painting or archery?"

"I'm not interested in hobbies. I want real action!"

"What did you do when you were on earth?"

"I was a King!" with glinting steel in his voice.

"A King, I see. Say, why don't you join one of the political parties we have on heaven? We have communists, republicans, we even have Nazis, but that's more of a costume party."

Contemptuously, "I'm not a grubby politician. I'm a King! Kings rule their Kingdom and invade and conquer other Kingdoms."

"I'm sorry, but I can't accommodate you on that. War is forbidden in heaven.

Though we permit re-enactments. Why don't you join one of those—Gettysburg, Custer's Last Stand, Hiroshima…"

"I'm bored of all the fakery."

"Why don't you get married?"

"I'm a fighter, not a lover."

"What's your job right now?"

"I'm a government clerk."

"Why don't you get a more interesting job?"

"I'm not qualified to be anything except being King."

"Why don't you go to university and get qualified?"

"I despise knowledge. I'm an unthinking beast."

"What interests you then?"

"I'm only interested in being an autocrat, a conqueror."

Darryl's eyes lit up. "I know! Why don't you become an actor? There are lots of roles for kings in Shakespeare's plays. In fact, I could introduce you to Shakespeare. Or should I say Edward de Vere, the true author."

"I hate actors. In fact, I'm the one who blew up Hollywood."

"Which Hollywood? The one here or the one down on earth?" Darryl looked anxious, as he loved movies, especially musicals.

"The one on earth."

He was relieved. "But why would you want to do that?"

"Because I wanted to reclaim reality. I felt Hollywood was making us forget about reality, the grandeur and glory of reality. Movies make us stop from grappling with reality. Reality is a bitch and she's the greatest fuck of all."

"Oh…" Darryl blushing. "But isn't heaven part of reality?"

"No! Heaven has no death! No pain! There was no struggle! No victory! There's only comfort and safety. I'm not alone anymore, fighting against fate. The search for truth, Love, Meaning, Purpose, has ended. There's nothing left to do but to be. But what is being? It's nothing! Gone are the things that thrilled and filled my mortal life. Immortality is just a great, vast emptiness."

"Hmmm…you are a peculiar case, Mr Steve Song. What, specifically, do you want me to do for you?"

"Please, let me return to my beloved earth. Please, I beg you!" King Prawn fell on his knees and cried on Darryl's sandals, which was bought cheap at Heaven's K-Mart.

"Now, now, King Kong, please get up and sit down. No, no, not on my lap, on the seat, please. I suppose I can send you back. I can manage that."

"Will you, really, really, send me back? Please!"

"But you will have to come back to Heaven eventually."

"I'm not ready for Heaven yet. I have not given up on the earth and its madness. When I do, I shall return here. I swear."

Darryl deliberated for a while, then he said, "I guess if I don't let you go back, I'll be condemning you to a kind of hell. So I guess this is your lucky day, King Shrimp. I am sending you back to where you left off. You won't remember a single thing about Heaven. However, you will return here when you die again."

"I thank you so much," said King Prawn, grateful, joyful, and bubbling in his seat like a fizzy coke.

"Now close your eyes, Big Bob."

"Okay," and King Prawn closed his eyes, clicked his heels like Dorothy in the Land of Oz, wished for home, sweet home, and fell into a deep sleep.

When he awoke, he was in the middle of a devastated Hollywood.

"How the hell did I survive that blast?" King Prawn said out aloud to the unhearing famous corpses. "Someone up there must like me."

"Someone up there must like me too!" sang out Gene Kelly's corpse.

"Someone up there must like Hollywood!" croaking voices rang out.

And then the corpses got up and performed a spectacular song and dance extravaganza. King Prawn, feeling joyous, joined in, linking elbows, swaying, kicking, and singing, although he didn't have much of a voice nor any rhythm. But he was just glad to be alive. So he could accumulate more conquests, more glory...millions will die, cities devastated, grieving widows and mothers, bereft children, horrific injuries, amputations, lost souls, lost minds, and lost innocence—thanks to Darryl's magnanimous gesture.

**END OF BOOK ONE**

# BOOK TWO

# PEACE

# CHAPTER 1

## Twenty Years Later

Twenty years have passed since that fateful forked day when King Prawn and Queen Clytoris went their separate ways. Unhappy women from all over the world rebelling against male domination joined up with Queen Clytoris. Likewise, unhappy men, sick of women belittling the male ego, joined forces with King Prawn. Thus, the world was sliced into two: the Kingdom of Men and the Queendom of Women. They were irreconcilable foes. Naturally, to continue the propagation of our wretched species, some men, who preferred to be among women, chose Queen Clytoris, while some women, who actually enjoyed the company of men, followed King Prawn.

The Queendom of Women underwent an amazing transformation. No longer was it a simple village hidden in a paradisiacal vulva-like valley, but a modern industrial empire spanning from one continent to another like the spreadeagled legs of a giant whore. Truly, a superpower that could match King Prawn's empire in military and economic power.

Carol Prag was responsible for this quantum leap forward. It would have remained a simple village if Queen Clytoris had her way. But Carol plotted, machinated, bullied, deceived, tricked, manipulated, and conspired until Queen Clytoris was reduced to a mere royal figurehead. The Queendom was now a republic ruled by President Carol and her Nationalist Democratic Conservative Liberal Party.

The world was now in relative peace, though violent wars preceded it. Twelve years prior, Carol had set up a woman's army after getting wind of reports of women being imprisoned by King Prawn in kitchens and forced to wash dishes and cook delicious food. This was an intolerable situation that called for military action. The prototype army was a ragbag of amateurish fumblers, but the military genius of Carol molded them into a dangerous military unit. She accomplished this through hard discipline, forging delicate hearts into steely armor. She trained her soldiers to slaughter without mercy.

How Queen Clytoris squirmed to see her women lose their softness to become trained dogs of Carol. This was not the type of women she had envisaged that would bloom from her Queendom, the flowers of wisdom and compassion, not these weeds of hate and destruction. Carol came and dug up Queen Clytoris's garden and built on it her castle of stone. Carol used fear to conquer the women's minds, making them fearful of King Prawn, of the future, and of reality; this fear drove the women to seek security through military, economic, and political means. Carol, the politician, promised the end of fear (although, deliberately, never fulfilling the promise); Queen Clytoris, the philosopher, promised the beginning of doubt (and its endlessness).

The women chose Carol and followed her into battle. Their first victories were essentially sneaky hit-and-runs. As they travelled from place to place, their army grew in confidence, and strength. Carol understood that she had to funnel all the nation's economic resources to the war effort. Industry and Science linked hands; soon the war became the battle of technology. The wars became bloodier and bloodier until it reached a stalemate. Thus, the war had to be settled on the negotiation table.

At first, King Prawn proposed giving women the bottom half of the world and men the top half, but Carol rejected the plan as sexist and immediately ordered massive bombing raids on populated male cities. King Prawn responded by counter-bombing. In one night, 1,500,000 souls were incinerated. The next day, King Prawn and General Carol returned to the negotiating table; this time, Carol requested that the women be placed in the upper half and the men in the lower half. King Prawn declined. That night, 2,000,000 people were blown to Kingdom Come.

The next day, King Prawn offered to give Carol the top on the condition that she give him a blowjob and pose for Vulva Magazine. Thanks to King Prawn's lewd gestures, 3,000,000 people died. But thanks to General Carol's sarcastic retort the next day that she'd give him the top if he allowed her to kick him in the balls, 5,000,000 men, women, and children died that night. Finally, after fifteen months of peace talks and more than 100 million dead, they agreed to halve the world vertically from the north pole to the south pole, and the war was declared over.

Carol was hailed as a hero and rose to become the world's most powerful woman, while Queen Clytoris faded in influence and relevance, with some even accusing her of treachery for her pacifism. Carol was eternally new, progressing endlessly like technology, whereas Queen Clytoris had become obsolete.

President Carol, elected overwhelmingly by women, built a royal palace for Queen Clytoris, against her wishes. President Carol insisted, arguing that the Queen was a prime target for terrorists and required a highly secured and protected palace.

The true political motive, however, was that President Carol wanted Queen Clytoris monitored and imprisoned in her palace, a lavish, opulent cage that would also serve to trivialize her in the eyes of the public. And she was trivialized, fodder for gossip mags that rhapsodized endlessly about the trinkets and baubles of her life.

President Carol did not want Queen Clytoris free to teach her iconoclastic teachings, which questioned everything. Her teachings undermined President Carol's philosophy of belief. President Carol needed people to believe in something, be it nationalism, God, Elvis, or Mammon. Belief keeps people ignorant and in a perpetual state of emotional immaturity. Queen Clytoris regarded belief as destructive to intelligence. Intelligence was a journey; belief was a cage.

And what happened to the next generation: Prince Jotel, St Claire, and Virginia? Prince Jotel was still in love with Virginia, although she was not in love with him at all. To complete the triangle, St Claire was still in love with Prince Jotel, who did not reciprocate her feelings.

As for their careers, Prince Jotel became a playwright, while Virginia, became a famous actress. St Claire was…um…a philosopher of sorts…technically, she was unemployed, but that is such a harsh judgmental word.

All were blinded by their emotions.

The years had not been kind to this trio, and, of course, the villain was none other than love. Love for the trio was the only God left in their empty lives. Love was the only avenue to Heaven. Everything else was a mundane Hell. Love was now their only reality, for they had rejected the transcendent reality of Queen Clytoris, the glorious battlefield of King Prawn, and the pragmatic chessboard of President Carol. While St Claire sought to dissect reality, Prince Jotel and Virginia, rejected reality, and their new world was of the imagination, with love as its' king. Unfortunately, lovers were human beings, imperfect and flawed, so that Prince Jotel and Virginia's fantasies of glorious love came to an inglorious thumping, bruising end in the real world.

Prince Jotel, skeptical and cynical, lived as if he had nothing to lose, and that life was all about pursuing pleasure (women) and avoiding pain (alcohol). He wrote plays in the same negative vein as his personality, monuments erected to his enormous self-lachrymose. To give you an example, here are some excerpts from one of his plays. This play is called "CRAP". The three protagonists are three turds trapped in the author's bowels. Yes, well…

# CRAP
## Or Three Turds in Search of an Anus
## By Prince Jotel

*SETTING: A stage, dim and bare, and everything is colored brown except for the black moon, which is both haunting and beautiful.*

A CHORUS OF WORMS: This is a tale of three turds, who live inside the inner rectum of an unknown man or woman, who might be you. It is a tale of their lives, their dreams, their despair, their struggles, and their deaths. Death awaits us all. This is guaranteed. We cannot guarantee love, happiness, health, or success, for life disappoints us, and death never does. Death will never ignore you. Death will never reject you.

Here are our three main characters: Bal, Jentil, and Yaya. There is Bal, alone, proud, and fierce. He separates himself from the other two, Jentil and Yaya, who are obviously in love with each other. There's the scene, and now here's the unfolding tragedy...

BAL: Once I did not exist, I was darkness. Then a rip tore a small hole in my fabric and ushered in the light, and I was able to see. Light came as a blessing and lingered like a curse. The beauty that surrounds me torments me because it excludes me for I do not belong to this beauty. My place is ugliness. I was born in Heaven, but my soul is Hell.

JENTIL: Black moon, black moon, do you live with envy at my happiness?

YAYA: No, it smiles upon our bliss.

JENTIL: One day we shall have to enter that black moon.

YAYA: Into the beautiful light!

JENTIL: Will it be a beautiful world out there?

YAYA: Of course, how can you doubt it?

JENTIL: I love and trust only you. I cling to you as if to stop me from falling.

122

YAYA: Don't doubt. This is a happy world created by a happy God.

JENTIL: You inspire me.

YAYA: When we enter the world outside, I want to become an artist! I want to create like God.

JENTIL: You're so full of beauty that you will create beautiful works.

YAYA: What do you want to become?

JENTIL: I'm just ordinary. I'll become an accountant or a computer programmer.

YAYA: There's nothing ordinary about you.

*Enter Bal, dark and brooding.*

BAL: You fools! There's nothing at the other side. And if there is, it's not meant for us. Out there is just a country of nothingness for us turds.

YAYA: And how would you know? You're only projecting your darkness on to the world.

BAL: None of us know what's out there.

YAYA: If there is nothing on the other side, then life is nothing. We were created merely to be destroyed. I believe we were created because the soul of this universe is creativity. I believe in this, not in your nothingness.

BAL: Belief does not make things true, it only consoles fools.


A CHORUS OF WORMS: As the saying goes, two's a couple, three's a crowd. That's the central law of life. There's never enough for everybody. This is what undermines the dreams of humanity and brings them into conflict. This is what makes Bal an enemy of Jentil and Yaya, and enemies always plot a tragedy for their art.

BAL: My eyes feel like seeds pecked by birds when I see those two lovers intertwined, which the more entangled they are, the greater their bliss. Happy, happy knot, and it behooves me to unknot them, and cast them to separate corners of the universe. Why doesn't Yaya love me? Why am I condemned to isolation? Nothing touches me, and I touch nothing. How could she love him, and not me? He is, to me, a mouse to a lion. His brain is mere feather stuffing to inflate his head. But she loves him and not me. I shine, but his dullness attracts her, wins her. Can it be that all that matters to her is his good looks? If that is so, their love is ice cream and cannot last and will melt when love gets too hot. Or what if it is just him, unconditionally him, loves him like one may prefer chocolate to strawberry. If that is so, I am doomed, a lonely strawberry in a land of chocolate lovers. Am I to do nothing? No! I shall be loved! I shall not die unloved, and if it means that I must kill to love, then Death, I will be your scythe.

*Enters a smiling Jentil.*

BAL: Jentil, must you always smile?

JENTIL: I guess I'm happy most of the time.

BAL: And I'm sad most of the time. Don't you think that I too deserve happiness, Jentil?

JENTIL: Yes, everyone deserves happiness.

BAL: Do you really mean that, or are they just words? I don't want advice, I want solutions.

JENTIL: No, I really want you to be happy.

BAL: Do you merely give words, or do you help those in need?

JENTIL: If you want my help, I will help you.

BAL: Yes, Jentil, help me, I want to be happy,

JENTIL: How can I make you happy?

BAL: I want Yaya. Give her to me.

JENTIL: Bal, I can't do that. I love Yaya.

BAL: I love her, too.

JENTIL: But she loves me, not you.

BAL: Don't you care for my anguish? I'm starving, and you deny me food.

JENTIL: I feel for your suffering, Bal, but I can't give you Yaya.

BAL: Why not?

JENTIL: Because love does not work that way.

BAL: Share her with me. Is that too much to ask?

JENTIL: Even if I agree, it's not up to me to decide, it's Yaya who must choose. And she's chosen me.

BAL: I'm up against a brick wall, and it's useless to argue a wall down. Now is the time to blast it down. I'm not going to ask you politely, I'm going to demand her from you. You are not listening to reason right now, you are hearing the voice of Death. Death! Death wins all arguments.

JENTIL: Bal, you are insane!

BAL: What makes a person insane? Because he does not obey the rules. Whose rules should he obey? The rules that protect the rights of the possessed to keep out the unpossessed.

JENTIL: You are not thinking of killing me, are you, Bal?

BAL: Yes.


*Later, Yaya finds Bal by himself.*

YAYA: Bal, where is Jentil? I'm looking for him.

BAL: Forget about him, Yaya? You don't love him. It's me that you need. Jentil is weak, he can't protect you. I'm strong, wise, and I love you, Yaya.

YAYA: Love! You can't love! You are the antithesis of love. You're the dark soul of negativity. You can't love nor can anyone love you.

BAL: I can give you more than that lover of yours. He knows nothing about life. I'll give you wisdom, passion, love, hate, joy, misery, peace, and terror. I'll give you the gamut of life. As long as you love Jentil, you'll never understand and experience life to the fullest. You'll always be a virgin.

YAYA: If ever I love you, you will destroy me. Do you know why? Because we are too much alike. You and I are twins of a dark soul. Your anger, your plunging abyss of despair, your contempt for God or gods, it is all in me. Loving you would make me twice as mad, twice as hateful. You are reality to me, Jentil is a dream, and I need him, for he gives me serenity and joy. He loves me because he is so full of love, but you and I love out of despair. We cling, we demand, we seek salvation, we seek glory. You should be glad we are not lovers, you'd find yourself in greater misery than you are in now. At least you can still dream. I would have taken sanctuary from you, and you'd be bereft. I'd be in your arms, and you would be the loneliest man in the world, without dreams and hope.

BAL: Very emotionally convenient for you to rid yourself of me. I guess we are alike after all, for I too am a practitioner of emotional convenience. I do love out of despair, and I also kill out of despair.

YAYA: You won't kill me. Jentil! Help me!

BAL: You don't think you can sweep me under the carpet and pretend that our dark souls can just go away. You have to deal with your dark soul because if you don't, it comes to deal with you.

YAYA: Jentil, where are you? I'm scared. Jentil!

BAL: You killed Jentil.

YAYA: What do you mean?

BAL: You killed him. Because you refused to save my soul. You fool! You never loved Jentil, but you loved me! But you were a coward. You refused to confront your deepest fears. You wanted to be safe and secure, so you chose mild, gentle Jentil to make things sweet and easy for you. But now all your security is gone, and before you is that abyss you ran away from. Hold me, the abyss is not as frightening as you think it is.

YAYA: Yes, I did love you, but I can't love you now. You killed Jentil. I'll never forgive you!

BAL: You will forgive me. Because you have to forgive yourself.

YAYA: Jentil! I need you now! I'm falling! I'm falling.

BAL: You don't need Jentil.

YAYA: Perhaps he's out there, at the other side of the Black moon.

BAL: There's nothing out there! I'm here. I'm reality

YAYA: Jentil is out there! I know! I have to go to him. I cannot stay in your hell.

BAL: No, Yaya!

A CHORUS OF WORMS: Yaya dives into the Black Moon. Where did she go to? As you humans know, turds go to the toilet bowl, are flushed, and hurled into the sewerage, which flows out into the deep blue sea. But Yaya did not know that, nor did Bal. Yaya knows now. Perhaps knowledge will console her, because she will feel complete, finished and therefore whole. Death makes us whole. In life, we travel through fragments in search of wholeness. We fool ourselves into believing that love can complete us, but it does not. We are separated from our souls. The separation is like a bleeding amputation.

BAL: Once more, I am alone. Oh misery, will you never end? Where is your happiness now? Through the Black Moon. I have only myself now, bereft of hopes and dreams. Only a saint can find joy in his isolation, for he has God to love him in his empty world. I have no God. Only darkness inside and outside of me. Black Moon, should I dive into your heart? But I can't. I am a coward, not because I fear, but because I can't take the leap from Reason to Faith. Faith is blind and is blind to darkness. Darkness is not a curtain spread across the light, it is greater than light. But what if there is indeed light out there? But why can't I believe that? The only way to know for sure is to see. No, I must stay here. At least I know misery. I am no stranger here.

*A giant rumbling sound, an earthquake. A flood is coming. Bal braces for what is to come.*

THE END

# CHAPTER 2

## Super Ranulfo

Help!!!! Will somebody rescue me from this novel!

"Stop whingeing!" my muse berates me. "And get back to work, you lazy wimp!"

"Leave me alone, you sadistic bitch! Can't you see I'm suffering? My mind is bleeding!"

"You're just plain lazy."

"Why should I write today? I don't feel like it. I don't want to be a writer because it goes against my nature, which is to be weak, lazy, stupid, and hopeless. Writing demands that I be strong, alive, intelligent, and creative. Writing demands that I be a hero, when in reality I'm a coward. I prefer to let things happen naturally, not force my will to get things done. I want the simple and easy life. Writing transforms me into Rambo, armed with a nuclear arsenal, and I have to take out the bad guys. A writer must be a superman!"

"Well, don your superman outfit and get to work!" shouts my muse, cracking a whip.

Tearing my shirt open, I reveal a blue costume with a big SR emblem on my pectoral rippling chest, and tearing off my trousers, I display my red undies over slightly bulging blue tights. Up, up and away! I smash through the library window and soar over the library lawn of the University of NSW into the blue yonder.

From down below the students gaze and gape at the flying superhero.

"It's a bird!" cries A Psychology Student, Hansuk Kim.

"It's a plane!" corrects a History Student, Clare Bonham.

"It's Super Ranulfo!" yells Alla Berson, a computer student

Yes, folks, I'm Super Ranulfo, great superhero, sent to earth to fight evil and defend Truth, Justice, and the Artistic Way. Faster than a sweeping statement, more powerful than a false premise. Behold, who is that dark, sinister creature clad in a three-piece suit flying my way? It's none other than my arch villain, the dastardly Super Normal Person, come to destroy my genius, and turn me into ...gasp!...a normal person.

"Hi, how are you?" he greets me, shaking my hand.

"Get thee hence, Evil One!"

"What's the matter?" asks Super Normal, and smiles, smiles, yet a villain.

"Keep away from me! You won't zap me into a computer programmer!"

"Why would I do that?" asks Super Normal.

"Because you pity me! Pity is death to genius!"

"Computer programmers earn an awful lot of money."

"Get away! I won't listen to your evil temptations."

"How much do you earn?"

"I'm a superhero. Saving the world is my reward."

"Hey, let's go have lunch. I know this great Chinese restaurant."

"Um…I don't have any money."

"Sorry, I didn't catch what you said."

"I said I haven't got any money!"

"Such a pity."

"Get away from me! You're tormenting me!"

"I was going to have some seafood chow mein, fillet steak, garlic prawns…"

"Aarrgh! Quiet my rumbling, ravenous stomach!"

"Aren't you having lunch?"

"I usually skip lunch."

He laughs. "Come on. Live it up. Let's buy some king prawns."

"I love king prawns. But I can't afford it. I have $5 to last me all week."

"You must be hungry."

"I'm starving!"

"Such a pity that you are a writer and have no money. Computer programmers make good money. It is such a shame that an intelligent guy like you is living in poverty when you could have been a lawyer."

"Yes, I could have been a yuppie."

"Money buys happiness. People who claim otherwise are lying to you. With money, you can go to restaurants, to concerts, buy a nice, fancy car, and live in a posh apartment. With money, you can get chicks."

"I'm so lonely. I can't afford to get out much."

"With money, you create opportunities, and opportunities mean life, and more, more life."

"Nothing happens to me. It's all fantasy."

"All because you're a writer."

"A god damned writer!"

"But there's no use trying to convince you to become a computer programmer."

"How long does it take to be a computer programmer?"

"Only three years."

"Three years! I can't wait that long."

"You can get a job."

"I had a job before. It's hell! It's excruciating boredom eight hours a day, five days a week. Never again!"

"There are other jobs."

"Let's face it! I'm a social misfit! I don't belong to this society."

"But you're not listening to your stomach."

"I want ambrosia—the food of the gods!"

He sniggers. "Ambrosia ha! I'd rather have a large steak and baked potatoes covered in sour cream."

"And lots of fried onions."

"Fried mushrooms in melted butter."

"Stop it! I won't listen to a word more! "

"For dessert, I shall have all the chocolate ice cream I want."

"Cold chocolate ice cream dancing on my tongue."

He continues, "And after that I'll make love to my girlfriend. It's so much easier to get a girlfriend when you're normal, but when you're an outsider, girls keep away. You're too different, too arrogant, and too poor. A writer needs a special person to love, a Beatrice to inspire him to create a masterpiece. Your search for true love is futile for rampant materialism has destroyed all our souls, no one escaping."

"Maybe there are still some left."

"Not very likely. Meanwhile how do you cope with your loneliness?"

"Aarrrgh! Leave me be! I can't stand it anymore!"

"You're destroying yourself. You're poor, hungry, and lonely. All for what? Truth? Art? Just because you want to be an artist does not mean you'll succeed. There are more mediocre artists than great ones."

"I don't care. I need to create."

"Can you create your own food as well?"

"I have to be patient. I shall discover the secret of happiness, the secret of life. In the meantime, I have to be an explorer, a learner. I shall discover the New World. I can't go back to being a normal person. I must sail the unknown ocean...?"

"You're just a writer in love with words. Truth, Art, New World—just words."

"I'll make these words real."

"Okay," says Super Normal, "you can have your fantasies while I go have lunch at a Chinese restaurant and eat some real food while you stay here and eat your ambrosia."

"Super Normal Person, before you go, there is one thing I have to give to you."

He smiles, "What?"

"This!" And I give him a big smackeroo, smashing his teeth in. "Now go eat your Chinese food, Super Toothless! Hahahaha!"

Through his mouth of loose teeth, he shouts, "You asole!!"

Once again, Super Ranulfo defeats his arch villain, Super Normal Person. Up, up, and away, Super Ranulfo comes to the rescue: making ignorant people read and think, showing the extraordinary to the ordinary, forcing politicians to repent and mend their ways and legislate against poverty and war, compelling big corporations to behave ethically towards the environment and people, teaching humility to the proud and arrogant, sowing doubt to the believers, creating more love, more wisdom, more beauty for the world...

"We love you, Super Ranulfo!" grateful people shout as they see me fly up in the bright blue sky.

My stomach growls back in hunger.

# CHAPTER 3

## The Fool

I am trying to awake from the nightmare of the self! I chose to become a writer because I desperately need to believe that there is in life a plot, a meaning, a greater significance, an ethical struggle, and that I, a sort of hero, am not a beetle on a dung heap. But life without literature would be utter desolation. I would be merely a germ floating helplessly and aimlessly across a void. But I am a writer, a spider to ensnare you readers into my web, so I can feed on you, get fat on you, to fill up my emptiness. You are trapped! You have read me thus far, the poison has set in, you are feeling faint...

"I'm bored! I'm so fucking bored!" screamed King Prawn to the whole world.

What now? Nothing. This great big silent monster devouring him. Help! King Prawn stood up, pacing the floor agitatedly. Pressing the intercom button, he asked his secretary to summon his Court Jester at once. And then he waited. Waiting was terrible. The boredom, this massive fat arse of nothingness sitting heavily on his soul.

Hurry! Where was that Court Jester? He checked his watch, how slow time was? How did he ever get to 50 years of age with time ticking by so slowly?

The Court Jester, clad in a motley robe, entered the court, and bowed to the King. "The Court Idiot at your service, my Royal Nothingness."

"I'm bored," said King Prawn, unemotionally.

The Jester replied, "Bored, bored, bored. Poor King Prawn a-bored. All the King's whores and all the King's gold can't put broken King Prawn together again. Boohoohoo. Try a hobby: take up attempted suiciding. Go out and have fun. Make love to a rhinoceros. Lick a baboon's bottom. Poor King Prawn all a-bored. His ship is sinking, and there's a hole in his soul. Abandon ship! Eat the sharks! Run naked around the North Pole!"

"It's no use. I'm bored with everything," King Prawn lamented.

"When you're bored with everything, go and have nothing. Everything is too much. Everything is an elephant that sits on your head."

King Prawn looked around at his sumptuous court with its golden and marble statues, magnificent tapestries, oil paintings by great masters. "I have everything, but I am nothing. While you have nothing, I think you are rich beyond measure. Tell me.

What are we alive for? What's the purpose, the meaning?"

"God created the world for pussycats. In the beginning, he created the pussycat, and to assist its survival, he created man and woman, taking a rib from the pussycat, of course. God never cared for these human beings, thinking them much too crazy, violent and presumptuous. God is a pussycat, you see. The purpose of human beings is to serve the pussycat. Nothing else. Any other purpose is a fantasy, a conceited and desperate fantasy."

"A conceited and desperate fantasy," echoed King Prawn. His mind revolved around such fantasies.

"Despair not, King Prawn, for despair is a figment of the imagination, an actor playing tears on the stage of his dark, empty theatre, pretending a purpose, a cause for grief. Tears are just water. Human beings are artists, creating their own unreal unreality. When we die, we do not die, for there is no death, since there is no such thing as life. We are nothing."

I am nothing, pondered King Prawn. Am I nothing? What has been my life?

He recalled Queen Clytoris, Harry the Farmhouse, Mammon's Arse. But that was all over, finished. Who cared about memories? Memories were ultimately nothing, just sands of time. He remembered his marriage to Queen Clytoris, their happiness. But where is their love now? Queen Clytoris might as well not exist. All that mattered was the present, and his present was not worth remembering.

"Gloom! Gloom! I'm tired of gloom!" bellowed King Prawn. "You're a Court Jester, tell me a joke or off with your head."

"I laugh at life, my Majestic Gloominess, jokes I do not find funny. What are jokes but words? Why laugh at words when one can laugh at reality itself? Words are for people who can't see reality."

"Must all comedians try to be philosophers?"

"But who understands philosophers but other philosophers? Comedians are the philosophers for the layman."

"Do you want to be King?" asked King Prawn seriously. Do you want to be me?"

"No, you are too ugly. Besides, my face is much too beautiful."

"And your soul too beautiful."

"I have no soul. Only pussycats have souls."

"Your wit is too quick for me."

"I fight words with words. Words can create illusions as well as destroy them. You have conquered worlds, but I have conquered words."

"And for my conquering, I have a Kingdom of Nothingness."

"Ditto."

"Let's blow up the world. I have the power."

"I blew up the world a long time ago. My wit willed it into nothing."

"Why haven't I a sense of humour?" asked King Prawn dejectedly.

"You must have a sense of absurdity. It's the ability to see that one is absurd, politics is absurd, religion is absurd, love is absurd, and most importantly, that cats are logical, and not absurd at all."

"Teach me to be funny," asked King Prawn solemnly.

The Court Jester asked for a mirror. King Prawn contacted his secretary to bring him one.

The secretary brought a bejewelled hand mirror. The Court Jester asked King Prawn to scrutinise himself in the mirror. "Look how serious you are. Now make a face. Destroy that face with a funny one."

"I can't...it's ridiculous," protested King Prawn.

"But that's what about humour is all about—destroying seriousness. Look at your serious face, that face is full of serious ideas and feelings, that serious face is of a King who has conquered half the world, and killed millions of people and all for what? It hasn't given you any fulfilment. Destroy that serious face, it is a murderer, a madman, a fool, a tyrant, destroy them all with a funny face."

King Prawn gazed long at his serious face. It was stiff, inflexible like stone.

"No, I can't...it's impossible."

"Poke that tongue out," commanded the Court Jester.

His tongue arched back, resisting any movement forward. His cheeks solidified. His mouth refused to open; it was shut like a locked caged door.

"Use your hands to shape and distort your face."

King Prawn raised his hands to his face. He pushed hard, but his face held firm. The face was solid like a statue.

"I'm made of stone," King Prawn said in final despair.

The Jester touched the King's face. Stone. He tried to grab hold of a fold of flesh, but there were no folds to be made.

"It's no use," King Prawn said.

'I'm sorry. Perhaps a jackhammer might help.'

"Leave me!" King Prawn hollered at the Court Jester.

He bowed, smiled, and got the hell out of there before he lost his head. He made his exit skipping like a girl.

Fury settled on King Prawn's brows like a winged predator. His life had been cursed by an injustice. Fate had enslaved him like cement, destroying his sense of humour and his sense of fun. This seriousness had always dogged him; it was his birthright. Memories of childhood regurgitated his poker-faced countenance staring at him. His child's face could not laugh; those eyes saw things darkly. The world was not a happy place; it was terrifying.

It dawned on him that all his present problems could be traced back to his childhood. The seeds that grew into this crooked tree. He tried to think back, tried to remember his parents. The last time he saw them was on a long-ago Christmas day. A magnificent banquet was held on that day. He was only a boy of five or six, and how excited he was about all the food and the gifts. He remembered his father drinking a golden chalice of blood red wine. Suddenly, he choked, then collapsed. There was a lot of commotion and noise.

"The King is dead. Long live the King!" And a pair of arms held him aloft to the audience; he cried as the audience hurrahed him, his innocent eyes watching blood trickle out of his father's mouth, nose, and ears.

Reliving that fateful day made him want to cry, but no tears could be squeezed out of his eyes. After all, he was a stone statue without a heart.

# CHAPTER 4

## The Andrews Sisters

President Carol sat behind her large, cluttered desk, thinking of King Prawn. As long as he was alive, he would always be a threat to her empire. He had to be removed, i.e., killed. She considered this a practical solution: killing people was an effective way of shutting up the opposition. Dead men do nothing, say nothing, and are nothing. A simple solution. When one becomes a ruler, one has no need for complex solutions with their knotted tangle of words, logic, and psychology. Just a clean slice of death at your command. To do her slicing, President Carol summoned Tessa Waterbottom, Head of the Secret Intelligence Network, otherwise known as SIN.

"Ms President, Project Prawn Night is failproof. The women I have employed are supremely skilled in the art of assassination."

President Carol asked, "But how will they go undetected in King Prawn's Kingdom? Women are under heavy surveillance over there."

Tessa smiled. "Ah, but only if women look like women. But have you seen the lovely ladies I have engaged? "She clapped her hands, and out came four tall, muscular men.

"Introduce yourselves, Mademoiselles."

The first woman curtsied and said in a low booming voice, "My name is Julie."

The other towering monsters were Karen and Janet.

President Carol was astonished. "I don't believe this. They look and sound just like men."

"Yes, it's incredible, but they are women without any doubt. I'll prove it to you. Ladies, pull down your trousers and your panties."

Simultaneously, the well-disciplined soldiers unbuckled their belts, unzipped their flies, and dropped army khaki trousers, revealing their very pretty panties. These panties were quickly removed and zipadeedodah they were truly women, labias and all.

"They are really women," gasped President Carol.

The three women stood at attention, their trousers coiled round their hairy ankles.

"How?" She looked quizzically at Gladys Waterbottom.

"Super steroids," she answered. "These women were once ballet dancers, thin, willowy, and light as a feather. Do you want to see them do the dance of the cygnets from Swan Lake?"

"Super steroids? Those pills did that to them?"

"Yes, indeed."

"Any side effects?" asked President Carol.

"Only minor."

"What are they?"

"The users become inorgasmic."

"Oh, just minor side effects."

"Yes, that's all."

"Women," began Carol, expounding on theory of hers, "have been oppressed for centuries, mainly because of their physical frailties and aesthetic worth. Women were naturally unable to challenge men physically, and men, seeing them as frail and beautiful flowers, deemed them as sex and art objects. Men, being taller and stronger, naturally felt superior over women, and women couldn't help feeling weaker. Men were built like lions and women like sheep. A woman's body has been her greatest oppressor. But now! With this marvellous new pill, we need no longer be weak or frail or even beautiful. Women will feel equal to men. Women will be able to compete with them in sports such as football, boxing, and weightlifting. No longer shall we be treated as pornographic fodder, for our bodies will have tall, male, muscular frames. There will be no more rape or wife bashing. There will be no discrimination, for men will not be able to distinguish a woman from a man."

Carol gripped Gladys's arms excitedly. "This will set women free forever!!"

"I do believe you're right," agreed Gladys, congratulating herself.

"We're free at last! We're free at last!" President Carol exclaimed, sounding a bit like Martin Luther King.

"Hallelujah sisters!" shouted Tessa, sounding black as well.

President Carol broke into a rap song. Behind her, the assassination team was dancing like the Pips of Gladys Knight.

*Get up, sisters!*
*We've been down too long*
*Raise your head up high*

*For we've got a new invention,*
*Which will make things right*
*It's a brand new pill*
*Which is gonna make you strong*
*That's right*
*It's gonna make you strong*
*So get up, sisters!*
*You don't need to get down no more*
*We've got a brand new pill*
*That's gonna make you strong.*

Julie, one of the assassins, rapped:

*I was once a Penthouse Centrefold*
*And had a bod so hot*
*That it made men quiver*
*I was slim, sexy, and my legs*
*In every page*
*Spread so wide*
*That my toes touched my ears*
*Yes, touched my ears*
*But now I am 6 feet tall*
*and I keep my toes on the ground.*

Janet:

*I was a petite housewife*
*Just 5 feet tall*
*My husband was a mean old man*
*I so trembled at his footsteps*
*Now that I'm big and strong*
*I'm scared of nobody*
*And take no shit from any man*
*And now my hubbie trembles*
*At my heavy footsteps.*

Karen:

*I was the prettiest little thing*
*In the world*
*But no guys ever listened to me*
*They thought I was too cute to think*
*Now I'm a giant hulk*
*with a giant voice*
*And everyone listens to me*
*With fear and trepidation.*

President Carol turned to Tessa and said, "Send me a bottle of super steroids. I like to try them on me. And if I'm satisfied with the results, I might mandate all women to take them as well."

"Good idea."

"Or perhaps doctor our water supply with it. After all, there will be silly women who want to maintain their frail sexy bodies."

"Yes. Maintain their inferior bodies."

"But I'll make them big and strong whether they like it or not. They'll thank me later."

"Indeed, they will."

"Say, Tessa," said President Carol, observing Tessa's slim figure. "You are rather on the thin and frail side. Do yourself a favour and try out these super steroids."

Stammered Tessa, "Ta...ta...take these pills?" Her face beaded with sweat.

"Why yes!" exclaimed Carol, making up her mind that Tessa should take the pills.

"Um...yes...I'll think about it."

"Don't think about it. Do it! It's an order!"

Carol turned to the girls. "You can all go now." They saluted her, clicked their heels, and marched out. Carol watched with excitement at their impressive bodies. Such steely buttocks!

President Carol gazed out the window, the long hall of cut grass suffused in light. Hardly anything flickered on this windless day. "Leaders must be powerful so that they can make the nation powerful. The nation gives power to the leader, and the leader gives power to the nation. Power is truth. It does not matter if the leader is a liar and his nation's ideals are lies: power is truth, and that is all you need to know."

President Carol's eyes shone brightly. There was a star of Fate shining inside of her…a star which she would follow all the way…

# CHAPTER 5

## The Cat said to the Mouse

*The cat said to the mouse*
*Let's be pals.*
*Let's end all enmity*
*Let's be chummy*
*Life's too short for wars*
*the cat said to the mouse*
*who agreed*
*Then ate him,*
*The yummy yummy mouse*
*Lalalalala*

"What a horrible song!' exclaimed the bearded lady Tamara to Prince Jotel, who was full of drink and song.

*Sleeping Beauty lay in bed*
*All fast asleep*
*Waiting for a Prince*
*To awake her with a kiss*
*A prince came along all right*
*He did not press her lips with his*
*Instead, he fucked her night after night!*
*Lalalalala*

"You are a fallen angel, Prince Jotel," said Tamara. "You are the son of a great woman, Queen Clytoris, yet you are a drunkard, a prostitute monger, a foul-mouthed degenerate. Why did you fall so low, my angel?"

"I'm a weak man, and the weak must fall."

"You don't want to be strong. You want to wallow in self-pity."

"I won't be happy until I get what I want."

"And what is it you want?"

"A woman called Virginia."

"Unrequited love, is it?"

"Yes, my inquisitive hirsute lady."

"You're pathetic. It's disgusting to love someone who doesn't love you back."

"I need disgust. I'm a disgusting pig. Oink! Oink!"

"Let's get down and dirty, my little pig."

"I didn't choose to love her. Nor did I choose to suffer. It just overwhelmed me…like a rampant disease. That's man's fate…to meet up with his disease."

"Oh shut up…you're so negative."

"I'm the prince of Darkness."

"You deliberately chase after women who can't replace your affections with Virginia. That's why you're with me."

"Virginia is irreplaceable."

"Why doesn't she love you?"

"It's one of life's major mysteries."

"Maybe it's because you are a negative, self-pitying loser," she suggested.

"Probably."

"Enough of this Virginia. Tell me about your mother. I adore her."

"I never knew my mother, the great Queen Clytoris, the wisest being in the world," said Prince Jotel with a tinge of sadness and sarcasm.

"Why?"

"She educated me to be alone. While she found her strength and peace in her aloneness, my aloneness destroys me…"

"Don't worry. You won't be alone tonight."

They went up to her apartment and made love. But Prince Jotel still felt alone. He longed to be with Virginia. While Tamara slept, he sneaked out of her apartment to see Virginia. He returned to his apartment to slip into his ginger cat costume. He gazed at the mirror, envious of the cat that stared indifferently back at him. The cat seemed to be existing on his own, a separate entity. A powerful, vain, cocky cat that lived dangerously with nine lives to gamble away. Did Virginia love the cat for his integrity and insouciance, and did she not love him because he was a confused and cowardly fool? The cat in the mirror sneered at Prince Jotel and hissed.

The cat jumped out of the window and landed hard in the alley below. Springing forward, the cat made for Virginia's house, dashing perilously across the street, weaving through the traffic at breakneck speed. The cat was far too quick for death.

It possessed bullet-like reflexes.

When the cat arrived at Virginia's house, she was asleep with a man in her bed. The cat leapt up on her stomach, waking her. She let out a frightened gasp. But after recognising her cat, she cheered and embraced him with great affection.

"I'm glad you've come," she said happily.

The cat mewed back.

"How are you? Are you tired? I'm tired too. I've just begun shooting a new movie about a woman who murders all her lovers by cutting off their penises. See that guy sleeping in my bed? He's one of my lovers in the movie. I hate him. Really, I do. I don't know why I sleep with him. He's so full of self-importance. Those guys who want to be loved but not to love anyone in return. He behaves as if he was looking at the mirror all day long. You know what? I want to blind him, to take a shard of a broken mirror and stab his eyes with it. His blindness might make him see. Oh, if only you could turn into a prince, if I kissed you."

Is this my chance? Prince Jotel contemplated. Shall I take off my mask? But it's my mask that she loves, not me.

"But I'm glad you're a cat. I really hate men. I really do. But I need my dreams. Though I bump hard into reality all the time, I'm a bruised soul. Sex is the only form of communication I can have with men. I can't relate to anyone. Women don't like me. I don't blame them since their lovers can't help but chase after me. Oh, but men betray all my dreams all the time. I'm so alone. You're my one and only friend. You know what? When the right guy comes along, I'd probably snub him. I don't have a clue what is right or wrong for me. I'm blind."

Virginia rose, dropping the cat on the bed, and padded to the wardrobe.

She took out a red scarf and blindfolded herself.

"Miaow?" asked the cat curiously.

Virginia put out her hand to feel the space around her. She inched her feet gingerly forward, trying to get to the bedroom door. Grasping the knob, she opened it and went out to the living room.

The curious cat followed her.

"I've shut out reality, and all I have now are just my dreams."

"All is darkness," she said, trying to interpret her invisible surroundings. "It's terrifying. It's exciting. It's challenging. It's so humbling because darkness dominates everything. Beauty does not exist at all...vanity cannot thrive...in the darkness one becomes a saint...selfless...yet one feels the rhythm of darkness...it carries you...it dances with you."

Tentatively, she danced in the arms of darkness, her true lover. She laughed.

Having gained confidence, she moved forward. Recklessly, she made a leap

…she hit a chair and fell. She winced in pain.

She ripped off the blindfold. "Oh silly me. Darkness won't be my lover. She got up and limped back to her bedroom. "Turn on the light! Turn on the light!" The room exploded into light when she flicked the switch on. Squinting, she scanned her bedroom. How depressing and meaningless were the objects of her life? "Is this life? Where is Love? Where is the truth? Where is joy? Is TV the meaning of life? Is this bedroom paradise? Is that man in my bed the Saviour? Is that light bulb God? Turn off the light! I do not want to see an ugly reality. Let me not see anymore. There is no beauty in this world."

"Will you shut up!" shouted the man in her bed. "I'm trying to get some sleep."

"Hark! My true love speaks."

Virginia turned to the cat. "You see how he loves me? The sound of my voice is not sweet music to his ears but grating noise. Nobody listens, everybody talks. The walls of our ego block our ears. Come, my wonderful cat, my real true love, come inside my walls and be my prisoner forever."

The cat jumped into the arms of Virginia.

Let me be your prisoner forever, said Prince Jotel silently to himself.

# CHAPTER 6

## Mort

King Prawn saw conspiracies around him, people from all walks of life plotting against him, craving his throne and lusting for his death. Thus, he had to be vigilant. To deter these plotters, he needed people to be afraid of him, so they wouldn't dare attack him. To implement his politics of fear, he set up a death squad whose duties were to detect enemies, real or imagined, and eliminate them. Everyone was a suspect.

The head of the death squad was Mort, an intelligent and cold-blooded man. Mort was a psychopath who saw the world through blood-stained eyes and relished his job as head terminator. To Mort, murder was a consummation, an answer to his prayer, which throbbed irresistibly in his mind. His actions invoked no remorse in his conscience, for he saw murder as a pleasurable function. Death was woven into life, creating a great tapestry. The art of living and dying was man's aesthetic obligation.

Mort was summoned by King Prawn for a personal interview. He looked forward to the meeting. He loved King Prawn and would do anything for him. King Prawn had given him freedom and legitimacy. Before King Prawn, he was an outcast, forced by society to restrain himself and feel guilty before he was guilty of anything. King Prawn had restored his manhood.

Mort was startled to find an old King Prawn sitting on the throne. He appeared old and exhausted. Nothing suggested the dangerous man he once was. But Mort still loved him; he was indebted to him forever. Time could not absolve his debt.

"As you see, I am too old to fight any more battles. My sword is sheathed for the remainder of my life. I leave it to men like you to wield my sword. You have been chosen to serve as the leader of my secret police. This requires that you make yourself know everything that is going on in this kingdom. You are to search for and destroy my enemies. Destroy all walls of secrecy, keep the populace naked and exposed, and always preserve the walls that fortify me. This is the castle, the brain of the kingdom, and you are my ears and my hands of death. I envy you, you can still be a man of action. My job now is to sit and be still in times of peace."

Then King Prawn shut his eyes.

Mort waited. He had hoped to converse with King Prawn. To tell him how much he admired him. To share his ambitions and dreams. To show King Prawn the man he had become.

King Prawn snored.

With great reverence Mort knelt and bowed to King Prawn. As he left the court, he stole a parting glance at King Prawn, who sat on his throne as motionless as a monument. His glory had passed, and like a monument to a hero, he was a convenient toilet for indifferent pigeons. Yet Mort was happy for himself. His days of glory were about to begin. The conquest of land might be over, but the conquest of human souls had just begun.

# CHAPTER 7

## Muscles

Who was that tall, muscular man looking at himself in the mirror? Was he a professional body builder, or maybe a sportsman, or perhaps a boxer? No, you silly twit, it was President Carol, who had undergone a stupendous transformation since beginning a course of high-dose super steroids. Lost forever was her small, slim physique, making way for her broad-shouldered, barrel-chested, slim-hipped, tree trunk thighs, a Mr Universe body. She was standing naked, and you would have mistaken her for a man if it weren't for the telltale sign that she was minus a penis. It was with approval and pride that she regarded her new body in the mirror. The mirror flinched as she threw a couple of punches at her reflection. She raised her dumbbell arms in triumph and bragged to the mirror, "Mirror, mirror, on the wall, who's the strongest person in the world?"

"Me!" Her voice, however, retained its shrill feminine pitch.

She put on male jockeys and a singlet before fitting into a man's suit. She found herself repelled by female clothing, viewing it as clownish. Her new body had made an enormous difference to Carol and her perception of life. She felt strong and powerful—well, she was strong and powerful, and that was the difference. Her strength was real, and she did not rely on mental energy, which was unreliable, a thing of moods. Gone were her fears of being assaulted and raped, those humiliating terrors of fragility and helplessness, those fears which undermine any feelings of strength. Those fears had dissolved, and a new citadel of confidence had taken their place. Even though she was strong and assertive, she derived her strength solely from her mind and its power of cunning and superior intellect. Her new strength was physical, and her mind, which to her had been an abstract thing, had taken on solidness—her new mind had become one with her body. This was a strange new feeling for President Carol. She had become more physically oriented. She delighted in the mindless pleasures of sport, hard manual work, and bodybuilding. President Carol was no longer that frail, but an intense thinker, eternally sitting and eternally splitting hairs like a metaphysical hairdresser. Her new body rejected thought, preferring to be just a body, sheer, alive, and full of virility.

Having dressed up and returned to her office to work, President Carol sat in her chair, unable to lift a pen, which seemed to her extremely heavy. Her mind was a burden. She did not want to think. Her body could lift 150 kg barbells, but her mind was too heavy for her. This abstract world was to her...a great meaningless mass, dragging her down. Her office impinged upon her like a cage that imprisoned her body, which was an eagle needing to soar into the skies and prey upon the creatures of the earth. She languished in her chair, bored with the dictates of her mind. She had to escape at once, away from this mental dungeon.

The Treasurer entered the office.

"Good morning, Ms President," her treasurer greeted her as she entered the room. She was a tall, skinny woman with glasses that made her look fish eyed.

"Hello, Leona," said President Carol, standing up and vigorously shaking Leona's skinny hand, hurting it. "Say, Leona, what are you doing now?"

"I'm working on the government budget. We need to make more cuts."

"Budget smudget. Let's go out and play football," suggested President Carol, her eyes excited.

"The Budget must be delivered to the public in one week's time. There is no time to play."

"You should see my sidestep. I scored a try last week with my sidestep," Carol boasted about her rugby prowess.

"A sidestep is of no relevance to the nation's economy. Now let me show you some of my budget proposals."

"Do you want to arm wrestle?" President Carol challenged her, sticking out her hand in an arm-wrestling pose.

Leona noticed Carol's bulging biceps.

"Please, Ms President, time asks us to serve the country right this very minute."

"Do you know what you are?"

"A Treasurer with an economy to fix."

"No, a sissy! That's what you are!"

"It doesn't matter," replied Leona with annoyance.

"I hate sissies!" grumbled President Carol.

"President Carol, you are most distracted today."

"I want to play football!"

"But the budget must be addressed."

"Do you know what I think about politics? Mere housekeeping."

"Nonetheless, politics is our job, and we have to get to work now."

"Later, we'll play football now." President Carol stood up, looking excited.

"Please."

"Sorry, but you don't have a choice." President Carol heaved Leona over her shoulders and hauled her all the way to the football field.

"Put me down immediately, I implore you."

At the football field, President Carol instructed Leona on the game of rugby league, a sport played mostly in Australia and England. "When you have the ball, you must try to score by touching down the football at the end of the field opposite your goal line, and you do this by avoiding being tackled."

"What, for heaven's sake, is a tackle?"

"A tackle is when a player grabs hold of the opponent to prevent him from running. Thus, when I have the ball, you must try to tackle me. Get it?"

"Yes, any moron can understand it, and only morons would play it," answered Leona, resigned to playing the game. She had no foreboding of what she was getting herself into…

"Good. I'll kick the ball. You catch it and run. Right?"

"I can't wait," said the innocent victim.

"Go down to your half."

Leona walked back to her half of the field. Besides her pink-rimmed spectacles, she wore a spotless white frilly shirt and a black skirt over her black net stockings to the edge of her black high heels. What else would one wear to play rugby?

President Carol kicked the ball, sending it rocketing up into the bright, glaring sky. Leona watched the ball grow smaller and smaller, then larger and larger as it made its downward plunge, heading straight towards her nose. Leona stretched her hands up, at first to retrieve the ball, then, defensively, as the ball chased after her aggressively. It landed on her cranium, and she sat on her bottom, the ball magically bouncing and dropping into her hands. And if she thought the ball was scary, what was far more heart-stopping was the looming sight of the big and hulking President Carol charging at her. Leona stood up with the ball and fled, not to score a try, but to flee from the rampaging rhinoceros President Carol. She darted diagonally across the field towards her own try line. The President was fast gaining upon her. A few feet away, she hurled her brick wall into the mushy body of Leona, who crashed heavily into the ground like a chicken run over by a truck. "Now, it's my turn to run, and you to tackle."

Leona was angry and entertained thoughts of revenge, but her thoughts dispersed into unconsciousness as the Panzer tank President Carol blitzkrieged right over her flimsy little body. She regained consciousness two weeks later in the hospital, with a broken nose, a broken rib cage, and a mouth sans teeth.

President Carol, instead of returning to work after football, visited the pub, enjoying the camaraderie of the men. She felt an affinity with their coarse and physical natures, enjoying their conversations, which were intellectually untaxing opinions that carried no logic but the threat of physical violence. She loved the ugly-tasting beer, which made her dumb and vulgar, destroying her intellect and any refinement of manner. It metamorphosed her into an unthinking animal like a lion that needed to roar and stalk prey and laze long hours in muscular indolence. She enjoyed asserting her physical self over the other men, like the wrangling of antelope horns. Her new body was always dignified and pure, even at its most violent expression.

Strangely, President Carol took to picking up women. She wanted to know what it was like to be a predator. She visited singles bars. The women she picked up were oblivious that she was a woman. To deceive them, she had worn a false penis, a huge monster, 12 inches long. It was an unsophisticated device, being in perpetual erection. The artificial penis fooled all the women she went to bed with, for it did look very authentic, the flesh made of the best rubber technology could provide. It even had special effects, like a sound box, which made the penis growl like a lion. Women were very impressed with President Carol's penis. However, they were hardly impressed with her sexual performance.

President Carol cared little about satisfying her partners; they were of no importance. Picking up women was like hunting, to devour their souls or hearts, to make them feel as if they were meat to her tummy...

# CHAPTER 8

## TRUTH and other stupidities

How does one meet the truth? Through the eyes? The mind? The heart? The genitals? What is Truth? I don't know! Why should I know? I'm a fool most of the time. I'm not one of those serene wise men who act so damn sure of their wisdom. I can never be sure of anything. There is too much of the unknowable to know what life is all about. And human beings are just too limited to experience the limitless.

St Claire woke up one morning, the birds singing, the cars rumbling by, sunlight streaming upon the bedroom floor, got up, went to the bathroom, peed, pooed, showered, shampooed, brushed her teeth, flossed, rubbed lotion over her body, returned to her bedroom, dabbed some make up on her pretty face, jumped inside her white lacy underwear, strapped on bra, blow dried hair, brushed her hair, put on polka dot dress, slipped on white low heel shoes, made toast and coffee, ate quickly, picked up shoulder bag, went outside, locked up, and began her search for Truth.

Queen Clytoris told her that if she wanted the Truth, she must search for it. When searching for Truth, it is advisable to wear loose clothes, comfortable shoes, and no makeup. St Claire found out on the first day that in a desert where one searches for Truth, panty hose and high heels are incompatible with the sun and sand. In the desert, she hoped to find Truth. The desert is pure, naked, cruel, and unrelenting; surely a place where Truth would abode in. When searching for Truth, don't search for cliches. The desert is a cliche.

In the desert, she found hot, hot weather.

In the desert, she met a philosopher. She told him she was searching for Truth.

He didn't speak English, shrugged, and went away.

Truth has communication barriers.

In the desert, she gave up searching for Truth and focused her remaining energy on finding water. She stared ahead, her hand saluting the horizon, and saw it was all white, hot sand, endless desert. She crawled on the ground like an animal.

Truth has no relevance to animals.

She was ready to give up and die when she saw an oasis ahead. Like a dog, she ran on all fours towards this watery paradise, the palm trees and cool pond beckoning her. She dived into the pool, quaffing the lovely water. Bloated like a whale, she beached herself on the banks.

She would have gone to sleep had it not been for the impertinent prodding by some wooden stick. She peeped up and saw the perpetrator was an old, long-bearded man with the sun radiating an aureole around his head.

"Who are you?"

"Aharazam. I am the guardian of this oasis, which is the source of all the religions of the world. Have you come here to find a new religion?"

"I'm searching for Truth."

"God is Truth."

"Is there a God? I want to know," she tugged at his white flowing robe.

"I'm glad you asked that question," he said, and then, in a loud TV announcer voice, he exclaimed, "Have I got a God for you!"

Materialising, a curtained stage with a long catwalk. On centre stage, a tall man, with a long, white beard, flaring nostrils, and scowling eyes, strutted down the catwalk, whirled a few times, and stopped for a grand divine pose...

"For this summer's God collection, this God is a must-have for people who fancy a bit of discipline, guilt, sex-hating, eternal damnation, and vengeance for one's enemies. This God is outfitted with cutting-edge surveillance technology, allowing him to see and hear everything you do."

"As an added bonus, you will also receive a mysterious gate which leads straight to...Hell!"

The curtain sprang up to reveal a flame-filled stage with sinners gnashing their teeth in agony and vicious devils whipping them along. "Wouldn't you love to see all the baddies and nonbelievers writhe in wretched agony?"

St Claire didn't clap for the departing God. She didn't like him at all. Appearing next was a small, rotund, smiling God who strolled down the catwalk cheerfully, as if he were on a beach promenade, waving at St Claire as if she were a close dear friend. St. Claire waved back. She liked this guy.

"However, if you prefer a more benign God, a kinder and gentler divinity, then this God will suit you to a tee. He's small and non-threatening, fat and cuddly, extremely caring, and compassionate, extravagantly generous, answers all prayers, and forgives all sins, no matter how heinous. And if you choose this God, you will also receive for free...Paradise!"

The risen curtain revealed a pastoral landscape populated by angels, children of various races, and animals, all looking cute and lovely. They all smiled, even the animals, the lion and the lamb, cheek to cheek. The fat and merry God departed to a loud applause and whistling from St Claire.

She drew back in fright when a large golden rhinoceros stomped on stage. In awe, she put her hands to her mouth.

"Tired of neurotic human gods? Then why not try some pagan animal worship? It's a big hit among primitive tribes and new age hipsters. Give your emotions and intellect a rest. Let's get physical and summon an animal god!"

After stomping the length of the catwalk, the Golden Rhinoceros turned around, relieved itself, leaving some golden droppings, then retreated backstage. "The God that excretes the golden poo. One compelling reason to follow him. And what's the harm in a little materialism?"

After the hoofs and horn, a giant shining ball of light hovered over the stage. St Claire squinted from the intense glare.

"Now this is designed especially for you intellectuals who prefer abstraction to reality. This God is the quintessence of the quintessence of the quintessence. It doesn't get any more abstract than that. Discard all your impure, imperfect, screaming, shitting Gods, and take this logical perfection home with you."

The light vanished.

Next, a woman waltzed onto the stage and glided gracefully down the catwalk. "Who says God has to be a man? God can be a woman too. Latest from our batch just released. This is a God to behold. Beautiful, maternal, and yet sexy. Her name is Queen Clytoris!"

"Queen Clytoris!" gasped St Claire. She looked at the woman, and, indeed, it was Queen Clytoris whirling around on the catwalk.

St Claire bounded onto the stage and gripped her arms. "Queen Clytoris! It's me, St Claire! What are you doing up here?"

But Queen Clytoris ignored her and continued modelling.

"Queen Clytoris!" she implored her. She took her arms again and looked straight into her eyes. Although her face was identical down to the last pore, it wasn't her. There was a deadness in her eyes. This was Queen Clytoris, perfect on the outside but nothing inside.

"Is she the God you want? I can offer you a good price for her."

"Gods for sale?"

"The price is your brain. Give me your brain, and you will have her to worship for eternity."

"My brain?"

"Sure. You sell your soul to the devil. For God, you sell your brain. Is it a deal?"

"No! She's a fake! Besides Queen Clytoris would never let me sell my brain to you or anyone else. They're all fakes! I don't want God! I want the Truth!"

"Sorry, I can't help you there. Perhaps you should try another mirage. I'm sure you'll come across another one in the desert. There are so many. They're in big demand from desperate human beings."

"A mirage?"

Immediately, the oasis had disappeared, and all around her was sand, hot, white, blazing sand. She groaned. She trekked on. The hot white sand was so fierce that it felt like she was walking on hot coals. Go back, go forward, it made no difference; she was in the middle of hell. She noticed a cluster of people clambering from behind a sand dune. Seeing her, they scrambled down towards her. They bore heavy wooden chests. A man laid a chest before her.

"We are going Nowhere. Will you take us there? If you guide us, we will reward you greatly." They opened the chests, and before her glittered mounds of diamonds, rubies, emeralds, and gold. How she would prefer to see a gallon of water instead.

"You are going Nowhere? That's crazy. Nowhere is…nowhere. It does not exist."

These words induced a wave of shock and indignation among the crowd. St Claire had touched a very raw nerve, and she was fearful for her life as they directed their fury at her. However, coming to her rescue, a man, appearing from out of the blue, shouted, his eyes gloating on the jewels.

"She's a liar! I've been to Nowhere. I'll take you there if you give me the reward." What a strange sight this man was in the middle of the desert clad in a three-piece Armani suit. How strange to see a man smile so professionally in this wretched furnace. He proceeded to shake the hands of all those present except St Claire. St Claire thought he was slimy and insincere and eyed him with contempt. But the others were generally impressed.

"Why should we believe you?" asked a man, not out of scepticism, but out of ceremony.

"Because I'm a politician. You can trust me." He smiled wider still, if that was possible, as it was wide enough already. He gazed at each person as if he cared for them all except for St Claire, whom he avoided making eye contact. He was nervous about her. He felt she could see through him.

"The last guide abandoned us and took some of our treasure. Why should we trust you?"

"Because I promise that I won't abandon you. And I never break a promise."

St Claire rolled her eyes.

The crowd cheered and applauded him loudly. He raised his arms like a giant V for Victory salute.

"You fools!" shouted St Claire. "You're not going to listen to this charlatan? He's a fraud."

Immediately, the crowd turned against the man and booed him. But he remained composed.

"It saddens me that you should doubt me. I am an honest man, a devoted husband to a loving wife, a doting father to three wonderful children, and a dedicated servant to the public. I am deeply hurt. But I am made of sterner stuff. I know that I won't allow my good name to be besmirched by this troublemaker, this outsider, this heinous depraved soul. She says that I am a fraud. Let me put this question to her..."

He had the crowd won over, and now they booed at St Claire,

"Can you tell me where you are going?"

"Actually, I'm searching for..."

"Aha! So you are going somewhere. How dare this woman, who is going somewhere, presume to question my expertise in Nowhere. I am going Nowhere while she is going somewhere. It is as simple as that. The fork is upon this road. Follow me and Nowhere will be upon you soon!!!"

They erupted in a great burst of applause. Leading the way, the Politician strode towards Nowhere, the happy believers at his heels. They trudged across the desert and disappeared into the sand and heat.

St Claire groaned. "I wish I was anywhere but here."

She kept walking and walking and walking until she leapt with joy at the sight of a great city bustling with life and more life. A white walled city, dazzling like a diamond. White crosses of a cemetery gleamed outside the city. The massive city gate beckoned her inside. Greeting her was a fountain, in the centre of which writhed the stone statues of naked orgiastic men and women, the men with their erect penises ejaculating in an eternal orgasm. St Claire jumped straight into the water, drinking madly from the cool, cool water. Water poured over her hot, dry skin, cascading like a waterfall over her breasts and between her thighs, seducing her. Water drenched her desert-parched skin.

After luxuriating a while in the fountain, she jumped out. A little man was watching her with lewd interest.

"What is this city?" she asked him.

"Eh, this city is called Azhmar. In deesh city we live and loove to our heart's content. We ple and ple and ple ool day long! Come, let's ple you and I."

"Play what?"

"Whatever you like to ple, my pretty dool."

"I'm starving."

''Then eat we shool, my beauteous dahling."

The little smiling man hooked his arm around St Claire's arm and guided her through the vibrant streets. Music throbbed in the air, people sang and danced without inhibition. The people in this city were so fun-loving that they shied not at all from making love in public. Beasts with two backs everywhere, prolific like grey pigeons. St Claire and the man entered a restaurant whose entrance was a giant gaping vulva.

A dress code notice required that all patrons must enter in the nude. Starving, she had no qualms stripping, despite the little man leering at her.

"I feel like a steak."

"Steak, noo, my bootiful missy, we eat no steak, for cows are people too. We have oonly ice cream."

"Then ice cream is fine with me."

"Then here we gooo!!!!" a chute opened beneath their feet and dropped them into a room of ice cream, which seemed to contain a kaleidoscope of flavours.

"Oh my God! I'm swimming in ice cream! This is heaven!" She dived mouth first into the ice cream.

Underneath, the little man grabbed her by surprise and kissed her. She wanted to resist him, but there was something about his kiss that was so irresistible. It was like kissing a rose, the lips soft like petals. She succumbed, and they started to make love. He was very good at sex. She clamoured for more and more, and he seemed to possess a limitless supply of energy and spunk.

In the next few weeks, she had the best sex she ever had (not that she got much of it previously). They made love unceasingly, everywhere, anytime. The ecstasy reached such heights that she felt she could explode. In fact, a couple who had been making love a few metres away exploded right in front of her eyes, their severed genitals copulating in the sky.

"Oh my God, they...blew up!"

"Dahling, it's when one has reached the ultimate orgasm that one exploooods! It's what every citizhen in our city longs for. To exploood! Cooom, my dahling, let's go kabooom!

"I don't want to explode!" He kissed her, down to the floor they went, bonking. St Claire found it impossible to resist this super sex machine, and every time they made love, it got better and better, and every time she had an orgasm, she felt she was going to explode into a million bits. She was terrified. But her passion overwhelmed her and compelled her to tempt Fate.

"I'm coming!" cried St Claire. "Oh God, I think this is it!"

"Yes, dahling! I feel that this time we explood like a nooclear boomb!"

Ecstasy surged through her body like jet propulsion. Her body vibrated turbulently. The orgasm was catapulting her to the stratosphere of bliss. She screamed so loudly it was like breaking the sound barrier. She was going to die, but the happiness was worth it. A white light flashed before her eyes. It was like the light of God. She opened her eyes expecting to see God. Instead, she found nothing. The little man was gone. She looked to the ground and found a mound of ashes. He had exploded and disintegrated. Miraculously, she had survived. St Claire ran out of the city gates, refusing to look back. She entered the white light of the desert. She longed for the purity of the light.

No need to say that the desert was hot. The desert was very hot. Although, I, the author, am writing in bed, in the cool of an autumn night, I imagine that the desert was very hot. I can say the desert was cold. I can say anything, willy-nilly, I've got the bloody pen. I am the creator of this novel! I can write whatever I please! The desert was wet with thunderstorm. The desert was deep in snow. Poor St Claire, hot, cold, wet, thirsty, it was all crazy when she entered

THE

land

OF

W O r D s.

The desert was an ocean. The desert was a pig snout.

"Help me, somebody!" she shouted.

"Permeating coruscation," answered:

a) an old man

b) a donkey

c) eggs and bacon

d) hepatitis C

"Huh?"

"Let's fandango bloop whiskey thought raddled balustrade!"

"I don't understand you!"

"Melancholic blood pewter!"

"Get me out of this place!"

Blustering

PanCREAS

calm

Ins    olent

the belacroisity boop

"Help me! I'm in the hands of a pretentious avant-garde artist!" she cried out.

st claire

sctilrea

S T CLAIRE

St Claire was gored by a Spanish bull, which was born and raised in Brooklyn, his parents, Jewish Intellectuals.

The guillotine blade was suspended above her; all she could see from her position was the empty bloody basket below her head. She could hear the impatient crowd jeering the executioner to release the blade. She wondered how dying would feel. Would she be conscious when her head falls into the basket? Would she see the crowd when the executioner holds her head up to them? Would there be life after the blade? She would know the answer soon. The blade falls. A sharp pain in her neck and the basket receives her head. What is the answer, St Claire, to the ultimate question?

Potato Chips.

The horse gazed into St Claire's eyes, and then he passionately kissed her. She swooned under his large head. "No, no, no, I can't...you're a horse, and I'm a woman...it can never work."

The horse neighed, then said, "Shut up! Just kiss me, damn it!" And they kissed, and everything appeared to be fine for St Claire. Ah, but they can't be kissing forever; soon she'll have to face society's judgement.

Ding!

This was the final round of the world heavyweight boxing championship, and St Claire was behind in points, having been knocked down twice.

To win, she would have to knock out her opponent, the great legendary Muhammad Ali. He loomed up to her, his punches crashing upon her fatigued and battered body. Her head snapped back, her nose flattened, bloodied. In the pained dimness of her consciousness, she continued to defend herself against the barrage of punches coming from everywhere. Bang! Bang! Bang! rang Ali's punches upon her. Bang! Bang! Bang! like bullets to her brain. But she refused to go down. She imagined herself as General Custer in his last stand, a lone figure surrounded by bloodthirsty Indians. She would fight to the bitter end.

St Claire was nailed to the cross. She screamed in excruciating agony. Tearful mules with bright halos knelt on the ground and prayed to her. A giraffe in a Roman soldier costume offered her a lick of an ice cream cone.

"What flavour is it?"

"Grass."

"No, thanks."

She vomited diamonds.

The cross blasted off. She was hurtling through outer space. Two spaceships pursued her, firing laser rays at her. She evaded the rays through clever aerobatics, whirling, looping, plunging, and rolling. However, one of the spaceships scored a direct hit and she was blasted into oblivion...

A stooped, shaky old woman shuffled across the floor. This bag of wrinkles and bones was none other than St Claire, hardly recognisable, her beautiful face ravaged by time.

"Is that you, St Claire?" I asked her.

"Yes," she gasped.

"What's happened to you, poor thing?"

"You...you...did this to me!"

"Me? I couldn't possibly do such a thing to you."

""Your words...your words!"

"My words?"

"You wrote this novel!"

"Well...yes."

"Help me, Ranulfo...don't leave me this way. I want to be young again."

"St Claire, my novel demands my characters to suffer."

"I beg you. Don't be cruel. Please."

She was crying, but she was so dry and withered that no tears came out.

"I can't help you, St Claire. A novelist has a plan, and the characters must follow. The plan is the whole purpose of your existence. Take away the plan and you are unnecessary."

"What is the plan?'

"I can't reveal it to you. Revelation would destroy my plan. I must keep you in darkness. You are not ready for the Truth."

I sent her back to the desert. The hot sand blistered her feet; the hot breath of wind parched her flesh. Wheeling high above, a buzzard waiting for supper. His winged shadow circling her as she trudged across the desert. And where to? Whatever the horizons bring?

A dot on the horizon. A dot became a man. A man digging a hole in the desert. The wind blowing to refill the hole. But the man continued to dig. St Claire was wary of meeting this man. She had had enough of desert crazies. Observing him, she thought he looked normal and innocuous. However, he was wearing a tie, despite the sweltering heat.

"Hi," greeted St Claire.

"Hello," he greeted back, unsmiling, without disrupting the rhythm of his digging. St Claire sat herself down on a red swivel chair, swinging herself around a few times.

The man paid not the slightest attention to her. She waited for him to stop and converse with her. But he kept digging. She was about to give up on him and leave when he stopped suddenly, dropped his shovel, and went to his bag, taking out a thermos.

"You want some tea?"

"No, thanks. It's too hot for tea."

"It's my morning tea break. If I don't have a morning tea, then I wouldn't need a break."

He showed her his steel watch. "Ten O'clock on the dot."

"So, what are you doing?"

"Digging a hole."

"Why?"

"It's my job to dig holes."

"But…can't you see the wind is filling up your holes…isn't it all rather futile?"

"They pay me to dig holes, and so I dig."

"Why bother?"

"Better than doing nothing."

"You are…doing nothing."

Failing to understand, "Of course. It's my tea break." He glanced at his watch. "I've got to get back to work in five minutes."

"Who's watching you if you don't go back to work?"

"Myself. I'm a supervisor."

"Where's your staff?"

"I sacked them all. They were slacking off."

"Ever thought of getting another job."

"No," he replied with conviction. He returned the thermos into his bag. "Tea break's over."

She watched him resume his digging. She wanted to continue the conversation, but he was adamant against it and ignored her. So she reluctantly greeted the endless horizon, not having the foggiest idea what she would meet next. So far, the journey has been exciting and enlightening, but only because I, the author, have made it so. In reality, she would encounter only dune after dune, ending in death. In Art, anything goes.

A temple of stone stood tall and magnificent. From afar, it seemed empty and spectral, but as she dragged her weary body forward, she observed a person standing guard at the entrance door, tantalisingly ajar. As she moved closer, this person, the guard clarified itself into a woman. This particular point gladdened St Claire. She believed women to be saner than men, and she was not up to having those absurd encounters with men she had been having. St Claire sized up the guard, considering the strength of the body and the character of the face. The guard was similarly built like her, and the guard's face strikingly resembled her. In fact, the resemblance was exact, for what St Claire was staring at was none other than…

"You're…me!" gasped St Claire. She was not only shocked but also curious about how she herself would look without the filter of a mirror to twist things inside out.

"Yes, none other but you," said the other St Claire.

"Why is that?"

"This is the Temple of Truth. I am here because the self is the barrier to the Truth."

"Truth!" St. Claire dropped back and imbibed the gleaming structure of Truth. She felt like a mother reunited with her long-lost child.

"Let me inside," she asked, excited and eager.

"No, you can't," replied the other St Claire.

"Why not?"

"I'm just following orders."

St Claire made a step towards the door, and, instantly, the guard responded by assuming an aggressive stance to scare her off. St Claire pushed her. This sent St Claire to the ground, flung there by the guard with quick jujitsu moves. Unfazed, she threw herself into the gap of the door, which drew heavy resistance. St Claire was hurled to the stone steps, grazing her skin, and bruising her bones.

"If I can't go in," cried St Claire, "at least tell me what's inside?"

"I don't know what's inside. I'm just a guard."

"Who's allowed inside?"

"That's classified information."

"Can historians come inside?"

"No historians. Historians are mythmakers and cannot be trusted with the truth."

"What about scientists?"

"The truth is too illogical for them?"

"What about priests?"

The guard laughed out loud.

"Politicians?"

"They worship at the Temple of Lies."

"What about the general public?"

"They get the truth from TV."

"What if I pay you?"

"The rich can't get inside for money is the only truth to them."

"Let me in! I order you! I want to know the truth!"

"Over my dead body."

"So be it!" Grappling arms, straining torsos, grimacing faces—a giant human ball rolling and bouncing about. They wrestled with all their might and determination, protracting the fight to its fullest agony. In this crazy tangle, St Claire noticed that the guard was deliberately trying to hurt her, biting and punching her viciously. She reciprocated pain with pain, but the intensity of the pain ascended, it would not get any less. It was a fight to the death. This mad aggression of accumulating pain and anger repulsed St Claire, so she allowed herself to be thrown back into the desert. Prostrate on the ground, she no longer thought of the temple but only of home.

She struggled to her knees and crawled homeward. Back to her sanctuary from the world. Fuck the Truth! Fuck God! Fuck it all! I want to go home! How many more horizons, St Claire, before you reach your home with walls to shut out all horizons? Crawl on, and may the sun be kind. The desert, or the Truth, is not your friend, go home.

# CHAPTER 9

## Home Sweet Home

Attention all Filipinos! Cast out all your Western Gods, Western heroes, Western values, Western clothes, and the rest of the Western bullshit, and find out who you are! What are you afraid of? Discovering that you have betrayed your soul, betrayed your gods that once inhabited the trees, the sky, the water, the fire....

For too long, we have accepted third world status. In other words, third-class citizens. We are invisible, insignificant, expendable, and worthless. We die in the thousands and millions, not as individuals. No longer. Hear us laugh and roar...

St Claire came to an extraordinary town, the buildings skewed and distorted like an Expressionist painting. Cars drove all over the streets, which had no traffic lights or rules to guide the traffic. Often, a car would crash into another, and the inhabitants would burst out screaming and gesticulating madly. Not only was the traffic chaotic, but so were the people. This was not your typical town with people suppressing feelings behind placid masks. The people's faces were amok with emotion—anger, laughter, sadness, all revealed, undiluted. St Claire was disconcerted by people's naked reactions to her. Some found her funny and laughed rudely; others found her repulsive and grimaced, avoiding her like the plague; and still others found her beautiful and swooned.

"Oh my God!" shouted a man, distorting his face at St Claire. "You're so ugly! Ugliest thing that I've ever seen in my life. Cut your head off and hide it in a bag! I could retch just looking at your face!"

Another man cried at her, "My beautiful Goddess! You are absolute perfection! Your beauty gives me an instant erection like the Empire State Building! I think I love you! Will you marry me?"

A woman screamed at her, "Get out of town, you bitch! Get out out out! We don't want you here!"

St Claire broke away and bounded down the street to escape from these mad people. She slipped inside a movie theatre, hoping for peace and quiet. Inside, an empty screen was being played to the audience, who, amazingly, were surprisingly entertained. They cried, laughed, and screamed. St Claire concentrated deeply on the blank screen and experienced nothing. After all, it was just a blank screen.

Exasperated, she yelled at the projectionist, "When is the movie going to start?" She was greeted with hissing and booing and told to keep quiet so they could enjoy the movie.

"What movie?"

"Sssshhhhhh!!!!!!"

St Claire slumped in her chair, red-faced.

She stayed quiet until the end of the movie when people applauded and cheered and left the theatre with pleased faces.

St Claire followed them out into the street. She yawned. A piercing scream split her brain. A woman was kneeling on the footpath. St Claire, concerned, asked what the matter was. "I've killed an ant! I've killed an ant! I'm a murderer! Oh, poor ant! Never more will you grace this footpath to experience the glorious rays of the sun! Never more will you meet your beautiful community of ants! Never more because I have killed you. I am sorry! Will you ever forgive me? I will take you with me, give you a funeral, and spend the rest of my life praying for your soul."

"This place is crazy! Get me out of this madhouse!" St Claire said to herself and ran towards the desert.

A crowd pursued her, their faces violent.

"Why are you running away? You hate me, don't you? You hate me and you want to get rid of me?"

"Let's run and play! Weee!!!!"

"Don't leave us! We need you! I beg you, please stay!"

"Get out! Filthy scumbag! Get out!"

"I love you! I love you!"

The streets ran into labyrinths, the streets obviously designed to render the traveller lost. She ran and ran and ran. People she passed along the street cheered her on as if she was a famous athlete. Some fled, screaming with fear. Finally, she was out of the city, and back to the desert, which she welcomed gratefully.

The next town she passed through was quiet. This was a relief for her nerves, shattered by the previous town. Yet there was something peculiar about the sun sitting up in the sky. It had hands. Well, not human hands, but the hands of a clock on the face of the sun. The citizens who traversed the footpaths constantly glanced at them to note the time, their gaits suggesting a rush to reach a certain place at a certain time, not a minute earlier or later. They bustled and hurried past the tardy St Claire. Being ignored was a blessing to her after all her perilous adventures. What a luxury to be left alone. No more stress from human interaction.

But St Claire was far from invisible as she strolled down the streets of this orderly town. Furtive eyes were upon her, eyes of judgement and vigilance. The soul of this town revolved mechanically around set rules, like a clock. Obedience to all rules, large and small, was demanded from all citizens so that the town would function with absolute perfection. The breaking of rules was not tolerated, and any misdemeanour was punishable. One rule which St Claire inadvertently broke was that one must not pick one's nose in public. St Claire was observed committing this heinous offence at the corner of Locke and Hume. Witnesses were:

Masha Bootnik, 48-year-old librarian: "Yes, your Honour, I saw with my very eyes her picking her nose and flicking its disgusting contents upon a street to be innocently trod upon by an unfortunate stranger."

Jonton Boog, 16 years old, plumbing apprentice: "She did it! She did it! I swear on my Mum's grave. Filthy outsider dirtying our good clean streets with her snot. Send her to the slammer and throw away the keys I say!"

Minnie Beep, 10-year-old sweet angelic girl: "Yes, your Honour, I saw her pick her nose. I was following her, you see, because she was a stranger in the town and strangers, as I was taught by my parents, are not to be trusted and should be put under video surveillance to record all evidence of their crimes, which I did with my pink handy camera."

For this criminal charge, St. Claire was found guilty and sentenced to 25 years of imprisonment.

"25 years! For this trivial, insignificant offence!" Defiantly, St. Claire picked her nose and flung the booger at the judge. Before she could assault the jury with her nosepicks, the guards grabbed her and dragged her away into the slammer.

Poor St Claire, thrown into a dark, gloomy cell, her home for the next twenty-five years. Light vomited itself through a rusty barred window and splattered itself on the dirty stone floor. Cockroaches and rats stirred in the shadows. She lay on her brutal bed and lamented how her life had been ruined. Youth, Love, Joy—she waved them goodbye. Only darkness was relevant to her now. Surviving in the darkness was her top priority. She pounced on the impotent light and prayed for some miracle to lift her from this nightmare. She grabbed the insubstantial light and knew her case was hopeless. The light could not help her. Only the darkness was her friend, whether she liked it or not. The darkness was now her world. The world outside was as remote from her as the sun. She must forget the light and think dark thoughts.

Thoughts of love and happiness would pain her. She must think of hate, death and revenge. She thought of how to get back at those who got her here. She thought of long, elaborate plans of revenge with painstaking details. Hate was now her passion. Hate was now her purpose of living. Hate made her strong in the Kingdom of Darkness.

She thought no more of Queen Clytoris, Prince Jotel, or her friends. In the darkness, you could not see faces. You felt the darkness, as if it were part of you.

When she walked out of the cell to mingle with prisoners for meal breaks and exercise in the yards, she was not afraid of them. They, too, were part of the darkness to which she belonged. Only people who lived in the light would fear them.

"What's your name, bitch?" a female prisoner confronted her at the mess area, determined to put St Claire in her place.

"St Claire," she answered indifferently.

"We've got a fucking saint in here!" she shouted for the other prisoners to hear.

They jeered and taunted St Claire.

"What's you in for, Saint?"

"Picking my nose. What about you?"

"Jaywalking. I'm here for 20 years. How long you here?"

"25 years."

"That's too fucking long to look at your ugly face!"

St Claire stood up and stared down at the woman, who was short, plump, had curly black hair, and wore thick glasses. "Who are you calling ugly?"

"You! You look like a baboon's arse!"

The other prisoners gathered around the two, forming a circle, and egged them on to fight, clapping and shouting.

"I don't like tough people," said the woman. "I'm the queen in this place."

Momentarily, St Claire felt nostalgic for Queen Clytoris and was weakening at her knees, her old self returning. But a shove jogged her back to the necessity of being tough.

"Sorry, my Majesty," said St Claire, "I didn't think you were a Queen, I thought you were the Queen's corgi."

The audience gasped at the insult, knowing that it would bring more ire to Meena (the bully's name, by the way, I nearly forgot!), increasing her savagery over poor St Claire. They now expected St Claire not to be spared life or limb.

"Why you..." and Meena grabbed and pulled St Claire's hair with both hands. St

Claire tweaked Meena's nose. The audience screamed for blood. The fighters let go with their open palms and slapped each other viciously. St Claire punched Meena on the shoulder, shocking Meena, and the prisoners, for they did not expect such savagery from St Claire. Retaliating, Meena hit her back on her shoulder. They traded punches, their shoulders reddening. St Claire stomped on Meena's foot, which made Meena shriek. They wrestled, a tangle of bodies on the stone floor, which grazed them. Gaining strategic position, St Claire bit into Meena's plump butt.

What a yell came out of little plump Meena. The fight was over; Meena was bawling her heart out.

St Claire stood up and glared at the other prisoners.

"Anyone else wants a piece of me?"

The prisoners, heads bowed, dispersed. Now St Claire was the Queen of Darkness. All the prisoners would respect and obey her. The guards, who watched and did nothing because they encouraged conflict, not unity, among the prisoners, ordered everyone back into their cells. For the first time, St Claire slept soundly in her cell.

Being Queen was good at first; prisoners obeyed her and did things for her. She could sit anywhere she wanted, she could take food from anyone's plate with impunity. But these privileges aroused jealousies, and her Queenship was constantly challenged. The early fights she won easily. However, each fight diminished her, her strength ebbing with each fight. It didn't do her appearance any good either; she saw in the mirror a rough coarse woman. She looked evil. Meena, the former Queen, not only lost her power but her confidence. The other prisoner no longer respected her and treated her with contempt. She shuffled about like a scared dog, cowering at any sudden movements or noises. This was St Claire's future. St Claire saw it coming. Maybe in the next fight or the one after. She had two choices: get stronger or escape. She couldn't get stronger, so she had to escape. Out of the darkness and into the light.

The prison was a huge, stony, monstrous protuberance made of thick walls and wrapped in electric fences. It protruded from the empty desert like a giant sand-covered turtle. There were four towers, guards roosting in their machine gun nests. At night, a roving searchlight glided along the ground and walls of the prison like a hungry moon, hunting for prisoners to eat. No prisoner ever escaped these walls.

St Claire devoured her time thinking of the perfect plan of escape. The wall was the obstacle. How? Get over, get through, get under?

While eating her baked beans breakfast, she noticed the eruption of wind among the prisoners. Immediately, she saw her escape. She demanded to eat everyone's baked beans. Plate after plate poured into St Claire's tummy. The prisoners watched bemused; they thought she had gone mad. They watched her walk out into the exercise yard and followed her.

She dropped her pants and knickers to reveal her naked arse to all. She grimaced as if she was about to shit, a few prisoners were disgusted and walked away.

Those who stayed to enjoy the show saw her strike a match and place the flickering flame behind her anus.

She let out a big fart, a massive one.

KABAROOOSHHHH!

A huge stream of fire and smoke blasted out from her anus, lifting her like a Saturn rocket and catapulting her into the sky and over the walls, beyond the desert, beyond the mountains, and into the sea, which was fortunate for her hot, red-hot bottom. She swam, her arms slicing and churning, to the shore. She was free! Free! Free!

She was determined to stay free.

The village she entered didn't care for her lack of pants. She had come upon a very poor village, so poor that few of its citizens could afford clothes, shelter, or food. Hungry villagers scavenged the garbage left outside its gates.

Pity and anger filled St Claire's heart as she looked upon the miserable starving people, while a stone's throw away, a rich family sat at dinner, indifferent to the suffering outside. She knocked (pounding like a hammer of justice) at the iron door leading to the mansion's gardens. After a long wait, a maid responded through a peephole.

"I demand to see the master or mistress of this house," said St Claire with restrained fury.

"Who are you?" asked the maid.

"I'm St Claire, friend of the great Queen Clytoris," she added to lend weight to her request.

"Please wait."

The peephole closed. After a while, the maid returned and opened the door for St Claire while beating off a group of beggars trying to enter. "They're human beings for God's sake!" shouted St Claire. The maid ignored her and slammed the door hard on the faces of the poor beggars. The maid, who had a proud countenance, led her inside the mansion, which was elegant and opulent beyond belief. Paintings from Rembrandt to Picasso stared at her from the oak panelled walls. Statues, both ancient and modern, passed her by like bystanders. The shiny marble floor was like a wide open, shiny sea, and they sailed for a long time before they reached the shores of the reposed silk-robed master, sucking indolently on a cigarette holder.

"You have no pants on," he remarked indifferently, like a man who had grown bored with the joys of female flesh.

"That's of no importance. What is important is that people are starving to death outside your walls, and you're not doing anything to help them!"

"Don't mind them. They're all right. Poor people are happy. They live on spiritual things. It's the rich people you must pity. I've been seeing a psychiatrist for the past 10 years, and I'm still unhappy."

"The people are wretchedly poor, and they must be fed!"

"You didn't even ask how I am? Rich people have feelings too, you know."

"Then how are you?" asked St Claire, exasperated at this insensitive buffoon.

"Well…not too good, not too good. I've been feeling a bit melancholic."

"Helping people is a good way of forgetting yourself. In fact, you might find in charity the happiness that has eluded you." |

"Oh, you have no idea how many charity balls and fund-raising dinners I've attended. And I always overeat and overdrink and return home melancholic. These charity balls are wearing me out."

"Real charity is helping the people starving outside the door."

"Do you know how lucky they are? Not having to worry about dieting. It's torture having to diet. Forgoing one's favourite fatty foods. These poor people must be so happy looking at a mirror and seeing a slim, happy creature. When I look into a mirror, I see flab, I see ugliness, I see despair. I wouldn't wish to give this torment to these happy, starving people. Let them starve and spare them the misery of weight watching."

"Will you stop thinking about yourself? Think of others for a change!"

"Perhaps that's their problem. These poor people should think more of themselves. If they wore better clothes, had a decent hair stylist, and brushed their teeth, they might get jobs and feed themselves. I mean, how the hell can they go to the opera if they wear these rags?"

"There's no getting to you. You're not listening to me. People are dying outside your gates!" St Claire was going blue in the face.

170

"Outside my gates! That's not very considerate of them. How am I supposed to drive to tonight's charity ball if I've got dead bodies blocking my gates? Surely, a clear driveway isn't too much to ask?!"

St Claire gave up and walked out in a huff.

The maid led her out the gates. St Claire cleaved through the dying people, their hands pleading for help, but she had nothing to give. The man in the mansion could help them, but there's nothing getting through to him.

Warning! Forthcoming indulgent narrator's comment: Fuck what's happening to our world! Who's to blame? Rampant, unchecked capitalism, I say! We're creating too many losers! Billions of sad, dying, starving, dying losers. It's not their fault that there must be losers. Hey, you guys, let's share the world, there's enough for everybody.

*MUSE: Ranulfo, can you remove this indulgent narrator comment? It's tedious and adds nothing to the narrative. Instead, it slows the novel down.*

*RANULFO: Oh please, pretty please, let me keep it in, please...*

She came upon a bleak, horrifying wasteland. An enormous black hole yawned in front of her. As far as she could see, it was a vast blackness. She peered right down and saw nothing.

She yelled, "Hello!"

Hellohellohellohellohello, echoed the hole.

She walked along the rim, which went on for miles and miles. She was tired, dizzy; the world whirled, and she tipped over the edge. Desperate fingers gripped the edge; she held on grimly. She was too exhausted to pull herself up. She thought of death. She thought of it not unkindly. She needed rest, and death seemed like a huge, comfortable bed. She just wanted to sleep. It had been a long, arduous journey.

Could she say goodbye to her life? Goodbye Queen Clytoris, goodbye Prince Jotel, goodbye misery, goodbye struggle. But then a hand said hello and lifted her out of the hole. It was a man dressed in a security guard uniform. He said nothing to her. He loaded her into his buggy and drove her away. She looked up at the sky and saw an enormous black cloud, like an atomic mushroom. The black cloud gobbled up the sky.

The smoke belched from a forest of chimney stacks. The buggy was entering a labyrinth of factories. Tall, towering chimneys raped the sky. She could hardly breathe. The air stank like a corpse. Trunks bustled in and out of the factories. She read the sign on the side of the truck: BAHO CORPORATION.

Cried St Claire, "They're digging a fucking hole as big as the moon. They're spewing poison into the air!"

But the man said nothing; he just drove her out of the corporation property and dumped her outside.

St Claire followed the road she was on and didn't know where it would take her. Seeing the horizon, she could hear the call of home. Home, sweet home, take me in your arms! On her way home, St. Claire met a woman and a robot. The woman, a scientist, pale, frail, depended greatly upon her robot to feed her, carry her, and do the physical things her feeble body was incapable of doing. The robot bore her on his steel arms; behind him, an exhaust pipe spluttered, puking great awful sulphurous fumes.

"Do you care for a ride? Hop on if you like?" said the scientist.

St Claire was exhausted; she clambered up on the steel arms of the robot and ensconced herself beside the scientist who introduced herself as Cloona. The heavy feet of the robot made great imprints on the ground, skirting nothing, crushing everything in his path as St Claire watched in horror. The robot kicked a cow in his path, the cow flying an arch and landing headfirst.

"Perfect, isn't he?"

"He's a bit destructive."

"He's very powerful. He follows my commands. I built him myself. I adore him. He's loyal, says not one bad word about me, and never deceives me. Behold the perfect man! Thanks to science, whose mission it is to obliterate human weaknesses."

"Does he talk?"

"Yes. Randy, say hello to St Claire."

"Hello, St Claire, please to meet you," spoke the robot in a low metallic voice.

"Hello, Randy."

"You may converse with her, Randy. If you wish."

"Thank you, Mam, it would please me greatly. Tell me, St Claire, what are your interests?"

"I'm a bit of a philosopher."

"Are you searching for Truth?"

"Right now, all I want is to get home."

"I can't search for Truth. I'm a robot. Robots have no souls and can only deal with facts. I wish I had a soul. Cloona did not build me one."

"I often wonder if we humans have souls. Or we're just really good at deluding ourselves."

They had a stimulating conversation; St Claire enjoyed it very much. She would have talked longer, but Cloona was getting jealous and ordered the robot to cease talking. The robot obeyed and kept silent, the only noise coming from his rambunctious exhaust pipe.

Nighttime, they settled down for supper, the robot murdering a cow and transforming it into beef stew. So lazy was Cloona that the robot had to spoon feed her, even opening her mouth for her, food dribbling down her throat like a baby.

"I don't know what I would do without him. I'd just be lost." Cloona sensually stroked the grey helmet of the Robot, who purred in response.

"Why did you call him Randy?" St Claire ventured to ask.

"Because he's also a sex machine."

Randy displayed his huge electric penis, which suddenly popped out.

"Oh," said St Claire.

The robot made a mattress out of horse hide and chicken feathers, ingredients he filched from a farm. St Claire shut her eyes while Cloona and the robot made love.

The sex went on interminably, Cloona erupting in a never-ending cascade of orgasms.

St Claire fell asleep. Her sleep was interrupted when the robot with one of his digits pried open her eyelids. "Excuse me, St Claire."

"Yes," drowsily.

"You want to have sex?"

"No, thanks. I want to sleep."

"I want to turn you on. It makes me feel like a human being and you a machine."

''Not tonight. I'm so sleepy."

"Okay." The robot released her eyelids, and after a few minutes, pried them open again. "St Claire."

"What is it, Randy?"

"Do you want me to be your robot?"

"You belong to Cloona."

"She's bossy and mean. I don't like her."

"She needs you."

"I don't care. I have needs too. I don't want to be her servant. She's driving me mad. She shows me no respect or consideration. Just because I don't have a soul."

"Then you must talk to her about it."

"I can't."

"Why?"

"I'm scared of her."

"Whatever for?"

"Because she's stubborn and dictatorial. She won't listen, and I can't argue and assert myself. I don't have confidence. Plus, she can turn me off forever."

"Look, Randy, don't be afraid. Be brave. Don't believe you don't have a soul. A soul is something to be earned. A lot of humans haven't earned their soul. You too can earn a soul if you show courage, goodness, love, justice, and wisdom."

"Thank you, St Claire. I shall go now and earn a soul."

The robot dropped her eyelids, and she fell asleep amid the hubbub of crickets, stirring leaves, the humming engine of Randy, and the obstreperous snoring of Cloona. In the morning, she woke up to the noise of argument between Randy and Cloona. The argument was about the robot demanding equality and Cloona adamantly refusing. The voices grew louder and harsher. St Claire fell asleep once again. The sound she awoke to was silence. A sinister silence. A silence that screamed with horror. She sat up and saw Cloona dead, her head crushed. She looked around for the robot and found him sitting under a tree, crying.

"You've killed her."

"I turn her off, and I can't turn her on again. Is this what you call murder?"

"Yes."

"Since a soul believes in justice, I must be punished. The punishment is death."

"Why did you kill her?"

"You told me that you have to earn a soul. I showed bravery and spoke to Cloona and demanded my rights. Then, before I knew it, I got so angry and lost control of myself. This has never happened to me before. I guess souls are crazy things."

"I guess they are."

"Goodbye, St Claire. I'll see you in heaven."

"Yes, perhaps."

With his right arm, he pulled off his left arm, then he yanked out his legs, then he heaved off his head and tossed it away. The right arm continued smashing the rest of his body. Finally, one finger disintegrated itself, and Randy was no more.

The road greeted her. Home was beckoning her. She was weary of Truth and Reality and Humanity. She wanted to snuggle inside her shell, and immerse her tired head on her soft, fluffy pillow on her giant, comfortable bed. Lock the door and shut out reality. That was what she wanted. No more adventures. No more crusades for Truth. She wanted to be alone. Home.

She hailed a bus, boarded it, and sat down next to a man.

"You look dirty, weather beaten. Where have you been?" he asked.

"I've been searching for Truth."

"Well, I can help you find the Truth."

"Really?"

"Sure." He drew out a pistol and pressed it against St Claire's temple.

"What are you doing?"

"You can only know the Truth after you die. After Death, all will be told."

"Then I don't want to know the Truth now. I'll wait. I'm in no hurry."

"I do. I want to know the Truth now." He turned the gun on himself.

"No!" and St Claire shut her eyes and covered her ears.

"Is there a God?" spoke the man. "Is there Life after Death? What is the meaning of Life? Why do we suffer? Will suffering end after Death? Will we live in Eternal Bliss? Do we reincarnate? Do animals go to heaven? Do they serve pizza in heaven? Will we have bodies? Is there other life in the universe? Can I return to earth as an invisible angel? Will I meet my parents and forgive them and talk to them? Will I find my true self? Will I find true love? All these and more will be known after death."

There was silence. St Claire waited for the loud bang.

"I just remembered," he said, "football's on TV tonight. I can't miss that." He returned his pistol back inside his jacket.

She pulled the cord and alighted, running excitedly to her home. She could remember the houses and trees that passed her. Then she stopped. Where her home was, was a blackened ruin. It had been burnt down. She dropped to her knees and cried. Is God or whatever so cruel? Must everything be taken away from me? Is there no sanctuary from pain and suffering? She cried and cried. However, she couldn't cry forever. She had to get on with her life. She would build herself another home and hoped Fortune would treat her kindly. And if it didn't, oh well, que sera sera.

# CHAPTER 10

## The Metamorphosis

Ranulfo awoke one morning and discovered that he was in a peculiar predicament. He had metamorphosed into a cockroach. He was not really surprised; he had been living an insect-like existence for a while. Two weeks ago, he had started clerical work to avoid the Social Security crackdown on bona fide dole bludgers, of which he was proudly one. He had contemplated fighting the SS, the new laws meant that it was illegal not to want to work. Only the rich had the privilege of shirking work. It was a de facto death sentence for dole bludgers. He considered going on a hunger strike. But he backed down. He got a job.

One morning, he woke up as a cockroach—an ordinary house cockroach—a tiny brown spear of ugliness, stranded in the middle of his now enormous bed. It had become a gigantic world around him. The blankets look like hills, the carpet like a vast plain, and the wardrobe like an enormous mountain.

Ranulfo tried to recall the night before, his final night as a human. He had worked overtime, and was home late, completely exhausted. His job was to count the whole population of Australia. He travelled from Western Australia to Tasmania vicariously through the census forms. He counted thousands of ordinary people with no artist to immortalise their lives. This was their recorded literature: Name, Religion, Sex, Occupation, Marital Status, Education, Dependants. In the end, the forms would be consigned to the fire, and the computer would know only statistics and acknowledge no individuals.

He had lost his freedom. Usually, in the now seeming distant past, he was free to do whatever he liked. Now he was paid to fix himself into a routine. There were no more choices. He was no longer a creator but a servant. This was the lot of the common man. No wonder he wanted to be an artist. That freedom was gone, he was now a cockroach. At night, when he should be burning the midnight oil and writing, he was too worn out to do anything. In the day, he worked as hard as a mule, in the night, he vegetated like a happy lettuce.

The night before he became a cockroach, he suffered a delirium, induced from the tedium of his life, hallucinating he was an accountant who lived in a four bedroom house with a colour TV, a video player, two children, a pet Burmese, a

wardrobe full of blue and brown and grey suits and trousers, a wife who spent his money on hats and one night his pet Burmese cat poopooed on his pillow and then he discovered that his eight year old son was a heroin addict and his seven year old daughter was a member of the Liberal Party Youth Club and his wife was cheating on him having an affair with a young graffiti artist with passionate eyes and his car was broken into and his car radio taken his house ransacked, pilfered were the TV, the video player, the microwave, his seven year old daughter, an explicit home video of him with his pet Burmese in compromising positions was sold in public and the thieves pissed on his clothes, socks, underwear, ties, shoes and his best friend felled by a heart attack and was half paralysed and the plumbing was flooding the carpet ruined and the grass was dying and bills kept piling up and the next door dog ate his Burmese cat and and and his eight year old son was arrested as a serial killer and and his wife was divorcing him and and his house burned down and and and his favourite tv                    show                    was                    cancelled andandandandandaaaaaaaaaaaaaaaaaaaaaaaaaaaaaaaaaaaaaaaaaaaaaaaaaaaaaaaaaaaaaaaaaaaaaaaaaaa aaaaaaaaaaaaaaaaaaaaaaaaaaaaaaaaaaaaaaaaaaaaaaaaaaaaaaaaaaaaaaaaaaaaaaaaaaaaaaaaaaaaaaaaaa aaaaaaaaaaaaaaaaaaaaaaaaaaaaaaaaaaaaaaaaaaaaaaaaaaaaaaaaaaaaaAAAAAAAAAAAAAAAA
AAAAAAAAAAAAAAAAAAAAAAAAAAAAAAAAAAAAAAAAAAAAAAAAAAAAAAAAAAAA
AAAAAAAAAAAAAAAAAAAAAAAAAAAAAAAAAAAAAAAAAAAAAAAAAAAAAAAAAAAA
AAAAAAAAAAAAAAAAAAAAAAAAAAAAAAAAAAAAAAAAAAAAAAAAAAAAAAAAAAAA
AAAAAAAAAAAAAAAAAAAAAAAAAAAAAAAAAAAAAAAAAAAAAAAAAAAAAAAAAAAA
AAAAAAAAAAAAAAAAAAAAAAAAAAAAAAAAAAAAAAAAAAAAAAAAAAAAAAAAAAAA
AAAAAAAAAAAAAAAAAAAAAAAAAAAAAAAAAAAAAAAAAAAAAAAAAAAAAAAAAAAA
AAAAAAAAAAAAAAAAAAAAAAAAAAAAAAAAAAAAAAAAAAAAAAAAAAAAAAAAAAAA
AAAAAAAAAAAAAAAAAAAAAAAAAAAAAAAAAAAAAAAAAAAAAAAAAAAAAAAAAAAA
AAAAAAAAAAAAAAAAAAAAAAAAAAAAAAAAAAAAAAAAAAAAAAAAAAAAAAAAAAAA
AAAAAAAAAAAAAAAAAAAAAAAAAAAAAAAAAAAAAAAAAAAAAAAAAAAAAAAAAAAA
AAAAAAAAAAAAAAAAAAAAAAAAAAAAAAAAAAAAAAAAAAAAAAAAAAAAAAAAAAAA
AAAAAAAAAAAAAAAAAAAAAAAAAAAAAAAAAAAAAAAAAAAAAAAAAAAAAAAAAAAA
AAAAAAAAAAAAAAAAAAAAAAAAAAAAAAAAAAAAAAAAAAAAAAAAAAAAAAAAAAAA
AAAAAAAAAAAAAAAAAAAAAAAAAAAAAAAAAAAAAAAAAAAAAAAAAAAAAAAAAAAA
AAAAAAAAAAAAAAAAAAAAAAAAAAAAAAAAAAAAAAAAAAAAAAAAAAAAAAAAAAAA
AAAAAAAAAAAAAAAAAAAAAAAAAAAAAAAAAAAAAAAAAAAAAAAAAAAAAAAAAAAA
AAAAAAAAAAAAAAAAAAAAAAAAAAAAAAAAAAAAAAAAAAAAAAAAAAAAAAAAAAAA

AAAAAAAAAAAAAAAAAAAAAAAAAAAAAAAAAAAAAAAAAAAAAAAAAAAA
AAAAAAAAAAAAAAAAAAAAAAAAAAAAAAAAAAAAAAAAAAAAAAAAAAAA
AAAAAAAAAAAAAAAAAAAAAAAAAAAAAAAAAAAAAAAAAAAAAAAAAAAA
AAAAAAAAAAAAAAAAAAAAAAAAAAAAAAAAAAAAAAAAAAAAAAAAAAAA
AAAAAAAAAAAAAAAAAAAAAAAAAAAAAAAAAAAAAAAAAAAAAAAAAAAA
AAAAAAAAAAAAAAAAAAAAAAAAAAAAAAAAAAAAAAAAAAAAAAAAAAAA
AAAAAAAAAAAAAAAAAAAAAAAAAAAAAAAAAAAAAAAAAAAAAAAAAAAA
AAAAAAAAAAAAAAAAAAAAAAAAAAAAAAAAAAAAAAAAAAAAAAAAAAAA
AAAAAAAAAAAAAAAAAAAAAAAAAAAAAAAAAAAAAAAAAAAAAAAAAAAA
AAAAAAAAAAAAAAAAAAAAAAAAAAAAAAAAAAAAAAAAAAAAAAAAAAAA
AAAAAAAAAAAAAAAAAAAAAAAAAAAAAAAAAAAAAAAAAAAAAAAAAAAA
AAAAAAAAAAAAAAAAAAAAAAAAAAAAAAAAAAAAAAAAAAAAAAAAAAAA
AAAAAAAAAAAAAAAAAAAAAAAAAAAAAAAAAAAAAAAAAAAAAAAAAAAA
AAAAAAAAAAAAAAAAAAAAAAAAAAAAAAAAAAAAAAAAAAAAAAAAAAAA
AAAAAAAAAAAAAAAAAAAAAAAAAAAAAAAAAAAAAAAAAAAAAAAAAAAA
AAAAAAAAAAAAAAAAAAAAAAAAAAAAAAAAAAAAAAAAAAAAAAAAAAAA
AAAAAAAAAAAAAAAAAAAAAAAAAAAAAAAAAAAAAAAAAAAAAAAAAAAA
AAAAAAAAAAAAAAAAAAAAAAAAAAAAAAAAAAAAAAAAAAAAAAAAAAAA
AAAAAAAAAAAAAAAAAAAAAAAAAAAAAAAAAAAAAAAAAAA!!!!!!!!!

The scream became a cockroach.

It was that time before the radio alarm went off, the time to savour those last luscious moments of sleep, squeezing as much sleep into those precious few minutes. Then the alarm went off, that annoying beeping sound piercing into his very soul. Must turn that damn thing off! Normally, a reach of the hand would suffice. However, he felt eight tiny limbs waving in the air. They were too short to reach the alarm off button. In fact, he had to travel quite a distance as the radio clock appeared to be miles away. It looked like a giant building with large neon lights, showing it to be 6 in the morning. Obviously, he was sick. He went back to sleep despite the annoying beeping sound.

He woke up later. He was gonna call sick. But the phone was gigantic, like a pyramid. He saw a reflection of himself and realised he was a cockroach. He wasn't surprised at all.

Famished, he crawled across his bedroom to scrounge for food. Fortunately, he lived in a dirty house and found food quickly. He nibbled on a large bread crumb lying on the carpet. Suddenly, he noticed a giant cockroach. At first, he was frightened before he realised he was the same size and that they were now of the same species. The cockroach proved to be quite amicable, and together they shared the bread crumb. Later, he followed the cockroach, and they journeyed across the carpet landscape full of strange large objects. It was really eerie. They came upon the towering wardrobe, and to his amazement, they started travelling vertically. At the top, he viewed the whole room, which was spread far and wide like a huge continent. He felt dizzy, it was so high up. Up there was also a small colony of cockies. They measured him up with their sensitive antennae, which seemed to detect good and bad vibrations. They accepted him.

Days passed, and he adjusted well with the cockroaches. He even adjusted to the silence. Cockroaches didn't need words. They understood. They ate. They slept. They fucked. They played. No illusions. No lies. Just reality. Take it or leave it. Ranulfo was shocked when one day a cockroach approached him and uttered words to him.

"I can't help feel you're not really a cockroach."

"How could you tell?"

"You're enjoying yourself too much."

"It's wonderful being a cockroach."

"That's what differentiates you from us. You have turbulent emotions. We cockroaches have calm and peaceful emotions."

"Can all cockroaches talk?"

"Yes, but somehow, we don't need to fill up the silence. We are content with the silence."

"We humans hate the silence. We call it Nothingness."

"Nothingness! Hahaha. But the silence is not nothing, it's music!"

"Yes, heavenly."

"I guess you are one of the metamorphosed?"

"What do you mean?"

"It happens occasionally. Usually, excessively sensitive individuals who feel they don't belong to the human world but lack the confidence to do anything about it. We have one former Franz Kafka living among us."

"Really."

"Yes. He's got three wives and is as happy as can be. Not a dark mood passes through his mind; he even smiles, which is strange for a cockroach."

"It's a great life."

"One has to be careful, however," he warned me.

"Why?"

"Humans—they don't like cockroaches. Nasty creatures they are. They're anti-nature. They step on us, poison us. Humans are obsessed with expressing their hatreds. They can't let be. They have no tolerance."

I got to know Conrad the cockroach very well. We became the best of chums. He was intelligent, witty, warm, and charming. It was through him that I met the love of my life: his sister Charlene. She embodied everything I sought in a woman. Smart, funny, kind, and sensual. Who would have thought that my ideal woman would turn out to be a cockroach? In fact, being a cockroach was my ideal life. Life as a cockroach was based on freedom. They never compromised on that freedom. Never! Unlike human beings who must enslave themselves to work, money, God, politics, and so on. But let us talk about Charlene: I love Charlene! She was not irrational, not self-centred, nor small-minded. It was not a struggle to love her. She was a delight. Not like my flatmate Nunta, who was most undelightful. Nunta personified everything that was wrong with the human race. He was selfish, hot-tempered, and unbearably boring. He was a physics student suffering from mental entropy. He had a dog called Satan, and together they barked all day long. I think they competed in barking...they both loved making raucous noises at the TV set as if the actors could hear them. But forget him, let's talk about Charlene...I could only think positively about her...I was so happy. How many times have I said that!

One day, Charlene and I took a trip to the kitchen. My bedroom had become food scarce on account that I, as a human, was not around to drop my food crumbs. The journey was long and dangerous. Outside my bedroom loomed the large and insane figure of Nunta. As a human, Nunta was frightening, but as a giant, he was downright terrifying. Amazing how many whackos there are among the human species. Animals or insects don't go insane. It seemed so easy to go crazy inside if you were human. The human mind was not built for strength...it was soft...ready to crack...from the weight of existence, the foot of God on one's skull...

"Watch out for feet," they warned us as Charlene and I made our trek across the living room to get to the kitchen. I noticed Nunta sitting in his armchair watching TV and puffing marijuana as usual; he liked to obliterate his consciousness. I hesitated to be in his diabolical presence.

"He won't notice us," Charlene assured me. "He's engrossed in his TV, and he appears to be oblivious to his surroundings."

"I don't trust Nunta at all. He's mean and despicable. The only thing he loves in the world is his dog Satan, and Satan is the only thing that loves him. They're both crazy."

"Let's wait till he leaves the room."

"Well, all right."

So we waited...and waited...for hours...days...there was no way he was getting out of that armchair...he ate there...he slept there...he pissed and shat there. He was in one of those drug and TV dazed state where his armchair had become his Throne in Paradise. We couldn't wait any longer as we were hungry. So we took our chances.

We scurried as fast as we could to the kitchen.

"Fee Fi Fo Fum I smell the blood of cockroach scum," Nunta bellowed. We looked above and saw Nunta's large and smelly feet descending fast upon us. We scrambled away, narrowly avoiding being crushed. We took cover beneath the refrigerator.

"I hate cockroaches!" shouted Nunta, peering under the fridge. His bad breath billowing upon us.

Nunta was the ugliest thing you'd ever seen up close. I embraced Charlene. Nunta had vanished, and we could hear him rummaging through the kitchen cabinets. We knew what was coming, so we made a break for it.

"You can't get away from me, you dirty cockies!" Nunta chased us, but this time armed with a can of lethal insect spray. We saw the door of my bedroom, so close and yet so far away. A burst of insecticide sprayed the air and rained down on us, searing our sensitive skins. We felt like we were on fire. Charlene gave me a quick kiss and a hug.

"I love you, Ranulfo. Hopefully I'll see you again in the next life."

But before I could tell her that I loved her, we both went into a spasm.

Charlene was squirming in pain, choking...we were dancing the dance of death.

Darkness descended upon us.

The insecticide must have caused a chemical reaction in me, for when I regained consciousness, I was in the living room, naked and human. Nunta was still embedded in his armchair, smoking dope and watching dopey television. I searched for Charlene in the pile of carpet. I could not find her. I returned to my bedroom and cried. I saw Conrad and called out to him. He didn't recognise me, so he fled.

"I'm sorry, Conrad. Your sister Charlene is dead. I didn't take good care of her."

Days passed. Then months went by. I had readjusted to being a human. It was difficult, but what helped me were my fond memories of Charlene, Conrad, and all those wonderful cockroaches I knew and loved. How I longed to be a cockroach again. So whenever I came across a lone star twinkling in the night, I would make a wish, that delicious wish, to be a cockroach again, free and happy. Set me free from the ball and chain of humanity!

# CHAPTER 11

## The Goodie Family TV Show

Welcome to the most perfect family in the world. Meet Greg, a great husband and dad, an architect, Mary, his wife, a loving mother, and devoted housewife, their two boys, Greg and Greg, and two girls, Greg and Greg. Let us meet their dog, Ralphie. Look at Ralphie. See how beautifully shampooed his shaggy white and black hair is. Sit Ralphie. Beg. Roll over. Play dead. Kill the intruder. Thank you, Ralphie. Good doggie woggie. The Goodie family is so perfect that they have their own television show, which airs every Wednesday night at 7:30 on Channel 6.

The Goodie family were having dinner. Mary had cooked them roast beef with nutritious servings of brussel sprouts, corn on the cob, and baked potatoes.

"This is really delicious, Mum," complimented the eldest son, Greg.

"Thank you, Greg."

"You're a fantastic cook," said father Greg, pecking a dry kiss on Mary's cheek, suitably free of germs and bacteria.

"Let's give a cheer for Mum," said Greg the eldest girl, lifting her glass of milk. "Hiphip!"

"Hooray!" roared all the Gregs.

"Hip hip!"

"Hooray!" their whiter-than-white teeth flashing.

All the while, the TV crew stood in the background filming all this wholesome activity. Watching this sitcom from outside the dining room window was a snake, long, shimmering, with gold and brown scales. Inside the snake was Mort, King Prawn's assassin; not inside the stomach, as the snake was only a costume. He had been watching this suburban paradise for the past three days, keeping an eye on their souls, searching for flaws in its structure. Mort the snake had selected this family to be dispatched to Hell. King Prawn was evil; good was his opposite. Mort had to destroy the opposition. There was no room for duality in the absolute world of tyranny. The Goodie Family presented an elephant challenge to Mort, for he did not merely want to execute them but also kill their souls. An elephant challenge indeed, for the Goodie family were an elephant herd of goodness. They were good, the snake analysed, because they were happy and contented with their lives. Therein lay the key to their ruin.

After the Goodie family said their goodnights to each other, said their prayers to God, thanking him for their joy and prosperity, went to bed, did not make love, or masturbate, slept without obstruction of insomnia, and dreamt without weirdness or terror, the snake crept into the master bedroom and slithered under the blanket where Mr. and Mrs. Goodie lay. The snake was examining Mrs. Goodie's exposed vulva, and proceeded to diddle her clitoris with his long, soft tongue. Mrs. Goodie was at that moment dreaming, and her dream was of the usual kind, stories of supreme saccharine. This dream was of her in the kitchen, making pancakes for her family (everything she did was for the family). Suddenly, the dream deviated from its wholesomeness when she started to orgasm explosively in front of her family as she sat with them at the table. She was emitting screams of ecstasy to the bewilderment of Greg, Greg, Greg, Greg, and whatshisname...Greg! Her body was writhing and convulsing, completely engrossed in pleasure. Her vagina was a pool of convulsive joy. She needed to be touched, so she ripped her clothes off, and lay on the table, hot pancakes with syrup on her back, and screamed for her husband. She woke up soaked in sweat. Her heart was pounding wildly, her vulva popping like popcorn. The pleasure was immense, and she allowed it to continue until she could not help but jump up and sit on her husband's startled face, her husband nearly suffocating, as she pressed down hard on his long nose. After the explosive climax, she collapsed in exhaustion. Her husband was left wondering whether it was all a dream. He went to sleep, and when he woke up in the morning, he decided that it had all been just a silly dream. Mary, too, decided that her sitting on her husband's nose, which was slightly bruised, was just a dream. She promptly dismissed the whole embarrassing event from her mind, and for the rest of the day she irreproachably pursued her duties and chores of being a good wife, mother and citizen. Later that night, she wanted to make love to her husband. This was very surprising, as it was a Monday night, and never in their entire relationship had they ever made love on a Monday night, if for no other reason than routine, which they regarded as a bulwark against chaos and madness. Her husband complied and gave her the standard fifteen minutes of foreplay, copulation, and manual masturbation. After coitus, he closed his eyes to sleep. He concluded that Monday night was indeed a silly night for making love. Usually, after the allotted fifteen minutes, Mary, too, would fall into an unannounced sleep. But tonight, sleep nagged at her that it would not arrive for a while. Mary was very awake with desire and frustration. There was a great hole in

184

her that needed to be filled with a flood of pleasure. There was none forthcoming, so she forced herself to sleep, pursuing sleep to anaesthetise her painful, unanswered desires. Later, while she was sleeping, the snake crept into her bed covers, and her dreams began to spiral into a sensual frenzy. She had been dreaming that she and her family were visiting the zoo and appreciating all the animals that came into view— the sad orangutans, the bored rhinoceros, the lazy lions, and the hungry zebras. Presently, they were admiring the elephants chewing hay on the stony floor of their Art Nouveau cage.

"Oh Mummy, look how big the elephants are," commented one of the Gregs.

"Yes," Mary drooled, her gaze fixed on the elephant's penis. "How wonderfully big it is." She felt a quivering between her legs, a feeling of expansion like a balloon being blown. It was a delicious sensation, and every movement of expansion brought greater dimensions of pleasure. She groaned and moaned, and her husband asked her if she was having indigestion from the ice cream sundae they had earlier.

A Greg laughed. "Mummy's put on a really funny face," and he made a funny face like her orgasmic mother.

This growing abyss inside of her craved to be filled, and it grew and grew until she felt one with the movement.

'Mama!' cried Greg, the youngest son. "You're a vagina!"

People around her screamed; she had transformed into a vagina, a huge, quivering, hairy, stinky, soaking, monstrous vagina with a maw ready to devour anyone within reach. She pounced onto the elephant's big cock and banged on the helpless creature. But that was not large enough. She needed something larger. Mary the Vagina enveloped the whole elephant. Then the other elephant was sucked into the vortex of her desire. Like a video game Pac-Man, she swallowed everything in her path, people, animals, buildings, ships. Eventually, like King Kong, she was atop the Empire State Building, riding it, screaming, "Fuck me, big boy!" while fighter planes buzzed around her trying to shoot her down. But Mary the Vagina was too strong, too powerful as it grew and grew, until the next day, the whole of New York was swept into her. Mary the Vagina was a cancer consuming the whole planet earth. Mountains, rivers, and whole nations were soon devoured. Not only was the planet doomed, but the solar system and perhaps the universe as well. The whole universe fucked to death by Mary's Vagina.

Mary woke up, totally exhausted, and she screamed, "What a funfuckingtastic dream!"

She returned to sleep, endeavouring in vain to bring back her orgasmic dream. The next day, Mary was happy and playful but absentminded. For breakfast, she served her family fried cornflakes, boiled bread, and sunny-side-up eggs in a bowl of milk.

"Mum, we can't eat these?"

But she didn't hear them; she was lost in another world, a world opposite to the world of the Goodie family. A world of selfish bliss.

When suppertime came, the food served was worse: raw beef, uncooked rice, and unboiled corn on the cob. Not only that, but the house was in disarray, pots and plates unwashed, carpets unvacuumed, and clothes unironed. No one could mention anything to her because she was unreachable, so dreamylost was she.

"Mary, the roast beef is…um…unroasted," bravely spoke husband Greg, who had been forcing himself to eat the raw beef for the past half hour out of politeness.

"Thank you, dear," was all she said, distractedly.

"The rice isn't boiled," ventured Greg the eldest girl.

And then, shock of all shocks, Mary exploded red in the face and yelled at her daughter, telling her not to whine or she would ram her hand down her throat and pull out her stomach.

All the jaws of the Gregs dropped. Was this Mary Goodie, the goodest mother in the world?

"What are you looking at?" she snapped. "You look like a bunch of kids mooning their arses out the car windows." She howled with laughter, one of those cruel, ego-hurting laughs.

All the Gregs cried. Mary came back to her senses, apologised for her behaviour, then cooked the beef, the rice, and the corn, and everyone was happy again.

However, the next morning, after a funfuckingtastic dream, Mary served them for breakfast bacon in a bowl of milk, toasted egg, and a glass of bread. After a fortnight of midnight trysts, the snake or Mort calculatingly ceased visiting Mary, and she fell into a great depression. She had become addicted to her sensuous dreams, and their cessation left her frustrated and bored. She became irritable and tense. Her temper was getting shorter and shorter. She lost interest in her home, children, and husband. Sexually, she demanded much more from her husband, who was politely obliging but ultimately unsatisfying. He lacked passion and imagination. Not only did she condemn him sexually, but she also began to scrutinise his overall personality, finding him boring, narrow-minded, and incredibly stupid. Although her dreams had stopped coming, she resorted to fantasies and masturbation as a substitute. One favourite fantasy of hers was of her possessing hundreds of vulvas, which covered her entire body, and she would make love to a hundred men simultaneously. Mary would masturbate for hours, lost in her fantasies. But fantasies were not real, so she despaired. Next day, she seduced Ricky the TV Repairman. Then Mel the Milkman. Soon, she was having affairs with George the Grocer, Peter the Politician, Angus the Accountant, Harry the Horticulturist, Paul the Pervert, Frank the Football Player, Michael the Midget, Sam the Soldier, Quinn the Quadriplegic, Zak the Zombie, Rodney the Rhinoceros, Henry the Headless Horseman, and Morton the Moron.

However, this spate of promiscuity did not make her happy or content. There was no man or enough men in the world to fill the void in her soul. Promiscuity was not a cure but a symptom. She was afflicted with the disease of discontent. Did Mort ruin Mary, or did it simply remove the buffets that protected her? Mary was a simple woman, and she had led a simple life. She was brought up by simple bourgeoisie parents, educated at Catholic schools, worked as a receptionist, and married Greg the architect who designed shopping centres. Everything was all right in the world of Mary Goodie until the snake came along, for the snake revealed to her a greater world than the simple but restrictive world she lived in. She sought out that greater world, just like Eve, the first woman, or Madame Bovary, and like all of them, she was cast out of Paradise. Perhaps the obstacle to the greater world was the men in their lives. Perhaps in a world without men, they could have reached the greater world.

Hmm...perhaps K would be better off without me. I can't make her happy. O when will she realise she should not depend on me for her happiness? No man in the world can reach into her soul and make her happy. Only she can do that.

The fall of Mary Goodie had also dragged her family down with her. Compensatingly, their TV show's ratings rose dramatically, as it was no longer a wholesome family show catering to the wholesome minority, but a sex and sin soap opera catering to the millions and millions. The world was not only interested in the amorous adventures of Mary Goodie but also in the sad fortunes of the rest of the Goodie family, owing to the neglect of love and food by Mary. Greg, the eldest boy, became a psychopathic punk, joined a punk group called "The Genital Mutilations" and was the secret assassin that shot President John F Kennedy. Moving along, Greg, the eldest daughter, became a prostitute, a cocaine addict, an actress in B grade Sri Lankan movies, and married a top underworld criminal, Jimmy Snot, who was involved in drugs, prostitution, and skin care products. The third Greg, the youngest girl, became a manic-depressive poet specialising in TV jingles, once attempted suicide by dressing herself up as a duck during duck season. She founded a conservation movement that advocated for the rights of flies, a movement that later took to terrorist tactics e.g. boobytrapping fly sprays which would explode in the hands of the users. Last but not least, the youngest Greg, the cutest and most loveable Greg of them all, became a cynical, self-centred, ruthless door-to-door salesman selling carpet cleaning products, who in his callous pursuit of power, profit, and plain nastiness, ruined countless carpets. He became a billionaire and married a beautiful woman who despised him but adored him only for his belly button. Yet compared to the other Gregs, he was still the cutest and most loveable Greg of them all, even though his friends, business associates, and wife considered him a low-down stinking rat who could not be trusted to be left alone with a pastrami sandwich.

And now let us speak of the lugubrious tale of Greg Goodie, the doting and dopey husband of Mary the Slut. Before the snake diddled Mary's clits, he was a happy and contented architect who was the leading designer of shopping centres. He was the famous architect of the greatest shopping centre in the world, CONSUMER CITY, a 100-storey department store situated in downtown Addis Ababa, the capital of Ethiopia. Greg Goodie was a happy man. He had a wonderful job, a wonderful family, and a wonderful home. What more could he ask for? It was his wife who started asking for more. It all began when one night, his wife mounted his nose and achieved orgasm. She changed dramatically after that. She became lazy, vague, moody, touchy, and downright mean. She began to demand more from him sexually. He was obliging, but he failed to satisfy her. Actually, she did not want satisfaction, she wanted to be overwhelmed. He was not the overwhelming type. She resented and even despised him. It took a heavy toll on him. He became impotent. His penis cowered before her powerful, insatiable cunt. He looked to his wife for sympathy and patience, but all he got was her withering judgement. Greg Goodie had always been a gentle soul and would never even hurt a fly of any religious persuasion, except Episcopalian. He was a person who kept his feelings to himself, and when he did speak out he expressed them in objective correlatives. Whenever he was hurt, he would refer to tragic historical events, such as the plight of the Red Indians, so that since he became impotent, the main topic of conversation during family dinner was the massacre of Pine Creek, where American soldiers scalped, mutilated, castrated, and burned the Indians, men, women, and children, and how some sadistic soldiers paraded about with mutilated vaginas and penises on their caps. All the Gregs would vomit their dinners, but gladly, since Mary would serve them rotten dinners. His sufferings affected his work adversely. His new designs for shopping centres were exact replicas of Jewish extermination camps, and he named them appropriately: Auschwitz, Dora, Buchenwald, etc. No need to say that they were colossal flops.

One morning, Greg Goodie tried on underwear three sizes too large, which he took from his bedroom drawer. He didn't let it worry him until the next morning, when he failed to get into underwear two sizes too small. Printed on the red underwear was "Big Where it Counts". He went to ask his wife, who was still asleep. She was shrouded in bed covers, so he removed them, revealing her naked bottom. There were some marks on her lovely posterior. He took his reading glasses and read the marks. On her left cheek was scrawled "You have a great arse" and it was signed "Lazarus the Born Again Christian", and on her right cheek was "George the Greek Gynaecologist loves Mary the Moll". Greg commenced to think about the poor Indians massacred at Wounded Knee.

"Help! Get me out of here!" screamed out a voice somewhere in the room.

Greg was startled and looked around.

"Help me, please. I can hardly breathe!" cried the voice.

Greg looked under the bed and inside the wardrobe.

"I'm here! Look!"

The voice appeared to be coming straight from his wife's vagina. That couldn't be possible, so he looked elsewhere.

"I'm inside here!" shouted the voice more desperately.

The voice did stream out of her vagina. He peered into her vagina and nearly died of a heart attack when he saw a man trapped inside. "Help! Get me out of here!"

"What do you want me to do?"

"Give me a hand and pull me up!"

Greg reached into his wife's vagina and grabbed the man's hand. He pulled hard, dragging the naked man out.

"Thanks a lot," said the man, looking very happy and relieved. "I didn't think I'd ever get out of there. I've been in there for over three days."

"Who are you?"

"I'm Brian the Bricklayer," he smiled, offering a handshake.

But Greg refused his hand; he was furious. "What were you doing in my wife's vagina?"

The bricklayer stammered, "Your...your...wife's...wife's ...well you see...it was dark...and I fell...and I didn't know it was your wife's...well, gotta go." The man ran and jumped out of the bedroom window, crashing through the glass.

Greg Goodie was stumped as to what to do next. All he knew was that it hurt real bad inside. And this hurt grew more painful till tears flowed from his eyes. But the tears would not wash away the pain, which he wanted to go away. He screamed, hoping the pain would fly out of his body, wafted by his scream. He screamed and screamed until his mind broke. He collapsed to the floor, unconscious.

When Greg Goodie woke up, he was no longer himself but Sleeping White Dick, survivor of the Pine Creek Massacre. Sleeping White Dick was wretched and wrathful for the white man had slaughtered his wife and children and his village. He was alone, and he felt he had betrayed his family by surviving.

"I, Sleeping White Dick, must avenge the spilt blood of my family, my wife, Big Cunt, my children, Ugly Shit, Little Degenerate, Heroin Addict, and Manic Depressive. I will kill all white men. I will kill until I die. Now I must find war weapon.

Sleeping White Dick failed to recall how he entered this huge flat walled cave, which had five bedrooms, a kitchen, a living room, a dining room, a laundry room, and a double garage. "Cave must be owned by very rich bear." Inside the bear's laundry, he found an axe. "Good tomahawk. Now must kill white men. But first must do war dance." He went out to the backyard, lit a bonfire in the middle of the lawn, using books, magazines, and furniture as firewood, and around the burst of flames he danced and chanted, invoking the gods for the power to kill plenty of white men. When he had completed his war dance, he was ready to kill...

However, he was hungry, and, fortunately, the bear that lived in the cave left three bowls of porridge on the dining table. He took a sip from each bowl. The first was too hot. The second was too cold. But the third one was just right, so he gobbled it all up. The warm porridge succeeded in making him a tad sleepy, upstairs he went to the bedroom to take a nap. The first bedroom was a mess, posters of punk stars were plastered all over the walls, and ouch the bed was made of nails. The next bedroom was bright red, like a brothel. A mirror suspended from the ceiling directly above the silk sheeted bed. The third bedroom was barren, except for a mattress and scores of paper filled with poetry strewn all over the floor. Misery, misery, misery, I love you, O misery, read one of the poems. The fourth bedroom was an office, cluttered with desks, files, computers, and the bed was a couch with a sign on it saying "Casting Couch". The bed was just right.

At that moment, the Greg children arrived home. They were hungry and went to the dining room, where they had left bowls of porridge.

"Some prick has left a strand of hair in my porridge!"

"Some prick has left some snot in my porridge!"

"Some silly prick has eaten up my fucking porridge!"

They marched up to their respective bedrooms.

"Some prick has blunted the nails on my bed."

"Some prick has come on my vibrating bed."

"Some prick has stepped on my beautiful poems."

"And there's a sleeping prick on my bed!"

The Gregs went to the youngest Greg's room to lynch the culprit.

"Get off my bed!" shouted the youngest and cutest Greg.

Sleeping White Dick awoke and stood up.

"White men!" shouted Sleeping White Dick in a rage. "Now I avenge the blood of my family and village!" He grabbed his tomahawk and swung it down on cute baby Greg, splitting his head, and, well, he didn't look cute anymore. Dislodging the axe from the dead Greg's skull, he charged at the three remaining Gregs, who were frozen with terror, and decapitated them all with one huge swing.

At that moment, his wife woke up and went to the bedroom to tell them to shut up. She saw blood and gore. She saw her husband with a mad look in his eyes and a bloodied axe in his hand. She screamed and ran. He chased after her. He thought Mary Goodie was General George Custer because of her long blonde hair. They ran over tables, chairs, and, finally, he cornered her just right in front of the TV camera, which was filming the very last episode of The Goodie Family.

"Now look here, Greg, I'm your wife, you promised to love me for better or for worse, and just because I've given you the worst does not cancel out your obligation. You must love me! Regardless how I make you suffer, cheat on you, insult you, neglect you, despise you, and do absolutely nothing to make you happy, you cannot break your vows. And if you kill me with that axe, I'm warning you, I'm going to divorce you!"

Down came the axe on poor Mary's head. At just that moment, the cavalry came to the rescue and blew the head off of Sleeping White Dick, formerly Greg Goodie, ex-goodest man in the world. Hmmm…Oh yes, it wasn't the cavalry that came, it was the Hollywood Police, who from next week will start their new series to replace the now defunct Goodie Family Show.

Mort was watching all this on TV from his headquarters. He had succeeded in destroying the souls of the Goodie Family. Who was next, pondered Mort. Mo believed that there was no soul on earth that could not be destroyed. Even perhaps Queen Clytoris. The thought intrigued him...

# CHAPTER 12

## Golderella

I'm sick of being single. I want a family to take to the moon for a picnic. I want to be disturbed by brats, not by ideas, which jolt me in the middle of the night. Time to get mellow. No more hacking at sacred cows with butter knives. K,K,K, let us pair up like a forever sandwich!

King Prawn, weary-sick of his self (isolation-heavy), decided to get himself a wife, a luminous kamikaze angel who would save him from his personal Hades. He had not thought of women for a long time. After Queen Clytoris, he lost all sexual desire for women, replacing it with a desire for conquest and glory. But his calendar of conquest and glory was over. His domestic days must begin. And to domesticate himself, he sought a wife, to ride the wilderness out of him, to put him to pasture. He arranged a Royal Ball, inviting all the eligible women (or not, he didn't care) in his kingdom.

The kingdom was astir with excitement. It was a chance of a lifetime. One excited family was the Stone family, a mother and her three daughters plus one stepdaughter. They were a good, affectionate family except for the stepdaughter, Golderella. She was one super bitch. Not only cunning and manipulative, but she was also the most beautiful woman in the Kingdom. Now she planned to marry King Prawn. For his Kingdom. Not King Prawn.

Golderella had a fairy godfather who was hopelessly in love with her, doing everything she bade him to do. For her, he turned people she loathed into toads. He even turned toads into handsome princes to satisfy her gargantuan lust. In return for these services rendered, he got absolutely nothing from her except the opportunity to gaze upon her beauty. She despised him; she thought him ugly and a fool. But let us not be too critical of Golderella. When young and innocent, she was abused by her uncle, and this experience embittered her. She was upon a fork in the road, and she had to choose to become either a victim or a victimiser. She chose the latter. Her uncle had wounded her, and all this pain inside her she chose to inflict on other people rather than upon herself. She had three stepsisters: Lucy, Kerry, and Sherry-Anne. They were the nicest women you could ever meet. Golderella loathed them; they were so plain. She believed that beauty was the most important thing in the world. It was power, like the sun, the ocean, these great forces of beauty, invincible, inhuman. Ugliness was weakness, like sickness, decay, rust, wounds, humanity. Beauty was immortality, ugliness was death. Her three stepsisters were death. They were wicked witches, spiders of dark will, villains to the heroes and heroines of beauty. But quite the contrary, these women were more like angels. Messengers of God. Servants of Truth. Golderella had no power over them. Her beauty was meaningless to them. They merely regarded her as rather vain and superficial. Golderella was merely gilded.

As usual, Golderella gazed longingly at the mirror. She was irresistible to herself. "Mirror, mirror, on the wall, who's the foxiest lady of them all?" she asked for the umpteenth time.

"You, of course, Golderella," answered the mirror.

"Stop drooling," said Golderella as saliva ran down the mirror.

"I can't help it. You're so beautiful. I want you, Golderella. I want you. I love you so much. Let's get married."

"I want to marry the King."

"Marry me, and you shall have the greatest love of all—yourself."

"How tempting," and she started to drool from the corners of her mouth.

"Will you marry me?"

"No, but let's fuck!" Golderella dived into the silvery mirror. Inside, she saw herself sprawled out in bed, naked, desirable, and full of lust. "Come to me," beckoned the other Golderella. "Come to me…"

Golderella gathered herself in her arms, kissed herself and flew away on the wings of desire.


### THE STORY OF THE MIRROR


Once upon a time, angels were like birds. They flew across the sky in patterns like a dance troupe. The approving sun touched their large, beautiful wings as they circled, swooped, and ascended the air. It was a happy universe, with no sadness darkening any spots. When Mirror was born, he seemed like an ordinary angel. But as he grew older, angels noticed how beautiful his eyes were. Angels came to gaze upon his eyes. One angel called Satan gazed a little longer at his eyes. Then he saw something and flew away in fright. The next day, curiosity drove him to gaze once more into Mirror's eyes. Instantly, he was overcome with fear. He wanted to fly away, but he was determined to get to the bottom of the mystery. He saw a strange face inside Mirror's eyes staring back at him. This strange face was also studying him. He tried to communicate with him, but the stranger merely aped his movements. Was he mocking him? This was rather rude, so he shot an angry glance. He became angrier, but so was the stranger. He shouted, and so did the stranger. He wanted to ignore the stranger, but he couldn't. He wasn't sure why, but he loved him. He hated him as well. He spoke to him once more. But again, he imitated him. Then, uncomprehendingly, he cried. The stranger cried too. This stranger knew everything that he felt. This stranger was no stranger. He then realised that this stranger was himself. He was trapped inside and couldn't get out, unable to communicate with the outside world. He was alone. Satan was so enraged that he shot up into the sky, freeing himself from the pattern of the angels. He wanted to blast out of the earth's embrace and lose himself in the dark universe. But he couldn't. He was weak. He fell, plunging headlong into the sea. He splashed into the blue mother. The sea was calm before exploding as he burst up into the sky. He flew directly into the flock of angels, scattering them in fear. He swerved and chased after an angel. When he saw the bright sun, he flew at it with all his might. He wanted to dive into the fire. But it was searing hot. It was too powerful. He stopped, turned, and shouted at the angels, "I am Satan! I am alone forever!" Satan flew away and never returned. Beyond the universe, he flew.

The angels were shocked and confused. This was most extraordinary. They were perplexed about what had happened. There were no easy answers. They dismissed it from their minds and flew back into their patterns. Their comfortable routines. As the days passed, everything was happy. Satan remained a vague memory. Then it happened once more. An angel gone amok. Smashed the pattern. Shouted his own name, and flew away, vanishing beyond the sky. It was as if a contagious disease afflicted the angels one by one, until there was only one angel left. It was Mirror. He was alone. He was afraid. He wept. Tears dropped from his eyes. These tears crystallised into mirrors. The humans crawling on the earth discovered these mirrors. They stood on their feet, proud, vain, and, just like the angels, went insane. Mirror led a long, lonely life. He flew a pattern of his own.

One day he left. The sky was empty when the humans looked up. The angels had gone.

## THE BALL

From his throne King Prawn observed the swirl of people on the dance floor. Women smiled at him, all endeavouring to catch his eye. King Prawn was unmoved, looking morose and bored. Before him was a glittering spectacle, the women arrayed in sparkling gowns of delicious colour, the men smart in tuxedos and military uniforms. Two large chandeliers bearing a myriad of candles glittered above the eddying dancers. But King Prawn was unimpressed. He had lost all concern for the external world; sinking was he into his interior twilight.

"My Royal Majesty," said the Court Jester, "a Ball for your balls but you bounce not. There are many great catches present, why not grab hold of one?"

"They're not women," growled the King. "They're girls. They think life is a fairy tale of handsome princes and beautiful princesses. They expect so much from life and get nothing. I want a strong woman. I am an ogre. I have caused the deaths of millions. I don't have tender hands."

"Maybe you want a woman with steel breasts."

"I'm a lion and I need a lioness to mate. A lamb is a lion's supper."

"Two lions on the throne. What a jungle our Kingdom would be."

"You are a coward, Royal Fool."

"Lovers are all cowards. Love always makes one anxious."

At this moment, the whole crowd gasped—entering the hall was Golderella, ablaze in a gown of gold.

"Conceited ass," muttered King Prawn.

She curtsied to King Prawn, and her large, sensuous mouth opened. "My grace, I hear that you are looking for a bride. Look no further, I am the one for you. I am Golderella, 20 years of age, the most beautiful woman in the world. Not only physical beauty do I possess, but I also have great intelligence. Intelligence, mind you, not wasted on Truth or anything abstract but focused monomaniacally on power. Power is what makes kingdoms. On the other hand, love is what makes peasants. Let them have all the love they want. All I want is power, and that is why I came here. I want to be Queen but not your silly obedient wife. I want to rule and make the peasants suffer!"

King Prawn was quite impressed with the honest but sick-minded Golderella.

"I will give your proposal great consideration."

"Excuse me, my Royal Majesty," a voice squeaked behind the glittering Golderella. Stepping forward was Golderella's stepsister, Lucy. "Um, I think you will be making um a grave error if you marry um Golderella. She, my Royal Majesty, is a cold, cruel woman who, um if given power, would be a scourge on you and your kingdom. On the other hand um I will make a great Queen because I care greatly for you and the Kingdom."

"What is your name?" asked King Prawn.

"Lucy, my Royal Majesty."

"Lucy and Golderella, Light vs. Dark, Good vs Evil. Which do I choose? Upon this choice, I decide the fate of my soul and my Kingdom."

## THE CONTEST

The Court Jester commenced the proceedings: "The contest to decide who will marry King Prawn will be determined by a series of questions. Whoever gives the most satisfying responses wins. The contest will be adjudicated by King Prawn. Let the contest begin!"

"Tell me, sweet Lucy, would you enjoy wearing leather knickers and whipping me into a frenzy?" asked the King.

"I wouldn't um do you the dishonour," she answered with a blush.

"Sour Golderella, if two mothers and a baby came to you, each claiming to be the mother of the child, how would you solve the problem?"

"Off with their heads! How dare they bother me with frivolous problems!"

"Lovely Lucy, if I were angry with you, and in a fit of anger I punch you in the nose, what would you do?"

"Go to the hospital and have my nose mended. Then um I shall ring the police and have you charged with assault and battery."

"Answer this riddle, grumpy Golderella. In the morning I walk on four, in the afternoon I walk on two, and in the evening on three."

"Who fucking cares!" shouted Golderella, with a great frown.

"Lucy, who fucking cares?"

"People um with intelligence um compassion and um responsibility."

"Golderella, does penis size matter to you?"

"Depends. If it's my lover, yes; if it's my husband, the size of his bank account matters more."

"Will you wake me up?"

"Depends um on your dreams."

"Will you die for me, Golderella?"

"You will kill for me."

"Lucy, what is a black hole?"

"It is um a dead star whose gravity's um power exceeds the speed of light, and um since nothing can travel faster than um light that whatever is in or enters the star cannot escape nor can be seen from um the outside. The dead star becomes um invisible like a black hole. Anything that enters the black hole becomes an um invisible prisoner forever."

"What is a black hole, Golderella?"

"A fucking hole that is black!"

"Who is Stanley Milgram famous for?"

"He is um a psychologist. He is famous for his um experiments on obedience and authority. His um experiments showed that a major percentage of his human volunteers were um willing to administer up to um 450 volts of electricity to another human being if ordered by an authority in spite of um the evident painful reaction caused by the um jolt."

"Why do we suffer?"

''Because humanity is divided into two groups: sadists and masochists."

"Lucy, why do we love?"

"Because love is glorious and wonderful. It is a challenge to the human spirit because love must be taken care of."

"Why do we die?"

"Because we deserve to die."

"Why do we fuck?"

"To make love, that is um to create love."

"Why do we hate?"

"Because hate is more real and more fulfilling than love."

"What is wrong with the world?"

"Um because we are not perfect. We go astray with our intelligence and our um emotions. We have a great capacity for um um error coupled with our great um capacity for believing we are not in error."

"Who is Ranulfo?"

Golderella laughed with disdain. "Author of this shitwritten novel. He's a man of reaction, not action. Things get done to him; he gets nothing done. He had spent the last eight months not working on this novel because he was too depressed to write.

He screams, cries, gets bored, and eats, eats, eats, but he does not work. A weakling! A coward! A loser! How his girlfriend K puts up with him, I can't understand. She's truly a saint! She deserves the Nobel Peace Prize!"

King Prawn stood up to make an announcement. The crowd was hushed, thick with suspense, wondering who the lucky bride was. "I have decided to marry Lucy."

Golderella fumed, smoke steaming out of her ears. Then, using incantations taught to her by her Fairy Godfather, she zapped Mary into a slimy green frog. Rebeep!

"On second thoughts," said King Prawn, his mouth open like a dead fish, "I shall marry Golderella."

That was how Golderella married King Prawn. And this, my dear readers, was the beginning of the end. But had sweet and sagacious Lucy been the Queen, she might have saved the soul of King Prawn and his kingdom. But that's life for you. Expect the worst!

# CHAPTER 13

## Tomtin

Watch out men, protect your penises, cup your balls because President Carol is gonna get you. It is the system that ladles out the roles, so to change the roles for men and women, President Carol changed the system. President Carol passed legislation to relegate men to second-class citizens.

Demolish their power bases! President Carol was going to strip power from the men.

For a start, in the work force, the central power base, men were to be discriminated against, given lower salaries and lower ranking jobs, mainly in secretarial, retail, and supermarket checkout operations. Furthermore, men were prohibited from performing physical labour; President Carol reasoned that for women to be superior, they must also become physically superior. From lack of hard labour, men's flesh would soften and weaken.

In education, the second most powerful power base, men were to be kept ignorant and stupid, barred from attending university. At school, men were to be brainwashed that they were inferior to women. Writing was impermissible. This included essays, treatises, fiction, poetry, and songs. Only recipes were permitted. In the new power base of social relations, men must be obedient and respectful to women.

Essentially, men must become women. It was decreed that men must wear female garments. The point of this was that female clothing was oppressive and degrading. How could women feel superior or even equal while wearing high heels and a skirt vulnerable to draughts and perverts? Female fashion was clothes for clowns. Let men be the new clowns. President Carol, the perfectionist, did not skimp on the little details. Men were mandated to wear nail polish on their feet and hands. Earrings were deemed a necessary appendage to men's ears. If a man were caught sans earrings...well, it would be sans ears. Women were given crucial control in the power bases of finance, politics, the military, science, sports, art, and education. Men were to be stripped of all power, being conditioned to see themselves as useless and irrelevant to society except as pretty accessories. Burdened by their feelings of worthlessness, they would, as an act of desperation, allow themselves to be used by women, to be objectified. By restructuring the political, economic, and social kebang whereby men felt helpless and inadequate while women were necessary and powerful, President Carol sought to create a psychological divide between women and men, like master and slave.

President Carol had expected the new topsy-turvy laws to incite men to revolt, and she was ready to crush any opposition. How surprised and amused was she when it turned out that the draconian laws brought only happy acquiescence from the men, as if they themselves had asked for their total demotion. The laws finally delivered them from the backbreaking burden of the male ego, which demanded unceasing struggle, competition, and vigilance. The men folded without a punch thrown back, just like the Roman Empire, whose citizens were weary and bored with their invincibility, sought relief in decadence, corruption, and annihilation, finding true peace in defeat, crumpling under the onslaught of the barbarians. The citizens of the dying empire weren't any longer the original conquerors; they were the spoilt, easy-living, cowardly children of conquerors. They were raised to take their strength for granted. They lived on the courage of dead soldiers. So when President Carol and her female warriors, who were building and gathering their strength in the wilderness, decided to dip their toes into the male empire, the men were ready to fall.

The men embraced their new roles with a passion. For example, they took up women's fashions like ducks to water. Men vied with each other for the best and latest wardrobe. Incredible to see tall, burly men, who only a season ago would be seen in pubs in singlets, stubbies, and thongs, now dolled up in the newest Paris couture. Men got hooked on looks. Fashion magazines such as Vogue, once catering to women, were now a thriving market for men. Beauty replaced valour as the foremost male virtue. Beautiful men were idolised in movies and fashion magazines. No longer could one watch a movie depicting men as heroic heroes battling heinous villains, but as frail, passive, ravishing, and ravished creatures in constant need of rescue by some heroic muscle-bulging woman with a cool demeanour and a big punch. As history has shown, events always proceeded to their logical conclusion, minor disagreements became bloody wars, history unfolding to the tiniest fold.

Thus, President Carol's revolutionary edicts reached their most grotesque conclusion. Men had become women so successfully that they probably made better women than women. It was as if the sexists' fantasies of the ideal woman were finally being actualised by the sexists themselves.

The new environment favoured evolutionary permutations. While men had become smaller, slimmer, and less hairy, women had grown taller, stockier, and unmistakably shaggier. Women relished their new position of power. There was more volume in their voices and a heavy leadenness in their movements. The new women enjoyed dominating over men who glided about timidly and lithesomely. Women sought dominance in all planes of life. Once you have power, you abuse it like an addict. Women were no longer content with being the gentle sex. Cruelty was the ultimate expression of power. Crime committed by women was on the rise; even the outrageous notion of women raping men became common tabloid fodder. President Carol annihilated the enemy, and reared a new enemy, more cold-blooded and grasping—President Carol lighted on the realisation that any danger to her political reign came not from men, but from her own sex.

Men posed no threat (only centrefolds) to President Carol. In fact, so safe felt she over men, she tied a knot with one, a lamb-groom for the lioness, President Carol. His name was Tomtin. Formerly, Tomtin was a typical example of a quasi-ape found in bars. Cull him out he's the one sloshed and picking a fistfight with anybody unlucky enough to bump into his personal hirsute space. Day time he worked in the meat factory, cutting cows' throats and hacking their torsos. Ugly was he, folded in fat like a doner kebab, hairy as a porcupine, quills sticking out of him ala St Sebastian. He was a missing link nobody missed. Then suddenly, the new laws whirled him giddy, he transformed dramatically—he lost weight, shaved his body as smooth as a Greek nude stature, rode women's fashions like a Phar Lap clothes horse—and lo and behold, he was a new man, soft and-tender-spoken, with exquisite silken skin, and a derriere, round, glowing, romantic, like the moon. Quickly, Tomtin became renowned for his delectable beauty. Model agencies snapped him up, and his face glimmered on the covers of all the best fashion magazines in the world. For an exorbitant fee, he dared to pose for Penthouse Magazine, very revealing photos indeed, angles and encounters from behind, between, and beneath him. This was where President Carol first noticed him, lusted after him, and arranged to meet him. Pornography for women boomed; it seemed that the new power brokers needed to keep seeing the powerless in defenceless, vulnerable, and degrading poses.

When they first met, Tomtin fell in love and Carol in lust. Revealing Tomtin might be in body, he concealed his heart's desires, and as he talked to President Carol, he played coy.

"You're very beautiful," was President Carol's millionth said opening line.

"Thank you, Ms President," with affected shyness.

202

"I really mean it. You are very beautiful."

"You must say that to all the men you meet."

"No, I don't. You have such beautiful skin." President Carol segues to lightly stroke Tomtin's roseate cheeks.

"I take good care of my skin."

"Taking good care of one's skin is very important. Doctors say touching is very beneficial in maintaining the health of one's skin." Another cue for President Carol to do some subtle groping.

"Yes, I see a masseuse every week."

"She must be very lucky."

"She's a professional."

"Do you have a girlfriend?"

"No."

"I find that hard to believe. Surely droves of women must be hopelessly in love with you."

"I have a very busy schedule. I have little time for a social life."

"I think I'm in love with you," another millionth-uttered line.

"I've had so many women telling me how much they love me. But I know they only want one thing."

"I want only one thing. You."

"I know women. They'll lie to get that one thing."

"I can prove my honesty. Marry me."

"We've only just met."

"I feel as if I've known you a very long time." President Carol commenced to stroke Tomtin's dulcet legs.

"Please don't."

"I want you"

"Please."

"I can't control myself. You're so irresistible."

"Please stop it," and Tomtin sobbed, tears trickling through her mascara and foundation.

"What's the matter, darling?"

"You're just like the other women."

"No, I'm not. I love you."

"I want you to respect me."

"I do respect you."

"Then be patient. I don't want to rush into things. I like to take things slowly."

"Well, I want to marry you now?"

"You'll get bored with me. You're so intelligent."

"No, I think you're wonderful."

"But I won't be able to talk to you about politics."

"Don't worry your beautiful face over such tedious topics. I'll be happy just being with you."

President Carol then kissed the bewitched Tomtin long and passionately.

"Will you marry me?"

"Yes! Yes! Yes!"

President Carol ripped Tomtin's dress off her like it was candy wrapping. Tomtin's pores begged for President Carol. Funny thing about the new sex-reversal laws, the act of sex changed somewhat. Men were no longer the aggressive, probing rhino horn and women the prostrate spread of flesh; now men laid back like a rug and waited. It was now common for men to experience no orgasms during sex. The will to orgasm was gone. The will now belonged to women, who determined the portioning of pleasure. The new power brokers hoarded all the pleasure for themselves.

It was a strange sight to see Tomtin resplendent on his back, his legs wide apart and feet aloft like balloons, while President Carol in between banging humping thumping like a charging beast. After President Carol came (precisely two minutes and thirty-four seconds after contact), she laid beside Tomtin and lit a cigarette.

Tomtin wanted much more, but he was too demure to ask, so he silently despaired, wondering if he was frigid. Nevertheless, he was happy for Carol. Sex was boring, but if she enjoyed it, he didn't mind putting up with it for a couple of minutes of frenzied hustle and bustle. He was in love. Love was more important than sex anyhow.

President Carol and Tomtin were married in the springtime (Carol cynically needed to boost her sagging popularity). Tomtin looked stunning in a white gown with a twenty-foot train. While President Carol was suave and debonair in her tuxedo. It was a grand wedding televised worldwide. The beautiful Romanesque cathedral was filled with the heavenly music of a symphony orchestra fronted by a one-hundred-member boy choir. The archbishop intoned the wedding ceremony, his voice wafting through the thronged streets via amplifiers. When the newlywed couple stepped out, thousands cheered; none had an eye unblemished by a tear.

They honeymooned at Niagara Falls. Like the Niagara, President Carol had an unending supply of spunk when it came to sex. She was insatiable. She demanded sex everywhere: elevators, cars, bathrooms, closets, and even during a "Message to the People" nationwide broadcast (invisible to the viewers was Tomtin's head between President Carol's wet thighs under the table and tangle of microphone wire). Sex as permanent verb. Yet not once did Tomtin experience an orgasm. President Carol never cared to give him one. One time, Tomtin, feeling exhausted and sick with a headache, demurred to President Carol's advances; Carol blew her top and hurled abuse and insults at him with such vehemence it was as if she truly despised him. Underneath the veneer of lust was a lava-core of hate for Tomtin. A hatred for an entire sex deemed inferior by Carol.

Tomtin relented, crying while President Carol banged between his legs like she was stabbing him.

"Hey, I'm sorry, baby," President Carol as she snuggled up to her.

He did not answer, sobbing.

"You have to understand. I need a lot of sex. Power makes me horny," President Carol explained.

"I can't see what's so great about sex."

At this remark, President Carol's eyes turned basilisk. "I don't satisfy you, is that it? You fucking liar! You fucking enjoy sex!"

"Yes, I enjoy sex," he timorously lied out of fear

"Good! Because I want to fuck you now! This time I want to do it behind you."

"Behind me?"

"Yes!" and President Carol showed her clitoris, which had grown massively. "I want to stick it up your arse!" Carol's eyes sick and desperate.

"No, please, please, Carol, please…No!" as Carol rammed her twelve-inch-long clitoris wholly into Tomtin's arse. It hurt Tomtin tremendously, but he obliged meekly for the sake of his wife, Carol, female chauvinist sow.

''You enjoy it, don't you, baby?"

"Yes, my love," he answered with a strained smile.

Then, without warning, President Carol plunged headfirst into Tomtin's arsehole and forced herself forward until she was head to toe inside, thrusting herself to and fro like a giant penis. Tomtin screamed. This wasn't sex, beautiful, mysterious, mutual; this was torture, this was an act of violence. President Carol was out to murder his soul through sex. Tomtin wondered whether he had married a monster. Then he realised he had simply married a woman. Women no longer expressed love; they expressed power. Love was man's terrain, love, the opium of the weak and powerless.

Tomtin contemplated divorce but found out, to his amazement, that he was pregnant. Somehow it happened. The feminisation of men had feminised their bodies. What was more feminine than having babies—changing nappies, interrupted sleep, constant care, and attention—babies were only appropriate for those who had no time for ideas and power, which were now the domain of women. Men bore babies because they were the bearers and caretakers of reality. Tomtin informed President Carol. She was happy, but her attitude changed towards him. Desire was dead. Pregnancy made Tomtin ordinary. He was no longer Beauty's King. He was a plain old househusband who led an unglamourous life of nursing the baby, washing dishes, and cleaning the house. He had become a maid in the eyes of President Carol's eyes. Her eyes began to roam in search of new conquests.

President Carol found new toys to play with. On one official occasion, Tomtin watched his wife spend a vast amount of time talking and flirting with young, single, beautiful men. He could see that the men were attracted to President Carol. He recalled how thrilled he was to know President Carol when he first met her. Powerful women drew Tomtin and all those other men. He had thought marriage to a powerful woman would make him feel secure and safe, for she would always keep things under control. She would ensure his happiness and joy. Tomtin failed to see that power could be evil, something gained through callousness and viciousness. Power was no Princess Charming but the Evil Ogre. Tomtin felt sorry for the young, beautiful men attracted to President Carol, for they were being lured into the cave of the Evil Ogre.

# CHAPTER 14

## Bus Trip

"Hello!"

I jump as if I am awakened from a falling sleep. A woman has taken a seat next to me in the bus, greeted me, and I can't recognise her face.

"Hi," I answer back, offering a nice-to-see-you-again smile as if I knew her.

"You remember me? I'm St Claire."

Double take. "Of course, I remember you. I created you."

"My creator. How's our novel going along?"

"Oh…it's going okay."

"What kind of an eloquent answer is that from a writer?"

"I'm a writer, not a speaker."

St Claire laughs genially. "So…what brings you on this bus so early in the morning?"

"I got a job. It's hell. I don't know how people want to sacrifice their freedom. Eight hours of my day down the gurgler."

"Why don't you quit?"

"The Government's cracking down on dole bludgers. They don't like people who value time more than money. They want to hunt us down. They want us to worship Mammon and kiss his arse. I can't see why it's considered a crime to be a dole bludger. It's a death penalty if you don't want to work. You're not entitled to welfare if you don't want to work. How the hell can I write if I don't have time?"

"You should stand up for your rights as a dole bludger."

"I'm a writer because I'm a coward.''

"That's not true."

"No. I'm a writer because I'm a stupid idiot!"

St Claire laughs.

She says, "I guess writers can't be perfect; they have to understand what it means to be human."

"Oh, I'm so sick of being human. I'd like to be God.''

She gives me a little laugh.

"So, how's your girlfriend K?" she asks me out of the blue.

I laugh at her bluntness. "I haven't seen her for two months."

"Have you broken up with her?"

"We break up all the time. I'm afraid K has little faith in me. She doesn't believe that I could make our relationship work and solve the problems that impede our path to Paradise. Do you know what destroys relationships?"

"Love?" quips St Claire

I laugh. "That's part of it. What destroys relationships is nuclear explosions."

"Yes, well, it also destroys everything."

"No, no, no," my head shaking. "I'm speaking metaphorically. Don't take me literally, I symbolise everything. Let me explain. What causes nuclear explosions is a chain reaction, right? You see, at the beginning of all relationships, everything is perfect. Then, one day, one of the lovers absentmindedly and unintentionally hurts his loved one, who, out of hurt, reacts and retaliates. The reaction goes on and on, each reaction bringing a worse reaction, until bang goes the nuclear explosion. End of relationship. The solution to the problem is simple: one must not react. To do that, one must be calm. One must forgive."

"Easier said than done. Self-control is too difficult. Life is a wave, and we get carried away."

"I think the world can do without the endless waves of human reaction. Let's have real peace and harmony."

"You're beginning to sound like Queen Clytoris."

"Another creation of mine."

"Is she just a fiction character? I still remember meeting you when I was a young girl. I was lost in a forest. You found me and took me home to where you lived. We then travelled into your imagination; we flew into outer space. I fell in love with you that night. I told you to make me grown up, and to marry me. You took me back to my home and made me think it was all a dream. I could never accept that it was a dream. It was too real. My heart could not deny it. And it hurt. What hurt me was the reason why you couldn't love me. Because I wasn't real. A mere fiction character. You can say what you like, but as far as I'm concerned, my feelings are real, and were real back then. You can't take those feelings away from me. I don't know if I'll ever forgive you?"

"Oh St Claire, I'm a novelist and I'm not supposed to get involved with my characters. It's like doctors not getting involved with their patients. Professionally, we have to be detached. "

"Aren't you allowed to have any feelings for your characters? Is it necessary to watch them suffer?"

I evade the sad and probing look of St Claire. I know I am guilty of deliberately making my characters suffer, and all for the sake of Truth. My characters are mere illustrations of the moral struggles of humanity.

"Can't you make us all happy?"

"I don't know. Maybe or maybe not. Depends on the requirements of the novel. You see, St Claire, you play an important role in the novel, you are the heir apparent to Queen Clytoris, you are the Messiah's apprentice. It's important to show the struggles of attaining wisdom. When Queen Clytoris dies, you will be the new saviour of humanity."

The author smiles at St Claire, expecting her to be happy, but instead, to his dismay, he finds her glaring at him, a mad, mad St Claire.

"You're killing off Queen Clytoris! You bastard! How can you do that to such a wonderful woman?"

I look around the bus, and notice people are staring at me as St Claire has raised her voice a notch too loud.

"She's only a fiction character," I tactlessly reply.

"Only a fiction character!" she repeats loudly. "You heartless bastard! She's an object, which you can do whatever you like. Am I an object, too? Maybe that's why you can't cope with K because you can't treat her as an object? She refuses to play the part you wrote for her."

The bus driver is glaring at me from the rear-view mirror. I feel nervous and uncomfortable on a bus full of fiction characters. My immediate desire is to plunge this bus down a cliff. But that would have killed St Claire, who I need for my novel.

"What do you want me to do? Write a sickly-sweet novel where everybody lives happily ever after?"

"Yes," answers St Claire quietly, her hard glare softening.

"I can't. Because that's not what life is all about. I wish it were so, but right this minute, people are suffering meaninglessly."

Her sadness penetrates me, making me feel so guilty and evil. I touch her hand.

"I'm sorry, St Claire. I'm sorry."

She looks at me, her eyes holding me. I turn away, afraid of the heart knowledge that she loves me, and more afraid that I want to reciprocate her love. Feeling spurned, she withdraws her hand from mine.

"I'm getting off in two stops," she tells me.

I do not answer her. I glance out the window and remember that there is a world outside me. The bus makes a stop outside a small apartment block, where from a balcony I could see an old man watching me.

"Well, I might bump into you one day," she says, preparing to leave.

"Yes...what's your phone number? Maybe we can have a chat sometime," I say to her.

"Yes, sure. You have pen and paper."

"Of course, I'm a writer." I take a page from out of my novel, which I carry in my bag.

"Who's Harry the House?" reading from the page.

"A minor character."

"Did he die?"

Reluctantly, "Yes."

"Figures." She jots down her phone number.

When I arrive at work and begin doing my boring and meaningless duties, I think of St Claire, and thinking of her makes my life appear more meaningful. Why can't a novelist fall in love with his characters?

# CHAPTER 15

## Inside the Vagina

Prince Jotel loved Karina's vagina. He loved its many moods, being inside, touching it, playing with it, and driving it crazy with pleasure. Perhaps he loved Karina's vagina more than he loved Karina. They were like two different creatures. Two crazy sisters.

"You should have become a gynaecologist. You're always between my legs, perving at it. What is so fucking fascinating about it, I don't know? I think it's ugly, to tell you the truth."

"Maybe I'll discover the secret of womanhood if I get to really know it."

"I don't understand you men. You want secrets, mysteries, truths, answers. You're always ripping everything apart to find out what is inside."

"How boring if life has no mysteries."

"Life is exciting as it is. A detective story needs a corpse and you're willing to turn the world into a corpse so you can dissect it to your heart's content."

"I love you, I love you, I love you," he whispered to the mouth of the vagina. Could it hear him? he wondered.

"Can I close my legs now?"

"No. The church doors must remain open at all times."

"Sorry, but my cunt is closed for the day." She kneeled and searched for her panties. She rummaged through the whirl of blankets and found it and slipped it on.

"Goodbye, my little furry animal," Prince Jotel said sadly.

The next morning, he crawled into her vagina without her knowing. She was asleep, snoring faintly. Inside, it was dark. Bats fluttered about him. He was scared at first, but he did not feel lost. He came upon a bright forest. Birds were singing, and animals were rustling in the bushes. The whole place bathed in incredible beauty. The colours were intense, ripe, delicious. Heading languidly towards him was a tiger, beautiful and magnificent in its orange and black coat. He wanted to pet it, but the tiger's eyes glinted with malevolence. Prince Jotel scaled up a tree. The tiger stared up at him and lay down. Prince Jotel was prepared to out-wait the tiger. So did the tiger.

Another tiger appeared and joined the waiting tiger. More tigers collected themselves around the tree. Prince Jotel was unconcerned until the tigers began to mutter among themselves, as if hatching some scheme to snare him. After a while, they agreed on something, and a group of tigers arranged themselves into a straight row. Another group of tigers leapt on their backs and formed a second row.

A third row took shape. A pyramid of tigers was being constructed. Eventually, the pyramid would reach him, and he would be smorgasbord. Climbing to the top of the tree, he saw the pyramid was still rising; on the ground, tigers were swarming to join them. He marvelled at their co-operation. But with all these tigers, there wouldn't be much of him to share around. One ear for one, one nose for another, and so on. Would they be as co-operative when they get to eat him? He didn't want to wait around to find out.

He saw an eagle flying his way, and if it got close enough, he could catch a lift. It all depended on luck. He concealed himself as best as he could; he didn't want to scare away his transport. "If it doesn't come my way, then I'm dead." The eagle was flying closer. He braced himself to leap and grab the bird. Only one chance. Now! But it was too soon, the eagle had seen him and made a sharp turn. He made a desperate plunge and was airborne. He grabbed hold of a talon, and he was aloft. He now had a new problem. Could he hold on or fall? He looked around and saw he was encircled by a green horizon and, below, his hanging shadow against the green treetops. For a fleeting second, the silhouette made him appear like an angel. Nothing to do but wait. He had to muster all his physical and mental strength to survive.

Mentally, he wanted to give up. Normally, he luxuriated in his weak character. He enjoyed squandering his life away. But Death was knocking at the door, and he refused to open it. The forest gave way to a lake; he let go and dropped himself into its calm blue arms. As soon as he fell into the water, it turned angry and vicious. Waves tossed him helplessly like a leaf in the wind. He thrashed his arms, trying to swim. A wave chucked him up into the sky, and he fell, only to be thrown up again.

He sank into the depths. Something bore him up. A smooth, strong, silver creature—it was a dolphin—raised him to the surface. He rode the dolphin, and it skimmed over the mountainous waves. Suddenly, the water was calm. He was relieved that it was over. Then, without warning, the waves rose again into a tumult, and he was in fear of his life again. As quickly as it started, it stopped. But he was not relieved, for he anticipated another seizure. The dolphin escorted him to the shore. He patted the dolphin's head but jumped back when he saw it was a shark with a great wide-open mouth. He ran as far as he could on the shore. He planted his face in the sand and fell asleep.

It was night when he awoke. He heard a woman screaming. Was it the pain of childbirth? Was it the pain of anguish? Was it the pain of bereavement? There was a chorus of screaming women, each expressing a different pain. It was terrible, horrific. Then all kinds of noises began to be made—groans, moans, sobs, shrieks, shouts—covering a wide range of emotions from happiness to despair.

The noise stopped except for one sobbing voice. The voice cut him to the heart. "I'm sorry," he heard himself saying. The sobbing went on, inconsolable. The crying was unbearable, as if he was guilty of an unforgivable crime. He wanted to stab a stick into his ear so that he could no longer listen to the voice. He ran into the woods, wondering if he could run away from it. The crying ceased. Now the noise was laughter. He heard female voices mocking, ridiculing, and humiliating him. The laughter pursued him as he ran. He was angry, breaking off a branch to swipe at the darkness. He wanted to burn down the whole forest to stop those cackling taunts. He ran and ran. Finally, the laughter stopped. All was silent, and above him was the bright white moon. Drops of blood appeared on the moon until the whole face was drenched in red. He closed his eyes and fell to the ground, crying. He cried for a long time. His emotions had never been through such a whirligig of extremes. He hated his emotions. He was alien to them. He didn't want to have any. He wanted peace. He found a cave and went in to have a rest. The ground was soft and soothing. Peace washed over his body, and his tears dried up. A sense of security and belonging pervaded him. He felt unafraid. Death, old age, illness, none of it scared him. The feeling stayed and lingered in his heart like whispers. He wanted to remain here for the rest of his life. Months passed. After many months of bliss, a great pain attacked him, as if he was being torn away from the cave. He fought to stay. But he was forcibly ejected. Outside, he cried and cried inconsolably. He turned to the cave, but its entrance was blocked. He knocked and knocked, but it stayed closed.

Nothing to do but to move on.

The seasons passed before his eyes in a space of minutes.

It was winter.

It was spring.

It was summer.

It was autumn.

The seasons besieged him; he sweated, he froze, his body's temperature rose and sank like a roller coaster. Nature dressed and undressed in the clothes of the seasons. In the middle of the forest was a bed covered in luxurious red satin. Scattered on the floor were headless skeletons. Moving closer to the bed, he realised the bed was not red satin, but blood stained. He touched the bed, which was sticky, and found he was attached to the bed and could not free himself. Using his foot as leverage, he stepped on the bed, but it too got stuck. He pulled hard, but he felt stuck to the bed. Out of the corner of his eye, he glanced movement. A spider! Oh Horror! To him, the spider was the incarnation of horror; his mind reeled and dissolved into pure terror. At a closer look, the spider was hairless. The four pairs of legs were definitely of the female humankind. Covering its body were breasts, delectable, scrumptious breasts. Such a beautiful spider she was, purely female, and seemingly possessed no head, just legs, tits, cunt, and arsehole. The spider crawled up on the bed, and Prince Jotel embraced it passionately. He kissed the legs and breasts. The soaking vagina summoned his penis, and he obliged. He was fervent in his lovemaking. The eight legs wrapped themselves around him, and as he was about to climax, a chasm opened up before him. The spider, growling, had a mouth full of sharp fangs and was about to rip his head off. Suddenly, he was lifted into the sky. He felt soft, slender arms carrying him, he felt breasts upon his back, he felt long, beautiful hair tickling his face, he heard a soft, white gown fluttering in the wind, and wings beating in flight. An angel had rescued him. He tried to gaze at the angel's face, but he couldn't twist himself around. She was taking him back to where he began. He landed at the entrance of the vagina. He turned to see his guardian angel, but she had flown away, a bright light receding into the distance. He wanted so much to see her face; he wanted so much to love her. Suddenly, he heard this loud roar. A massive wave of blood surged through. Before he could escape, the blood swept him forward. All he could see was red. Blood, blood, everywhere. He had no will to resist. He was floating down a long, tortuous tunnel, like a river gushing its way to the waterfall.

The blood flushed him out of the vagina.

"What's happened to you?" Karina asked Prince Jotel, covered in blood.

"I've been to heaven, hell, and back," he answered. He gazed studiously at Karina's face. She was a woman. And not a man. She had eyes, a nose, a mouth.

But it was all so incomprehensible.

# CHAPTER 16

## Mary Roses

Let's kill Queen Clytoris. I'm feeling quite tragic today, and besides, I want to get this novel moving along. Towards the denouement. Towards the apocalypse. Let's kill King Prawn, Prince Jotel, Virginia, President Carol, and the whole lot of them. Let them die, after all, we have to die sometime. Let them suffer, life is not a bed of roses, eh? Not only is God evil, but humanity, animals, plants, planets, galaxies, and the rest of the universe—evil, evil, evil! And what is goodness? But suffering without the opportunity for revenge.

The assassin of Queen Clytoris was a woman named Mary Roses. Let us say she had less than admirable parents. Her daddy was a businessman who cared only for his career. Selfish, arrogant, narrow-minded, miserly, and dull, he was definitely no role model for the young Mary Roses. Mummy dearest was a sad and obese housewife—a TV addict, food addict, nag addict. Long-suffering, Mummy had become indifferent. Her parents epitomised the debasement of life. Mary Roses was brought up to believe that life was a shabby thing. Not very bright, she never doubted the wisdom of idiots—teachers, politicians, journalists, economists, rock stars, movie celebrities, and religious messiahs. Not very beautiful, she found no love or vanity to make life bearable. Untalented, she became a non-entity, seen and heard by nobody. Poor, she possessed only rage, lots and lots of it. She was a whirlpool of hate. Reality shunning her, she retreated into her crazy fantasy world. Uneducated, she developed great powers of irrationality. Mistreated, she developed no sense of goodness. The whole world was bad so there was no point in being good. Revenge she longed for.

She must make society suffer. What better way to retaliate than to take away one of their idols, their false idols who symbolised the crudeness and vulgarity of our sentiments? What were famous people but Mammon incarnate, who had attained their riches through their ruthlessness, their dedication to their egos, and their need to shove their superiority down people's throats? These people were loved by millions. Ugly and mediocre, Mary was loved by nobody. The crumbs of life were for her. Condemned to the poverty of the heart. Yet she had loved so much. Her imagination evoked wonderful vistas of ecstasy, a world of photogenic happiness. But no lover or friend came along to make those dreams come true. Loneliness made her life empty and senseless. She saw the beauty of life, but it was all outside her—people, nature, God—all outside her. She was ugly, her life was ugly. Eventually, she learnt to hate beauty. Beauty was the great divider...

In the eyes of Mary Roses, the most beautiful person in the world was Queen Clytoris. Queen Clytoris was physically attractive, intelligent, and happy, and Mary Roses loved her dearly. She read her books, tried to understand her teachings, hoping she too would find the wisdom and serenity of the Queen. For years, she read Queen Clytoris, but the joy and the wisdom never came. How could she be wise? She was too consumed by despair and rage to be peaceful, which was the springboard to wisdom. Her emotions, battered by reality, had made her stupid. Yet would wisdom cure her of her loneliness, her misery, and her rage? Why care about Truth when the people around her were full of lies? This was an evil world she lived in. To be good was to be a victim, exploited and destroyed. Crazily, she wanted love from this world, this world of selfish egotists who had turned love into a rat race, making the Machiavellis the best Romeos and the Catherine the Greats the best Juliets. Love was no longer a gentle, wonderful feeling which radiated itself like a warm spring sun, but a commodity in a cutthroat market. Love was not love anymore, but a status symbol of success, a drug, a power game, a material thing. Love spilling from the ego and not the heart.

Mary Roses despised the world yet was crushed by it. Unlike Queen Clytoris, who stood strong and formidable. Thus, Mary Roses resolved to stop loving Queen Clytoris and to hate her with all her passion, a passion as great as if she loved her. According to Mary Roses, Queen Clytoris, far from being good, was, in fact, evil. She had turned Truth into a narrow gate, and it seemed a gate wide enough only for her to enter. She was at the pinnacle of success. She was top dog who outbarked the rest. She was no victim. Born rich and beautiful, she never had to struggle. At 17, she won a beauty contest. Her suitors were the cream of society: rich, handsome, and powerful men. Then she got the cherry on top when King Prawn fell in love with her, courted her, and married her. She had never done an honest day's work, thought Mary Roses in her cliche-bound mind. All her life, Queen Clytoris was pampered like a pet poodle. She had all the love and money to give her happiness, and to give her time to philosophise, the time to understand. Mary Roses never had the time, wasting all her time in the office doing meaningless work, and spending her hours of recreation in misery. No, she had no time to understand. Time was power, and the poor and the powerless had no time. Thus, Mary Roses planned to take away all the time of Queen Clytoris. Killing her would be taking away one of the idols of our success-worshipping society. Killing her would be revenge. Killing her would be her "success". She would become a celebrity, lionised by the media, books would be written about her, the masses would know her now that she had lost her invisibility. She had been trained for this all her life, to be a vicious rat in this rat race. She would be successful, and like all successful people, she would be a prisoner of success. But it would all be worthwhile because successful people were content with their empty glories.

## Queen Clytoris World Tour

Queen Clytoris's World Tour was a huge success. Mort had organised it. Pretending to be a businessman, he visited Queen Clytoris at her palace. He observed that she felt trapped in that opulent cage, and he offered to set her free. He saw the opportunity to destroy Queen Clytoris's soul with money, success, and idolisation. Everywhere she went, she was greeted with mass adulation. She was a media phenomenon. On TV, you could see millions of people gathering in the streets, theatres, and stadiums to see her, if only for a glimpse of a dot in the distance. See their faces and you see faces of hysteria and excitement. They had to see her, their Queen, their idol. Seeing her in person was like making real the image on the TV screen. It was the consummation of one's marriage to the TV set. It was like getting inside the TV.

The crowds came not to understand her words. They came not for the Truth. They came for the realisation of the image.

"We want Queen Clytoris!"

"We want Queen Clytoris!"

"We want Queen Clytoris!" chanted the 100,000 or so people in the President Carol Sports Stadium. This was a special event because it was a homecoming. The little commune she founded twenty years ago had grown into a sprawling metropolis outfitted with fifty McDonald's franchises. Five pillars of light flooded the stadium, which was a giant basket of people; the huge stage stood at one end, flanked by massive amplifiers and two large video screens. On stage at present was the supporting act—a troupe of poodles performing, directed by a man dressed in a cat's costume. The poodles danced on their hind legs, jumped through flaming hoops, added simple arithmetic sums, and did slapstick routines. But the audience was bored; people wanted Queen Clytoris. It was her they paid for. Queen Clytoris sat in her dressing room with her dresser, make-up artist, and entrepreneur Mort, who had coaxed her into doing the world tour.

She gazed at her face in the neon-lined mirror as if she was taking one last look at a very dear friend who was departing for a far-away land. She had a sense of foreboding. In the morning, as she looked outside her hotel window, she saw nine black crows flying in the formation of a cross. Queen Clytoris wasn't superstitious, but she did believe Nature always sought to communicate with humanity.

Prince Jotel was in town, so he dropped by backstage for a visit. He was rather tipsy.

"Hello, Mother. How's things?" he asked her, his eyes like slits, his body imperceptibly slipping off the leather upholstered chair.

"I'm fine, Joey. How are you?"

"Okay, I suppose."

Conversation ended, and silence dominated the space between them. Prince Jotel found it hard to converse with his mother. He felt that he had nothing to say that might interest her. He was too convinced of her superiority. But tonight, he felt compelled to talk to her. He was superstitious, and in the morning, he saw nine black birds flying towards this stadium. Finally, before she had to go on stage, he asked her a question. "Mother, have you ever gotten drunk in your entire life?"

"Let me remember...when I was 16. I was at a party and my boyfriend was flirting all night with a beautiful girl, so I drowned myself with drink, well, I thought it was punch. And after that, I smiled and laughed all night, even though there was nothing to smile and laugh about."

"A happy drunk. See how perfect you are, you even get drunk perfectly."

Queen Clytoris laughed. "But I didn't tell you I vomited all over the birthday cake in front of everybody."

"And I thought you were a classy lady."

### The Four Battles

When Queen Clytoris stepped on stage, the audience exploded into a fusillade of cheers. The whole platform was a chasm of light, while the audience was a huge hole of darkness. She saw faces glimmering in the darkness, like objects bobbing in the water. Reaching the microphone, she stood before the audience, which was still an explosion of welcome. After a lengthy time, the cheering subsided. The stage darkened; two bright lights struck her. She was standing on the moon of light. The audience was now quiet in excited anticipation.

"Why have you come here? For entertainment or for wisdom? For those who come here for wisdom, they can leave the stadium now. For those who come here for entertainment, they can stay and watch me sing and dance. If you want wisdom, seek it within yourself, start at the beginning, in the vacuum of thought, without preconceptions. You won't find wisdom in me. You have to find it in yourself. I am just an entertainer! Like Socrates, Jesus, Buddha. Truth is just show business, and I'm just a pop star. You have come here to cheer and not to learn. (*Loud cheering, standing ovation.*) You will not begin to understand until you have rid yourself of all the idols, including me. There is no one in the world but you. Grab that reality! No one can see through your eyes but yourself, no one can feel your pain but yourself. You are entirely alone. I am merely external to you. I don't know you. You must know yourself. You must carry the burden of your own self; no one else can."

"I declare war! (*Loud applause.*) These are the four great battles we need to fight."

"Our first battle is against Words. Find out what words control you? Is it God? Is it Truth? Is it Duty? What are words but made of air? But such airy beginnings lead to walls, castles, bombs, and prisons. But words plucked out of the air will ultimately lead you to nothingness. Shut your mouth and kiss the ground. Words have destroyed reality. Look around and you see concrete, iron, electricity, and plastic. It is all nothingness. This civilisation of nothingness. This empire of nothingness. This politics of nothingness. This religion of nothingness. And this nothingness grows and grows like a black hole, sucking up everything. Reality is dead! You are dead! Words have killed you! (*Cheers.*) Shut up! (*Deafening cheers, hoots, whistles*) Words bar you from the wisdom of silence. Kill words, and the silence will be your victory."

Thundering applause. The crowd was ecstatic.

Queen Clytoris waited awhile for it to subside.

"Our second battle is against Control. Don't let politicians, industrialists, and priests run the world. Do not relinquish your power to them. Do not vote for them, give money to them, or obey them. Do not let these vampires drink your blood. Do not let them turn you into shadows. Look at this Hell they have created, the institutions of torture to ensure the eternal misery of our souls. War, hunger, poverty, pollution, and environmental destruction overwhelm this poor earth. We must fight these misery mongers. The only person that should control you is yourself. Control yourself—be aware that you are a dangerous human, so you must try to limit the damage you cause."

Claps, cheers, and whistles.

"The third battle is against Greed. We crave too much of everything, such as money, power, sex, love, happiness, entertainment, food, religion, and even knowledge. Greed is devouring the world. Greed is creating a big void inside of us, sucking up our souls. Yet Greed has given us little, and the world is much smaller. End Greed and Eternity is yours."

People reached for the skies as if for eternity.

"Our fourth battle is against Hate. It is the enemy within. It is the enemy of Life. It is a cancer which grows and kills. Hate controls and shapes your life, hurts and twists and breaks you. Hate creates fear, despair, anger, isolation. Hate destroys you within and without. Hate festers division, discrimination, sexism, racism, walls, tanks, guns, missiles, and nuclear bombs. This wheel of hate must be stopped from leading us to the abyss when the whole world is destroyed. To achieve this, we must learn to love. Learn to give. Learn to be kind. Learn to forgive. Forgive yourself and everyone. Forgive God. He knows not what he does."

The audience rose in a thunderous ovation. Amid the roar, a loud bang sounded, which frightened no one, a bang which the Queen did not hear so that when she dropped to the floor, she had no clue why blood was soaking her dress. People watching from the wings rushed to her aid, and they, too, were ignorant as to why she was on the floor. Did a wrathful God strike her dead? they wondered. The audience stopped cheering, and cries of horror erupted among the hushed silence.

"The Queen's been shot!" someone screamed.

"Oh my God, she's dying!"

"Someone call the ambulance!"

"Don't worry, Queen Clytoris, you'll be alright."

"Please God, don't let her die."

Queen Clytoris felt herself slipping away, and she could not resist it. It was pulling her away. She could only submit. The world she was entering was dissolving her being, and she was becoming pure.

Prince Jotel sat beside his mother in the ambulance, holding her hand. He was studying her face, seeking a clue to Death. Her face was graceful and calm. Death seemed like an alright place. If Death was alright, then Life was alright. Strangely, Prince Jotel felt strong. He was surprised. He knew he was distraught, but he had to pull himself together. Right now, he wanted beauty, happiness, joy, peace, wisdom, all the things written on his mother's face.

He wanted a drink. He fought the urge to succumb to the darkness.

Mort stood on the empty stage in the middle of Queen Clytoris's pool of blood. He looked at the empty coliseum and bowed. He was going to turn her into a pop saint, all glitter, hollow to the core. The religion of Queen Clytoris. Soon there will be a holiday named after her, with much drinking, celebrating, and consumption. Her words will be trivialised, cheapened. She will have followers without an original thought in their heads.

# CHAPTER 17

## The Story of Death

When Death was born, his parents thought he was the ugliest baby in the world. They queried the doctor as to why their baby, whom they named Death Thomas Smith, had no flesh or muscle or inner organ to speak of; Death was just a skeleton.

The doctor admitted that he didn't really know why and hypothesised that his condition was brought about by an angry cow giving them the evil eye. Since Death's parents were idiots, they readily believed the doctor. They brought their controversial baby home and were so ashamed of him that one day they fed him to their pet dog, Fifi, who then buried Death in the backyard. Death was dug up a few years later by a pirate called Captain Twain, who was searching for buried treasure. Captain Twain, needing some deckhands, took Death with him back to his shop. The captain took a liking to Death and decided to make him the ship's mascot, and even went so far as to put Death's face on the flag. He treated Death as if he was his own son.

When Death turned 10, Captain Twain thought it best that he shouldn't spend his formative years on a pirate ship but in a private school in England and perhaps one day go to Oxford and study law. Death loved Captain Twain, the crew, and the pirate life, and did not want to leave them. Amid sad and lugubrious farewells, Death was sent to England to receive a gentleman's education.

Not only did he receive a gentleman's education, but he also received a very ungentlemanly physical and emotional beating from his classmates, who teased him and called him names like Bonehead, Dog Munchies, and other horrible monikers. Death reacted by retreating to the world of the intellect. He devoted his time to science, wishfully thinking that one day he might become a great scientist and discover a cure for his dermatological problems, or lack thereof. He did become a great scientist, not in dermatology, but in the social sciences. The time between his adolescence and his success was a lean period for his hungry heart. He had no friends or lovers; he was completely alone.

At that period of time, the world was experiencing a serious problem of overpopulation. This was brought about by the fact that there was no such thing as death. Everyone lived forever. The world was so overcrowded that walking across a street would take a whole day. In fact, the most effective form of transport was the catapult. When Death graduated from Oxford University, he set out to solve this particular problem. His first attempt at a solution was to shrink people to an average height of 7 inches. This experiment failed; instead, he inadvertently discovered the secret recipe for Kentucky Fried Chicken. His second attempt was to flatten people like wallpaper, but one human experiment blew away and was lost on one blustering day. Death worked on the problem for twenty years and never came close to succeeding. He was greatly depressed and felt his whole life was a failure.

One morning, he chose not to go to the laboratory. He wanted to stay home and…he wanted to do something…but he did not know what it was particularly. It was a desire to cease, to stop, not work, not eat, not even breathe. Suddenly, Death realised he was on to something. Would not the removal of people be the solution to overpopulation? But how could they be removed? People were immortal, even indestructible. How does one make humanity mortal?

Death found the answer by asking the opposite question—what makes humanity immortal? Timelessness is the essence of immortality. By creating Time, one destroys immortality. How does one create Time? Death achieved this by inventing the wristwatch. Thus, Death created death. His invention of Time changed the whole world. For starters, people were furious that they could only have one hour for lunch; previously, lunch could last for months and years. Some sadist invented the alarm clock. There was now a time for everything, a time for work, a time for sleep, a time for fun, a time for each and everything. Gone was spontaneity, everything was scheduled and measured. Somehow, everything became small and limited. Mortality was a prison. Changes also occurred in the cosmos. The sun, which formerly roamed all over the sky whenever or wherever, had now taken to rising and setting regularly. Flowers, which were in eternal blossom, began wilting and shrivelling into decay, into death. Everything was doomed to die. People died, as did animals, vegetables, and even the universe, eventually.

Death, our hero, did not become a celebrity for his revolutionary invention of Time. Rather, he was pilloried and ostracised by society. They blamed him for all the woes and misery that had befallen them. People did not take to dying kindly. Although Death discovered the solution to overpopulation, he was never in his lifetime hailed as a great scientist. Defamed as a mass murderer, a mad butcher; overall, an evil man.

Death was plunged into misery after his invention. He was abused wherever he went. To make matters worse, his surrogate father, Captain Twain, was arrested and hanged at the gallows. Death retired from science and took up the profession of alcoholism. He committed a slow suicide for ten years. When he died, he was buried in an anonymous grave. Not one soul came to the funeral except the rain and the gravedigger.

After his death, he became the stuff of notoriety. Writers mythologised him into a terrible and gruesome monster, which we know was far from the truth. This lonely, shy, kind, intelligent human being became a byword for horror. Humanity had done little justice to Death, for he was by far the greatest scientist who had ever lived.

DEATH

(1713 - 1758)

And that was the story of Death Thomas Smith.

I, too, must be grateful to Death. Art seeks conclusions, or else there is no final movement to a symphony, no frame to a picture, and no last chapter to this damned novel! This novel must end! All my characters must die! Show no mercy! Mwahahahaha!

*MUSE: Ranulfo, don't you think this chapter is irrelevant?*
*RANULFO: Everything is a concept: Life, God, Love, Death, and even Ranulfo. This novel*
*seeks to undermine our concepts so we can face the silence of reality. This novel is a journey to*
*the Void.*

# CHAPTER 18

## Fatso

The death of Queen Clytoris was a media bonanza. Newspaper sales rocketed, TV news ratings exploded, and books written about her became million-dollar sellers. There was now a movie to be made about her life, starring Madonna as Queen Clytoris. That is, if the producers and Madonna succeeded in agreeing on her salary. If not Madonna, then another superstar had to be found to play the superstar Queen Clytoris.

Hardly had the Queen been buried and eaten by worms, when people were claiming that they had seen her alive. One sighting had her in a tryst with Elvis Presley. But as you well know, superstars bring out the looneys out of the woodwork. As for the big looney Mary Roses who assassinated her, she became a superstar herself, attracting massive attention. This attention outed her submerged personality. She developed confidence and a talent for knowing what to give to the media, who could count on her to say something outrageous and controversial. She was the philosopher of darkness, the spokesperson for all the loonies in the world: the outsiders, the rejects, the not-haves.

The death of Queen Clytoris shattered St Claire. The world had lost any meaning for her. The Queen made her feel intelligent, strong, and alive. Queen Clytoris had brought her out. But now she was shut in her shell.

So she ate.

And ate and ate and ate. That was what life was all about. Eating. The earth is a restaurant. We're no better than cows browsing in the pastures waiting for the abattoirs. We're just conceited cows with grand illusions. So she ate. She no longer sought fulfilment, but merely to be filled.

Weight she gained.

But she was oblivious to her weight gain as she never looked at a mirror, losing all interest in self-awareness. She lost interest in the human or natural world. Seasons pass by without acknowledgement.

But her observational skills were unfaltering when watching television. TV was her saving grace, rescuing her from boredom and despair. Whenever she switched on the TV, life switched on. How she loved TV. Pure meaningless entertainment, nothing to provoke her to great thought. She loved American sitcoms like Gilligan's Island; they made her laugh even though the jokes were inane.

But as soon as she turned off the TV, all the fun, drama, and excitement vanished, and she was left alone with her boring, boring, boring self. She was lost. She would walk around the house trying to do something. Usually, she would visit the refrigerator and devour a morsel or ten. Or she would read the TV guide, hoping that there was a good show on. Planning her watching schedule excited her; it gave her something to look forward to. Instead of waiting for Godot, she waited for Gilligan...

If there was no food or TV, she would go out and watch movies, eat out, go shopping...anything but meet people. Real people bored and depressed her; they weren't as entertaining as TV. St Claire read no books. It was too actively intellectual. She rejected thought. She was getting lazier and lazier. The fantasy of suicide visited her frequently, even consoling her, comforting her, delighting her. Death was the ultimate refuge for laziness—lying in a coffin, having no thoughts or feelings. The ultimate holiday. Living was too difficult and strenuous. She wanted the struggle to end; it had gone on for too long. She wanted peace. She wanted death. She wanted food. She wanted TV.

Weight she gained...

She slept a lot; sleep quickened time. Sleep ushers in the future, annihilating the present. She was sick of the present. The future always gave her hope. Like Sleeping Beauty, she waited to be awakened by Prince Charming. No prince came, not even Prince Jotel, but she enjoyed sleeping.

Weight she gained...

One morning, St Claire got dressed to go out to buy groceries. None of her jeans could fit her anymore, so she put on a big blouse.

At the supermarket, she met an old friend from university. At first, she didn't recognise Claire underneath the layers of fat.

"Don't I know you?" queried her friend Miranda.

"Hello, Miranda," reluctantly answered St Claire.

"You're...you're ..."

"I'm St Claire." Feeling ashamed.

"St Claire!" shock of all shocks. "You've...changed." An understatement.

"Yes, well."

"So, tell me, St Claire, how's things been with you?"

"Feeling a bit sad. My best friend passed away." Without emotion. She was merely talking perfunctorily with Miranda.

Meanwhile, as they walked down the supermarket aisle, St Claire put into her cart: 3 cheesecakes, 2 chocolate bavarians, 5 packets of lemon meringues, 10 packets of pineapple donuts, 12 apricot Danish muffins, 20 chocolate eclairs, 10 apple pies. Miranda watched with disbelief.

"Are you working, St Claire?"

"No. How about you?"

"I'm a lecturer at the University of NSW. I'm also married and have two kids. Are you married, Clare?"

"No," wishing Miranda would just disappear.

"I'm married to Bob. You remember Bob at university. He's now an economist at the Reserve Bank."

"Bob! An economist! But he was a radical leftie at university."

"I kicked all that socialism out of him after we got married. I told him that I wouldn't marry him unless he earned more than I did."

20 kgs of sirloin steak, 20 kgs of chuck steak, 10 kgs of beef mincemeat, 20 frozen chickens, 5 topside roasts...

"And what have you been doing lately?" she asked St Claire.

"Nothing. I don't care much about doing anything really."

"But you're so intelligent."

"What good is it being intelligent? Look what they did to Queen Clytoris."

"Surely Queen Clytoris didn't live in vain. Her wisdom lives on."

"If she was stupid, she'd still be alive."

"If she was stupid, you wouldn't have cared to know her."

...potato chips, cheezels, Pepsi, fruit juice, Mars bars, frozen pizza, assorted frozen dinners, chocolate this and that, ice cream of this flavour and that, Chinese instant noodles...

"Stupidity wins all the time. What help was reason to Socrates? Stupidity is rich, powerful, stupidity wins in love, stupidity finds happiness, stupidity has all the fun, stupidity has all the friends and lovers in the world. Look at lonely wisdom, poor, impotent, ugly, starving."

"St Claire, pull yourself together. You deserve a better fate. Don't sink in your bitterness and self-pity."

Together they went to the checkout table. Miranda's groceries cost her $32.40

and St Claire's $548.35.

"St Claire, don't give up," Miranda said to her as they parted. "Use your intelligence."

St Claire went off to visit McDonalds for a little snack. "5 Big Macs, 5 Mcfeasts, 2 Fillet O Fish, 12 Chicken nuggets, large chips, and a diet coke, please."

"Eat here or take away."

"Eat here? No, I'll eat at the table."

Next day, St Claire discovered, to her dismay, that there was no food left in the house; she must go at once to replenish her supplies. She got into a blimp of a dress. She stepped out of the door and headed to …um where are you, St Claire? …oh, you're stuck in the door, you can't get out, you poor thing. The door was much too narrow for her too wide self, and she was wedged between the doorposts. She tried to heave her way out, but nothing worked. After a lengthy period of vain effort, she burst into tears.

"Queen Clytoris, please help me, I can't go on. I'm so unhappy without you."

She cried and cried until she realised that crying didn't solve her problems.

After three days, she lost some weight to free her from the door posts. Instead of heading to the supermarket, she jogged around the block. She made up her mind to lose more weight and get her act together.

She was St Claire, and she was no loser, except as a loser of pounds.

228

# CHAPTER 19

## The Return of the Village Idiots

A starry night looked down upon the castle of King Prawn and his new wife, Queen Golderella. The walls were dark, the windows lit like stars. Music and revelry rocked the castle and were heard by a lone sentry guard who paced in front of the large iron gates.

"Halt! Who goes theyere?" he shouted at the approaching footsteps somewhere in the dark.

No one answered, but the footsteps kept coming.

"Haltyhalt, dastardly footsteps!"

"Only one person can speak like that. Is that you, Suck?"

"Yeyes! And who are youyouse, answer now speaking feet?"

A face appeared, smiling. Suck recognised him at once and embraced the man. "My friend, Fart. It's so goody to see yuyu again."

"Suck, it's been ages since I saw you last. You didn't have wrinkles and white hair then."

"How are thee, Fartyfart?"

"Fine, fine."

"It's been a long timey. Do yuyu missey the oldy days when we were village idiots togethery?"

"O those crazy days. I used to go around in funny costumes. What good times we had."

"Yeyes. We had such funfunfunny days."

"I've been a serious man for a long time."

"Yeyes. You lookie your smile has gone. Tell me, whatsa been doing to your elf?"

"Elf haha. After the great wars, the elf went into real estate. I'm well off, a fine house, a fine car, and a fine family. Everything's fine. And what about you, Suck?"

"I'm a sentry guard as yuyu see. I likey doing nighty shift. Dayeydreams are better than nightydreams. It's less scarey."

"Bad dreams, Suck?"

"Just scary meanymonsters chasing me."

"I've been having bad dreams as well. I've been wandering the past few hours.

I'm afraid to sleep."

"Yeyes."

"I'm old."

"Soso am I."

Fart gazed pensively at the stars, then, worn by its great weight, cast his eyes on the castle. "I see, there's a party going on. Is it true what I have heard? Our brave King reduced to a strumpet's fool."

"Yeyes. 'Tis sad but trooey. Ever since Queen Golderella took up residence, theyere has been nightly wassailing. She is determined to drain our King empty of money, power, and dignity. Behind his backsy she cuckolds him. His power she steals, she decrees, and he agrees. He dotes on the bad wench, worships her little toes, listens enchanted to her froggy voice. His headsy in the clouds, and his ballsy are in her pockets. Yeyes, poor King Prawn. he's goney. The King is kaput! Long live the Bitchie!"

"He's a fool in his old age. I don't blame him much. Facing decay is not easy."

"Sayie! You don't want to be a village idiot againie?"

"You mean turn my back on everything and go back to being a village idiot," a smile materialised on Fart's face.

"Let's have fun againy."

Then the smile quickly vanished. "I can't. I've got responsibilities. Besides, being a village idiot is a strenuous mental and physical job. My health is not up to it."

"Remember how we tried to overthrow King Prawnie and Queen Clitoris all those yeyears ago. Let's throw this Queen Goldie out."

"Haha. It's all coming back to me. That started everything, didn't it? We sure were crazy young men!"

"Comey, Fart. Letsa do it! For our King! For old time's saki!"

"Haha. You're still crazy, Suck."

"Come on, what have you got to lose? We're old, letsy go out in a blazy of glory!"

"I don't know. I wish I could."

"There! The light's on her bedroom window, let's go belowie and vovociferate!"

"I heard she's a real termagant. She has people executed at her whim."

"Comesy, we aint scaredsy of any bitchy."

"No," shaking his head, sadly, "I don't want to die or go to prison. My family needs me."

"Let's disturb her while she's in the middle of cuckooing her husband."

"I'm sorry, Suck. Maybe, if I were younger. But...anyway, it was great talking to you again, Suck."

They gazed fondly at each other, imagined their younger selves, then laughed.

"Yeyes, nice seeing you agensky, Farty."

"Take care of yourself, Suck."

"I wiwill. You take care."

"Goodbye, Suck."

"Byebye, Fartyfart."

Suck watched his friend slowly get swallowed up by the night. He gazed up at the sky. The universe was so huge and endless. We are but dust compared to the stars. Why should we miniscule creatures amount to any importance? As man is to a cockroach so is God to man. A hierarchy of feet. Small smelly feet begging mercy from big smellier feet. Abruptly he laughed, his body reverberating. He burst into a scramble, crossing the palace's garden. He did a few flips. Picking up a stone, he flung it at the window door of the Queen's balcony. The stone cracked the glass. The door banged open, out came Queen Golderella, furious, in a sexy red gown.

"Who is that?" she shouted at the night.

"It is Suck!" he shouted. "You're the wrongy bottom on the throne!"

"A traitor before our midst," said Queen Golderella. "You are a brave soul pitting yourself against the mightiest Queen of them all."

"Yeyes, get your bottom off the throne or else I'll kicky it to where it belongs. To the dunny!"

A shadowy man stood beside Queen Golderella. Suck was happy, thinking at first, he was King Prawn. But the man was young, wore an officer's uniform, and had in his hand a black gun, which he raised, pointed at his direction, a loud bang, a puff of smoke, and suddenly there was nothing to see from Suck's dead eyes. Suck was now an insensate and imperceptive carcass. Insects gathered around his blood and the banquet in memory of Suck had begun.

"Now, let's get back to what we were doing." The man caressed the Queen's neck with his lips, making her smile.

"'Mo, my darling Mort, it's not my neck you want, it's King Prawn's."

Aghast, "I can't possibly..."

"Wouldn't you like to sit next to me in the throne, King Mort?"

"King Mort..." the words were like an incantation.

They entered the bedroom and closed the door behind them, the lights were killed, and somewhere in the night walked Fart, lost in his reminiscences. He had heard the gunshot but thought nothing of it. He was smiling, he had not been happy for a long time. "Tomorrow, I'll visit Suck, and we'll be good friends again. I want to spend my old age with my dear friends. Friendship—that's all that matters in our short, short life."

# CHAPTER 20

## Death talks to Virginia

Phew! That was a close call. Nearly got crushed to death by Harry the Farmhouse. I was just heading to the shops when I bumped into him. He didn't look convivial the way he was seething and fuming, so I bolted, and he chased after me. He was just about to run me over when I crossed an intersection and a semi-trailer smashed straight into Harry. Poor Harry. I hope he's okay.

One night, Virginia was awakened in her sleep by a man she thought was a man she went to bed with but could not remember. She was not afraid. He did not appear to be a stranger.

"Hello, Virginia."

"Do I know you?"

"I'm Death."

"Sure you are. Now tell me. You look familiar?"

"I'm Death," the stranger repeated.

Death pulled back his hood and revealed his skeletal countenance. Virginia drew back, terrified.

"I want you," Death whispered to her like a lover.

"I don't want you."

"Yes, you do."

"No, I don't."

"You've been waiting for me a long time."

"No, I haven't."

"You've had hundreds of lovers, but it's me you've longed for."

"That was sex. I wanted love, not you. I wanted a best friend. I wanted someone to dream with."

"I don't understand."

"Someone I can dream being a princess and he a prince."

"I'll let you sleep the eternal sleep, and you can dream as much as you want."

"But you won't love me. You won't be my friend."

"How do you know?"

"I don't know. You tell me. What is Death like?"

"You will find out very soon."

"No! I don't want to die."

"It's over. It won't make a difference if you live an extra 20 or 30 years, nothing will change. Nobody loves you, nobody ever has, nobody ever will. Your search for love has been in vain. I'll mercifully end that vain search."

"I want to live, please," she begged him.

"Why?"

Life, that basket of goodies, was being snatched from her. Death was a void of possibilities, an end to desire.

"There are so many things I want to do," she implored.

"Such as?"

She couldn't focus, desire flooded her as always: she was desire. She stumbled out the words, "I don't know...like running in a forest...naked..."

"Then do."

In a blink Virginia was standing naked in a forest bright and shimmering with sunlight. Quickly she blotted out the scene by covering her eyes with her hands.

"Why don't you run?" Death asked her.

She hated the dead tone of his voice, without a hint of humanity. "I feel as if I've been given my last meal before the execution."

"You see, you'll never begin to live. You are an emotional bureaucrat."

"Just leave me alone! Go away!"

"Your temper has no effect on me. In fact, your temper has not served you well in your life. You've screamed and shouted, and it's gotten you nowhere. Your temper has stopped you from understanding yourself and other people. You've never learnt to get off the stage and watch life with detachment. You were always the actress in a drama."

"I don't like this scene very much. I won't play this scene!" Virginia ran, wishfully thinking that somehow she could outrun Death. Even though she was afraid, there was a part of her that was aware of her nudity and the sensation of running, the colliding of senses that delighted her. She was out of breath when she noticed Death waiting for her.

"Are you having fun?"

"Go away!" she screamed at him, her face distorted but yet achingly beautiful as always. Virginia carried beauty with her.

"I'll make a deal with you, Virginia. You find one person in the world who truly loves you, and I'll let you live."

Virginia said nothing, daunted by her impossible task.

Alone. The ground was brown crunchy with autumn's dying leaves. The sky was cloudless cerulean. The trees were half bare. This was certainly Death's country.

Virginia walked on, sniffling, terrified. She was unsure whether she was in the real world. It was too beautiful to be real, or perhaps she had never noticed how beautiful nature was. The ground was soft and cool, the leaves underfoot crackled as she threaded forward. Light, soft light suffused the forest, light which seemed to emanate from the air and not the sun. Everywhere was silence. The breeze had gentle fingers. Nonetheless, the beauty could not shake off the chilly dread in her heart.

Virginia walked for hours as the forest rolled on and on. Dead leaves floated down on her and crunched beneath her feet. Tired, she sat down on a bed of leaves and cried tears and tears. The cruelty of life she hated. There was nowhere or nobody to go to for love and comfort. She lay down on her stomach, how sensual the earth was, her nakedness feeling more and more naked. Yet the joy ended there. Life was only comfort for the senses. Her heart was a planet blasted by asteroids. The grass delighted her, but it could not talk to her, protect her, or love her. Like her lovers, who loved her body but shunned her heart. She could not bear the isolation of her being. The human mind an aberration in this mindless universe, a mind impotent against the cosmos, which grew larger and larger, creating more mindless spaces.

"Help!" she screamed. "Help me! Please somebody help me!"

But there was no reply. There were no ears in this forest. She was all alone. Resilient, she stood up and continued her trek into the forest, which went on and on. She was aware of time, irrevocable, ineluctable, moving, rolling, throbbing with the beat of her heart. Maybe life was tragic, but she did not want to wallow in its mud. She wanted happiness. And nothing could take that away from her. She commenced to dance and laugh and sing, as if to spite everything. She stopped singing. What was lacking in her life? Love? Truth? God? Or perhaps it was her mind that misled her, that deceived her, a mind that ruined any chances for her happiness, a mind that was not under her control, a mind that was controlled by its fears, lies, and hates, a mind built on sand.

She noticed a glimmering gold-like object ahead of her behind the trees and bushes. She approached it curiously and was astonished to see a golden rhinoceros browsing on the grass. Shining gold, it gazed indifferently at her. She moved forward to pet its forehead. It didn't respond to her touch.

She wondered what this beautiful creature was doing here. Did this imply that she was no longer on the planet? Was this another world? Was she dead? Whatever it was, she didn't want to find out and hastened away. She dared not look at this otherworldly symbol. Further on, she was surprised to see a well-dressed man in a tuxedo holding a blue folder. He smiled with shining teeth and shining eyes. His hand, with a shining gold ring and watch, extended to shake her hand.

"Virginia?"

"Yes."

"Miss Virginia Prag, this is your life!"

A cameraman jumped out from behind the trees, pointing a TV camera at her. The trees flew up like missiles; in fact, the trees were a painted curtain, which rose to reveal a dark throb of audience clapping and cheering and whistling. She felt embarrassed to be naked on television. But nobody minded. She was a public personality. They thought her nakedness was not real. It was just a movie, the audience thought.

MAN: Do you remember this voice?

VOICE (*a child's voice singing*): Virginia the Vagina, Virginia the Vagina!

VIRGINIA: Sorry, I don't know.

HOST: It's Raphael Merlo. A childhood friend of yours!

(*A little fat boy comes out.*)

RAPHAEL (*snivelling*): Virginia, long time no see.

VIRGINIA (*surprised*): It's been twenty years. You haven't changed at all.

RAPHAEL: That's because I'm part of your dream.

HOST: Raphael, tell us what you remember about Virginia?

RAPHAEL: Virginia was famous in our neighbourhood. She wouldn't wear any knickers under her short skirt and always sat down and revealed herself for anyone's innocent eyes to see.

VIRGINIA: That's a lie!

RAPHAEL: From where I am you haven't changed your exhibitionist ways. (*leers at her nudity*)

VIRGINIA: I'm an artist. An artist always reveals himself.

RAPHAEL: An artist? I thought you were just a nympho.

VIRGINIA (*defensively*): I like to make a lot of people happy. I gave myself, but everyone took, and nobody gave in return. (*Then, with a sudden shift, she puts on a coquette smile.*) Tell me, Raphael, did you love me?

RAPHAEL: Heck, no, but I sure wanted to fuck you!

VIRGINIA (*hurt, furious*): Well, fuck off then.

(*Raphael attempts to grab Virginia but is tackled and hauled away by burly security guards.*)

HOST: Moving along, Virginia do you remember this voice from the past?

VOICE: Get your knickers off!

VIRGINIA (*thinking*): It's not my ex-boyfriend, Michael Potty, is it?

HOST: That is correct. Michael Potty, come on out!

(*Enters Michael in a penis costume*)

MICHAEL: I'm coming! I'm coming!

VIRGINIA: You came quickly. As usual.

(*The audience laughs. The audience are inside cans*)

MICHAEL: I couldn't wait to tell my mates.

HOST: You had a love affair with Virginia, Michael Potter. Tell us about her?

MICHAEL: She was one hell of a good lay.

VIRGINIA (*imploringly*): But you did love me then, Michael? Didn't you?

MICHAEL: It was better than love. It was pure absolute lust.

VIRGINIA: Why didn't you love me?

MICHAEL: I thought you didn't want love. You never gave me the impression that you even cared about me. You were so...unreachable...in the mental sense.

VIRGINIA: Well, I wanted love. Nobody cared to reach into my heart and find out.

HOST: We must move on. Virginia, do you remember this voice?

VOICE: Her acting shines like polished wood.

VIRGINIA (*extremely annoyed*): No, not him, please!

HOST: It's the famous movie critic Henry Blum!

VIRGINIA: I don't want to see him! He hates all my movies!

HENRY BLUM (*enters in an electric mobile armchair*) Look who's here, its Mrs Pinocchio. Tell me, darling, how are the termites?

VIRGINIA: Go away! Who are you to judge? You critics love to destroy, but you can't create.

HENRY: You destroy Art with your acting.

VIRGINIA: I am an artist! I create happiness for people.

HENRY: You are a demagogue. You pander to the vulgar sentimental emotions of the public. You do it by acting like a corpse to be pitied.

VIRGINIA: Go away! Leave me alone!

(*The electric armchair goes haywire, smoke coming out, races and crashes into the fake backdrop, Henry Blum screaming.*)

HOST: All right. Do you remember this voice, Virginia?

VOICE: I love you, Virginia, I love you so much.

VIRGINIA: Somebody loves me. Bring him in.

(*Enters a teenage male fan, acne-ridden, eyes goggling at her nudity, and munching popcorn.*)

FAN: I love you, Virginia.

VIRGINIA: Thank you. It's for you and all my fans I live for.

FAN: My favourite movie of yours is Tender Cruelties,

VIRGINA: Thank you. But why I didn't get an Oscar nomination, I don't know?

HENRY (*suddenly reappearing as his armchair races by*): That's because the Oscar statuette is a better actor than you.

VIRGINIA: Shut up! I didn't ask for your opinion. All I care about is what my fans think. Tell me (*to the popcorn munching fan*) why did you like me in that movie?

FAN: I like that spanking scene with Michael Douglas. Was that your real bottom or a stunt?

VIRGINIA: I do all my stunts.

FAN: You must have been sore. Your bottom was so red.

VIRGINIA: I must say I don't believe in gratuitous nudity and sex. I will only take my clothes off if I feel that it is artistic and meaningful and important to the plot.

FAN: Can I have your autograph, Ms Prag?

VIRGINIA: Yes, I love to.

FAN: Can..can…can you sign it on my pppenis? (*He takes out pen and penis.*)

VIRGINA: Oh go away! You disgusting creature!

FAN (*starts masturbating*): I masturbate to all your movies. I have a well-worn pause button on my VCR.

VIRGINIA: Stop that! Get him out of here!

VOICE: Hello, Virginia, I'm back.

VIRGINIA: I know that dreadful voice,

HOST: Of course, you know that voice. It's none other than the voice of Death!

VIRGINIA: Don't let him here, please…

DEATH: It's time now.

VIRGINIA: No! Keep away from me!

DEATH: You've lost the wager. Nobody loves you, Virginia.

VIRGINIA: You didn't give me enough time.

DEATH: That's everyone's excuse.

VIRGINIA: Please…please…I'll do anything.

DEATH: It's too late.

VIRGINIA: What about my mother? She loves me.

DEATH: President Carol? She loves her ambition more than she loves you.

VIRGINIA: What about my cat? He loves me, I know he does.

DEATH: Pets don't count.

VIRGINIA: Don't you have any feelings of sympathy?

DEATH: Death has no heart.

VIRGINIA: Then who has? Life hasn't.

DEATH: Let's go

VIRGINIA: No!

Virginia woke up screaming, her blankets coiled around her body like snakes. What a horrible nightmare! All her life she found solace in dreams. Dreams were her sanctuary from reality. Now it had turned against her. Not wishing to believe her dreams had betrayed her, she visited a doctor for a rigorous medical check-up. The tests were to reveal she had terminal cancer. From that moment forward, she no longer dreamt or even fantasised. There was now no escaping from reality. Death was real, chewing up her bones, her organs, her life.

# CHAPTER 21

## Postcards

Taking the plunge, I curl the numbers up with my finger.

"Hello," spoke a voice sweet as candy.

"Hello, can I speak to St Claire?"

"Speaking."

"Hi. This is Ranulfo."

"Hello, Ranulfo!"

"Hello, St Claire, how are you?"

"Fine. What about you?":

"Okay."

"How's your novel getting along?"

"It's a slow boat to China."

"Why, what's the matter?"

"Misery, mainly. I broke up with K once again. We had a fight over the phone, and I hanged up. Neither of us rang each other back. So, I guess it's over."

"Don't you want to ring her back?"

"Anyway, I think it's about time I admitted to myself that our relationship just doesn't work. We're simply incompatible. I can't delude myself any longer that I can make things perfect. If I pursue this relationship, I'll have to struggle for the rest of my life. I want a relationship where my girlfriend and I simply get along well with each other. No more forcing a square peg into a round hole. You know what I mean?"

"Yes, I guess so. It's what I've been learning. I'm not Queen Clytoris and can never be. I'm me and I'm stuck with that for better or worse."

"We are what we are. My problem is that I'm too deep. All my life I've always concerned myself with Truth, God, and Beauty."

"Instead of Money, Food, and Sex."

"If only."

"Yes, I understand. I have the same problem myself. To be thine self be true."

"What a curse? Say, tell me, you want to meet for coffee? It'll be nice to talk to you."

"Yes, I'd like that."

After the call I lay on my bed thinking sweetly of St Claire. How nice it is to enjoy being alive without shadows visiting one's dreams and thoughts. To enjoy the vistas like a bird winging in the breezy sky. Strange, happiness made one unvigilant, one trusted opening one's heart to the world.

I meet St Claire for coffee at the University of NSW. St Claire is looking as beautiful as ever. We have a wonderful time together. What I love about her is her sense of humour. I enjoy hearing her laugh. She reminds me of my best friend at High School; his name was Gary, and together we joked and laughed through our teens. My best friend and I haven't seen each other for a decade, but that's because life's seriousness caught up with us and made us both forget that we were alive to enjoy life to the dregs. It is great to laugh once more. That's what's missing in my relationship with K. She is terribly serious and cannot see the funny side of life. Life is not fun for her, it is tragic and dramatic. I have to get out of her desolate world and onto the sunny side of life. And how sunny St Claire is. I love her smile; it's so refreshing and authentic. While K smiles as a sort of theatrical pose, like smiling for a camera, expecting me to see her smile and say how beautiful she is. Her smile is all for effect, like a painted sun on a stage backdrop. She is much too aware of her beauty and its effect on men. Everything is a movie. She gives her love as if it were tangible and could be allotted. Unlike St Claire, whose love is like sunshine that beams from her and is felt by all around her. For K, love is a switch that she can turn on and off at will. Another different thing about St Claire is that she does not argue senselessly like K.

K loves fighting, arguing, and inflicting defeats. Life is polarised for her: allies and enemies. She sees the world as a warrior with weapons and armour. Our clashes get very emotional and painful. She knows how to inflict wounds. As for St Claire, she sees the world as a lover. She accepts that we are all human and vulnerable. I enjoy talking with St Claire. Neither of us needs to prove how right we are; we listen to and respect our differences. K hates what differentiates me from her. It threatens her. She trusts no one. Oh K...why can't you trust me? You know I love you.

Being with St Claire makes me happy. We don't fight; we accept each other.

"What immediate plans do you have?" I ask St Claire, wanting to know her future, which I wanted to share with her.

"I'm going to India for a holiday."

"Oh..." I am quite startled and saddened by the news. I want her here in Sydney. I want to tell her I love her and want her to stay with me. St Claire looks at me as if she wants direction from me about her future. But I'm afraid I can't. I'm not one you'd call an ardent lover who demands immediate satisfaction. I can wait. Patiently like a novelist. I am sure she loves me. Her going to India will not destroy our tacit love for each other, it is sealed.

"Send me a postcard," I say to her.

"Yes," in a tone of disappointment.

We talked for a while. Then it is time to go, and I accompany her to the bus stop. I want to invite her to come home with me. But no words came out of my mouth. When the bus arrives, she kisses me on the cheek.

Back home, I try to convince myself that everything will be all right and that my inaction will not alter the future St Claire and I will share.

A few weeks later…


*Dear Ranulfo,*

*Hi, how are you? India is beautiful. I adore the silly monkeys that prowl the streets. But enough touristing, I want to visit the spiritual spots of India. Perhaps I might attain Nirvana. Time is so different here, it's slow and indolent, unlike Western Time, which goes by so quickly that it's unnoticeable—the un-Time, so to speak. I must say that the natural scenery is religiously inspiring. Nature is my God. Yet the poverty in the cities saddens me. Yet all this misery makes me more human and less alienated. I know now that we all need each other. My brothers and sisters are hurting, and I must help.*

*Love,*

*St Claire*


My work has been extremely productive since I last saw St Claire. Despair is not there to kill my time by monopolising my thoughts and feelings. It's so hard to believe that I can do so much work. I am confident of finishing this novel at long last. I am also confident in the future. I'm happily creating as an artist. I am determined to marry St Claire as soon as she returns from India. That will be soon. Two more weeks. Yet I cannot forget K, she haunts my mind from time to time like an unhappy ghost. Strangely, when I think about her, I never use my memory, instead I fantasise about her. It has always been my fantasies that have kept our relationship alive. The artist in me believes in my fantasies. That I can sculpt reality into the image of my fantasies. But reality always proves unwieldy. It resists my willpower. Or rather, K refuses to play the role I allotted her in my movie. I don't like to give the idea that I am the goodie and K the baddie. I am drawn to her. She is unique, and I crave uniqueness, seeing it as a prophylactic against banality. We are both anarchists. The only difference is that I express my soul through Art and she through Life. In Life I am conservative, though in Art I am willing to play, control, and destroy my characters. In Life, she behaves like a novelist, and I feel like I am a character in her novel, subject to her narrative tyranny.

I receive another postcard from St Claire.

*Dear Ranulfo,*

*Hi, how are you? I'm fine. I've been working as a helper for this organisation that helps the poor and the sick. It's hard and distressing work. Guess who I met here in the hospital? Prince Jotel. He's changed so much. He's no longer a drunkard, or a self-pitying neurotic. He's said he's come to India to learn to love and care for others. He seems to have found some strength and wisdom. I wonder if Queen Clytoris is now his guardian angel. How's your novel coming along? Are you writing a happy ending? It's completely up to you.*
*Love,*
*St Claire*

The following week, I received another postcard.

*Dear Ranulfo,*
*I proposed to Prince Jotel, and he said yes. I'm so deliriously happy. We're making arrangements.*
*Love,*
*St Claire*

Goodbye, St Claire.

# CHAPTER 22

## Death Ward

They called this room the "Death Ward." People come here to die. Virginia was one of the patients. Had she wanted to, she could have had a private room, but she did not want to die alone. There were five other dying people in the room. One young 18-year-old youth, one 100-year-old man, one 40-year-old woman, one 10-year-old girl, and one age-indeterminate screamer, a man (or woman?) mummified in bandages, who screamed all day long in unutterable pain. This man was shrinking all the time; the doctors amputating his body limb by limb, organ by organ. So far, they have amputated both his legs and his right arm. Next week, his liver will have to go. What disease he was dying of was a mystery to the patients.

But in the ward, nobody cared to know each other's diseases. Dying was everyone's disease.

"I wonder if he could hear us," said the young man about the screaming mummy.

"I think he's only aware of his pain," answered the old man.

"That's terrible. What's the point of living?"

"What's a good-looking boy like you doing here? You should be out there in the world sowing your wild oats?" said the old man.

"What do you think killed me? Youth? You know how traumatic being young is? Youth is like those baby turtles freshly hatched on the beach, scrambling to the safety of the mother sea while hundreds of winged predators gobble them up one by one. When one is young, one is most vulnerable."

"I know what's killing you. Your virginity?"

"Does it show?" asked the boy, feeling ashamed.

"Yes, I can tell. You're terrified of life."

"I'm a wimp, I can't argue with you on that."

"Why don't you escape and lose your virginity? Better to die on the battlefield than to die in this rat hole."

"It's so easy to say those things. But, old man, I'm not built to make my words come true. I'm weak inside. When I plan to do something, I can't go through with it because I get scared and stop myself. You understand?"

The old man shook his head. "I've reached the age of a hundred by avoiding injury to myself. I've achieved this by inflicting injury on others. In my hundred years, I've broken thousands of hearts and thousands of bones. And remorse I've none."

"You're lucky. I still remorse over things I wasn't guilty of."

Virginia was listening from her bed. She hardly spoke; she just wanted to listen. Listening enlarged her world. Her loneliness had imprisoned her. She was, in a sense, now practising dying. She was relinquishing herself to make way for the greater world.

"Why don't the both of you shut up and let me die in peace!" shouted the middle-aged woman, glaring at the two men.

"Don't tell me to shut up, lady!" exploded the old man, his fury belied his feeble broken body.

"Shut up, you old fool!" the woman taunted his impotent male body.

"What are you angry about? You're so angry inside that when you die, you'll never rest in peace. You're damned to walk the planet earth as a ghost forever."

"I'm sick of your fucking opinions. You think you're so wise, but no, you're an idiot."

"We're all idiots, lady."

"Just shut up!"

"Please, everyone, don't fight," cried the little girl, who could pass eerily for Margaret O'Brien, the famous 1930s Hollywood child weepie star.

"I'm sorry, little girl," apologised the old man, smiling through his black rotting teeth.

The woman shot a poisonous gaze at the little girl. "You shut up, too, you false little bitch!"

"Leave the little girl alone," mumbled the youth timidly.

"This is a fucking conspiracy! Everybody hates me!" shouted the woman, pulling the blanket over her head.

"I don't hate you, Miss," said the little girl.

"Well, I hate you, you nauseating little brat!" pulling her head out of the blanket and sticking her tongue out, which was a sickly green colour.

"Please don't hate me, I want to be your friend," the little girl pleaded, smiling an irresistible smile like Shirley Temple.

"You make me puke!" She put her finger in her mouth. "Little girl, grow up. You think these guys like you? Not a dot. They want to sexually molest you."

"Hey! Don't talk that way to the little girl!" snarled the old man.

"You feel guilty, do you?"

"I've made love to thousands of women, but I've never molested a child," he declared.

"What's the difference between molesting a child and molesting a grown woman? Women got feelings too, you hypocrite!"

The old man did not reply.

"Now all of you shut up and let me die in peace!" Then she added, "And especially you!" throwing the bedpan at the screaming mummy. Strangely, it made him quiet...momentarily.

Virginia never took sides in any of the arguments. She listened for the sake of understanding. Understand the madness. Not actually a verbal understanding, but it was like she was capturing a spirit, a bird in one's hand, understanding the essence of life. Because she kept quiet all the time and looked very interested and concerned, the patients in the ward confided in her. Even the angry woman spoke to her.

"I kept waiting...waiting to live happily ever after, you know, meet Prince Charming who'll marry me...and that's what made everything endurable. I hated my whole life...I hated me...I hated people...I hated God...this universe was ugly and terrible, and I was ugly and terrible. I looked at the mirror and do you know what I saw...an ugly woman. I was no beautiful princess that Prince Charming would use his charms to win over...how could God torture me with this face...how could I ever find happiness...even if there was life after death, it would be hell because I would be stuck with my ugly face forever...I'll never be beautiful...I'll never be happy. Oh I wish I could die and end it there. No more consciousness, no more soul, no more face. Nothing. That is my Prince Charming—Prince Nothingness."

The nurses wheeled out the bandaged man one morning and in the evening he returned minus a few organs. His screaming continued incessantly. The little girl sat beside him and talked to him, but still he screamed. The little girl hugged him but this only hurt the bandaged creature, who screamed louder. Everything was painful for him. There was no medication, no sleep that could relieve him. Pain would not let go of him.

"No legs, no arms. What's the next thing they'll cut off? His head!" said the old man, outraged.

"At least they can't surgically remove his soul, that is, if we have one," said the young man

"He's better off dead," the woman said.

"Don't say that," cried the little girl. "Nobody deserves to die. Nobody!"

"He's not going to die, little girl," said the old man.

"How can you lie to her? Tell her the truth. We're all in this ward fucking dying!"

"Shut up!" shouted the old man.

"Are we all dying?" asked the little girl.

"No, we're here for a fucking holiday," the woman scoffed.

"Don't we go to heaven after we die?" she asked hopefully.

"Of course," said the old man unconvincingly.

"Bullshit! There is nothing after death. There is no God, and even if there was, he hasn't indicated that he cares a bit about us."

Then a nurse and a doctor arrived. They had come to speak to the old man. They drew the pale blue curtains around him. Everyone in the ward looked on with fear, even the hateful woman. They were terrified of doctors who went about like white, sterile, unsmiling messengers of death. This was the face of death. Utter sterility. Devoid of germs. Germs, which carried the disease called Life.

When they left, the old man put on a bravado act. "I've just been told that I'm pregnant."

When everyone was asleep that night, the old man spoke to Virginia. "It does not look good. I'm afraid I'm a goner. I want to share something with you that I've never shared with anyone. When I was 19, I was very much in love with a young woman in our village. We had known each other since we were children. She was four years younger than me. I loved her madly. One day, she went out to the countryside for a walk, and when she returned to the village, she was hysterical. After she had calmed down, we asked her what had happened to her. She wouldn't tell us. In fact, she wouldn't speak. She was silent for three days. I went out into the countryside looking for clues. I was sure she had been raped. When Bella began to talk again, she told us that she had seen God and that God had spoken to her. I tried to make her give more details. I was sceptical. But she wouldn't elaborate. She told me there were no details. It was God, something indescribable. I was sure she misinterpreted some natural phenomenon. But what shocked me was her announcement that she was joining a convent. I pleaded with her, I threatened her, but it was useless. God had taken control of her brain. I went crazy. I got drunk night after night. I fought with everybody. After a year, I set out for the convent where Bella resided. I entered the church and desecrated the religious icons. This God was the man who took my Bella away from me. I wanted to prove to him I was the better man. I entered the quarters where the nuns were sleeping. It was all very hushed, everyone was asleep. I chanced upon Bella's room. I woke her up. She was surprised to see me but glad, as if I was her friend or brother. How humiliating to be looked at by a woman and not seen as a flesh-and-blood man. I told her I was going to take her away and marry her. She refused to go, expressing how happy she was. I couldn't believe it. She chose to devote her life to a fantasy, a lie! She smiled, and this happiness cut me to the heart, so I hit her, hoping she'd become human again. But it wasn't her who was smiling at me. It was God mocking me. God, the invisible, the unknowable, the perfect. How could I, a mere mortal, a limited, ludicrous human, compete with a woman's imagination of perfection? I could not fight against invisible monsters! I beat her and I raped her. It was God whom I beat and raped. God was the enemy."

"And you know what she did? She started to pray, invoking God to forgive me and to enlighten me. I was so enraged that I placed my hands around her neck and choked her as hard as I could, imagining that I was choking God to death. She died. I fled the convent and travelled all over the world by land and by ship. And all that time, I never felt guilty about her death. You only feel guilty if you have gained something at someone's expense. I gained nothing. I simply gave her to God. I was the loser."

"Now that I'm dying. I feel God's hands on my throat. Yet sometimes I feel his hand on my heart filling me with love and forgiveness. I resist that feeling. I don't know if I could ever forgive God for taking my Bella away from me."

Virginia was quite disturbed by his confessions. She thought about it through the night. His story was not in itself unique or grotesque, it rather epitomised life itself. This story was about love, hate, despair, man, woman, and God, and all these elements converged into tragedy.

All roads lead to Rome, and Rome was a city of madness.

Next morning, they took the old man to the operating table.

"Now we can have some peace and quiet," said the woman callously.

"He'll come back, won't he?" said the little girl.

"Yes, as a ghost!" and the woman burst into cruel laughter.

The young man intervened. "If he doesn't come back, he'll be going to heaven, and that's a beautiful place to go."

The girl asked, "Is there heaven? Is there God?"

The woman couldn't resist. "There is no life after death. And especially no life before death."

The youth answered the little girl, "No one knows, child. It's a secret."

"I'm scared."

"Don't be scared."

"I'm scared." And the little girl cried softly.

"I want to puke!" the woman shouted, grimacing.

The young man went to the little girl's bed and held her hand, "Hey, it's all right. I'm here. I'm here. I'll protect you."

The old man never returned. No one mentioned it. The little girl's health took a bad turn very soon afterwards. She lay in bed, delirious half of the time. She kept screaming about a big bad wolf trying to eat her. The youth stayed faithfully by her side. Her moments of lucidity came less and less. The Big Bad Wolf was devouring her.

"Please someone help me," cried the little girl in a last moment of clarity. "The pain is so scary."

"Don't be scared," the boy comforted her.

"God is a big, bad wolf. I saw him in my dreams."

"Dreams are not real."

The little girl made an ugly face and screamed at him, "Go away! I hate you! I hate everybody! Stop eating me! I want to be left alone!"

"You don't mean these things you say. You're suffering from a lot of pain."

"Leave me alone! I hate you!" shouted the little girl with ferocity. "Go away!"

"No, I won't go away. I'll hold your hand and protect you from the big bad wolf."

The little girl's health deteriorated, and her screams grew louder and more horrible. "Stop eating me! Stop eating me!" she screamed at some unseen creature...or was it the Big Bad Wolf?

The little girl stopped screaming, her face serene in death.

The woman visited Virginia that night. "I'm really shook up about the little girl. I might be bitter and cynical and all, but things like this, you know, terrify me and sadden me. It's like some great horror. And I thought my heart was dead. I felt for her. I even cried. That's what frightens me. To me, the Universe has no room for sentiment. All the space has been taken up by a devouring logic. The Big Bad Wolf, as the girl would say. Hell, I don't know what we were created for if it weren't for great lashings of sentimentality, you know, getting teary-eyed about sad things and happy things. We weren't meant to be strong, to understand, to cope. We human beings were designed to be crazy. I guess we're just an aberration in this logical universe. Truth is not a human thing."

The woman's personality altered dramatically after the little girl's death. Gone were her anger and her bitterness. She wanted to open her heart and never shut it again. She was friendly and helpful, and she even struck up a good friendship with the young man. One day, they wheeled away the bandaged man, and they returned him without his body. He was just a head, an octopus with tubes as tentacles.

"Poor man, isn't he ever going to die?" said the woman.

"This is the future of medicine—doctors would have found a cure for death. The only side effect is that we'd be vegetables forever."

"They can't let him live this way. This is terrible."

"Death is more the terrible," said the youth.

"Is it? Why can't death be beautiful like getting born to a new world."

"There's no logic for life after death. The only reason is compassion."

"Personally, I'm a bit wary of expecting compassion. Look at our religions, there's no compassion after death, only judgement. Judgement expects too much from us mere humans."

"Crazy," the woman said. "The universe is a most intelligent, sophisticated, complex creature, and yet we think it's not capable of compassion. There has to be compassion. I hope that it's out there…"

Next day the bandaged man was 'out there'. Out of compassion, the woman picked up his head, tearing it from his life support, and threw it out the window. The police came and arrested her. Rumours were bruited that she had died in prison before her trial. The young man prayed, as if hoping that the compassion in his heart would reach out to her "out there" and spark her into being.

"I guess I'm next," said he.

"Are you prepared for it?" asked Virginia.

"How could I? I'm 18 years old. I haven't begun to live. I never had a girlfriend. I never experienced fatherhood. I never had a chance to succeed in this world. I might as well not have been born. I look back at my life and it's all childhood memories. When I look back at my childhood, I was just a happy idiot. Being an adult—that's what life is all about. The opportunity to choose your happiness…or your idea of happiness."

"What are you doing here? Get out there in the real world."

"I'm scared."

"Are you scared?"

"It's not that. I want to stay here."

"Why?"

"Because I'm in love with you."

"Oh."

"I shouldn't have said it. But anyway, you're the first woman I've ever said it to. I guess that's some sort of triumph, isn't it?"

"Why don't you ask me out for a date?"

"Where? They won't let us out."

"We'll find a way."

"All right."

"Haven't you forgotten something?"

"What?"

"Aren't you going to ask me out for a date?"

"Oh. You wanna go out on a date with me?"

"Sure. I'd love to. We'll make it really special. A candle-lit dinner, some wine. Can you arrange that?"

"I think so. Wow. My first date. With the famous actress Virginia Prag."

"I'm not just a famous actress. I'm human like you."

Later that night, she waited for him. He had sneaked out of the hospital to buy some things, smuggle in some Chinese food, wine, dessert, and get some hot new gear to wear. She waited for him for what seemed like an endless amount of time. She was worried. Did he collapse and die? Did he chicken out? Or did he meet a girl and fall in love? Before the next question entered her head, she was asleep.

Next morning, she woke up to bright, dusty light streaming through the window. She immediately looked towards the young man's bed. It was empty, unslept in. He never returned. Now she was alone. She was alone and had nobody to listen to. She hated being alone. She had thought she had found some inner peace by listening to her friends. She thought she was free of herself. Now there was nobody to imprison herself to. Now she was the observed, the sad creature in the zoo. She sobbed uncontrollably, tears gushing out of her. But it was tears of sadness, not of pain, as she remembered how much she missed her friends in the ward, how much she missed all the people she had met and loved. She wanted so much at this very moment to tell them all that she loved them and to ask for forgiveness for having caused them pain from unnecessary emotional drama. The drama had ended, and all that was left was to thank everyone for having taken a part in her life. She reflected on her past, and it all seemed sweet to her, there was no bitterness, no hatred, and she was grateful for having lived and loved. She remembered the good times and she laughed at the bad, how unnecessary all that conflict was, when deep down all she wanted was to love and to care. And if they didn't love her, it didn't matter, she loved them anyway. After all these years, her heart still remained intact. Death no longer seemed scary; she was no longer alone for her heart, shining, burning, was within her, still loving, each and every beat....

Virginia was so exhausted; she knew she couldn't hang on to life anymore. She drifted in and out of consciousness. She thought she saw her cat come to her and hug her and cry. She wasn't sure if she had been dreaming it; after all, cats don't cry.

Or maybe this one did. A faint smile came to her face, and it lingered even after she died.

# CHAPTER 23

## Baby Adolf

I'm fed up with myself. I think there's a conspiracy by my brain to screw my life up. I wish I just didn't think or feel. It leads me nowhere. My brain gets in the way of my finding happiness. K, I'm sorry, I let you down all the time. I am too often ill-advised by myself. Of course, it doesn't help you too are ill-advised by yourself. You are much too hot tempered and vindictive. Don't you realise that anger is like a cloudburst, it comes, vanishes, and then it's sunshine? But you intellectualise your emotions and make the storm a permanent idea. You're bellicose, and I'm morose.

What a great pair! The Bitch and her Wimp! Oh K, we love each other so much, but we're so fucked up! Why do we hurt each other so needlessly? But that's the human condition for you. Shut up, Ranulfo, and write. The readers don't want to know about your problems. Act like a man and write!

Tomtin's baby was born, and President Carol called him Adolf. President Carol had big plans for Baby Adolf. This baby would be no computer programmer, no artist, no plumber, no, he would be raised to be a leader and nothing less. President Carol was going to teach him power: how to gain it, how to use it, and how to keep it. Power was the only thing you needed to know in this crazy, confused world. Her daughter, Virginia, did not understand that. She got lost in the Void of Art and paid the price. My poor Virginia, but I won't mess up with Adolf, thought President Carol. Baby Adolf appeared to have the goods. He was one hell of a screamer; he screamed and screamed all day; he wasn't crying, for there was no fear on his cherubic face. There was method in his screams. He relished the annoyance, pain, and despair he could drive his nurses to. His father, Tomtin, had given up on him and life and turned to the solace of Valium, alcohol, TV, talkback radio, and Elvis Presley records. Mentally he was gone. But President Carol adored Baby Adolf. She would hold him face to face and they would scream at each other in a contest of volume and persistence. Baby Adolf never played with toys; viciously, ecstatically, he dismembered toys. Forming a bulwark around his crib was a gruesome display of decapitated teddy bears, their cute heads impaled upon sticks, their stuffing- free bodies lying limp on the floor. His nurses, bruised and cut from his playful games, naturally, never stayed long in their tenure.

Eventually, it was necessary for President Carol to hire the strongest woman in the world, a woman 7 square feet in size. Next morning, the nurse was found dead, dismembered like one of Adolf's teddy bears. People suspected Baby Adolf, but they could not believe that a tiny baby, and oh so cute, could do such a heinous thing.

In the baby's third month on planet earth, he learnt to stand and walk, well, actually, goosestep. President Carol presented him with a military diaper and knee-high baby boots. Baby Adolf cherished it and grew a moustache to complement the outfit. He was sent to a childcare centre at the Presidential Palace so he could be with other children and reveal his social place—leader, follower, or outsider? He immediately demonstrated that he was a natural leader all right. The other babies and young toddlers stood at attention to him like soldiers, and he made them march and follow orders. Well, he didn't speak yet, but somehow the children understood the gist of his gibberish.

"Goooggooga!"

"Yes, sir!" replied a child in a quaking voice, and immediately did one hundred push-ups on the spot.

"Googooogooogee!"

"Yes, leader!" replied a 4-year-old girl, who immediately jumped on the push-upping boy and bashed him black and blue. And she was the sweetest child one could ever meet. Baby Adolf had a mental hold on the children, who needed to please him and obey him. He had a presence that made one feel immediately inferior, and obedience seemed natural. One did not hate him, for he seemed to know your soul and where you wanted to go. Obey and he will take you there. The children in the childcare centre became his gang, which terrorised the palace. It started off as harmless pranks, but it turned more and more serious. He became involved in protection rackets and blackmail. He developed an intelligence network, which somehow knew everything about each and everyone in the palace.

President Carol sent Baby Adolf to school since she felt he was being cramped in the little world of childcare. She wanted him rushed to the wider world. President Carol had little patience for the slowness of childhood. She wanted to see quick results. Baby Adolf didn't mind. At school, he had the same effect on the children. Children of all ages were enchanted by him. Except for two bullies who picked on him and called him a brat. The two bullies later became his bodyguards when he blackmailed them by having photos of them in bed cuddling with their teddy bears. Quickly, the school came under his control. He had the principal twisted around his little finger, for he knew that the principal had a sexual preference for sheep. He forced the principal to decree that there should be no homework. In the end, it was a complete overthrow. The teachers were all routed and were humiliated in front of the school by having their exposed bottoms caned. Baby Adolf and the children celebrated their victory by torching the school library.

One school wasn't enough for him, so he spread his revolution to other schools. Children everywhere were spellbound by him, who represented a vision of liberation: freedom from adults, freedom to play, eat, and watch TV all day long. Children were tired of adult oppression. For so long, adults were in control, and children had to obey, obey. Children were being brainwashed into becoming future replicas of their obnoxious parents. Children had no say in their future. For far too long, adults have abused children, teaching them lies, emotionally scarring them, driving them into a straitjacket, and crippling them as adults.

Well, no longer. Baby Adolf was going to set the children free. The future would belong to the children, and the future would not be shackled to the past like a ball and chain. The past was not the present was not the future. Children would not become the cracked mirror of their parents. Seeing Baby Adolf as their best hope for freedom, children willingly gave themselves to him. He incited children to sow dissension in their own homes. Talk back to your parents, don't do your chores, don't clean your bedrooms, disobey, disobey. Then start a campaign of terror. Destroy Daddy's golf clubs, destroy Mother's vibrator, flush down Grandpa's medication, bust Grandmother's rocking chair. Children no longer felt alone, vulnerable to the authority of their parents; they were part of a movement, a straw in the broom which would sweep away the tyranny of adults. The broom was Baby Adolf.

President Carol was unconcerned about this new tide of affairs; she was proud of her son. She had taught him well. Nonetheless, her cabinet ministers were very anxious. They felt like dust soon to be swept away into the bin of history. Aha, if the dust rallied together to form a stone, it could be hurled to knock out Baby Adolf.

"President Carol, your son is posing a serious threat to our nation. The children are up in arms. We must quell their revolution or else we shall face ruin." Spoken by Linda Tetchnik, Head of National Security.

"But he's only a cute little baby. A little headstrong perhaps." President Carol smiling stupidly, as only a doting parent could.

"He's a political anarchist!"

"Baby games! It won't come to anything."

"He's threatening the stability of our nation. You must do something."

"What do you want me to do? Ground him?"

"He must be controlled."

"You worry too much," and President Carol dismissed her away.

Later, Linda Tetchnik met with the other ministers to plot the death of Baby Adolf.

"He must die. Otherwise, he will endanger our nation and everything we have worked for."

"How should we terminate him?"

"First, we must get him alone."

"I know when he is alone. 3 o'clock. That's when he takes his afternoon nap."

"Tomorrow then? Shall we agree on that?"

"Yes."

"How shall we kill him?"

"He will leak to death. We shall knife him many holes."

"How do we explain his death to President Carol?"

"We'll have to kill two birds with one stone."

"You mean?"

"Yes, we must also kill President Carol."

"Yes, I agree. President Carol will kill us if she finds out we have killed her beloved son."

"Yes, I understand."

"Then tomorrow it is."

At 3 o'clock the next afternoon, Baby Adolf slumbered in his crib, dreaming of cakes, angels, talking animals, and concentration camps. Everything seemed okay until he dreamt he was Julius Caesar, just about to be sheskebabbed. He opened his eyes only to see that the nightmare was real. The room had darkened as the ministers loomed over him with their raised knives. Baby Adolf let out an ear-splitting shriek. Before the assassins could plunge their knives into Baby Adolf's blubber, they were soon attached to biting babies. Hundreds of babies swarming around them in a biting frenzy like piranhas. The ministers were trapped in the room. Babies charged into the room to join in the dental frenzy. Linda Tetchnik tried to kick and hit her way out of this sticky situation, but there were too many for her to deal with. As soon as she would dislodge a baby, another would latch on immediately to the vacant space of scrumptious flesh. She screamed for help until one baby flew into her face and bit her tongue off. All the other ministers were in an equal predicament: babies, babies, babies, biting them to death. The nursery room was bespattered with blood. The bodies of the would-be-assassins were mangled like chewing gum.

Baby Adolf was incensed. This was an attempt on his life. If he died, then the movement would die with him, the children losing their voice and guiding spirit. No one else could shape all the children into a wedge which would rip apart the structure of society. His death would mean that oppressed children all over the world would remain abused by their parents for generations to come. Baby Adolf knew that his life was vulnerable until he assumed the mantle of power. He must tarry no more. He was ready. Then he delivered this historic speech:

"Googooogaaageeegeeegooogoogoogaagaagaagaagoogoogoogoogoogaageeegeegaaa geeeegaa!!!!"

The babies had been waiting for this speech for a long time. It was a speech calling for the overthrow of the government, which was his Mum. The babies cheered, and without any dillydallying, they charged out of the room, crawling headlong at breakneck speed towards President Carol's office.

In the meantime, President Carol was in her office, showing baby photos to an African leader. "Isn't he adorable?"

"Yes." Yawn.

A huge roar like a tsunami.

The door flung wide open, and babies blasted into the room as if a maternity hospital had blown up and flung babies everywhere. A baby leapt and attached itself to President Carol's nose. Baby Johnny on her left ear, Baby Cathy on her right nipple, Baby Ivan on her right bottom cheek, Baby Nguyen on her right big toe and and and…President Carol was well aware that this was it. Her death.

The pain was excruciating as the babies gobbled her up. It had all come to this. This ignominious exit. All those years of building and constructing, all to be toppled by this grotesque humiliation. Yet she had secretly foreboded this; she had chosen to walk the path of pragmatism and always knew that her real and superior enemy was the shadow of absurdity that dogged her every step, and now the shadow was to overtake her, consume her, mock the solemnity of her soul, her whole life degraded and ridiculed in the final moments for which she had never prepared in her pragmatic paradigm. And who was to ring down the curtain on her but her child, Baby Adolf, the child of her being, who imbibed her soul and understood that Power was Truth, and Truth Power, and all he needed to know…

"Goo goo!" shouted Baby Adolf.

Baby Adolf had spared his mother's life. President Carol was shocked; didn't he know power had no room for sentimentality? It was love, love for Baby Adolf, that had brought her downfall, and now love, she foreboded, would bring down Baby Adolf. She had failed, after all, to teach him about power. Yet she didn't feel like a total failure as they led her away to the tower; Baby Adolf's love consoled her.

Baby Adolf sat in President Carol's chair, his head barely visible above the desk, but he knew he was in the right place.

"Googoogaagooo!"

The new President was saluted in Nazi style by a room full of babies.

## CHAPTER 24

## King Prawn Goes Crazy

Yes, dear readers, it's poetry time! Perhaps the novel restricts my ability to express my relationship with K.

### THE GAP

*Sometimes it gets to me, the weather,*
*who pleases only herself, too cold, too hot,*
*Nature, the poet's beloved is a beautiful woman*
*without a heart.*
*Sometimes it gets to me, loving you,*
*you, who is married to your fears,*
*and can never be free. I, who is bound*
*to my dreams, can never understand you.*
*I judge reality, you justify it,*
*I seek solutions, you deny it.*
*Can we find sympathy, I in your fears,*
*and you in my dreams, and in that sympathy*
*create a bridge to unite us.*
*Often it gets to me, the gap*
*separating us, this great gap of sympathy*
*which makes our love into islands*

King Prawn went crazy. It was inevitable. He had exploded and created a great empire. Now there was nothing left to do but implode. Floor after floor of sanity came tumbling down.

One morning, King Prawn woke up at the ungodly hour of 6 am, suffering from delusions of normality. He got up, washed, and dressed himself in a smart businessman's suit. Rudely awakened at so early an hour, Queen Golderella was upset. She cursed King Prawn, asking him what the hell was he doing up so early in the morning.

"I'm going to work, honey. I must hurry or else I'll miss the bus and train. Don't want to be late. You know how the boss gets angry with late employees. As he says, 'A late employee is a fired employee'."

She had no clue what he meant and was certain it was all a dream. Queen Golderella hated dreams because she had no control; in reality, she was in charge.

"What are you talking about? You're King Prawn, ruler of half the world."

Mr Prawn laughed. "Sure, I'm King. A King of my little castle in the suburbs. Goodbye, my lovely Queen. Don't get up, I'll fix myself breakfast."

He laughed as he walked out the bedroom. "Me a King. That's funny."

Mr Prawn ate with relish the bowl of Coco Pops cereal. Soft on the kitchen floor, miaowing and circling Mr Prawn's legs, the cat looked up with pleading eyes.

–Mkgnao!

–There you are, pussy wussy, Mr Prawn said. You want a bowl of milk, my cutie pie.

– Miaaw, the cat politely asked.

Pretty cat. My father hated cats. Then again, my father didn't like anyone or anything much. Rising, Mr Prawn twostepped to the refrigerator opening and culled out the carton of milk wedged between the orange juice and the bottle of Coca-Cola.

Bending over the empty cat bowl on the floor, he poured the milk, white and cold as his wife's bottom. The cat scurried and drew his head to the milk, sniffed it, and darted out quick laps of his pink tongue.

– Miaowthankyou.

– You're welcome, said Mr Prawn. I like cats. You can judge a person by the pet they keep. Cat lovers are vain, selfish, independent, lazy, and snobbish. Dog lovers are dependent, fascist, subservient, hyperactive, and stupid. What's the time? Raise wristwatch to eye range. Quarter to Seven. Must rush.

At the bus stop, underneath a silvery grey cloud mantle, his eyes alternately watching the road and his watch, Mr Prawn waited. Should have brought an umbrella. Don't want to get wet. Shall I rush inside and get an umbrella? Will I make it? No, it's too late. Or maybe it's not too late. Um…no…yes…no…no…yes…no…oh here comes the bus. Right on time. Paying the bus driver, coins plucked from wallet, Mr Prawn searched the bus for the best seat available. A young brunette and an old white-haired woman both had vacant seats next to them. Choosing beauty over age, he seated himself cosily next to the fragrant young flesh who gazed dreamily out the window. I could smell her. Love women and their fragrances. Like flowers. Let me be a bee and sip your nectar.

Strike a conversation. Impress her with my worldliness and my intelligence. Women like older men. We're more mature and more in control. A young man's chaos. Yes, I remember. I was a dream machine. Horizons to conquer. Ha! I conquered the office all right. Oh no! I'm about to fart. It's a big one. Must silence it. Don't want to make a fool of myself. Press my buttocks solidly together. Shut down anal muscles. Tight. Tighten. It's approaching. Restrain. The will to power. Nietzsche, I beseech you.

– BBBBRRRRRRHHHRRTTTTTT!!!!!!!!!!!!!!!!

Pretend it's not me. Look innocent. People are giggling. Must pretend nothing happened. Woman next to me is covering her nose. I'll never catch this bus ever again. Never! I'll never live it down. A fart can ruin a person. Strange, historians don't record farts. Perhaps famous people don't fart. Geniuses must have great anal control. Geniuses don't make fools of themselves. Shouldn't have drunk the milk. Lactose intolerant. Oh my God, another one is on the way. A major one. Maybe I should get off the next stop. Too late. It's coming. Battle stations! Resist! Resist! Will to the utmost power!

BRAGGKEKDKDIDKELDIKELDIDKSJSJHSQLSLOELSLSLNNZXHBBBBBRO FOSJSKSIWLSOLSOISJDFUDJDUIDJDUASKWUWJSJZOQKDIKWSOIZIPADO ODAYOWATAWONDERFULDAYKDKDIDKDIEKDIILSLSOLROSLQPPA!!!!!

The bus erupted with O's of mouth, guffaws of laughter.

HAHAHAHAHAEHEHEHEHEHEHOHOHOHOOHAHAAHHAHEHEHEHH OHOHHIHIHIHHHAHHAHAHAHAHEHEHAHA!!!!!!!!

Red as a prawn.

Mr Prawn entered the Hook and Crook Accountancy Office, situated ten floors up in a modern glass skyscraper. From outside, one would think from the windows that clouds inhabited the interior. The clouds were mere reflection, just as one could not see the madness inside Mr Prawn's bright shining eyes as he entered an air-conditioned office and sat himself behind a desk, believing it was his cubicle. A woman with long, straight, shiny, black hair parted at the middle stood up from her receptionist desk and asked Mr Prawn why he, a stranger, was sitting in a desk that belonged to Mr Wilkins, an accountant in the firm.

– Are you my new secretary? asked Mr Prawn. Good looking sort she.

– I'm not your secretary. But this is not your desk. You don't work here.

– This is my desk, said Mr Prawn. I'm positively sure.

– I'm sorry, said the woman. But you are mistaken.

Mr Prawn raised one eyebrow, his right. He was most indignant, after all had he not dedicated thirty years of his life in this firm.

— My lady, he reprimanded her, how rudely you speak to me after the many years of industry I have given to this office. Please depart, or else I shall see the boss and have you terminated.

Mr Prawn was proud of himself, voicing his mind to the young disrespectful woman. The youth of today have no respect. The insolent woman strode with angry swinging hips to the office of the greatest accountant that had ever lived in the history of the world. A little man appeared at the doorway glaring at Mr Prawn, the little man's pallid skin giving contrast to his killer blue eyes, which threw shafts and even hand grenades at Mr Prawn, who had now cast his eyes blissfully on the work for the day.

To Mr Prawn with long angry steps the little man marched, the taller woman keeping pace with hasty little steps. Mr Prawn was now conscious of a shadow darkening his ledger. He looked up at the little man and beamed an affectionate, respectful smile.

— Good morning, said Mr Prawn. I was just about to see you about the Yi account.

— I don't know who you are, spluttered the diminutive but greatest accountant, spraying large spheres of saliva on Mr Prawn's face. But I would like it if you were to leave this office right now or else I shall call security?

— Are you firing me? asked Mr Prawn, taken aback like JFK's head shot.

— Get thee hence from this time forth from this Paradise and live beyond the walls where forever you will fend for yourself, struggle in pain and futility, and suffer disease, old age, loneliness, and death.

— Please forgive me, beseeched poor Prawn, my soul is in torment.

— You have sinned most terribly, a sin that is beyond redeeming. Nothing can save your damned soul. Out! This Paradise cannot bear your odious presence any longer. Out! Hell awaits your black soul! Out! Death, pain, misery, are now your only fit companions. Out!

Mr Prawn wept gigantically, and his tears precipitated into a flood which flushed him out of Paradise. He looked around his new surroundings and saw all was ugliness. He had arrived in the City of Sorrow.

*Night. A cobbled street, wet, glistening, weeping. Wreathes of fog creep in tardily and wrap themselves around the expressionistic buildings and forlorn figures. The shimmering lampposts* outshine the dazed full moon. A colourful, rowdy bar, where a fracas is raging, men cursing and punching each other. A gaudy brothel guarded by an unsmiling whore. Mr Prawn walks down the street, his elongated tie trailing twenty feet behind him. His grey business suit is five sizes too large. His tight trousers hitched short, exposing white socks and hairy shins. Like a wolf, he howls at the fogveiled moon.

MR PRAWN: All is lost! All is lost!

(A little boy wearing chequered golf pants, pointed velvet shoes which curl upwards, a brocaded frock coat over a lace-frilled shirt, a top hat ten feet high, tugs at Mr Prawn's tie.)

LITTLE BOY: Excuse me, mister, is anything the matter?

MR PRAWN: My life has lost its meaning.

LITTLE BOY: I have a dictionary. (*Takes out Samuel Johnson's Dictionary.*) Maybe I can help you find the meaning?

(The dictionary bursts into a flock of doves fluttering through the night sky.)

MR PRAWN: O woe is me. What lies ahead sans job?

(A prostitute, multivaginal, dressed in a short red silk cheongsam, her boa, a boa constrictor, and six-inch cork platform shoes.)

PROSTITUTE: For $30 I can give you a blowjob.

BOY: A soul job is what he needs.

(From the night descends a nun capped in a 727 tail fin.)

NUN: (*to Prostitute and Prawn*) Pray to God and repent all your sins before it is too late.

(A hideous polymatous, dolichopodous, carminative, podobromhidris monster hovers before King Prawn.)

MONSTER: I am your soul, Mr Prawn. I beg you make me well, I want to be beautiful again.

MR PRAWN: O most horrid, horrid soul. I can't bear to look.

PROSTITUTE: (*to the monster*) Have you tried cosmetic surgery?

MONSTER: Which doctor would you recommend?

NUN: Repent of all your sins, Mr Prawn.

PROSTITUTE: (*to Nun*) Beat it! This is my corner!

NUN: I was lost, and I have found my way! Thanks to the shopping centre directory.

MR PRAWN: Show me the way. I am long lost.

(*An Aussie copper riding on the back of a red roo hops around Mr Prawn.*)

POLICE: Mate, go to jail and receive free meals and free accommodation.

MR PRAWN: Must I be punished for my sins?

POLICE: Fart the crowbar! There are no freebies outside the slammer. Tom, Dick and Joe must cough up. So, pull out your onkas, mate, and shout me some VBs. (*A massive spectre rolls into the streets bulldozing away the incoming traffic. It is a two-storey farmhouse in diaphanous apparel. The front door swings open and from the messy interior bellows a voice.*)

THE GHOST OF HARRY THE HOUSE: You've killed me, King Prawn. You've killed me and my future children and my future grandchildren and my future great grandchildren and etcetera and etcetera.

MR PRAWN: Please forgive me. How can I make amends?

HARRY: You cannot! I died a virgin! There is no greater hell than being an eternal virgin, which you have rendered me.

MR PRAWN: Surely in heaven you can have sex.

HARRY: Are you kidding? We kneel and pray all day. The horror! The horror!

MR PRAWN: O most tormented timber, nothing I can do for you, but can you not help assuage a tormented soul as mine and forgive me.

HARRY: Never!

(*A man in a tight checkered suit carrying an alligator's head suitcase. He carries a smile on a stick, which he screens in front of his sour mouth.*)

THEATRICAL AGENT: Sell your soul and be a famous celebrity.

MR PRAWN: I want oblivion. Sweet Nothingness Hallelujah!

AGENT: (*produces a 200-page contract written in Swahili*) Sign on the dotted line and I'll produce an album no one listens to, a movie no one watches, a book no one reads. A failed artist! What greater oblivion could there be?

MR PRAWN: To never have been born!

(*Swooping like a bird of prey, Elvis Presley in rhinestone studded white cloak and jump suit.*)

ELVIS: Don't sell your soul, man. You soul is all you have. (*To Nun*) Hello, baby. You want my autograph?

NUN: No, but can you get God's autograph?

ELVIS: There is no God. I'm the best there is.

MR PRAWN: If there is no God, then who will teach humankind?

ELVIS: Learn how to live, that's all you need to find out.

MR PRAWN: If there is no God, there is nothing to learn. All is futile.

ELVIS: Living is all we have.

MR PRAWN: I don't want to live.

(*A tall man in green velvet coat and breeches sniffs a plucked sunflower. Arrows protrude from his body like St Sebastian.*)

OSCAR WILDE: What indeed is an Elvis Presley? I'm afraid that this century is in dire need of my impeccable taste.

ELVIS: I did to myself what society did to you.

OSCAR: All artists need to be crucified. There's no greater thrill. Nothing penetrates better than nail upon flesh. It is the ultimate orgasm.

ELVIS: Food is the ultimate orgasm. Everything else is loneliness.

(*A giant juicy tomato sauce-soaked hamburger materialises before Elvis.*)

HAMBURGER (*growling*): Come to Mama!

ELVIS: Mama! (*He swan dives to the bun opening burger and sinks inside the melted cheese.*)

HAMBURGER: Yummy! Rock stars are scrumptious!

MR PRAWN: Sure, I'll get myself a job. I'll get a job. I'll show that Mr Crook.

OSCAR: Work is so unbecoming to a beauty in repose.

(*A beam of light drops before them. A bearded man comes out of the light. He wears a long white tunic and blue mantle. A halo shines around his head.*)

NUN: Is it the Messiah?

MR PRAWN: Will you save me?

NUN: Save us all, O Lord!

D H LAWRENCE (*throws off his halo*): Messiah my arse! What society needs is a good kick in the arse! It's about time messiahs crucify the masses. Save Christ and damn Christians!

NUN: You're not Jesus.

LAWRENCE: Kiss my unholy arse!

OSCAR (*lifts up Lawrence's robe*): Tis a pity that the beautiful moon is scarred and cratered at closer look.

MR PRAWN: I want to die!

OSCAR: Death is the last refuge of a bad plot.

NUN: Death is the Master's bedroom.

LITTLE BOY: Death is angels and cake.

POLICEMAN: Death is a down to earth fellow.

PROSTITUTE: Death is most likely an anti-climax.

*(Cowled Death with sickle tap dances over a stage of skeletal remains.)*

DEATH (*sings*): That's entertainment!

AMBIVALENT AUDIENCE: Boo! Hurray! Boo! Hurray!

DEATH (*to King Prawn*): Conclamatum est. Hahahaha!

MR PRAWN: I must get a job.

*(Enter a hydra-headed monster crawling upon its large slimy belly. The heads are of nine employers.)*

EMPLOYER 1: I'm sorry. We're looking for a great poet to fill in our vacant managerial position.

EMPLOYER 2: Your nose is too small.

EMPLOYER 3: You are a worthless good-for-nothing scum. If we have a vacancy for a managing director, we will give you a call.

EMPLOYER 4: I'm afraid the vacancy has already been filled with cement.

EMPLOYER 5: My advice to you, old man, is to stick your other foot in the grave.

EMPLOYER 6: Not once during the interview did you comment on my good looks.

EMPLOYER 7: There has never been a vacancy. I advertise so I can humiliate people.

EMPLOYER 8: I'll hire you on one condition. That you kiss my arse once every workday.

EMPLOYER 9: Sorry, I wasn't listening. You bore me senseless.

MR PRAWN: Nobody wants me.

PROSTITUTE: $40 I'll say I want you. $1,000,000 to say I love you.

OSCAR: For nothing I'll say I love you. For your soul I'll say I want you.

D H LAWRENCE: I'm sick of these personal singulars. The ego is a disease. Let there be love but let there be no lovers. Deliver us, O Lord, from personality.

EMPLOYER 1: Mr Lawrence. You're the man I want in charge of our sales department.

LAWRENCE: Damn your money. I shall have no merchants in the temple.

EMPLOYER 1: You're hired. When can you start?

LAWRENCE: When you replace the profit motive with the life motive.

*(He finds a sword and hacks off the heads of the nine employers.)*

MR PRAWN: This cruel, cruel world. It has no place for old men. But where can I go? There is only Nowhere. Perhaps Death will be my sanctuary. But will Death shed away my sordid flesh and wretched mind? I want Death, but not if I have to live again.

*(Prince Jotel in embroidered black doublet with white ruffs, padded trunk hose, black stockings, and peaked black and white shoes. He is reading a dusty old tome in his velvet black glove.)*

MR PRAWN: My son, my son. Have you come to take care of your old father?

PRINCE JOTEL *(glances up from his book and studies Mr Prawn)*: I know you not, old man.

MR PRAWN: Surely you are Prince Jotel, begotten of my loins and the late Queen Clytoris.

PRINCE JOTEL: I am the famed spawn of the immaculate Queen Clytoris. And pray, who are you? Your loins I recognise not.

MR PRAWN: I am Mr Prawn. Your very father.

PRINCE: Not my father, you are a mummer!

MR PRAWN: Do not deny your creator.

PRINCE: I don't need a creator. I am an artist!

MR PRAWN: My son a creator! He created while I destroyed.

PRINCE: Come, I believe I have a part for you in my new play.

MR PRAWN: A job for me?

PRINCE: Your pay will be a pittance, of course.

MR PRAWN: Oh, thank you, thank you. I am useful once again.

PRINCE: How dreary you are. But never mind. The curtains, please, ring it up.


## DJEIDLDKILAELDX

### by Prince Jotel

*(An old man in rags enters. He sees the audience. He takes out his penis and pisses on the people in the front rows.)*

OLD MAN: Deishlsloos! Dfododohlkowopapsoilloshjlsjhlwoidkwi!

Didjwlsososlwoapp! Llaosirhoahclkhoolelsosis! kdidkdisksidis! Idkdidididisidi! Deslsos!

*(He bends over, drops his pants, and moons at the audience. He farts.)*

### THE END


PRINCE JOTEL *(clapping)*: Bravo! Bravo!

MR PRAWN: Thank you. Can I be paid now?

PRINCE: Here's your fee. *(He kicks Mr Prawn in the guts. He doubles over in pain.)*

MR PRAWN *(groaning)*: Why did you do that?

PRINCE: The artist must suffer for his art. I must speed. Thank you very much, Mr Prawn. I'll call you, don't call me.

MR PRAWN: Where are you going?

PRINCE: The play is over.

MR PRAWN: What about me? I have no home. I am your father. Aren't you going to take care of me in my dotage?

PRINCE JOTEL: You are mistaken. I have no father. My Mother is an immaculate virgin.

MR PRAWN: Queen Clytoris is no virgin!

PRINCE JOTEL: What was lost can be found. It has been nice talking to you, Mr Prawn, but I must dash. Farewell, old fool.

MR PRAWN: Goodbye, my son.

THUNDER: Boombaraboom!

MR PRAWN: Hark! The sounds of war! But I longed for the sounds of peace. The war in my head I cannot win.

LIGHTNING: Karazzzzz!!!!!

MR PRAWN: No more fire and thunder, sing birds, sing wind, sing sun.

RAIN: Pitterpatterpitterpatterpitterpatter...

MR PRAWN: I am abandoned by all.

(Swinging from a chandelier, Errol Flynn lands. He is dressed in swashbuckling attire, with a prop sabre in one hand and a bottle of whisky in the other. He parries with the rain and lunges his sword into the imaginary heart of the night.)

ERROL FLYNN (offers a swig to Mr Prawn): Have a drink, friend. There is no better companion to misery.

MR PRAWN: Can drink kill my misery?

ERROL: Every day misery is born, so every day you must kill misery. With a drink!

MR PRAWN: Give me a sip of this nectar.

ERROL: Nectar of the Godless.

*(A loud thumping sound. Massive shoes appear. Seven feet high, a greenfaced subhuman, sutures stitched across his large forehead, and rusty bolts riveted on the sides of his neck. Yes, you guess it, it's Frankenstein's Monster. Thanks to TV, we have monoculture to bind us human beings into one happy American world. Come on down, Mr Frankenstein's Monster!)*

MONSTER: And can this drink make me more human?

ERROL: Drink is the panacea. It gets at the root of all our misery—consciousness!

MONSTER: If only I am not aware of my ugliness, my loneliness, my soullessness, I can cope.

ERROL: The mind is a cursed gift of the gods.

MR PRAWN *(drinking):* I feel better now.

ERROL: Drink and drink and drink until you have drunk a sea of wine.

MONSTER: This drink makes me feel a most loved man. This drink shall be my soul.

LAWRENCE: I drink life. That intoxicates me. Are you all so dead that you cannot longer see and feel beauty?

MONSTER: I can crush this man's body but not his soul. People ask me do I have a soul? I tell them that it depends on the creator. Since a monster created me, I have no soul.

ERROL: Perhaps God is a monster. Perhaps there is a god that makes everybody happy.

MONSTER: This is a most wonderful God that makes his own creation happy.

ERROL: God is guilty of neglect. Let us worship a God that loves us. I drink a toast to our new God.

MR PRAWN: I am not guilty. God is. *(He shouts)* God is guilty!

HARRY THE HOUSE: You are guilty, King Prawn. Guilty of murder!

MR PRAWN: I did not invent death. God did. God is guilty!

NUN: Blasphemy! God is Love!

MR PRAWN: What is Love? I don't know what Love is. I don't know anything. I'm tired. Let me rest.

LAWRENCE: Your self-pity disgusts me. Stand erect like a phallus and flow with the rhythm of the cosmos.

MR PRAWN: What is there left for me? Just rot away and wait for death?

LAWRENCE: You either choose or let society choose for you. Don't fall prey to society's so- called wisdom.

OSCAR WILDE: My advice to all sad people is to sit in lotus position and contemplate their navels. Bellybuttons never fail to amuse me.

ERROL *(to Mr Prawn)*: Lie down, friend, you are tired.

MR PRAWN: Lie down where?

ERROL: In the gutter. It's the church for drunks, losers, and scum.

MR PRAWN: It's so dirty and smelly.

ERROL: The better to enjoy reality.

MR PRAWN *(sits down)*: It is wet.

ERROL: Your body cannot suffer as much as your mind.

MR PRAWN *(lies down, stretches to his full length)*: It is indeed a bed of roses.

ERROL: Good night, His Royal Majesty, King Prawn.

MR PRAWN: I am no King. I am scum.

MONSTER: Good night, scum.

MR PRAWN: Good night, everybody. *(He clenches his eyes shut, he forces himself to sleep, his face grimacing like a reptile.)*

*Through the curtain of mist emerges a large figure. It wears an armour of gold and carries a large golden sword. A soldier from Hell or Heaven come to kill King Prawn? People, terrified, disperse into the night. As it comes closer, we find that it is not a soldier but, in fact, a rhinoceros. A Golden Rhinoceros. It heaves itself towards the prone King Prawn. Standing beside the fallen King, it cocks its legs and pisses upon him. King Prawn does not respond. He is fast asleep. Good night, King Prawn, sleep and spare your kingdom from your living nightmares.*

## CHAPTER 25

### New Eden

I have to admit it. It's finally over between K and me. Although our relationship has been on and off for the past five years, I think it will remain off. I have no more energy left to make it work. Our relationship was much too combustible. Nothing for me to do but move on. Perhaps I'll find a gentle girl more suitable for my delicate sensibilities. A girl who won't fight me. I don't want to fight anymore. I want peace. In this novel, I've fought God, Truth, Love, Art, Men, Women, and Society. But I'm hanging up my sword. It's time for me to love. I unknot my fists and, with open hands, I reach out…

Hallelujah! The end of this novel! Goodbye, my characters! Goodbye, King Prawn, sleep well! Goodbye, Queen Clytoris, wherever you are! Goodbye, President Carol! Goodbye, sweet Virginia, sweet Prince Jotel, and sweet, sweet St Claire! Goodbye to all my minor characters, Harry the House, Mammon's Arse, Greg Goodies, goodbye! From this time forth, you will live in Art, your creator will have no more to do with you. You are now on your own. Don't invoke me, pray to me, scream at me, I will not listen, I will move on to other novels. Please, if you can find it in your understanding heart, forgive me for all the lousy things that I have done to you. But a novel must have suffering characters, and a novelist must provide them. It's the way of Art, for Art reflects the human condition. And goodbye, dear readers, may we meet again in my next novel if there is one. I dedicate this novel to all the confused souls out there looking for a way out. But before I go, there are some loose ends I must fix. One last chapter and my job will have been done. Get to work, St Claire and Prince Jotel, yours is the last curtain act, get on the lighted stage, say your lines, take a bow, then piss off, back to the shadows we must all return to…

The world was all blue, the sky, the ocean, except for a small yellow yacht sailing on the gentle waves. On board this vessel were the naked newlyweds, Prince Jotel and St Claire, sunning themselves on the deck like eggs on a frying pan.

"Aren't you going to miss the world?" asked Prince Jotel.

"This is the world," replied St Claire, "you and me, and it's perfect."

"Won't you miss civilisation?"

"No."

"Do you think we'll live happily ever after?"

"Yes," unhesitatingly answered St Claire.

"You think so?" asked Prince Jotel, the eternal sceptic.

"We are Romeo and Juliet without the Montagues and Capulets. Good riddance to them all."

"You're so positive. I'm used to negativity. I guess bad habits die hard."

Prince Jotel felt vulnerable in this large shark-octopus-piranha-infested ocean. He never trusted Nature. Nature was powerful and could gobble up all of humankind in a second.

"I'm tired of misery. I want happiness," said St Claire, her body drinking up the sun rays.

Prince Jotel kissed the flesh on her shoulders. "Is this what we are going to do for the rest of our lives? Make love."

"Yes."

"What about Art, Science, Philosophy and Politics?"

"No more traps. I want to be free of all that."

"The spider in me still longs to spin his web."

"Too many spiders trapping innocent people in their webs. King Prawn, President Carol. How many people have died for them? If you want to spin a web, make sure the gossamer is stick-free."

"There are spiders that have created beautiful webs. Mozart, Shakespeare, Beethoven."

"That's true. But I ain't them. But I'm tired of talking right now. Stop worrying. Just listen to the silence. It's so peaceful."

Prince Jotel tried to listen to the silence. But he had too many thoughts in his head. This constant noise drumming away like Keith Moon of The Who.

They reached a deserted island, not unlike Gilligan's Island. Hey, my imagination has been fed by non-stop television, so give me a break. They anchored in a lagoon and rowed ashore. Prince Jotel was relieved to touch solid ground.

"This is beautiful," said St Claire ecstatically, looking up at the tall coconut trees, and the mass of green beyond, lots and lots of green stuff. Stuff...I like that word.

"It's a jungle," said Prince Jotel, anxiously noting the thick tangle of green stuff. "There'll be snakes and tigers, too. I should have brought a machine gun."

"And shoot what? Attacking bananas?"

"Just in case."

"Trust Nature. She's kind and will look after us."

"What if there are cannibals?"

"We shall have to eat them," giving Prince Jotel a playful bite.

Brave St Claire followed a track in the jungle, with cowardly Prince Jotel traipsing close behind her. They went deeper and deeper; strange animal and bird noises greeted them. St Claire wasn't afraid, sure of her instincts. They saw a clearing, and Prince Jotel made a run for it, desperate to get away from the jungle. He stopped at the sight of a large edifice. It wasn't ancient, it was modern—in fact, it was a shopping centre. It was so weird it being here in the middle of nowhere.

"What is this?" wondered Prince Jotel. "I don't see people, cars. It's an abandoned shopping centre."

There was a big neon sign at the front: THE GOLDEN RHINOCEROS. The automatic doors slid open as they stepped on the rubber mat. The centre was well lit inside, muzak filled the air. Inside were all kinds of shops: clothes, records, food, a supermarket and so on. It had everything one could want. But there were no shopping assistants to greet them, even though all the shops were open.

Prince Jotel went inside a supermarket to get fruit juice loaded with sugar and preservatives. He twisted off the cap and took a tentative sip. It was fine. The expiry date was stamped ETERNITY.

"This is Paradise!" shouted Prince Jotel. "All the food we can eat, everything to keep us comfortable. We have all the luxuries of suburban happiness at the tip of our fingers."

"There must be a catch," said a wary St Claire. "There must be people around here."

"Paradise don't need more than two people."

They had lunch at a Chinese take-away where all the meals had authentic monosodium glutamate. Then to further abuse their digestive systems, they had large scoops of rich chocolate ice cream from an ice cream parlour called Heaven.

At night, they slept on a Queen size bed at a furniture shop.

Next day, St Claire insisted on investigating the island, certain there was a town or village out there. It was illogical for a shopping mall to exist without a town of customers. They followed a track full of prickly encounters that led to the highest part of the island. From that vantage point, they could see that there was no sign of civilisation at all. Just verdant nature, except for the shopping centre, which protruded like a giant acne. When they returned to the centre, Prince Jotel was jubilant.

"You see. This is Paradise for you and me."

"But who built it then?"

"Don't know, let's just be grateful."

"Why is there electricity?"

"I don't know, and I don't care. It's magic as far as I'm concerned."

"This is eerie."

"This is home sweet home."

St Claire laughed gently at Prince Jotel. "You are an incurable modern spirit. I was rather looking forward to becoming a noble savage, living on bananas, coconuts, and fish, building ourselves a hut, and making love on the beach, with insects biting our bare arses. Instead, we're living inside an air-conditioned shopping centre, eating packaged food."

"I wonder if this place has Kentucky Fried?"

"I should burn this place down!"

The next few months, Prince Jotel and St Claire lived happily in this electric Eden, eating takeaway food, watching videos, playing squash and bowling, reading novels, staging plays, poetry readings, and karaoke nights, dressing up in all kinds of clothes, or not wearing anything at all. They were extremely happy until an unexpected visitor arrived. It was Darryl, the Creator of the Universe and this shopping mall.

Both Prince Jotel and St Claire were naked when they bumped into him at the record store. St Claire had wanted to listen to some Michael Jackson.

They were shocked to see someone. "Who are you?"

"Darryl, you know, Lord of the Universe."

Prince Jotel and St Claire exchanged glances, both thinking this man was insane.

"Of course, you don't believe me. I get this reaction all the time. They expect someone taller, white, and with a beard. But hey I can't help it that I'm Filipino."

Since they still looked sceptical, Darryl decided to prove that he was Darryl by making the entire shopping centre vanish with the click of his finger.

"Is that proof enough for you?"

"Yes." They were very impressed.

With another click, the shopping centre rematerialised.

"I've created this shopping centre," Darryl explained, "for you two. This is paradise, and you are the new Jason and Kylie. Paradise has been modernised, to keep up with the times. The point of all this is that you are the last two human beings left in the world. While you were both off gallivanting around in your yacht, the world erupted into a nuclear war and hence destroyed itself."

"How did the war start?" asked St Claire, shocked.

"Baby Adolf spread the children's revolution around the world. Queen Golderella was ousted. Children took over everything. Unfortunately, a 7-year-old child was placed in charge of the nuclear arsenal, and like any curious child, he played with the buttons, which triggered off a nuclear war. Everybody was wiped out except you two. You may call it the end of the world, but I see it as a new beginning. A fresh start. As you remember, Kylie and Jason failed in their task, bringing misery to the world. This time, you can redress that catastrophe. I shall set one condition for your staying here. Just obey one rule or else I'll have to boot you out and force you to fend for yourself, like get a job."

"So, what is this rule?" Prince Jotel asked.

"You must not eat corn chips."

"I love corn chips," Prince Jotel protested.

"You eat one corn chip, and you are out of here, kiddo."

Prince Jotel thought about it for a second. "I guess I can survive without corn chips."

St Claire was angry, "I resent these rules. I don't mind rules that are good common sense, but rules that are trivial and petty, I think, are abhorrent. It's an abuse of power."

"Well, tough titties, St Claire. You must understand that I am Darryl, and I can do whatever l want. So there!"

Before St Claire could make any further argument, Darryl vanished.

"Now we can rectify what Jason and Kylie did. This is the world's second chance to get it right," Prince Jotel said, bright with optimistic fervour.

"We're doomed," said St Claire ruefully.

"Don't say that!"

"This is nothing but bureaucracy! Totally unnecessary. This is irrational and will lead to further acts of irrationality. In other words, the history of the world will repeat itself with the same illogical brutality."

The next day, guess who they ran into? Right. The serpent, Shane.

"Look here, Shane," warned Prince Jotel, "you are not going to trick us into eating corn chips. We ain't listening to you."

"You silly people," laughed Shane. "As if I care whether or not you eat corn chips. Unlike Darryl, I spend my time on meaningful activities such as Philosophy, Art or Science. Darryl, you see, is Philistine, narrow-minded, authoritarian, and basically a prick. He wants to be loved, worshipped, and adored like he was a Hollywood celebrity. How shallow is that! I'd rather have people talk to me in a stimulating manner rather than kneel before me in ridiculous reverence."

St Claire nodded her head in agreement. "You're right. It's stupid of Darryl to create this stupid rule. Doesn't he know it is human nature to break rules? Is he so inept at understanding the human psyche? Of course, we're going to eat corn chips. It's inevitable."

"No, St Claire," protested Prince Jotel, disappointed by her pessimism.

"You feel it, don't you? The tension is in the air. This wasn't here before Darryl came along. We were happy."

"We can still be happy."

"I don't know. All I am aware of this anger seething inside of me. It's this invasion of my privacy. I feel I'm being watched every minute to make sure I'm a good girl."

"Let's not think about it. Let's enjoy ourselves like we used to." Prince Jotel pulled St Claire to himself and held her. "We'll forget about Darryl and corn chips."

"In fact, I'll destroy every corn chip in this shopping centre."

But corn chips they were forced not to forget. Bombarded were they by corn chips advertisements. The TV played constant corn chips commercials raving about how crunchy and yummy they were. Posters of beautifully photographed corn chips were adorned all over the walls. Even though Prince Jotel burned and buried the corn chips stocked at the shopping centre, they kept reappearing, strewn all over the place, some packets open, allowing the aroma to pervade the air. One morning, St Claire woke up to find a packet of corn chips under her nostrils. She screamed as if she had discovered a horse's head.

"I'm sick of this!" screamed St Claire.

Prince Jotel woke up. "What's the matter?"

St Claire flashed her eyes at Prince Jotel. "Darryl won't leave us alone! He's determined to make us eat corn chips."

"We'll overcome all obstacles. We have to accept the situation. We can't change Darryl; we can only change ourselves."

"No, there's another option. We can change our address. I'm leaving this island."

"Leave all this behind. We have everything here."

"Everything but us. As long as we're here, it will be Darryl, you and me. I married you, not him. Besides, I don't even believe in him, I'm an atheist!"

"Think this through, St Claire. I don't think I can survive out there."

"I'll survive. And if I can't, I'll die trying. Are you coming?"

Prince Jotel hesitated, thinking of the merciless jungle, with a boa constrictor coiling around his neck.

"Great. You can stay here with Darryl. You'll make a great couple. Bye."

Prince Jotel said nothing. He continued to say nothing when he watched St Claire pack her things. He wanted to do something, but he was paralysed, as if all his mind and body had shut down.

Standing, with suitcase in hand, St Claire glared at Prince Jotel. She waited.

Prince Jotel said nothing; St Claire walked away in a huff.

It was like a Ball and Chain holding him back.

The next morning, he woke up with Darryl lying beside him. "Just you and me, eh, Prince."

Prince Jotel nodded.

"Do you play chess?" Darryl asked him.

Prince Jotel shook his head.

"I'll teach you one day. We'll have lots of fun together."

Prince Jotel stared blankly before him, tears welling up in his eyes.

"Hey, don't feel bad. You made the right decision. Many years from now, humankind will be thanking you for saving them from the curse of freedom. From now on, everybody will be happy, everybody will find love, everybody will have the answer to everything. You're a hero, dude!"

Darryl laid back on the pillow where once St Claire's pretty head nestled in and closed his eyes. He was pleased that the history of Jason and Kylie had not been repeated. The future appeared bright: no wars, no poverty, no suffering. Now he could rest; things would be smooth sailing from now on.

Prince Jotel saw that everything in his life had led to this moment. He was weak and incapable of making decisions. The Ball and Chain, the Past was the Present was the Future. Deep in his damaged psyche, he believed that he didn't deserve to be loved. Perhaps it was King Prawn's and Queen Clytoris's fault for never having given him enough love. Perhaps he had to pay for their sins for the rest of his life.

"I love you, St Claire," he uttered, hoping the words would drift along and catch a wind that would carry them all the way across the ocean waves to St Claire's ears.

Darryl snored obstreperously beside him.

Prince Jotel stood up. He started running as fast as he could. Past McDonalds. Past Woolworths. Past Sanity records. Past Riverrun pharmacy. The front entrance automatically opened for him, and the heat outside hit him hard. He followed the familiar trail in the forest. He saw the splendid blue strip. He heard the soothing sound of waves. He scrambled towards the beach, onto the sand, removed his clothes, and dived into the waves, starting to swim. The waves kept trying to push him back. He would swim to St Claire and join her. She was just beyond the horizon

A memory came back to him. They were up on the castle battlements: King Prawn, Queen Clytoris, and himself, a mere babe.

King Prawn, cradling him in his arm, pointed to the horizon and whispered, "The horizons of conquests."

The smile on St Claire's face seeing me when we meet. The glory of that.

**THE END**

# ABOUT THE AUTHOR

Ranulfo is the author of Nirvana's Children, Joker, Danika in the Underworld, and Danika vs the Monster Slayer. He lives in Sydney, Australia.